MW00978141

a Blood Angel novel
by Nina Soden

This is a work of fiction. All of the characters, organizations, businesses, and events portrayed in this novel are either products of the author's imagination or are used fictitiously.

AWAKEN. Copyright © 2012 by Nina Soden.
All rights reserved.

ISBN: 978-0-9858853-0-4

http://www.ninasoden.wordpress.com

Editors: Ula Manzo, PhD., Jamie Aitchison, and Nicole Smith

Cover Design by: Julie Csizmadia

DEDICATION

For my husband, Eric Soden, who never let me give up.

ACKNOWLEDGEMENTS

I want to acknowledge my amazing friends and family who read and re-read with smiles on their faces, and encouragement in their constructive criticism. I appreciate your kindness, generosity, creativity, and honest feedback. Thank you Nicole Smith, Clara Tapaninen, Britney Malone, Kim Holmes, and Andy Pinon.

Thank you to both Ula Manzo and Jamie Aitchison, for your excellent, sometimes frustrating, yet thorough proofreading and editing skills. I hope to work with you both again in the future.

EPIGRAPH

For someone like Alee, death is a common occurrence. It
permeates, intertwines, and feeds everything she does.
Everything she is. That may seem strange considering she's
only seventeen years old, but given her history she wouldn't
have made it that far in life if she had been scared of what
was around the corner or if she had run from the boogieman.
She embraced it. She embraced everything over which she
had no control, and used it to her fullest advantage. Can you
say the same?

1

It was after midnight when the police got the call: shots fired, possible domestic violence. Lucky for Loraline they lived in a small town with very nosy neighbors. Officers Manfra and Tandy were banging on the door in less than ten minutes. "Police. Open up!" The fifteen seconds of silence before they broke down the door seemed like a lifetime. "Stand back, we're coming in." The house was old, and the rusty hinges snapped off with little resistance, sending the wooden door slamming against the interior wall, only to end up broken on the floor.

"Oh man! Tandy, get in here!" They stood motionless in the doorway, not knowing where to begin. The house had been torn apart. Bookcases lay on their sides with their contents strewn about. The couch cushions had been ripped open and stuffing was spread everywhere. There was a trail of bloody shoe prints leading from upstairs down through the center of the living room and into the kitchen. Officer Manfra slowly made his way through the living room, gun raised at the ready the whole time. He pointed to the stairs along the opposite wall. "You take the upstairs; I'll clear the first floor." Officer Manfra moved toward the kitchen as Officer Tandy headed up the stairs trying to avoid the bloody footprints along the way.

The kitchen was in even more disarray than the living room had been. All of the cabinets had been ransacked and emptied, broken dishes covered almost every surface of the counters and floor. The refrigerator had been pushed over and the door hung open. There was a pile of unopened mail on the island in the middle of the kitchen, and Officer Manfra offhandedly flipped through it. Everything was addressed to a Ms. Loraline Wenham. "Wenham?" he said out loud to himself. "I know that name. She's from Atlanta. That…" His thoughts were interrupted by the sound of the wind that had suddenly started to pick up outside, and a loud clap of thunder overhead. Glancing around he noticed that the window on the back door was broken, and the door had been left ajar. There was a closed pantry door large enough for a person to fit behind and, hesitantly, Officer Manfra swung open the door. It was empty, aside from the cans, jars, and boxes of food covering the shelves. He turned to the back door and just as he was taking his first step out onto the patio, he heard Officer Tandy yelling for him from upstairs. "I got something. Get up here!"

Officers Tandy and Manfra were new to the force in McBain. They had grown up together like brothers, in

Atlanta, Michigan, and had gone through their academy training together with hopes of working in the same precinct after graduation. Officer Manfra had graduated at the top of the class and had offers from several major cities; Officer Tandy, on the other hand, barely made it through, graduating with the lowest ranking in their class. He received only one placement offer: McBain. It was only two hours from Atlanta where they had grown up—not nearly far enough, in Officer Manfra's opinion, but they had made a pact to stay together, and he wasn't about to let his best friend down. The position was for only one recruit. One of the six officers currently working in McBain had recently passed away. But Officer Tandy and Officer Manfra came as a package deal and the town's Sheriff, who was ready to retire anyway, was happy to have the extra help. Their plan was to work in McBain for a few years, until Officer Tandy had built up a solid reputation, and then transfer down south to one of the larger cities like Detroit, Lansing, or maybe just back home to Atlanta. If they weren't able to escape it they figured they might as well embrace it.

Rushing upstairs, Manfra noticed the photos arranged along the stairway wall, and instantly recognized Loraline. She had been two classes behind him in high school, but Atlanta High, "Home of the Huskies," was not very large, and everyone pretty much knew everyone else. Besides, the Wenham name was almost like royalty in Atlanta, although not in a way that anyone would mention to strangers. He and Loraline had even gone out on a date or two.

When he reached the top of the stairs he could see Officer Tandy standing at the end of the hall peering into one of the bedrooms.

"Did you clear the floor?" he asked. But Officer Tandy didn't move, let alone answer. "Tandy! Did you clear all the rooms?"

"Yeah, yeah everything's clear, but…" His face was as white as a sheet, and you could hear the rattle of the gun in his shaking hand.

"Step aside." Manfra made his way through the door. "Oh God," he whispered.

The room was in the same chaotic state as the rest of the house, but that wasn't what shocked him. Lying on the floor at the end of the bed and covered in blood were two seemingly lifeless bodies. One was Loraline—Manfra recognized her immediately. The other was a man. He had dark-brown hair and appeared to be only a few years older than Loraline, but not anyone he recognized. "Are they dead?" Officer Tandy didn't answer. "Did you check the bodies?"

Officer Tandy just shook his head. "I… um."

"Damn it, Tandy, get it together." Officer Manfra made his way over to the bodies. With the amount of blood on the floor around them he wasn't expecting either of them to still be alive. He wasn't able to find a pulse when he checked the man. "Nothing, he's dead. We need to look around—see if we can figure out who he is—her husband—friend. Hell, maybe he's the one that broke in." His brain was working a mile a minute as he moved on to Loraline, not paying any attention to Officer Tandy, who was still standing frozen in the doorway. Manfra checked her throat, her wrist, and finally her femoral artery, in search of a pulse. "I think I feel... Ugh, I can't tell." He pulled out a small mirror from his utility belt and placed it under her nose and then her mouth. The condensation was slight, but it meant that she was still breathing. "She's alive, she's alive! Call an ambulance!" She wasn't conscious, and her breathing was faint but she was alive and it sent a surge of adrenaline through his veins. "Seriously man, call an ambulance, NOW!" Not knowing the extent of her injuries he didn't want to move her, but he didn't think she would last much longer if they didn't get her to the hospital quickly.

Officer Tandy quickly grabbed the radio off his belt and franticly pushed the buttons, but in a pause in the howling storm outside, they heard a cry coming from the closet across room. Manfra held his hand up, indicating to Officer Tandy to be quiet. Then, raising his gun, he moved through the room like a football player, dodging the patches of blood in his path. When he swung open the door, he was surprised to find not a closet, but a small nursery inside. There were no windows, but one small lamp lit the small interior room in a soft amber glow. Lying in the crib was a red-faced baby girl, and she was screaming as if her life depended on it—which it did. "We got a child in here!" Manfra called out. "Call it in!"

With the radio already in his hand Tandy hit the call button. "This is Officer Tandy. We got a 10-83 here, and are going to need—."

"STOP!" Manfra shouted, scooping up the crying child and stepping back into the bedroom. "10-83? 10-83 is hazardous material, what the —." He bit his lip to stop from swearing in front of the child.

Tandy looked up, "It's just Marsha at the call desk. She knows what I—."

"Tell her we need an ambulance – Tell her there is one DOA, one wounded, and one child!" He needed to get away. He was pissed as he made his way out of the room, and down the hall. "Then start processing the room—and watch Loraline!" He called back over his shoulder practically barking the order at him.

"Loraline? Who's Lorali—?"

"The woman, watch the woman." He snapped, not wanting to deal with his partner any more right then.

When the ambulance finally arrived, about twenty minutes later, the baby was sound asleep in Manfra's arms. Hearing the sirens, Tandy hurried downstairs to direct the paramedics.

Tandy stepped aside as they rushed in. "Upstairs—last door on the left. Her pulse is faint, but she still seems to be breathing," They were already up the stairs before he could finish his sentence.

"Tandy, can you come in here please." Manfra called from the living room.

"Yeah, what's up man?"

Manfra was clearly disappointed in his friend, and having a hard time disguising it. "I think you should go with them—back to the hospital I mean. You can make sure the

baby gets to protective services until they see if Loraline is
going to make it. I'll stay here, and process the scene."

Tandy took in the situation, as what his friend said
slowly sank in. "You're putting me on babysitter duty? What
the hell!" Officer Tandy turned to walk out, but stopped
himself. "You know what, you may think you're all that, but
you're not. I was the one who worked with you late every
night at the range to get your scores up. I was the one who
stayed back during the runs to help you finish. You may be
smarter than me, but that doesn't make you any more of a cop
than I am. You'd do well to remember that!" He headed for
the stairs just as the paramedics were coming down with
Loraline. They had already begun an IV drip and one of the
paramedics was administering oxygen to her. "What about
the guy? We didn't feel a pulse—you get anything?"

"Uh…" The paramedic didn't quite know what to say.
"The guy? What are you talking about? She was the only one
up there."

Manfra always followed his impulses—those gut
feelings that usually made people run in the opposite
direction but for him forced him forward. This time was no
exception, and without thinking twice he handed off the baby
to his partner, confirming Tandy's babysitting duties, and
took off running up the stairs.

Sure enough, as he stepped into the room, he saw that the
floor was bare where the man's body had been only minutes
earlier. He scanned the room and noticed a fresh set of bloody
shoe prints leading straight to a window that was standing
half open. Manfra was sure that the window had been closed

before. The sound of the wind and rain was much louder now, with the window open. He also hadn't noticed that the window glass had been painted black, or the bloody handprint, still wet and sticky, on the white windowsill. Bending down to look into the back yard he saw that with no lights on in the back of the house it was pitch black. He knew there was a thick tree line about ten yards back from the house. Anyone could have easily have escaped into the trees without being noticed. Hell, someone could have been standing in the open yard ten feet from the house and you still wouldn't be able to see them.

The only reason Manfra could think of for a person to flee the site of such a horrific crime was if he were guilty. It took only seconds for his instincts to kick in, and he continued processing the room. With one of the victims having disappeared and the other unconscious and headed to the hospital, the evidence in this room was his only lead in the first real case they had come across since moving to McBain. He wasn't about to let it slip through his fingers.

He had followed procedure. The crime scene had been secured and the house and yard had been roped off so that no one could tamper with any physical evidence. CSI had been called in, photographs of every room in the house had been taken, and he even had a sketch artist preparing a diagram of the scene. All physical evidence had been collected and when the bloody handprint was fully dry he was able to recover a perfect print. Unfortunately, after scanning the print into IAFIS, the Integrated Automated Fingerprint Identification System, it led nowhere. The mystery man was like a ghost.

As for the rest of the house, the only sign of a man having lived there were the clothes hanging in the closet and filling the laundry hamper. Manfra found a wire basket filled with household paperwork amongst the items that had scattered out from the fallen bookcases. The mortgage, the bills—everything was in Loraline's name. Even the baby's birth certificate, which was also in the pile of papers, didn't have a father's name listed.

After everyone from the CSI to the blood pattern analysts were done, Manfra finally turned the crime scene over to one of the other officers for the final survey. He wasn't ready to officially release the house. He knew reentry would take a warrant once that was done, and he didn't want to have to go through the paperwork involved with that. But, if he had one of the other officers complete the final survey and stationed him outside the house for the rest of the night he could be sure that the house would remain secure, and he would be able to get in again later that night, or the next day if he needed to.

The drive to Mercy Hospital in Cadillac only took twenty minutes. When he arrived at the hospital, Manfra was directed to the floor where Loraline was being cared for. He made the rounds with one of the nurses, questioning the doctor on duty and the nurses in the labor unit where Loraline had given birth only weeks before. Although they all remembered seeing a man visiting with Loraline, none of them could remember his name or even what he had looked like, aside from saying that he was tall, and had dark brown hair. They could have been describing half of the male population of McBain.

"You're telling me he was here practically the whole time, and you never once asked his name?"

The nurse was flustered. It was her job to check guests in and out when they visited the patients' rooms, and Officer Manfra was making it perfectly clear that she had not done her job. "I'm sure I did. I know I did. I'm sorry; I just don't have record of it." She was sifting through a pile of papers on her desk. "I don't have anyone signing in to visit Ms. Wenham. I'm sorry."

"Not even her parents? No siblings or anyone?"

"No sir." Her hands were trembling as she flipped through page after page.

Officer Manfra placed his hand on hers. "It's all right. You can stop looking. I'll find him another way." Of course, he had no idea how he was going to do it, but somehow he knew the hospital records were going to be a dead end.

When he finally made it to Loraline's room, Tandy was sitting at her bedside, just staring down at her. Her skin was pale and fragile. She was hooked up to about ten different machines all checking different things—heart rate, blood pressure, body temperature, and who knows what else. They were beeping and buzzing all around her, and Officer Tandy was in a daze listening to them all at once.

"How's she doing?"

"What?" He was startled out of his haze. "Oh, hey man. Not well. The doctor says she's in a coma. They have no idea when she'll wake up, or even if she will."

"What about the baby?"

"They have her downstairs on the labor and delivery floor, in the nursery. The doctor said she seems all right, but they can't seem to get her to eat anything. Her body temperature is a little lower than normal, so they're worried about possible infection. They've got her under one of those baby heat lamp things. I think they're going to run some tests before releasing her to Child Services."

The two of them sat there in silence for a while before Tandy spoke up, "Hey, listen, about earlier—."

"Don't worry about it," Manfra shrugged. They had been best friends practically since birth, and he knew that although Tandy was tough on the outside, when it came to death he just didn't have the stomach for it. When Tandy was in the third grade, he had come home from school one day to find the living room window broken and the front door wide open. As he made his way through the house he found his mom lying unconscious on their kitchen floor. She had been beaten so badly that she suffered from brain damage. She was in a coma for almost seven years before his dad had finally made the decision to pull the plug. This was one of the many reasons why Manfra never understood Tandy's eagerness to join the police force. Tandy always said it was his calling—to help others, when he hadn't been able to help his own mom.

"Thanks. Oh and here." He held out a piece of scratch paper with some scribbled writing on it. "I looked up that number you asked for."

It hadn't been too hard to locate Loraline's family back in Atlanta. The Wenhams were well known and highly admired within the community—had been since long before either Manfra or Tandy had been born. Manfra made the call shortly after eight in the morning after he got the call that the final report from crime scene had been completed, and the doctors had been in to check on Loraline. The phone rang only once before someone picked up.

"Hello, you've reached the Black Onyx. How may I help you?"

"This is Officer Manfra of the McBain Police Department. I'm calling for Mrs. Elizabeth Wenham, is she available?" There was complete and utter silence on the other end of the line. "Hello?"

"Yes, um… This is Mrs. Wenham." Her voice wavered, as if she were about to crumble at any moment. "What can I do for you officer?"

"I'm sorry to be the one to have to tell you this, but there has been an accident. Your daughter, Loraline—."

"Oh no!" She cut him off before he could finish his sentence. Manfra heard her take a deep breath, and he heard a sob. Clearly, the thought of her daughter's death sliced through her heart.

"Mrs. Wenham, she's alive!"

"What? She's alive? Then what happened?" She sounded frantic. The words tumbled out of her. She couldn't find out fast enough.

"She's alive, but she's been admitted to Mercy Hospital in Cadillac." The news was supposed to be of comfort to her, but Mrs. Wenham didn't take it that way at all.

"Cadillac? Why Cadillac? No, that won't do. Cadillac is two hours away. I want her closer. You'll have to have her moved to Mercy Hospital in Grayling. That's only an hour away." Mrs. Wenham's thoughts were racing—she didn't have time to think, let alone really process everything.

"I'm sorry, but she can't be moved just yet. Your daughter is in a coma. They're going to have to keep her here in Cadillac for observations, until they can determine…"

"We'll be right there," she interrupted, then she hung up the phone without even so much as a goodbye, or a thank you.

Officer Manfra stood at the nurses' station just staring down at the receiver. "That went well." He hung up the phone and smiled down at the nurse who was pretending not to listen in on his conversation. "Are you working the day shift Mrs.…?"

She blushed at the question, wondering about his intentions. "Ms., actually—Ms. Evans – Jamie Evans, but you can call me Jamie. And yes, I'm working a double. I got in a few hours ago, when Ms. Wenham was brought in. I'll be here till eleven this evening. I'm on call and working a double shift. If you can't find me I'm probably in one of the break rooms sleeping. Any of the other nurses can come get me if you need me."

"Great. My partner is going to be outside the Wenham room today, and I'll be returning this evening." He nodded toward an empty seat just outside of Loraline's room. "I have a feeling her parents might show up. If you see anyone aside from myself or my partner going in or out of that room you notify me right away." He slid his business card across the counter into her hand and his fingertips gently brushed the top of her hand. "Can you do that for me?"

She felt like a giddy schoolgirl as his hand slid away. "Yes sir, but all visitors on this floor would have to sign in here with me before going into a patient's room anyway. I'm sure I-."

"I am well aware of how well that process works around here."

Obviously insulted, she turned her focus away from him, and back to the computer screen in front of her.

"I'm sorry. I didn't mean to offend you. It's just that the visitor logs throughout this hospital haven't been all that accurate in the past. I'm not blaming you by any means. Please don't take it that way. It's just that we still haven't found the man, I mean the person, responsible for her accident." Jamie looked up in alarm, and she quickly glanced left and right.

"Don't worry, Ms. Evans, there's no cause for alarm," Manfra assured her. "We have no reason to believe he would even try to come here. It's just a precaution. But, you can see why it's important that we're informed of anyone who comes to see Ms. Wenham while she's here. You do understand don't you?"

"Yes, of course." That soft and almost playful voice was gone as she answered, and she went back to the stack of patient files that she had been in the process of uploading into the computer system. "I've got your number." She waved his card without looking at him. "I'll call if anyone stops in to see the patient."

"Thank you." He stood there for a few seconds, waiting for a response before it dawned on him that he had burned that bridge, and he quickly made his exit–from the nurse's station, and from the hospital. In order to be ready for the search the next day, and to talk to Loraline, when or if she woke up, he needed to go back to the station and start writing up the report he knew would take him the rest of the night.

It was only a few hours later, though, that Tandy called him from the hospital. "I think you need to get back over here."

"What's going on? Is she awake?"

"No. But her parents are here, and they're not happy." Then, lowering his voice, Tandy stepped into the hallway so Loraline's parents couldn't hear him.

"Dude, I know her parents. I went out with her sister in high school, and ah, they don't like me."

"Of course they don't. Just don't leave them alone with her. And don't let them check her out of the hospital until I get there." Already cranking the car engine he slammed the door closed. "I'm on my way."

He could have gotten there in five minutes or five days. It wouldn't have changed the results. Her parents had clout in Atlanta, and with that came a lot of powerful friends. They were loading Loraline into the back of an unmarked ambulance when Officer Manfra pulled up, and they weren't about to stop just because the local police department said to. "I understand that you want her closer to home, but—."

"She's coming with us. Don't try to stop me, or you'll find yourself answering to them." Mrs. Wenham stepped aside and Manfra realized there were two Atlanta black and white squad cars parked on the other side of the ambulance, and four of the largest officers he had ever seen.

"I can't stop you, but please understand that this isn't over. We will be looking into what happened tonight..." The newborn baby girl who was already in the back of the ambulance started to cry, pulling Manfra's attention away from Mrs. Wenham. "...and your daughter is our only witness. I hope you understand. I'm only doing my job."

Mrs. Wenham, walking very slowly, closed the gap between them. "Nothing happened. My daughter is fine." Officer Manfra kept glancing back toward the sound of the crying baby. She reached out and with the tips of her fingers on his chin she turned his head and eyes back to hers. "Everything is fine. There's no baby... it was only a burglary... no one was hurt... we won't be pressing charges... nothing to concern the police." She was standing only inches from him, looking deep into his eyes.

"There is no baby?"

"That's right. There is no baby." Her smile was soft, and he felt warm all over as she watched him.

"No one was hurt." His voice was monotone and dry.

"No."

"Everything is fine."

"That's right. You can call your officers and tell them to release the crime scene."

"I can release the crime scene."

"That's right." Lowering her arm she took a step back. "Have a lovely evening Officer Manfra." Then she turned and made her way into the back of the ambulance, which drove off before he even had a chance to respond.

The only call he made was to Tandy. "Hey man, you can go on back to the house and let the others go. There's no need to secure the site any longer."

"You sure?"

"Yeah, the family doesn't want to press charges. No harm no foul."

"No harm no…"

"Just do it!" He hung up. It had been a long night and he was ready to head home.

Eric showed up at the hospital emergency room around seven o'clock that evening. His hair was a mess and his clothes were stained with blood. "Sir, are you all right?" A security guard standing just outside the hospital entrance called out and rushed toward him as soon as he saw Eric walking up the driveway. "Are you hurt?"

"I need to find my wife and my little girl." Eric pushed past the guard, and into the lobby.

"Sir, maybe you should sit down. I think——."

Eric pushed the guard aside again, and the man fell, hitting his head on the edge of a magazine rack just inside the waiting room. Without so much as a second glance to see if the man was all right, and without stopping at the desk, Eric forced open the door at the back of the emergency room and started searching the patient rooms.

"Loraline? Loraline, where are you?" It didn't take long for Eric to realize that she wasn't there. "Loraline Wenham, where is she?" He barked at a young woman sitting at the nurses' station.

"I, I don't know." She could feel her lower lip starting to quiver as she spoke. "I'm sorry."

"Never mind, I'll find her myself." He started toward the elevator, but noticed another security guard creeping up slowly behind him. Eric spun around inhumanly fast, and was standing face-to-face with the officer in an instant. "Don't follow me!" He said quietly. Then, as he turned away, the elevator beeped and he was inside in a flash. He disappeared, leaving them all behind—aghast.

Following only his instincts, Eric found himself standing outside an empty patient room a little while later.

"Can I help you sir?"

"What? Oh." Startled, he turned to find another nurse standing at his side. She was pretty and petite but, noticing the way her lips turned down at the corners, he thought she seemed a little sad.

"Um…" She was wearing a hospital identification badge with her name typed in under an awkwardly stiff photo. "Ms. Evans, do you know where the patient that was in this room is now?"

"Oh, I'm so sorry. She isn't with us anymore." She was staring into the room, and didn't even notice as Eric's expression changed from desperation to horror at the thought of Loraline's death. "I believe she's been moved to——." But by the time she turned around he was already gone.

Eric turned his attention to a frantic search for his daughter. He searched every floor, every unlocked door, from top to bottom, but couldn't find her anywhere. He begged nurse after nurse, but no one knew anything about a baby girl. He couldn't go home—his wife was gone, and there was no sign of his little girl anywhere. Although he dreaded it, he had no other choice but to contact Loraline's family. He wouldn't do it in person; he already knew how they felt about him. When Loraline had made the decision to leave her family for him they all but disowned her. The only person who was still speaking with her was her sister Jacinda, and even their relationship was strained.

He left the hospital and found a payphone outside a small diner in town. He placed the call and the phone rang and rang, but just as he was ready to hang up Jacinda's familiar voice answered. "Hello, you've reached the Black Onyx, how can I…"

"Jacinda?" He hesitated to tell her who it was at first, for fear that she might hang up on him.

"Yes, who is this?" Her voice was trembling. Jacinda had been with Elizabeth Wenham when her mother had received the call earlier that day. Although she had wanted to go to the hospital with her mother, Elizabeth had told her to stay at the house in case the police called back before she made it to the hospital. She had already been through so much, and didn't need any more bad news, but Eric couldn't have known that she already knew about Loraline.

"It's Eric. Please, before you hang up, just hear me out."

"What do you want, Eric?" She spoke quietly, almost hushed and distorted, and he could hear her closing a door as she spoke.

"It's about Loraline—she—."

"We already know. The police called. Mother left hours ago, she should be home shortly if you want to talk with her."

"You know I can't talk to her." Eric slumped down against the wall with the phone held close to his ear. "Not now. Not after this."

"What happened? What did you do?"

"It wasn't me!" He yelled it, defending himself and their relationship all in one breath. "You know I love her. I would never hurt her."

"Then what happened? How could you let something like this happen to her?"

"I wasn't there." The events of the attack played over and over in his head. "I got home late, and she was lying on the floor by the bed. There was blood everywhere. When I knelt down to help her, I was attacked from behind. I didn't see who it was. When I woke up, the cops were there. I had to get out before they figured out who I am."

"You're her husband; don't you think they'll eventually figure it out?"

"We're not married."

"What?! But, when you left... Loraline told us—."

"I know what she said, but we never got married. Just a little while after we moved away we found out she was pregnant." Eric's voice dropped and he let out a long sigh of exhaustion.

"Pregnant?"

"We decided to wait until the baby was born to get married. Loraline thought that maybe, with the addition of a child, your family would welcome us back. That was two weeks ago, but now this—."

"I'm an aunt?"

"Yes, but..." How could he tell her now, after just learning that her sister is in a coma and that yes she's an aunt, but that the baby is missing? "...she's gone."

"What do you mean she's gone?"

"The nurse at the hospital said that Loraline is dead, and no one could tell me anything about Aleerah–she's just gone. I searched the hospital and no one has seen her or has any record of her being there."

"Aleerah that was the name of my mother's great grandmother I think... or her... I don't remember, but I like it."

"Jacinda, you're not listening. She's gone!"

"That sounds like..." Jacinda stopped herself. "I have to go, but I'll be in contact with you soon."

"Wait, what do you know?"

"I'm not sure yet. I'm sorry, I have to go."

2

The Wenham family owned a little over a hundred acres of land just inside the city limits on the outskirts of town. Although they had a business to run, they enjoyed their privacy, and didn't mind being somewhat out of the way. Besides not many of their customers were going to take the main roads to get to them anyway.

Their property housed five different homes. The first was the Black Onyx, owned by Elizabeth and William, though they had always intended it for their daughters Loraline and Jacinda when they eventually took over the business. The second and oldest of the houses was Granny Edith's house, which she now shared with her daughter Estelle since their husbands had been killed. The third was Estelle's home, which had been all but abandoned since Estelle moved in with her mother. The forth was the home in which Elizabeth and William were living, just up the road from the Black Onyx. The last was a quaint little ranch style home that Jacinda and her new husband Thomas had moved into shortly after Loraline left Atlanta.

Although no one actually lived at the Black Onyx it was never vacant. Elizabeth and William still hoped that their daughter Loraline would one day change her mind and decide to move back home, and when that time came the Black Onyx would be there waiting for her. The shop had always been her vision—something she had talked them into opening when she was just a young schoolgirl, and even though they didn't really need the money it generated, they kept it open for her. Until that time came, the rest of the Wenham family ran the shop and used the Black Onyx as their 'central meeting place' if you will. It was in close proximity to every other house on the Wenham property, and it housed all of their essential items. Even in the late evening hours it wasn't unusual to find Jacinda, Elizabeth, or even one of Loraline's grandmothers reading quietly in the study by a fire, or brewing tea in the kitchen.

From the outside the Black Onyx looked like your average Victorian style country home, except for the wooden sign planted in the flowerbed beside the front porch, engraved with the words "Black Onyx" in script and a large pentagram in the center. And, the once lush front lawn had been replaced with a large gravel parking lot.

Inside, the lights were dim but welcoming as you entered a living room that had been completely renovated into a modern day apothecary with floor to ceiling bookshelves filled with books, jars containing assorted liquids and other such items, and stones of every kind. The center of the room held a large hand-carved wooden table covered with bowls of crystals, dried flowers, and crystal orbs of varying sizes and color. Toward the back there was a small countertop, home of an antique black cash register, and behind the counter another bookshelf held ancient-looking hand bound leather books organized neatly and clearly with great care.

A back door led to the kitchen, and although it wasn't part of the shop, it still had the same home remedy type of feel. The cupboards were filled with small glass jars of spices and herbs, neatly labeled, and the pantry contained things in glass jars and canisters that would make the average person call an exterminator. Alongside the cash register, back in the shop, there was a beaded curtain that separated the shop from the rest of the house. Beyond the curtain was a long hallway that extended much farther back than the outside appearance of the house would have suggested to be possible. From somewhere down that hall faint cries could be heard in between the loud claps of thunder that shook the walls.

It was the middle of the night and only the pitch black sky could be seen through the thin slits of glass on either side of the glowing fireplace in the back room. The rain came down in sheets outside as the howling wind threatened to tear off the roof and bring down the trees that surrounded the quaint little shop.

"If it were up to me you would have been killed for your crimes…." Edith Wenham, a fragile looking woman of seventy-eight years old, was standing in the small study with her daughter Estelle and her granddaughter Elizabeth behind her. There was a man in his early fifties and a woman in her mid to late forties kneeling on the floor in front of her, with their hands tied tightly behind their backs. "…but luck has been with you, this time. You will repay your debt through service—."

"Thank you so much—." Martha cut in, but her husband quickly stopped her.

"Do not thank her! You have no idea what it is she wants us to do."

"You would rather die?" Edith snapped nearly spitting in his face. "Is your life worth so little to you?"

"I would rather die than serve you or any of your kind."

"David, please." Tears were running down Martha's face as she pleaded with her husband, praying he wouldn't do anything to get himself, or her, killed.

"Your wife, she longs for a child. Does she not?" Edith was gazing deep into David's eyes, and Martha's crying stopped instantly. She had their full attention, as she had known she would. "And you can't give her one, can you?" Stone cold, David didn't move, but the answer was written all over his face as a single tear escaped his eye. "Would you rather die than see your wife happy, with a child to care for?"

A gasp of air escaped Martha's lips as she sank lower to the ground. Her whole body was trembling at the thought of a child. She wanted to scream out, cry, beg, but she couldn't move, let alone speak.

"What? Granny Edith, No!" Disbelief washed over Elizabeth as she realized why her grandmother had called them there.

"Hush child. This is not your decision."

"I am not a child; I'm thirty-nine years old. She is my grandchild, my responsibility! You have no right!" Elizabeth's eyes were wild and frantic as she begged her grandmother.

Edith may have looked frail and delicate to the unsuspecting eye, but by no means did she behave that way. Leaving Martha and David kneeling there, confused and afraid, she stood as tall as her old bones would allow, and faced Elizabeth head on. "Thirty-nine is a blip in the span of my life, and your child of only eighteen lies practically lifeless in a hospital bed with child of her own. Pitiful!"

"How dare—."

"The last time I checked I was still in charge of this family! That means the welfare and safety of everyone falls on me. If I say this is what shall happen than this is what shall happen! Do you understand me?"

Elizabeth swallowed hard and lowered her eyes to the ground. "I understand." Someone else might have simply taken the baby and walked out, but that wasn't the way you did things in the Wenham family. You minded your elders. You listened to and respected their commands, no matter how hard they were to swallow.

"Good."

As Edith turned back toward her eager 'guests' Estelle, Elizabeth's mother, grabbed her daughter's hand and, squeezing tightly, whispered something in her ear that only Elizabeth could hear. Elizabeth straightened up, wiped the tears from her eyes, and let out a yielding sigh of capitulation.

"Bring in the child!" Edith called out over her shoulder. Then turning back to Elizabeth she didn't ask, but ordered, "Untie them!"

As Elizabeth knelt behind the couple, slowly untying the restraints that had left rope burns across their wrists, her oldest daughter Jacinda walked in, carrying a soft pink blanket snugly wrapped around the porcelain-skinned newborn baby girl. The baby was sound asleep, unaware of anything happening around her, yet, as Jacinda handed her to her great grandmother she began to cry in her sleep.

Elizabeth attempted one final plea. "Granny, please. I'm begging you. Just let me keep her. They can't possible take care of her not knowing—." That was when Jacinda realized what was happening.

"Granny, are you actually giving Aleerah away?" Jacinda asked.

"Aleerah?!" Edith turned in shock. "She named her after my mother?" Looking down at the sleeping baby she struggled with her own decision. "It doesn't matter—" she said quietly to herself. Then back to her grandchild, "How do you know her name?" Edith's eyes were fixated on Jacinda's.

Then, for the first time—ever—standing up to her grandmother, Jacinda drew a line in the sand. She made a conscious decision that she would no longer blindly follow the leadership of her Granny Edith, not if she was willing to pull their family apart like this—willingly and deliberately. "I—what if Loraline wakes up? How will you—."

"Enough!" Edith commanded. "What do you think the Founders would say if they found out there was an unapproved birth in our family? Would you like to be the one to tell them?" Edith asked.

"I don't know, but I don't care. They will kill her, that's what they'll do. What if she has powers, how will they even—?"

"Stop. This is how it must be." Edith didn't let Jacinda continue. So much for standing up to Granny Edith.

But this decision hadn't come easily for Edith either. Even though she knew the baby's chances of survival were minimal, she couldn't chance the exposure she would surely bring to the family. Dealing with Loraline's situation was going to be hard enough without the addition of an unreported child of questionable descent. "If the time comes that her powers develop, she will find us. The goddesses have a way of working things out. You must have faith." Edith had had enough of her granddaughters' interruptions. "No go home, both of you. We will discuss this in the morning."

"No! You can't just send us away," Elizabeth cried.

"Yes, I can." Then waving her hand toward her great granddaughter she all but dismissed them.

Jacinda took her mother's hand, and helped her up from where she knelt behind Martha and David. "Come on Mom. We have to go."

Elizabeth looked down at them and spit the words at them, "I promise you, I will get her back and if you harm her in any way you will not only pay for what you have done to my family but you will die for hurting her. I'll be watching you. Don't forget it!"

Elizabeth and Jacinda could hear the baby's cries as they reluctantly walked toward the front of the house. "What will Loraline do? What will she say when she wakes up?" Elizabeth was crying too.

"If she wakes up," Jacinda corrected her mother.

"She will. She has to."

Back in the study Edith handed the baby off to her daughter Estelle as she spoke to Martha and David. "Now, you see how passionate my grandchild is about this child." She waved her hand back toward the crying baby. "Although I do not share her feelings, I will not stop her from killing you, if you hurt the child."

Martha's arms were already up waiting to hold the baby. "Do we really get to keep her?" Tears of joy and fear flooded her face.

"Martha, please!" David scolded.

"David, stop. We get to live—we're together—we finally have a child. I don't care what else they make us do. This is a gift; no matter who or where she comes from this child is still a gift from God."

Edith moved toward them, slowly but with fierce determination, and Martha stopped her rambling. "She is not your child. You will raise her as your own. You will care for her. You will do anything and everything to keep her safe. That is your charge, but she is *not* your child." Martha's expression fell. "Her true identity will remain a secret to her and to everyone else in town. And, remember, although you have no roots here, you are now forever bound. You are not to leave Atlanta, under any circumstance, without direct permission from me!" She took the now sleeping child from her daughter's arms. "Do you understand?"

"Yes." Martha's arms trembled slightly, as she reached for the baby, but her eyes were fixed on the baby girl.

"You will *not* hunt! If I get word that you have killed even once, you will die. Do you understand?"

"Yes, yes we understand." Martha pleaded, "Please," as she reached out again for the baby she so desperately wanted.

"Know that we will indeed be watching, and any wrong move will result in nothing short of death." Nothing seemed to faze Martha, as she nodded in agreement with everything Edith was saying. Edith held the baby out to Martha, and Martha gathered her into her arms and held her close to her breast. "You will call her Alee. When people ask, you will tell them she was a long-awaited adoption, one you choose to keep quiet for fear that it would fall through."

"I understand." Martha's face glowed with excitement, yet David still didn't move—didn't even turn to look at the child.

Edith was beginning to feel little patience for David's cavalier attitude. "If you would rather not take the child, we can make arrangements for you and your wife to face a more just punishment."

For the first time he lifted his eyes to meet Edith's. "For my wife, and no one else, I will do this."

"Very well then." She turned to walk out, but not before leaving instructions with her daughter. "Get them settled in somewhere close to town. Any of the properties will do." Then she was gone.

Estelle was a short plump woman only fifty-eight years old. Unlike her mother, she was a nurturer, and seeing her great grandchild given away was hard enough—having to be the one to arrange it was almost killing her. "As you've already been told, you will remain here in Atlanta."

"But we have no family here." It was the first time Martha had said anything that could have been seen as argumentative since the mention of the child.

"Your only other choice is death." Estelle wasn't being mean, or trying to scare her. She was simply stating a fact. Martha nodded, and Estelle continued. "We will have a house set up for you to live in, but you will be required to get jobs here in town to pay the rent and all other bills. Any expenses related to the care of Alee will be taken care of. You will receive compensation and instructions on a regular base, but you must also remain in contact with us at all times." Estelle moved past them to get a hand-carved wooden box from the mantel above the fireplace. A picture of a rose was carved and burned into the lid, and along the stem the word "family" was engraved. "Take this for Alee. It belonged to her mother. It is only fitting that it should be hers now."

Estelle led the couple out of the study, along the long hallway and into the shop. It was dark, save for a dimly lit lamp in the corner. "There is a car waiting out front. Go quickly, before she changes her mind."

Martha and David made their way out into the rain, and climbed in the back of the only car in the empty parking lot. The driver didn't hesitate—he drove off into the dark as Estelle stood silently on the porch, watching it go, weeping softly.

From the very first, Martha realized that something wasn't right with the little girl. She wouldn't take her bottle, and on the rare occasion when she did she would throw up more than she kept down—and she cried inconsolably both day and night. However, on the morning of the fourth day, Martha woke up to a silent house. David was already gone—he spent most of his time away from the house searching for work—at least that was his excuse. Martha was convinced he just didn't want to have anything to do with Alee. She prayed he would come around sooner or later, but was willing to give him the time he needed.

When she went into Alee's room, Martha moved as slowly and quietly as possible, not wanting to wake her if she was finally getting some restful sleep. Peering down at the baby, wrapped snuggly in her soft pink blanket, Martha gasped, and cried out in fear. She had to catch herself on the side of the crib to keep from collapsing to the floor. "NOOOO!" She screamed in horror. She knew that she must MOVE. She picked up the baby and dashed downstairs to the kitchen. Struggling to one-handedly manipulate the receiver on the wall phone, she managed to dial 911.

"911, what is your emergency?" A friendly operator answered the call.

"My baby, she isn't breathing! Her lips are blue—she's so cold." Martha was crying and frantic.

"I have an ambulance in route now ma'am. What is your name?

"Martha, Martha Moyer."

"Good, now Martha, where is the child now?"

"I have her here, in my arms." Martha was clutching Alee tightly in her arms, rocking her back and forth.

"All right. I need you to lie her down on the ground. Have you ever performed CPR?"

"Oh God. No—no I haven't. Please hurry."

"How old is the child?"

For a second Martha wasn't sure what to say. She had been so focused on Alee that night at the Wenham house that she hadn't actually paid as much attention as she should have. She made her best guess. "She's... she's only two weeks old. Please hurry."

"You'll want to make sure she is on her back. Put your phone on speaker, and lay it down next to her." She didn't say anything for a second. "Are you there?"

"Yes, yes I'm here. She's on the ground, the phone is on speaker. Now what?"

"Using just the tip of your index finger and middle finger you're going to do 30 chest compressions, but make sure you tilt her head back as you do them." Martha's hands were shaking, but she followed the instructions as she counted under her breath. "You're doing great. The paramedics should be there shortly."

"…twenty-five, twenty-six, twenty-seven, twenty-eight, twenty-nine, thirty."

"Now, you're going to cover her mouth and nose with your mouth. I want you to breathe two times trying to fill her lungs. Watch to make sure her chest rises." The operator's voice was calm as she walked her through every step. "Now, repeat the chest compressions."

"I hear the ambulance. I can hear them. Should I go open the door?"

"No. Martha. Stay with your daughter and continue the chest compressions. They will get in on their own." Several long moments later Martha heard loud pounding coming from the front door.

"I'm in here. Please hurry," Martha screamed from the floor of the kitchen. Then there was a crash as the window on the front door was broken. The front door flew open and two paramedics ran in, medical bags in hand, determined and focused. They took charge of the situation, moving Martha aside and taking over the compressions seamlessly. Everything seemed to move in slow motion for Martha as she watched, prayed, and hoped for the baby to hang on to what little life she seemed to have left in her. Finally, the silence was broken by the soft sound of Alee's shallow breathing that quickly turned into loud cries. Slowly, color began to fill her pale cheeks. The medics strapped her to a gurney, and lifted her into the back of the ambulance. Martha climbed in with them. The ambulance raced down the road, lights flashing and siren blaring.

Once they were settled in at the hospital Martha made the dreaded call to the Black Onyx to explain to Edith Wenham what had happened, but only after calling her husband first. Although he wasn't happy, he was there sitting next to her at Alee's bedside within the hour. Alee was still alive, and that meant that their job, as defined by the Wenham's, was not done. David wasn't about to let his wife suffer alone in the hospital.

Martha spent the next two weeks of sleepless nights in the hospital neonatal intensive care unit. She had been drawn to this baby the minute she laid eyes on her—now, she couldn't tear herself away. She spent every moment she could rocking her, feeding her, singing to her, and praying with all of her heart and faith for her recovery. By the end of the first week, even David was spending most of his days at Alee's bedside. The doctors finally diagnosed Alee with Aplastic Anemia, a rare blood disorder in which her body's bone marrow wasn't able to create enough new blood cells.

When Alee was released from the hospital, Martha and David, with full understanding of her condition, made a private agreement with one another to take full responsibility for the her care in every regard. They had grown closer to her with each passing day, and although the Wenhams were providing financial compensation for her care, the Moyer's refused to use it. They preferred to accept Alee as their own child in every way, no matter what the Wenham's decided to do later. They opened a bank account for Alee, and deposited the Wenham's money for her to use later in life, giving her an opportunity for a better future then they alone would be able to provide. Martha had the details of the account added to their wills, but secretly hoped that one day she would be able to tell her daughter the truth about how she came into their lives.

This small baby girl, Martha realized, had the power of love and life in her laughter, and her smile touched everyone who saw it. There was something special about her, and Martha had every intention of doing everything in her power to protect her.

The Moyers spent thousands on Alee's medical bills in that first year of her life. She was in and out of the hospital, and the doctors gave her five years to live—ten at the most. The Moyers knew that Alee would spend the rest of her life, however long or how short that might be, going from one doctor's office to another. She would be in and out of hospitals, and undergo tests, painful treatments, and thousands of blood transfusions. But at least now she would never have to do it alone. She had parents who would be with her every step of the way. She had parents she could trust— parents who would make sure she always knew how much they loved her. No matter what happened, she would feel safe with them. At least that was their goal.

The Police station was unusually quiet. Not that much ever really happened in McBain, but tonight felt different. The Ward family sat in a small room behind closed doors. Everyone passing by paused at the small window into the room and tried to get a glimpse of what was going on inside. The young mother and her beautiful five-year-old twins, Victoria and Damian, were waiting to speak with the next available officer. They seemed like a nice, normal family. However, upon closer examination, Damian's blood-soaked pajamas and tear-stained face, Mrs. Ward's puffy red eyes, and the eerie way Victoria stared straight ahead, silent and still, suggested a more sinister family portrait.

When Officer Manfra entered the room, his eyes met Mrs. Ward's and he instantly felt her pain. He stopped in his tracks for a breath, not knowing what to say. Taking a deep breath, he proceeded to the table, and sat down across from her.

"I'm very sorry for your loss. I know this can't be easy, but if you could just explain to me what exactly happened this evening prior to your calling 911. We need to get your statement."

Mrs. Ward took a deep breath. She didn't really know what to say, or how to describe it in a way that anyone would believe. She knew that any sane person was sure to think her crazy and lock her up.

"I don't—. My son was the one. I mean—. He was the one, he was there. He saw him." Tears began to flow in a steady stream down her cheeks but she didn't seem to notice—she somehow maintained control. "I was in my bedroom upstairs. I had gone to bed early because I had a headache." She looked at her children, wrapping her arms around them and pulled them closer to her. "I'm so sorry."

Officer Manfra waved to someone outside the window. An older woman, dressed in a conservative skirt and blouse came into the room within seconds. "Can you take the children to get a snack please?"

"No. Please don't take them," Mrs. Ward cried, pulling them closer still.

"Karen. Can I call you Karen?" he asked softly. Mrs. Ward nodded in response.

"Karen, it will be easier this way, and they won't be far. They're just going down the hall, I promise," Mrs. Ward nodded reluctantly. The woman escorted the children out of the room and down the hall while their mother watched through the window. When she finally turned back to the officer, he prompted her to continue.

She took a deep, steadying breath. "I had gone to bed early. I could hear James giving the children their baths and putting them to bed. I usually gave them their baths, but since I wasn't feeling well he offered. I—. I decided to read for a little while to see if it would help with my headache. I must have fallen asleep because the next thing I knew I heard a loud crash, and then Damian screamed. I ran downstairs, and—." She closed her eyes, and with her hands over her face she sobbed, shaking her head as if trying to dislodge the image from her memory.

"Would you like a tissue?" Officer Manfra asked, but Karen continued to sob. "Do you need something to drink?" She wiped her face with the sleeve of her flannel pajamas and just shook her head. It was late, and almost everyone had gone home for the night, but the few people still remaining started to gather outside in the hall, no longer trying to hide their curiosity. With her back to the window, she couldn't see them, but she could feel their eyes on her. She took a few slow, deep breaths to calm her nerves and slow her racing heart. Not wanting to acknowledge the judgmental eyes of those behind her, she forced herself to stare down at the table in front of her.

"I'm sorry. I'm sorry. I'm fine," Karen said, taking a tissue from the box on the table. She cleaned her face, and blew her nose. "I ran down the stairs, and a man, a tall man was running out the front door. I didn't see his face. I couldn't see his face." She was almost pleading with herself as if she could force herself to remember, to know what he looked like if she just tried hard enough. "It was dark, and he was wearing all black. His back was to me. I—. I couldn't see his face. I couldn't," she said, crying.

Officer Manfra reached across the table and took Karen's shaking hand in his trying to calm her down. "It's OK. Just try to remember what happened next."

She looked up and their eyes met. She took a few slow breaths. "He was gone so suddenly. The door slammed behind him as soon as he ran out. He moved so quickly, as if he were running, but faster, and he didn't make a sound. He just vanished." She knew it sounded crazy, but she didn't know of any other way to describe it. "I turned toward the living room, and Damian was sitting on the floor, kneeling over James. James was just lying there. He wasn't moving.

"I heard something behind me, and I turned around. Victoria was coming down the stairs. I ran up and grabbed her before she reached the landing. I didn't want her to see— she shouldn't see him. Not like that." Her hands started to shake as she tried desperately to continue.

"What happened next?"

"I told her to go back to her room, and to stay there until I came to get her. I told her to lock her bedroom door, and to hide in her closet." Karen began to lose focus. "She's such a good little girl. She always has been. She listened so well. I didn't even have to tell her twice. She just—she just went." Karen began to tear up again, and her hands started to shake. Her throat felt tight, and she couldn't speak.

When he looked up from his paper where he had been writing down every word, he realized she was having trouble breathing. "Karen? Are you all right?"

Reaching across the table she grabbed his hand and pulled him toward her. "What if, what if he had gone up there? Oh God, what if he had gotten her?" She was shaking her head trying hard to catch her breath as she started to hyperventilate. Her grip on Officer Manfra's hand was so tight that her knuckles started to turn white. He pulled himself out of her grip, rushed to the door, and called out to another officer sitting at a desk nearby. Moments later his partner, Tandy, ran in with a small brown paper bag in hand, and quickly placed it over Karen's mouth. Her breathing slowed down, and she started to relax. "What did I do? Why did I send her by herself? What was I thinking?" Head hung down in her hands she was sobbing uncontrollably.

"She is fine," Officer Manfra said firmly, his deep voice rumbling in Karen's ear. "Victoria is fine, and I'm not going to let anyone hurt her. OK?" Karen looked directly at him again and nodded. She allowed herself to calm down enough to look up and see that her children were safe, sitting quietly just outside the room. "Now, you said she went back upstairs. What did you do after she was gone?"

"I went back into the living room. Damian was still there, kneeling over James. I rushed over and when I got there—Damian was—James' blood—it was everywhere." Mrs. Ward wasn't crying anymore, and she looked him straight in the eyes, "Damian was covered in James' blood. He was holding James' head in his lap, and had his hands around his neck. I thought he was—I didn't know what he was doing. It looked like he was trying to strangle him, but when I grabbed his hands away, the blood—it just started to come out even faster. James—he looked like he had been attacked. No, that isn't right, not attacked. Mauled, he looked like he had been mauled. His throat—it was torn open. *Ripped* open."

"He shouldn't have seen that. Why did he see that? He shouldn't have seen that. I should have protected him." She continued talking to herself as Officer Manfra moved around the table to sit next to her.

"He's going to be all right. Damian is going to be all right, and so are you."

"You don't know that. You can't know that, you weren't there."

"You're right, I wasn't, but we have people who can help. Please, you have to try not to worry. We're going to talk to Damian, and we're going to get him help. We're going to get you both help. But right now, I need for you to be strong. I need you to try and calm down so that we can bring Damian back in here to talk to us. Can you do that for me?" She shook her head, but even as she did her breathing became steadier, and she stopped crying. "Yes you can. I know you can. See?" As she used the back of her hand to wipe the tears away from her face he slid the tissue box across the table in front of her. Then, moving back to his seat on the other side of the table, he nodded toward the window. One of the officers who had been watching the children from a few desks away got up and made his way to their side.

Damian was escorted back into the room, holding an unopened bag of chips. He sat in the empty seat next to his mother. Karen smiled down at his innocent face, trying to stay focused when really all she wanted to do was hold her son, and cry. Her husband was dead and she felt lost, alone, and scared.

"Damian, do you think you could tell me what you saw tonight when your father was attacked?" Officer Manfra didn't have a lot of experience dealing with children, and as the words came out of his mouth he realized the question may have been a little too direct. He was used to dealing with older witnesses and suspects, not five year-old boys.

Damian just looked at him. He wasn't crying any more, he wasn't making a sound, he wasn't even blinking. Save for the fact that he was still breathing and fidgeting with the chip bag, you wouldn't have known that he was awake.

After many silent minutes without Damian so much as coughing, let alone talking, Officer Manfra decided to take a different approach. He left the room for a few minutes hoping that Damian would talk to his mother.

Over and over, Damian's mother told him how sorry she was. "I'm so sorry, sweetie. You shouldn't have seen that. You should never have seen that. I should have been there." She sat facing him with his hands in hers and, looking into his eyes, and she asked the question she prayed he didn't have an answer to. "Sweetheart, did you see what happened? Did you see what hurt Daddy?" Suddenly, something changed within Damian, as if a light had been turned on behind his eyes. "Did you see who hurt Daddy?" Damian furrowed his brow and cocked his head. Karen repeated, "Did you see what hurt Daddy?"

He nodded, desperately trying to blink back tears and failing. His mother grabbed him and pulled him into her lap, holding him, cradling him in her arms like a little baby. She rocked him back and forth trying to calm him just like she used to do when he was a baby, but it was no use. Damian couldn't have controlled the tears. They weren't going to stop any time soon.

At six years old Alee was tiny, with wiry arms and legs, and skin so fair it looked translucent under the florescent lighting. It was the summer before she would be starting first grade, and she hadn't been in the hospital in over two months. Martha was sitting on the porch watching as Alee's carrot red hair glistened in the sun. Alee was as happy as could be, playing jacks on the walkway leading down into the front yard. "Mommy, look!" Alee was pointing to a large moving truck driving slowly up the road. "Who is it Mommy?"

"I don't know sweetie. Maybe someone is finally moving in next door." The house next to theirs had been vacant for the last three years. Prior to that, tenants had come and gone, never staying longer than a few months. Rental properties in Atlanta never lasted long. The housing market was pretty reasonable, so people usually only rented until they could find something better to purchase.

The truck made the left turn into the driveway next door, and Alee jumped up from where she was sitting, leaving her jacks on the ground and nearly hopped the whole way up to her mother's side. "Do you think they'll have a girl my age?" She was so excited at the idea that Martha hated to disappoint her.

"I don't know sweetie, but you know you can't—."

"I know, I know, but I'm not sick now. What could it hurt just to go over and see?" Sure enough as soon as the truck doors opened Alee flew across the yard and was nearly pummeled by a large Great Dane that jumped out of the truck.

"Alee!" Martha ran to Alee and wrapped her arms around her.

A young man stepped out of the driver's side door, and rushed around the truck. "I'm so sorry. Is she all right?" He was stocky, with short brown hair, and was wearing jeans with a flannel shirt. The wedding band around his finger gave promise to a young family moving in.

"She's fine, I think." Martha turned back toward the house, carrying Alee the whole way. "It's time for your nap now Alee."

"But I don't want to nap." She didn't whine often, but she was in bed so much of the time when she was sick that the last thing she wanted to do when she wasn't sick was nap. "Please—."

"No, you need your rest." Just as Martha was pulling the door open a blue minivan pulled into the driveway behind the moving truck, and out jumped a pudgy little girl with light brown hair down to her butt and black-rimmed glasses. Alee waved, but the little girl didn't see her. When the door shut behind her Alee knew that her chances of getting back outside before taking a nap were over. She conceded, going straight to nap so that her mother would allow her to go out and play for just a little while longer after she woke up.

The end of nap time couldn't come quick enough, but when she saw the numbers on her clock change from two fifty-nine to three o'clock she jumped out of bed and ran straight down stairs. "Mom, can I go outside and clean up my jacks?"

"I already took care of it while you were sleeping, sweetheart. They're in your room on your desk."

"Oh." Alee's voice dropped, disappointed, as she tried to think of another way to get outside.

Martha knelt down in front of her daughter and smiled. "Would you like to meet the neighbors?"

Alee's eyes lit up like Christmas morning. "Really! Can we?"

"Yes, but you have to stay with me."

"I will, I promise. Thank you, thank you, thank you." Alee jumped up, hugging her mother around the neck so tightly that Martha had to peel her off.

Alee wasn't a shy little girl. It probably had something to do with meeting so many new people all the time—doctors, nurses, other patients. Every time she found herself in a new hospital she was quick to make new friends—although, of course, those friendships never lasted long. Alee didn't hesitate to start pounding on the door as soon as she reached the porch. "Not so hard sweetie. I'm sure they can hear you."

Suzi, a round-faced woman with light brown hair, opened the door. "Hello!?"

"Hi, I'm Alee." Alee was holding out her hand.

"Well, hello Alee," Suzi said with a big smile. "I'm Mrs. Brown, but you can call me Ms. Suzi." Mrs. Brown knelt down and clasped Alee's hand affectionately.

Two seconds later Danielle raced down the stairs and squeezed into the doorframe at her mom's side. "My name's Danielle, but you can call me Dani."

"Hi, I'm Alee."

"Want to see my room?"

Alee turned to her mother, with pleading eyes—and Martha nodded. "All right, but don't be long." The girls were off, running up the stairs as quick as lightening.

"Would you like to come in for some tea?"

"Oh, no thanks—I don't want to intrude."

"We're just unpacking." Suzi held the door open, inviting Martha in, but Martha shook her head declining. "Well, if you don't mind, it's all right with me if she stays and plays for a while."

Martha was hesitant to leave Alee there, but she was just next door. "All right, but please, if it becomes a problem don't hesitate to send her home."

"It's not a problem at all."

Martha took a deep breath, staring past Suzi up the stairs, where she could hear the girls giggling. "Thank you. I'll be back in a little while to get her."

"Take your time," Suzi called as Martha started back home.

Back home, Martha busied herself preparing dinner and folding and putting away laundry. Putting clothes away in Alee's room, she noticed the small wooden box on the dresser, with the rose engraved on the lid—the one that Estelle Wenham had given her that night.

That box was the one concrete connection to Alee's past, and it haunted Martha's dreams. The thought that they could take her away at any moment scared her more than the idea of losing her to her illness. Somehow she thought she could deal with the illness, but never the thought of her going back to the Wenham's.

The doorbell startled Martha out of her thoughts. "Alee?!" She ran down the stairs, anxious to know that her daughter was home again, safe under her own roof. But Alee wouldn't ring the bell, would she, and with that thought Martha opened the door to find a tall slender man wearing all black and looking like he had been living on the streets for years. He was leaning toward her with his hands on each side of the doorframe. Martha didn't open the screen door, but instead quickly locked it. "Can I help you?"

"I'm sorry if I startled you." He stepped back from the door, and smoothed his hair back out of his eyes. "My name is Eric, and I'm looking for my daughter." He leaned in sniffing at the air coming from inside the house.

"I'm sorry, but I can't help you." Martha stepped back starting to close the door behind her when he stopped her.

"She would be six! If she looks like her mother she has the most beautiful red hair in the world, eyes as blue as the ocean, and skin as fair as a porcelain doll's. Perfect in every way." Martha's heart stopped beating for only a second, but Eric's eyes went straight to hers. "You know where she is!" He hadn't said it like a question, but she answered anyway.

"No, I'm sorry I can't help you." She shut the door and ran to the phone and dialed quickly—only hesitating a moment before deciding who to call first—her husband or the Black Onyx.

"Hello?" David answered on the first ring.

"Oh thank God you're there, David. It's happening, they've come." Martha was shaking and looking frantically back down the hall toward the front door.

"Martha! Who? Who's come?"

"I don't know. A man, he was asking about Alee. Please David—please don't let them take her." Tears spilled down her cheeks at the thought.

"Where is she now?" Martha didn't even hear David's question at first. "Martha!" he shouted. "Where is she now?!"

"Oh God, she's next door." She dropped the phone, and ran out. At the Brown house she knocked urgently, scanning the street behind her, but no one was there.

"Hi—. Martha! What's wrong?"

Wiping the tears from her face, Martha pushed past Suzi and started up the stairs. "Nothing," she called back. "I'm sorry, I just need to take Alee home. Her father just called, and he needs us to meet him right away." She didn't even bother to say goodbye as she rushed Alee out the front door and back to the safety of their own home, slamming and locking the door behind them.

"Mommy, what's wrong?"

"Nothing sweetheart, everything is fine. We are just going home for a little while, OK?" Martha grabbed the phone that was still lying on the floor in the kitchen, and could hear David screaming her name before she raised it to her ear. "I have her," she said. "Everything's all right, she's safe."

"Martha, you need to call them. If they've sent for her we're not going to be able to stop them."

"I know."

The next fifteen minutes were the hardest she had ever lived through. She knew the number by heart but had to force herself to push the buttons on the phone. The phone rang for an eternity, echoing in her ear. Alee just sat patiently in her mother's lap, not knowing what was going on, or why her mother was so scared.

"This is Elizabeth, you've reached the Black Onyx. How may I help you?" Silence filled the air. "Hello? Is anyone there?"

She couldn't speak right away, be it fear or be it pride, but desperation finally pushed the words out of her. "Yes, hello, can I please speak with Estelle Wenham?"

"Can I tell her whose calling?"

"This is—."

"Ma'am?"

"Tell her it's Mrs. Moyer." A gasp came through from the other end of the line.

"Yes of course, right away." Elizabeth set the phone on the desk then called. "Mother! Mother, come quick."

True to form, Estelle ran into the shop with Jacinda close behind her. "Elizabeth, what is it?"

"Mom, what's wrong?"

Elizabeth picked up the phone and handed it out to her mother, Estelle. "It's Mrs. Moyer." In the six years that Alee had been in the Moyer's care they had only called the Black Onyx once. That was the first time Alee had been admitted to the hospital. From that point on they had assumed full responsibility, only giving updates when requested. The idea that after so long a time Martha was now reaching out to them scared Elizabeth to the core. It wasn't as if the Wenhams didn't keep up with the child's well-being, because in fact they were a much larger part of Alee's life than the Moyers suspected, but always from a distance.

"This is Estelle." She spoke quietly.

"Estelle, this is Martha. A man came to the house today, asking about a child." She was struggling to get the words out, and held her daughter close to her chest covering Alee's ears so she couldn't listen in.

"What man?"

"He said his name was Eric, but he didn't—."

"Martha, you are *not* to let him into your home. Do you understand me?" Pulling her daughter closer, Estelle whispered to Elizabeth, "He's still looking for her."

"Why? Who is he?" Martha asked. To say that she was scared would have been an understatement.

"That doesn't matter. It is your job to protect her. In order to do that you must not allow him to see the child. Is that clear?"

"Yes. I understand, but he says he's her—."

"Good, I'll be in contact." Then there was a click and the phone went dead.

"—father." Martha sat there for a while, cradling Alee in her arms, rocking her back and forth as she sang softly in her ear.

"It's OK Mommy," Alee whispered. "It's OK." Martha heard the deadbolt on the back door click shut, and looking into the kitchen, she saw one of the chairs slide across the room, and jam itself under the doorknob.

"Wuhu-uh-uh-uh-uh." Martha couldn't breathe. She knew what it meant, but instead of facing it she just closed her eyes and held Alee close.

Later that night Martha and David sat talking in the living room, like they had done so many nights. Eric waited, watching the house from a safe distance.

"David, he was a vampire. I have no doubt."

David lowered his voice, "Did you recognize him?"

"No, only his kind." Her nose wrinkled in disgust.

"And he thought we had his daughter? How is that possible?" David was talking more to himself than to Martha, as he stood up and crossed to an old wooden desk that sat in the corner of the room. He unlocked and lifted the roll top and took out a photo album—the old fashioned kind, where the photos are held in by small tabs at each corner. Only, instead of photos it held newspaper clippings, snapshots, and hand written notes. He brought it over to the couch and sat back down next to Martha. "We need to be sure he—."

"David, why do you have that?" She grabbed the book out of his hands. "If they caught us with this, they would kill us."

"They're not in our home, nor will they dictate what I can or cannot have." He grabbed it back. "Besides, I'm not hunting. I'm merely keeping it for our protection. This book is the only record that remains of our family history. For the last six years we have been stagnant—that doesn't mean we will stay this way forever."

Martha jumped up. "That part of my life is behind me now. For our daughter's sake you should put it behind you too." She turned to leave, stopping briefly at the bottom of the stairs. "Protecting our family is one thing —so find out who he is—but please, don't do anything that will get you or us killed." She turned to go, but stopped before leaving the room.

"Martha, are you all right?" David asked, concerned.

"No. There's something else."

"What is it?"

"She's—." She couldn't look at him. "I think she's one of them—."

"One of—?"

"—a witch. I mean, we knew it was a possibility, more than a possibility. But, I think she has—powers."

"Ooh." They sat in silence. "Did you tell them?"

"No."

"Good."

"I guess I always hoped that maybe—maybe she wouldn't change."

"We both did."

After Martha went to bed, David stayed up for a while longer. He sat on the front porch, breathing in the fresh night air, trying to calm his shaken nerves. Just as he was getting ready to go back inside and head up to bed he noticed a man standing in the shadows across the street. They locked eyes and, as if prompted—or summoned—David made his way across the lawn and crossed the street. His hands were sweating, his skin tingled under his clothes, and every nerve crackled with fear and adrenaline.

"I'm not going to hurt you." Eric's voice was calm, almost gentle, and David's body reacted instinctively as his muscles relaxed on their own. "You've taken good care of her—for that I cannot thank you enough. But she isn't yours to keep. You know that don't you?"

David nodded.

"I know what you are, as I'm sure you know what I am as well."

"I do," David answered.

"Then know this. I have unfinished business to attend to, but she is my blood, and when I am able to care for her I will be back. For now, I will leave her in your care." Eric turned to go, but stopped himself. "You mustn't tell anyone of my visit. Do you understand?"

David breathed in, holding back a scowl. "I understand."

"And, do not try to keep me out. In her veins flows my blood. Therefore, as long as she lives here, I do not need an invitation to enter your home. And I will know if you have made any attempts to block me." Turning away he called over his shoulder, "Now you can go."

David didn't move for almost five minutes, staring into the darkness that had enveloped Eric. When he finally made his way back into his house, a heavy weight had fallen upon his shoulders and, too tired to climb the stairs, he lay down on the couch and drifted off to sleep.

Estelle hung up the phone, and turned to her daughter with somberness in her eyes. "We need to talk to Jacinda. Call her in."

"Should I get Granny Edith as well?"

"No. For now, let's leave your grandmother out of this. She hasn't been feeling well, and the last thing she needs right now is added stress." Estelle moved to the bookshelf along the back wall and sifted through book after book as Elizabeth went to the shop to find Jacinda.

"Sweetheart, can I speak with you for a moment?"

Jacinda was straightening the shelves, and organizing the crystals. "Of course—what is it?"

"Not here." Elizabeth gestured toward the colorful beaded curtain that separated the shop from the living courters. They walked together down the hall and into the sitting room.

"Mom, what's going on?" Even now that Jacinda was in her mid-twenties, her mother's silence could send chills down her spine.

The three women sat together, and Estelle looked pointedly at Jacinda. Getting right to the point, she said, "I thought you said that Loraline had moved on from Eric?"

"I'm sorry—what's this about?" Jacinda looked back and forth from her mother to her grandmother.

"You told us that before your sister ended up in the hospital, you and she had been in contact. And though you never told us she was pregnant, you did tell us that she and Eric had gone their separate ways. I overlooked the fact that you knew Aleerah's name all those years ago, assuming that Loraline herself had told you about her, but that isn't the case, is it? I think that you had been in touch with Eric. You had told us that Loraline was thinking about coming back home. Is that what she told you, or were you just trying to put her in a more positive light?"

Jacinda stood, offended, and ready to defend herself and her sister. "Loraline had no reason to feel guilty for her choices. I get that no one here could accept her decision, but that doesn't make it the wrong decision." She paced the room. "What does it matter anyway? That was six years ago! Loraline is in a coma. Who knows if she'll ever wake up. Granny Edith gave her daughter, my niece, your granddaughter—away! Yet, you sit here, six years later, questioning me?" Her fists were balled so tightly that her nails were starting to cut into the palms of her hands. The fireplace self-ignited, startling everyone.

"Jacinda please," her mother moved to her side, pleading with her. "We can't change decisions that were made in the past; all we can do is move toward our future." She sat her daughter down. "But, we can't do that without *all* of the information. Eric is Alee's father, isn't he?"

Jacinda swallowed hard, not really knowing why it mattered so much. "No. Yes. I don't really know. Loraline never told me, but he said he is. I guess I never really thought about it."

"Sweet goddesses above, what happens if he finds her?" Elizabeth whispered.

Estelle just shook her head. "I don't know."

"How is it even possible that he could be the father?"

"It's rare, but it *is* possible." Estelle opened the book she had been cradling. "Your grandmother would call her an abomination, but if she really is what I think she is, she is a miracle. It could explain her medical condition and point toward the cure, although it is not something one would want to have a child subjected to."

"Granny, what are you talking about?" Jacinda only understood parts of the conversation, and, having young children of her own, she didn't like the sound of it.

"There is a chance that Alee could be the first surviving dhampir."

"Dhampir? What is that?" The word sounded foreign to Jacinda's ears.

Estelle never answered Jacinda's question. She just sat back in her seat and let the idea sink in. "It may be time to call the rest of the family."

They had driven all night, but they finally made it home shortly after midnight, just like her dad had promised they would. Alee had spent the last thirteen days in the children's hospital four hundred miles from home, and she wanted so desperately to wake up in her own bed on the morning of her tenth birthday. When they got home, David carefully lifted her from the back seat where she slept, covered by the small pink blanket she had slept with every night since they had brought her home. He carried her into their comfortable old home: with all the lights off, it felt like a private sanctuary, apart from the everyday world.

The house was warm, and welcoming. David carried Alee up the stairs, placed her gently in bed, and covered her with a blanket. Putting her little stuffed white lamb in her arms, he kissed her forehead and said sweet dreams my precious. Alee rolled over and quickly fell back into a peaceful sleep, unaware that she had even been moved at all. David stood in the doorway, watching her sleep. The corners of her lips curved upward slightly into an innocent little smile, the same way they always did. What she could possibly be dreaming of he had no idea.

Martha sat in the dim light of the kitchen drinking a cup of tea, waiting for them to get home. David joined her, and they sat downstairs together for the next five hours, watching the sky through the open window, waiting for the sun to come up. The doctors had always said not to get their hopes up. "Don't get too attached." Every time Alee ended up in the hospital again they warned them that the end was near. "You need to be prepared. No matter how hard it is to think about, you can't fool yourself into thinking her time won't come." They had been hearing this for years now and it never got any easier. But Alee was a fighter. She had always been a survivor. From birth, it had been challenge after challenge, but she had survived them all. When the doctors told them she would most likely die before her fifth birthday, their hearts broke. By the time she did turn five, they knew how strong Alee could be. Now that she was turning ten they were convinced that nothing would stop their little girl from growing up. They sat in the living room eagerly waited to see her face when she woke up and realized that she was ten years old.

At ten years old, Alee was more mature than most people twice her age. She had known more pain, more fear, more sadness, and more challenges than most people know in a lifetime. Yet, she was still a child, and she still longed for the things that other children had—something her parents had to keep reminding themselves. So this year they had gone all out for her birthday.

Reluctantly, but with the encouragement of her husband and Alee's team of doctors, Martha had come home from the hospital a couple of nights early to get everything ready. It was worth it to make Alee's tenth birthday one of the most memorable days of her life. It was the first birthday her parents had actually allowed her to have a real party with other kids from around the neighborhood, instead of just dinner and a birthday cake with her parents and her best friend Dani.

When Alee woke up the next morning, the house seemed quieter and a little chillier than usual for a summer morning. It was a Saturday, and summer break had already started so she didn't have school, church, or—best of all—no doctor's appointments. She pulled her robe on, slipped her feet into her fuzzy bunny slippers, and went downstairs.

"I can't believe she's really ten," Martha said, a sigh of relief in her voice that Alee recognized from every other time she had come home from the hospital still breathing. She often wondered if things would have been easier for her parents had she never been born. They wouldn't have such high medical bills to pay, her father wouldn't be losing job after job because he had to travel back and forth to the hospital so often, and her mother wouldn't spend countless nights crying alone in the kitchen when she thought no one could hear her.

Alee stayed in the hallway just out of view, and crouched down against the wall listening to her parents' whispers. Although Alee didn't fear death anymore, she still felt the same relief she heard in her mother's voice just at knowing she had survived another year. Alee wasn't blind to her medical issues. She had lived with them all her life, and her parents and all of her doctors had always been open and honest with her about her condition, no matter how scary the truth was.

Her father had always been the strong silent type. She'd never even seen him cry, but today she could almost hear his voice tremble as he spoke. "Ten years... and she's still our little girl."

"I don't want to lose her, David. I can't" Her parents were always worrying about her, and she understood why, but at some point even Alee had accepted the idea that it would have to end eventually. In the meantime, she just wanted to live her life fully while she still could.

"We're not going to lose her." That was her cue to change the mood, and cheer her parents up. Alee ran into the living room and jumped on her dad's lap, embracing him tighter and longer than she ever had.

Her father's laugh filled the room. "Happy birthday, sweetheart!"

"Happy birthday, to ME!" she shouted up to the ceiling, and then hugged him again, laughing the whole time.

"Alee, it's almost eleven o'clock. You need to run up and get dressed before everyone starts to get here." Martha had always been the sensible one of the family, and although David knew she was right, he continued to hold Alee tightly, tickling her until she was laughing so hard she could barely see.

Between laughing and gasping for air, Alee managed to squirm away from her dad's grip. "Arrive for what?" she asked as she sat up and looked around the living room for the first time that morning. The ceiling was covered with balloons, pink and white streamers hung from corner to corner. Across the room, party hats and a big princess cake sat in the center of the dining room table.

She couldn't contain her excitement. "Oh. My. God! I get to have a party? A real party?" Martha and David just smiled back at her. "Thank you, thank you, thank you!" She hugged her parents and she almost toppled them over on the couch. Then she was off. After the quickest shower of her life Alee changed her clothes at least five times before turning to see her mother standing quietly in her bedroom door holding the perfect outfit for her party. It was the prettiest dress Alee had ever seen, sky blue, just like her eyes, with a white sash that tied in the back. She had a matching white hair bow and fancy little white sandals to complete the outfit. She felt like a princess as she danced around the house waiting for the party to start.

When the doorbell rang in the middle of Alee's dance, she almost tripped trying to get it. She opened it to find Dani standing there on the porch holding a small pink box in her hand. She wrapped her arms around her friend, and pulled her in close for a tight hug. "Happy birthday—I've missed you so much!" Dani took in all the pink decorations. "Wow, how cool!"

"I know, right? Can you believe they've actually invited kids from school and everything?!"

Dani pulled Alee to the corner of the room where Martha couldn't hear from the kitchen. "Do you think your mom would be upset if you opened just one present before the party starts?" Alee glanced back toward the kitchen, and then back at Dani shaking her head with a guilty little smile on her face. The box was small, fitting perfectly in the palm of Alee's hand, and tied closed with a single white ribbon holding a card in place. When Alee pulled the end of the ribbon the card slid off into her hand. She read it quietly, not wanting her mother to hear.

"To a friend who's always true, this shows how much I care for you!" She smiled as she read the card. True to form Dani had made it a poem. She loved to write poetry, and was always scribbling new poems in her notebooks at school and on her book covers.

Inside the box were two silver charm bracelets, each with a single half heart charm, one with the word 'friend' engraved in the center, the other with the word 'best.' Dani and Alee had been best friends in every sense of the phrase, since the day they met. Alee clasped the 'friend' charm bracelet around her own wrist and then clasped the 'best' charm bracelet around Dani's.

"I love it." Tears were starting to fill Alee's eyes as she hugged Dani.

"Well don't *cry*. This is a party, or at least it will be soon."

"Hello Dani." Alee's dad had come into the living room without their noticing. "I see you convinced Alee to open one of her gifts early," he said smiling.

Dani just giggled.

"Look Daddy, look." Alee ran up and jumped in his lap, while wildly shaking the bracelet in front of him.

"It's beautiful, sweetheart." He kissed her forehead and lifted her off of his lap. "Go show your mother. I'm sure she'll love it too." Dani's eyes lit up and she didn't even wait for Alee to respond before turning toward the kitchen and pulling Alee behind her as she started running. "Mrs. Moyer, come quick. Come see what I got Alee for her birthday."

Soon the Moyers had a house full of children running around, playing games, and eating cake. Alee's parents couldn't be happier and neither could she. Everyone sang "Happy Birthday" as she blew out the pink crown shaped candles, closed her eyes, and silently made the same wish she made year after year. I wish I knew the reason. But, when she opened her eyes, no revelation awaited her, no fortune cookie to tell her the answer she longed to hear. She was still surrounded by the same people who had been there when she closed her eyes. A deep breath, a sigh, a smile to her mom, and then she took a big bite of cake as everyone clapped and cheered, enthusiastically waiting for their own pieces.

There were screams of delight when Alee sat down in front of the pile of gifts wrapped in pretty pink paper. One by one she opened them: dolls, games, music, lip gloss—and so much more.

Alee appreciated her friends' generosity, but inside she knew that the real gift she wanted wasn't in that stack. She knew she would find it later that night, when all her party guests had gone home and she was alone in her room. In the meantime, she enjoyed every moment as if it were her last, basking in the excitement of her first real birthday party.

When the gifts were all opened and her friends started to leave, she realized how tired she really was. A day of running around and playing was more than she was used to, and her body didn't really know how to handle it. After a light dinner of her mom's famous chicken and dumplings, she said goodnight to her parents and went upstairs.

After her shower, Alee stood in the hallway just outside her bedroom listening—waiting. The hair stood up on the back of her neck and a shiver shot down her spine. There wasn't a sound to be heard as she slowly opened the door and scanned her room. There on her pillow was a small black box and a velvety red envelope. Her heart jumped and she ran to the bed, tearing open the envelope that read, Sweet Alee, in the same handwriting as every year before. She knew what to expect as she pulled out the small white card with the hand drawn sketch of a single rose. It was drawn in red ink, the same every year, and on the beautiful snow-white paper the red lines were like veins spreading throughout the petals. It was a rare blood rose. Every year, a new message, a single word, was left for her along the stem of the flower, in handwriting so beautiful she couldn't imagine the pen that had created it. This year it read, PROTECTION!

On the dresser across from her bed sat a small wooden box, carved out of red pine. The top of the box was engraved with the outline of the same beautiful rose. The top was connected to the base by an elegant silver hinge in the back and an ornate silver clasp in the front. She had had the box since birth, but it wasn't until the night of her sixth birthday that she really paid it any attention. She had just come up after dinner to get ready for bed, and noticed a small black box and velvety red envelope sitting on the little table out on her bedroom balcony. "Mommy!" She yelled out her bedroom door, just as the phone started to ring downstairs.

"I'll be right there sweetheart," Martha called back up to her.

"Mommy, come here." Alee, could hear her mother answering the phone downstairs, and passed back and forth outside her bedroom door before deciding that she didn't want to wait. She slid open the glass door to the balcony and stepped outside cautiously. Alee's parents had always told her not to go out onto the balcony by herself, but she had just turned six, and she thought surely that was old enough. She quickly picked up the envelope and box then stepped back in the room shutting the balcony door just as her mother was coming into her room.

"Alee, what were you doing outside?" Martha was still clutching the phone in her hand, but it was hanging down by her side. Alee could hear the steady beeping through the receiver indicating that whoever Martha had been talking too had long since hung up.

"I just—. There was a—." She held her hands out in front of her showing her mother what she had found. "Is it from you?" she asked eagerly.

Martha froze for only a second before going to her daughter. "Have you opened them yet?" She hadn't answered Alee's question, but Alee was so fixated on the gift that she didn't even notice.

"No. Can I?"

"Of course sweetheart," Martha's voice was trembling. "They're for you." Alee's eyes lit up and she tore the envelope open, pulling out the small white card. Along the stem of the rose was the word 'LOVE'

She recognized the rose instantly. "This is the same…" She ran over to her dresser and pulled down her little wooden box. "…look, it's the same!"

"You're right it is—do you like it?" Martha swallowed, holding back a lump in her throat, but Alee didn't notice. This was the first time the Wenhams had done anything to make direct contact with Alee, and Martha was afraid of what it might mean. The idea of losing her daughter now, after six years of caring for her and standing by her bed in and out of hospitals, was unbearable. It didn't seem fair.

Alee's attention was focused on the gift. "What's inside?" she asked but didn't wait for an answer before pulling off the top. Inside the box was a small velvet bag pulled closed with a black cord. It was lying on top of a half a dozen small stones, no larger than marbles. When Alee poured them into her hand she noticed each one was a different color—. A different shape—. A different texture. "They're so pretty." She spread them out on the bed and then pulled open the velvet bag to find a tiny crystal charm in the shape of a rose. "Oh Mommy! Can I wear it?"

There wasn't a necklace in the box, so Martha unlatched the thin silver necklace she was wearing and slid the charm onto the chain and then clasped it around her daughter's neck. Her hands were shaking as she smoothed Alee's hair back in place. "It's beautiful, just like you." She managed a smile and kissed Alee softly on the forehead. "You should go to bed now. I'll see you in the morning." After her mother left, Alee sat in her room with the lights off, just holding the tiny crystal rose close to her heart.

Now, four years later, as she sat on her bed holding the familiar wooden box in her hands, she took a moment to smell the fresh pine scent—the same scent that would waft through her open windows in the early summer evenings. She slowly opened the box. Inside were the cards from her last four birthdays. Written in the same graceful handwriting were the words LOVE, STRENGTH, COURAGE, and DESTINY. And now, PROTECTION. She ran her finger across each word, reading them quietly to herself before slipping all five cards safely back into the box and placed the box back on her bedside table.

She sat back on her bed and picked up the small black gift box, her heart racing with excitement. She leaned against the pillow and a soft smile came to her face. No matter how tired she was, she always looked forward to this moment every birthday. This was her favorite birthday tradition, a gift left by her parents for only her to see. When she lifted the top off of the box she found the most beautiful silver necklace. It was strong yet delicate, not thin and fragile like the one she had been wearing. She unclasped the necklace she was wearing and slid the small crystal rose off into the palm of her hand. Then she unclasped her new charm bracelet and slid the rose onto it, next to the silver charm Dani had given her for her birthday. Pulling the new necklace out of the gift box she found that it held a smooth, shiny, circular pendant about the size of a quarter, and made of black hematite. It was thick, with a hole that ran straight through from one side to the other, and carved in the middle, on both sides, was a star. Hematite had always been one of her favorite stones: sleek and mysterious, it always felt cool to the touch. She slipped the chain around her neck, the pendant resting gently on her chest. The cool touch of the hematite radiated through her body, and she knew she would never take it off again.

Every year, she received a handful of small raw gemstones or crystals along with a small gift. The stones were always different, unique, and lovely in their own way. Some were in their natural form: untouched and unchanged, raw and edgy. Others were perfectly smooth—polished as if someone had taken great care to make them beautiful. She collected them just like other children might collect dolls or baseball cards. She loved each and every one of them, and kept them safe in a jewelry box on her dresser, pulling them out whenever she started to feel sick, sad, or lonely.

Somehow, they made her feel better, and made the bad stuff seem to melt away—if only for a little while.

Over the next four years, Alee's birthdays had brought four beautiful, clear quartz crystal wands, each between four and five inches long, smooth to the touch on each side but sharp at the tip, almost like a dagger or a stake. They reminded her of icicles in the wintertime, but they felt oddly warm in her hands. Each year, the new one came with a card inscribed with one word, in the same elegant handwriting, and each wand was wrapped at the base with a different color twine: green twine around the one that came with the message EARTH, yellow twine for WIND, blue twine for WATER, and red twine for FIRE.

Alee had always found her gemstones and crystals to be fascinating, but by the time she received the third crystal wand she began to feel an urgency to know more about these precious gifts. She went to her mother first—it seemed like the logical solution. She had been the one to give them to her, after all, but anytime Alee brought up the topic her mother just brushed her off saying, "Really Alee, they're not important, just pretty rocks is all." Alee's mother had never had an obvious passion for crystals, but anyone who saw her on a regular basis would recognize her love of jewelry. She practically had a different necklace for every outfit, and she loved to dress up and show them off. But Alee had never figured out the connection—the reason her mother would give her such unique gifts. Alee's raw gems and crystal wands were a far cry from the elegant pieces her mother wore, and she began to wonder if they had even come from her mother at all.

Alee decided to do some research at the public library downtown and the local used book store, but the only books she could find about crystals were written by new-age healers or practicing wiccans. Alee hadn't grown up in an overly religious household, but they did attend church a few times a month. When she was in the hospital her dad would often sit next to her bed and read her passages from the Bible. So the mystery of why year after year she received crystals and stones on her birthday seemed to matter even more as she got older. It was kind of like the scavenger hunts her dad used to set up for her when she was little as a way to get her to clean her room, do her homework—or just for fun: the crystals seemed like another such puzzle.

By the time her fourteenth birthday arrived, she already knew what her gift would be. She even asked Dani to stay late that night to open it with her—something she had never done before. Alee paused as the girls went into her bedroom. She hadn't yet told Dani what she expected to find, but there on her pillow was the familiar black box and red envelope. "Dani—umm—you know my crystals?"

"Yeah?" Alee had shown them to Dani before, but all she had told her was that she collected them, nothing more.

"Well, I get them for my birthday every year..." Alee was looking at her feet, hoping Dani wasn't going to think she was odd or weird. "...and I was wondering if you wanted to stay and see what I get this year."

"Really? Yeah!" Alee was happy to hear how excited Dani was.

Alee spread the crystals out on her bed and placed the black box and red envelope in the center of the gems and quickly filled Dani in about what little she really knew about this birthday ritual. She picked up this year's gift and hesitated, looking at Dani, who clearly was fascinated. Alee wasn't the least bit surprised when she un-wrapped a fourth crystal wand, but it didn't lessen the excitement of seeing it for the first time. Both girls were stunned at how gorgeous it was, and the way is sparkled in the dim light of Alee's room. "Wow. It's like something from that show 'Charmed.'" Dani was holding the four wands up to the light and watching how each one sparkled in a different way. "Earth, Wind, Fire, and Rain… I ask you now to heal Alee's pain!"

"What are you doing," Alee asked, snatching the crystals out of Dani's hand.

"I don't know—making a rhyme? It just seems like there should be more to them then just being pretty rocks."

"They're not rocks" Alee corrected her.

"Fine, crystals, sorry" Dani apologized.

By now, Alee had spent countless hours studying all the different stones and crystals. She knew which crystals had healing powers, such as hematite, which can be used to increase the health of your immune system. She knew that amethyst and amber helped to ease the pain of headaches. She often carried a small piece of kunzite with her to calm her nerves whenever she went to the hospital.

The crystals had become more than just a hobby or collection. They were an important part of her life, and Dani was the only one Alee was willing to share it with. "They aren't magical Dani. They can help with some stuff—circulation, headaches—you know, small stuff. At least *I* think they can, but no crystal wand is going to cure me if that's what you're thinking!" She said it, and she probably believed it, but somewhere deep down she hoped she was wrong.

When Alee and Dani had turned thirteen they had begged their moms to let them sign up for yoga classes at the youth center downtown. Although Martha wasn't excited about the idea she told Alee that if Suzi let Dani join then she could join too. Sure enough Suzi signed the girls up the next day and drove them to the class herself. The yoga helped with some of the pain Alee would get when she was sick, and her instructor worked privately with just Alee and Dani on breathing techniques and meditation exercises. The girls practiced daily during the summer months, and whenever they could throughout the school year. Alee's increasing knowledge about crystals and stones helped her to enhance her meditation sessions. Little by little, she was coming to see the world in a different way. She was beginning to feel that maybe she had more control of her life than she often felt. Maybe things weren't all planned out for her after all.

And now she was fourteen. After Dani left, Alee looked at the four crystal wands laid out in front of her. Earth, Wind, Fire, and Rain... I ask you now to heal Alee's pain!" Dani's poem echoed in Alee's mind. She thought about what Dani had said about how there should be more to them than just pretty rocks. Alee had done her research—she knew that many cultures believed in their healing powers, and others believed even more deeply, but Alee had never considered magic as a possibility.

She held up each crystal as she spoke, "Earth, Wind, Fire, and Rain… I ask you now to heal my pain!" Alee looked around the room, but nothing had happened. "Earth, Wind, Fire, and Rain…" A crack of lightening outside, and then thunder shook the house. "I ask you now to heal my pain! Earth, Wind—." The roar as the winds picked up and blew the tree branch against her window startled her, yet she continued. "Fire and Rain… I ask you now to heal my pain!"

"Alee, are you OK?" Martha said as she opened her bedroom door. "What are you doing?"

Alee, gathered her crystals on the bed in front of her. "Nothing, just—." What *am* I doing? She thought to herself. "—just looking at my stones."

Martha was watching her closely. "I just wanted to check on you. It looks like the weather is going to be bad tonight. I wanted to make sure you're all right."

"I'm fine. I was actually just going to go to bed."

"All right, sweetheart." Martha leaned down and kissed Alee on the forehead and smiled. "Sleep well—and, happy birthday." She turned to leave as Alee gathered all of her crystals into the velvet pouch and it back into her jewelry box, laying the crystal wands on top.

Before climbing into bed Alee stood at her window for a little while, watching the steady downpour, and the bright flashes of lightening.

7

The sound of fighting downstairs woke Damian up, and he jumped out of bed and run down to the living room. At only five years old, he wasn't thinking about how he could help, but his instinct kicked in and he was ready to fight if he had to. At the bottom of the stairs he turned into the dark living room what he saw was not at all what he had expected. The sounds of scuffling had stopped, and before Damian decided whether to enter the room what looked like a large black panther leaped off the couch and flew through the air to the opposite side of the room where it crouched, and turned its eyes toward Damian. There was a moment of recognition in the creature's eyes before it flew back to the couch—and its prey.

Standing in the center of the room was a tall, slender man that Damian didn't recognize. He was dressed in all black with a long trench coat that hung to his ankles. He wore thick leather gloves and old scuffed work boots. The bottoms of the boots were covered with dried mud that had left a trail from the front door to where he stood. His perfectly styled brown hair was inconsistent with his ragged, worn appearance. His sunken eyes were the color of burning lava—bubbling, swirling, and ready to overflow. He opened his mouth in an evil grin revealing two long, sharp fangs.

Damian almost fell as he jumped back in disbelief and fear. A scream of terror and pain poured out of him as he hit the wall behind him. Distracted, the panther lost focus and the man was on top of it in seconds, his teeth digging into the panther's throat, ripping its flesh. It gasped a few short breaths and the struggling stopped. The man backed away from the pile of motionless black blood-soaked fur on the floor. The fur of the lifeless animal began to fade away as the figure slowly became more and more recognizable to Damian. There in the middle of the floor, he could see clearly, was the limp body of his father, blood pouring from his neck like a faucet that wouldn't turn off.

Damian rushed to his father's side, kneeled down, grabbed his throat, and squeezed as tightly as he could. He tried desperately to stop the bleeding, but it was no use. It was already too late. Looking up, his eyes locked on the now *blue* eyes of the man in the trench coat. "Why," he whispered.

The look in those piercing blue eyes burned into the young boy's mind—a look that would scar his memory forever. Damian heard his mother Karen rushing down the stairs as the stranger in black disappeared out the front door without a sound.

With a gasp, Damian woke up in a cold sweat. Breathing hard and looking around, he found himself lying on the familiar charcoal grey leather couch of Dr. Malone's office. She had been his therapist for the past two years, and although Damian's mother was unconvinced, Dr. Malone felt very confident that Damian was showing progress during their sessions.

Damian clasped his shaking hands together and focused on taking long, deep breaths. He felt the warmth of the fireplace across the room, and smelled the apple-cinnamon scent that puffed every few minutes from an air freshener. Dr. Malone was sitting silently in her chair in the gentle glow of a dim lamp behind her. He wasn't alone, and that brought a flood of relief.

"Don't worry, it was just a dream," Dr. Malone said. Her voice had a way of calming him. Maybe it was because she always seemed so confident, or maybe it was because she really did care. Whatever it was, Damian didn't care. All he cared about in that moment was that she was there, and he was safe.

Damian had gone through eleven therapists in the first eight years after his father's death. The third therapist had diagnosed him with selective mutism, a communicative disorder in which the patient, most often a child who has suffered a severe trauma or extreme anxiety, is physically and medically capable of speech but is inexplicably unable to speak, either in given situations or to specific people. However, in severe cases such as Damian's, the patient completely withdraws and ceases verbal communication altogether.

Damian's mother was desperate by the time she brought him to Dr. Malone. Karen had done her research. She knew that Dr. Malone was known for her work in hypnotherapy, and was renowned for her work with young children who had suffered severe trauma. Karen had hoped that Dr. Malone would be able to help her son in ways that the other doctors had not been able to, or hadn't tried. She was willing to try anything at this point, even treatments that had low success rates or may have been considered foolish. Maybe she was hoping for a miracle or maybe she was too stubborn to give up. Either way, Damian was her son, and she wasn't ready to accept defeat.

When Dr. Malone had first told Damian about the possibilities of hypnotherapy he was reluctant, not ready to re-live what he believed had happened to him. But he didn't really have much of a choice about that, when his memories kept pushing themselves into his dreams on their own. At least re-living those memories in the privacy of Dr. Malone's office he wouldn't have to do it alone.

Dr. Malone explained that these things take time, and she wasn't going to push him faster than he was willing or able to go. During their third hypnotherapy session, she was able to get him to tell her about the events of the previous day. Considering that he hadn't spoken a word to anyone, including his mother, since his father's death eight years ago, the mere fact that he spoke was almost the miracle Karen was hoping for. During their ninth hypnotherapy session, Damian finally mentioned his father, but only in small details: playing catch in the back yard, riding on his shoulders watching the Thanksgiving parade, and sitting in his lap watching the Christmas tree lights blink on and off.

After each session, Dr. Malone would carefully tell Damian what he had just told her. When she told him about the Christmas tree and sitting with his father, tears filled the little boy's eyes. The memories of his father brought out intense emotions in Damian, and the doctor sensed not only sadness and loss, but anger and frustration. He cried as though his heart were broken, until he just hid his face in the crook of his arm, curled up on the couch. Dr. Malone called softly to Damian's mother in the next room. Instinctively, Karen gathered him up, holding him, talking to him and trying to comfort him, but nothing seemed to work. Looking into his tear-filled eyes and knowing there was nothing she could do for him was unbearable. But Dr. Malone insisted that they were making progress, and the only answer was to push forward with the sessions.

This was their twelfth hypnotherapy session, and despite the seemingly slow progress, Dr. Malone was extremely pleased with how the sessions had gone so far. She had been able to take Damian deeper into his mind than she had expected after such a short time. She had finally heard in the boy's own words what he saw on the night of his father's death. As unbelievable as the story sounded, it was still a major breakthrough that he was even talking about it. She didn't want to halt his progress just because his imagination may have exaggerated the facts, allowing him to believe what he thought he had seen. She knew that in time the fantasy would be sorted from the facts, and he would be able to dismiss what had been a young child's misunderstanding and learn to accept the still-terrible reality. Dr. Malone believed that the panther was a physical metaphor created in Damian's mind to explain the rage his father must have displayed as he fought the intruder. She gently brought Damian out of the trance.

When he woke up on her couch this time, everything was different. Over the years, Damian had grown used to waking up afraid and empty inside, but he never felt that way when he woke up in the safety of Dr. Malone's office. This time, though, he saw something different in her eyes. She knew more about him now than she had ever expected to know. He had told her all the secrets, all the details he was too afraid to admit, even to himself. It had been the same nightmare he had been having night after night since it happened, and still he couldn't convince himself that it was real. Why would she ever believe him? He made her promise never to tell anyone, not even his mother, about what had happened that night. He knew they would never believe him anyway, and didn't want people looking at him with their judging eyes even more than they already did.

The dream was always the same, save for a few added details that would come and go. Damian never really knew how much of it to believe. He couldn't seem to separate what was real from what was created by his overactive imagination. All he knew for sure was that the image of the fierce panther wasn't something he could have just made up, like Dr. Malone suggested. What five-year-old boy makes up a story of his father turning into a panther only moments before being brutally killed in his own living room? But at *fifteen* years old, he also knew it wasn't something he could expect anyone to believe. More likely, he would end up locked away in a padded room somewhere instead of just lying on the leather couch of a psychologist's office twice a week.

Life for Damian had never been the same after his father died. He had gone through periods of deep depression, preferring to remain alone—another side effect of his selective mutism. He spent a lot of time looking through boxes of his father's old things, or at the library, reading and researching. He worked hard to trace his ancestors back through his father's family line, but always came up empty handed. Every new lead he found always came to be a dead end. But that didn't make him stop looking. It only made him more determined to learn more. His grades had fallen and his attitude at school slowly gotten worse, until his mother finally decided that he needed more help than simple therapy could provide.

A few weeks before her fifteenth birthday, during the
summer before her sophomore year in high school, Alee was
back in the hospital for what the doctors had thought would
be just another routine blood transfusion. However, her health
had been slowly declining over the past few years, and the
time between transfusions was getting shorter and shorter:
from six to eight months for a long time, but now between
four and six weeks. This time Alee arrived at the hospital
after her energy level had suddenly plummeted, and she had
become unable to keep down any food or liquid. The doctors
decided that they needed to be more aggressive in their
treatments. A simple transfusion would no longer help her.

Her doctors decided that in addition to the normal blood
transfusion needed for now, they would need to do an
allogeneic transplant. Since Alee didn't have any siblings to
turn to they were going to have to rely on the National

Marrow Donor Program to find her a match. Alee and her
parents were told that it could take months, if not years, to
find a suitable match for the transplant. The allogeneic
transplant would utilize stem cells from a host donor, which
are transplanted to the patient. The new cells would make
their way through the blood and into the bone marrow where,
if the engraftment was successful, they would start producing
healthy white blood cells, red blood cells and platelets.

Alee was in the hospital for only about four weeks before
a donor was found. However, during that time, word of her
illness had spread like wild fire throughout town. A number
of the Moyer's neighbors, co-workers, and even just
acquaintances, went in to be tested. All of them wanted to
help if they could, but not a single one was a match.

As was expected, Alee's health took another blow during
the chemotherapy and radiation process. Although the doctors
had told her the treatment would have serious consequences,
she was not prepared for the extent of the side effects that
included loss of appetite, constipation, diarrhea, fatigue,
nausea, pain, and worst of all—hair loss. Alee's energy level
dropped to the point that just sitting up in bed was taxing. She
was drained physically, emotionally, and psychologically.
The only time she got any relief from the constant nausea,
vomiting, fever, and diarrhea was when her extreme
weakness got the best of her and she slept.

Today she awoke, and slowly realized that the new
transplant procedure had been completed. Now, she knew, the
real critical part of her recovery was about to begin. She was
beyond scared for what was about to happen to her. Her

immune system was all but destroyed, and as she waited for the bone marrow to engraft in her system and start to produce normal blood cells, she was more susceptible to infections than ever before. Every time she heard another patient sneeze or cough from down the hall she cringed in fear.

Every precaution was taken to reduce her exposure to viruses and bacteria. This included limiting visitors to strictly her mother and father, and requiring *them* to wear protective gowns, gloves, and masks at all times while in her room. Her diet was carefully monitored to reduce the risks of food-borne illnesses, and she was given high doses of antibiotics, and constant blood and platelet transfusions over the six weeks following the transplant.

Late one night, as she sat alone in her hospital bed, Alee heard the nurses talking in their station down the hall. She wasn't tired, and had nothing better to do, so she listened, straining to hear what they were saying, but she couldn't make out anything more than a couple of words. Then the talking stopped and she clearly heard a deep voice that resonated through the hall. "Which room is the Moyer girl in?"

She fell back onto her pillow and pulled the blanket up around her. Who is looking for me this late at night? She could feel the palms of her hands become sticky and clammy, but didn't understand why, as she tried harder to hear what he said next.

"She's in room 412, sir," a nurse answered without hesitation. "Would you like me to show you the way?" The other nurses giggled as she said it.

Is she flirting with him? Alee wondered. And why were they directing someone to her room when she wasn't supposed to have visitors.

"That's all right, I know the way."

"Are you sure? I don't mind," she said eagerly.

From Alee's experiences, and there were many, she knew that hospital nurses didn't normally behave that way; which is to say, although they knew how to do their job, they weren't always so eager to jump up and help. The last time she had gotten sick enough to be transferred all the way to the University of Michigan Hospital, over four hours from home, she and her mom had referred to her nighttime nurse as the Ice Princess.

One night when Alee was, for once, sleeping peacefully, she was startled awake by a command, "Wake up!" And the overhead lights snapped on. "It's time to take blood."

"Mom, wake up," Alee had called out to her mom. Martha stirred on the hard couch a few feet from Alee's bed and rolled over to see the Ice Princess standing over her daughter's bed tying a tourniquet around her arm.

"What's going on?"

"The lab needs more blood," the Ice Princess snapped, then turned away from Martha, and slid the needle in without any warning.

"Ouch!"

"It doesn't hurt, just don't look at it."

"It does too hurt," Alee said more to herself than the nurse. Martha squeezed her other hand and rubbed her forehead gently.

"She's almost done baby girl. It's almost over." Martha and Alee had been there over two weeks by then, and every night was the same. They had requested a different nurse, but it didn't seem to do any good. They were always awakened by the Ice Princess every night around three o'clock in the morning.

She snapped the tourniquet off of Alee's arm, shoved her gloves into the trashcan, and gathered her supplies. "See you tomorrow night."

"I half expect her to cackle when she leaves," Alee said. "It's like she enjoys hurting me."

"Don't worry about her sweetheart. We won't be here much longer, and the Ice Princess will be a distant memory." They both laughed at the nickname, but Alee had never disliked a nurse as much as that one.

Now, sitting here in the dark room, Alee waited, but the man with the deep voice seemed to have vanished. He must have left—Alee could hear the nurses carrying on like schoolgirls fawning over the star quarterback.

But no, now, Alee clearly heard heavy footsteps coming toward her door. The door hinges squeaked as it was pushed it open. They were in serious need of WD-40 around here.

The privacy curtain that surrounded her bed was closed, and Alee closed her eyes and lay still as a corpse. Her mouth was dry and she longed for a drink of water, but didn't dare move without knowing who it was. He pulled back the curtain slowly and stepped inside, close to her bed. Even with her eyes closed she could feel him leaning over her, watching her, and she focused on keeping her breathing calm and steady. Just breathe, just breathe, just breathe——. The mantra that repeated itself over and over in her head. She could feel a small tug on her IV, and her eyes flew open. "Ouch!" then a warm sensation ran through her arm.

"I'm sorry, I didn't mean to wake you." A tall slender man, wearing a white lab coat was standing there looking down at her.

"Um, it's all right. Are you one of my doctors? You look familiar, do I know you?" He seemed harmless enough, with his brown hair, and chiseled jaw. He was tall, and actually quite handsome.

He didn't answer right away, but looked back over his shoulder toward the hallway. "You *did*, and when the time is right you will again."

"What does that mean?" OK, cryptic male nurse, was all Alee could think.

"Alee...." He paused, and she saw kindness, and sadness, in his crystal-blue eyes. "...you're not like other girls your age. You're special." He paused again for a long while, as if about to say more. Then he stood back up and, as if nothing had happened, turned away. "Your physician requested that I switch your medication, that's all."

"Oh—um—what are you giving me?" She tried to turn back to see the IV bag, but it was too far back, and the lighting wasn't that good.

"Don't worry about that right now. Just close your eyes and try to sleep." The drugs were already working, her eyelids were starting to feel heavy, and she could feel that sleep was coming on quickly. It felt like the drowsiness that comes over you after a particularly satisfying meal.

The next morning Alee waked up later than usual, having slept well, and soundly. The sun was already shining through the window, and she could hear patients and hospital staff bustling about through their morning routines. "Good morning Sweetheart." Martha was sitting in a rocking chair watching television with the sound turned off.

"Hi Mom, when did you get here?" Now that Alee was a little older, Martha and David took turns staying with her during her hospital visits, and more often than not they spent their evenings at the nearest hotel, only coming into the hospital during the daylight visiting hours.

"I got in last night. Dad had to go back to work." Martha turned the television off. "How are you feeling?"

"Actually, I feel great." She pulled herself up in bed, and glanced back at the clear liquid slowly dripping out of the IV bag and into the tube leading down to her arm. "Has the doctor been in yet this morning?"

"No, why?"

"I was just curious who the new night nurse is." Alee swung her legs off the side of the bed, rolled the IV stand along behind her, and went into the bathroom.

"What new nurse?" Martha asked, standing up to look at the chart at the foot of Alee's bed. "I don't see anything in your chart about a new nurse."

"I don't know Mom. Give me a minute, I'll be right out." Alee shut the bathroom door. After brushing her teeth, changing into a fresh pair of pajamas, and pulling her hair back into a ponytail she inched her way back into the small room she had called home for several weeks.

Martha was standing with a nurse just outside the door, whispering. "Who do you think it was?"

"I'm sure it was no one. No one signed in to visit your daughter last night, and we have no new staff assigned to your daughter's case, or on the unit for that matter."

"Then what do you think it could be?" Martha was insistent now, and starting to sound a little less upset and a lot more freaked out.

"Oftentimes patients going through chemotherapy will experience chemo-induced dreams. I'm sure that's all it was, but if it would make you feel more comfortable I can have her doctor stop in this morning before she's released."

"Released? So soon?" Martha was shocked, and not at all prepared for the process of caring for her daughter after the transplant.

"Don't worry, Mrs. Moyer, everything will be fine. Over the past week we have seen remarkable improvement, more than we could have expected so soon. Now, go back in and spend some time with your daughter. I'll be back shortly to go through all of the discharge information with you." The nurse walked away, and Martha, silent and shaken, made her way back into Alee's room.

"Did she say I get to go home?" If Alee had even one ounce more energy she would have been jumping up and down.

"Well, we're just going to have to wait and see what your doctor says when he gets in," Martha explained, but it didn't subdue Alee's excitement in the least.

Later that morning, a team of doctors came in to handle her discharge and say goodbye. "I really get to go home?"

"You get to go home..." Alee almost screamed she was so excited. "...but it's not going to be as easy as it has been in the past. Your recovery has only just begun." Her release was not without numerous warnings and a list of instructions including things she must and must not do. Her parents were determined to make sure she followed each and every rule. Alee had had many blood transfusions in the past, but this being her first bone marrow transplant, she was shocked and devastated when they told her that she would not be able to return to school, and that she would have to spend the next six to nine months locked up in her house to avoid any and every possible infection that she might come in contact with. On top of that, she would be home schooled. All of the work, and none of the fun.

"No, you can't be serious. Six months cooped up in my room? I'll look like Rapunzel by the time they let me out."

Everyone just laughed, and one of the younger doctors patted her softly on the shoulder. "They're not locking you in a tower somewhere hidden in the woods. Besides, at least you don't have to eat hospital food any longer, and I'm sure your mother's cooking is far better than the cafeteria food at school." He did have a point about the school food, but it didn't make it any easier for Alee to accept her fate.

She thought her parents had been strict after her previous blood transfusions, but that could not begin to compare to the twenty-four hour watch she was under now. She felt like a prisoner in her own home, and after only a few weeks she was already going crazy. Over the years she had become a pro at knowing what her parents wanted or needed to hear when it came to her health, but this time was different. They didn't listen to her when she said she was feeling better or when she asked to go out. Her request and pleas just fell on deaf ears. It wasn't an option, and they were not even remotely interested in entertaining the idea, or giving her false hope.

"No Alee, and don't ask again. You know you're on lock-down until Dr. Mitchell tells us different," her mother would say.

Dr. Mitchell, an elderly man in his late sixties with silver grey hair and faded blue eyes, had been Alee's doctor for longer than she could remember. He came by occasionally to check on her. Every time she saw him she pleaded with him to let her leave the house, to just go outside for a while, but he never budged. So it would be a tremendous understatement to say that she was surprised when, four months into her confinement, he told her that it would be all right to have a friend come by to visit "Your last two sets of lab results came back great. Your red and white blood cell count is perfect, and your platelets are normal too. So, I was thinking…" Alee sat up in bed and she could feel her checks blush with anticipation. "…if you wanted to have Danielle over—."

"Are you serious? Really? Oh. My. God." She jumped out of bed and ran to the door. "MOM!!!" She screamed. She wasn't going to take a chance that her mother wouldn't believe her after Dr. Mitchell left. "MOM!!!" She wanted her mother to hear it straight from Dr. Mitchell's mouth.

Martha ran into the room like something was on fire. "What? What's wrong?" She stopped short when she saw the smile that lit up her daughter's face. "What's going on?"

"Dr. Mitchell said I can have Dani come over. Can I call her now, please?"

"Honey, I don't know." She was shaking her head. "Frank, can I talk to you—." She quickly pulled the doctor into the hall to discuss it further; Alee could only hear whispered bits and pieces of the conversation.

"Frank, I trust your opinion, you know I do, but," Martha's voice faded ever so softly, "we've made it this far. We need to protect her. Are you sure we shouldn't wait just a little while longer? I mean, the doctors in Ann Arbor did say six months."

He always had a way of making her mom listen—maybe not always agree, but she always trusted him and listened to what he thought was best, "Martha, you know I'm not going to do anything to jeopardize her recovery, but at some point you have to not only trust me, but also start trusting her. She's going to be—."

What—what did he say? I'm going to be what?

After saying goodbye to Dr. Mitchell in the hallway Martha came back into the bedroom. She didn't look happy, but she didn't look angry either. She looked tired. "OK, I give in. You can have Danielle over, but no one else," she sighed. It was as if her mother had given her the stars right out of the sky.

Alee was so excited that she couldn't even wait for her to leave the room before she was on the phone with Dani. Dani was quiet when out in public, but alone with Alee she could never stop talking. Before Alee had gone to the hospital for the bone marrow transplant they rarely went more than a day or two without seeing each other, let alone not talking on the phone. However, the treatment had taken such a toll on Alee this time that she hadn't had the energy most days to pick up the phone let alone hold a conversation. Lately, they had been talking maybe once a week, if they were lucky.

So when, after the two months in the hospital and the four months locked in her house, now that Dani was actually finally allowed to visit, it took only three words on the phone. "Come over now." And Dani started running. In less than a minute, she was bouncing up the stairs and into Alee's room. They spent the rest of the day talking, laughing, eating, watching movies, and enjoying each other's company. Alee told her everything that had been happening with her health and Dani filled Alee in on everything she was missing at school. The hardest part for Alee was hearing about the new friends Dani was making, and feeling left out because she couldn't be a part of it all.

They talked for hours, as they had done so many times over the past nine years. But after a while, Alee's energy started to drain and she began to drift off. Dani didn't mind, though. She was very nurturing by nature, just like her mother, and she had a way of making Alee feel comfortable. Even when they were little girls she seemed to be able to calm Alee down when she was worried, afraid, or anxious. Alee always said it was Dani's calm nature—she had never once heard Dani yell and honestly didn't believe she had it in her to get mad at anyone. Many times, when she was facing new health challenges, it was that simple, soothing quality that helped to put Alee right to sleep and allowed her to get much-needed rest.

When Alee woke up from her light sleep, Dani was still there sitting on the floor next to her bed. The lights were off, and she had lit a small white candle. She was holding something tightly in her hands and quietly whispering something to herself.

"What are you doing?" Alee, asked.

"Oh, you're awake." Dani looked up over the soft glow of the candle that reflected in her black-rimmed glasses. "How are you feeling?"

"OK, I guess." Then, gesturing to the candle, "What is all this?"

"Um…" Dani was hesitant, although if anyone would understand her new obsession it would be Alee. "…well, when you told me you were having a bone marrow transplant, I started looking into holistic healing—and other things." She opened her hand to reveal a smooth, light-purple stone.

"Amethyst? Dani, what other things are you—?"

"Don't freak out OK!" Alee didn't answer. "I was reading on the internet about crystals, and I found this site with all these Wiccan spells that use crystals for healing. I thought maybe—."

"Wiccan spells? You mean witchcraft? Do you seriously believe in that stuff?"

"I don't know. I guess I, don't *not* believe in it."

She watched as Dani shifted uncomfortably. "OK." Alee wasn't freaked out, nor was she surprised. She accepted Dani for all that she was, and didn't judge her like some people might. Besides, it wasn't like she hadn't thought about it herself.

Over the next five months, Dani was by her side whenever the doctor would allow it. She helped her get through some of the hardest times of her recovery, helped her celebrate the good days, and together they even learned more about the Wiccan religion that had become Dani's new obsession and, by association, Alee's.

Despite Damian's inability—or unwillingness—to participate in class, he was a well-behaved student. However, he had been kicked out of school after school for reasons labeled "aggressive tendencies," "anger management issues," or anything else they could think of to make him someone else's responsibility. No one wanted to take on the responsibility or the challenge of having him in his or her school, let alone in their class. No one knew how to communicate with him, and no one was willing to try.

When Karen finally decided it was time for a new start, a fresh beginning for all of them, she uprooted the family and they moved two hours away to Atlanta, a small town where she herself had grown up. The twins were already in the middle of their sophomore year and transferring wouldn't be easy. Karen made it clear that this time things were going to be different: this was Damian's last chance before being sent off to boarding school.

Atlanta was literally in the middle of nowhere—at least that's how it felt to Damian and Victoria. Not that McBain had been a big city, but it was close enough to Traverse City and Mount Pleasant to at least feel like there were things to do. Atlanta had a population of under a thousand people. There was one school that housed both the elementary grades and the high school students, unless you counted all the families that banded together to "home school" their kids.

Saint Mark's Episcopal Church was in the center of the town, and it seemed as though the whole town had been built around it. The courthouse, post office, and even the hospital were all within walking distance of the church. The roads downtown were made of cobblestone, and the buildings were excellent examples of the federal style architecture of the late 1700s to early 1800s. They were beautifully maintained, if a little out of place in such a small town.

Karen registered the twins for classes at Atlanta High, and they started within days of arriving in town. Just like everyone at all of his previous schools, everyone judged Damian right from the start. He had always been the quiet, misunderstood type. Victoria was the polar opposite: a social butterfly who never noticed when her brother was being ostracized again and again. Or at least after so many years of him being different, she just stopped caring—until they moved to Atlanta that is.

Damian wasn't a bad kid, but he had seen things that a child should never see, and it affected him in ways no one could explain. He didn't know how to express his feelings so, more often than not, they came out in frustration or anger; and, more often than not, he didn't really care. He had never hurt anyone, at least not directly, but during his freshman year in high school, pushed to the limit by the other kids' ceaseless subtle taunts, he had thrown a trashcan through the window of his homeroom class. It had been accidental, actually. He had meant to pull the can back from another kid's grasp, and it had slipped. But the principal insisted that he was too much of a liability, and the school board decided that he would be better suited at a prep school where they were set up for handling his "specific behavioral issues."

Victoria had known for years that her brother was often considered different, or odd. In fact, *she* thought so, so why wouldn't anyone else? Over the past ten years, they had grown further and further apart. Their relationship was nothing like the twin connection they had had in the distant past, but that didn't mean she didn't love him, or that she didn't still feel the need to protect him somehow. She had seen the change in him more than anyone, even if she had tried not to. She had felt him pulling away after their father died, and she never really knew what to do to get him back. For a while she thought that maybe it wasn't so bad; they were siblings—they weren't *supposed* to like each other. But no matter how hard she tried to convince herself that everything was OK, she never really believed it. She was determined that this year was going to be different. She had a plan—or at least she planned to have a plan, which is about as far as Victoria ever got with anything. Although Victoria was quite the planner, she lacked follow-through.

The school wouldn't allow siblings to be in the same classes together, but that didn't mean they couldn't spend time together. They had the same lunch period, and Victoria made sure that Damian knew just where and when to meet her. She took charge, as always, like an older, protective sister. She always said that even though they were twins, she was the oldest because she had been born a whole twenty minutes earlier than he was. And of course there was the small technicality of their birth dates. She had been born at eleven forty-eight on a Saturday evening, and twenty minutes later at eight after twelve on Sunday morning her "little brother" Damian had been born. So they were twins with different birthdays—a very rare occurrence. Victoria took it as a sign that she was meant to lead. Damian took it as a sign that she had been pushy right from birth, and had no intention of slowing down. Even as children, she insisted that her birthday party—which was usually just the three of them sitting around with pizza they ordered in and a movie from the local video story—be a day before his every year. On the rare occasions that their mother could afford an actual party with their friends, they would celebrate on the same day, but Victoria would make sure that she got to open her presents first.

On the very first day of classes, Victoria started to make friends. It didn't matter where she was, people just naturally congregated around her because she had a way of making them feel comfortable. And of course most people were drawn to her looks and her incredible self-confidence. Victoria was stunning, and she knew it. She had never played on a school sports team a day in her life, but every year, no matter what school she attended, she was always asked try out for the cheerleading squad. She would just laugh and wave them away, telling them she had better things to do then memorize poorly written rhymes, and bounce around with a bunch of girls.

Boys of all types flocked to her, trying to get the seat next to her in class, wanting to carry her lunch tray through the line, and even offering to pay. While she liked being the center of attention, she was very selective in who she actually allowed to get close to her. She rarely dated the same boy for longer than a couple of weeks, and she picked her friends wisely, and with care. When she wanted to, she could be very gentle—a behavior she normally reserved for her brother. But when she got mad, even he knew that the last place on earth you wanted to be was within fifty feet of her wrath.

During their lunch period on that first day, Damian found her at the back of the cafeteria right where she said she would be; only she wasn't alone like he had expected, or hoped. Her table was full, save for one spot still open right next to her. After standing in the long cafeteria line, he paid for his food and, dubiously, made his way to the table. Hoping nobody would notice him he quietly slid into the empty seat next to his sister and started to eat. As if on some secret cue, everyone at the table went silent, stopped what they were doing, and stared.

This is where Victoria's plan came into action. Her brother, if it was up to her, was no longer going to be the outcast. If they were going to have any chance at a normal life, a stable life, then she was going to have to take matters into her own hands and help him to adjust, adapt, and acclimate.

"This is my brother, Damian." Victoria's calm voice drew the attention away from Damian and back to her. "Yeah I know. I got the looks, he got the brains. I still think I got the better end of the deal."

It wasn't a very funny joke, at least not to Damian but, like always, everyone started laughing, and she nudged Damian slightly with her elbow. He took a deep breath and let out a quiet sigh of relief, and the table filled with conversations again as everyone started talking almost simultaneously. He just sat back and watched, no longer the center of attention. For the first time in years, there was no pressure to be someone he wasn't or to act outside of his comfort zone. He knew the feeling wouldn't last, but he was happy just knowing that during his lunch hour he would be able to relax.

Eventually people stopped looking at him as if he was different. In fact, they didn't really seem to look at him at all. Except for the occasional lab partner, or class group project, he pretty much kept to himself without anyone taking notice. To him, this was much better than the alternative. He would rather be left alone than be seen as a point of conversation or curiosity. Damian allowed himself to blend into the background and all but disappear, aside from the rare moments when he got to enjoy the comfort and ease of his sister and her new friends. He even began to enjoy listening to their silly banter and repetitive conversations. He found himself looking forward to lunchtime at school, and Saturdays when she had them all over to the house.

Sitting in the living room just to be a part of the group was never something Damian would have done before they moved to Atlanta. However, something had started to change in him. He stopped getting up whenever the doorbell rang and vanishing into his secluded quiet bedroom. He began to spend more time out in public then he did in front of his computer. He even allowed his sister to drag him to a couple of Tyler's parties. Tyler was one of the few guys Victoria let sit at their lunch table, and occasionally let walk her to class, probably because he was good looking, and complemented Victoria well, and she knew it. He was a star player on the basketball team, but was fairly shy when he wasn't on the court. Damian saw Tyler as just another guy soon to be a cast off, joining the long line of guys his sister had left behind.

Danielle, or Dani as she liked to be called was the only other girl who regularly sat with them, although there usually was the occasional girl trying to convince Victoria that she should try out for the cheer squad, the upcoming play, or just about any other club or sport at the school. From what Damian could tell, Dani was cool, pretty smart, and easily influenced which is why Damian thought Victoria kept her around. Besides, although she was pretty, Dani was a little overweight, and that meant that Victoria looked even more beautiful in comparison.

Kyle was another guy who hung around with them during lunch. Damian's first impression of Kyle came about two minutes after stepping foot on school property. Damian and Victoria were walking up the sidewalk toward the main doors when Kyle came zooming by on his skateboard, almost knocking Damian down. "Oh man, I'm sorry. I didn't see you there."

"Didn't see him? How could you not see him, we're walking right in the middle of the sidewalk." Victoria never wasted time expressing her opinions.

"Wow, I said sorry."

"Just watch where you're going next time." Victoria stormed off, but Damian hung back, a little embarrassed by his sister's overreaction.

"She your sister?" Kyle asked as he elbowed Damian. Damian only nodded. "What an excellent day for an exorcism." Then taking off toward the school he called back. "See you around." Later that day Kyle plopped himself down at the lunch table across form Damian. It was probably more to annoy Victoria than anything else, but he seemed perfectly comfortable anywhere he was. While most boys were drawn to Victoria like a moth to a flame, Kyle just seemed to like to push her buttons. And that intrigued Damian. After realizing that Kyle was also in his history and math classes, and that he was just as much a movie buff as Damian, they became pretty good friends. The fact that Kyle liked to talk and Damian didn't also made them the perfect friends.

For years, the only thing that had kept Damian going was his hatred for the man who killed his father and his determination to find out what really had happened. But by the time summer came around, and they had completed their sophomore year at their new school, Victoria was starting to see a change in her brother's behavior and attitude. She was finally starting to see the brother she remembered and the twin she missed. She hadn't really thought that she could change him, or fix what had been broken inside of him so many years ago. She had only hoped that with time and patience she could help him see that there was more to living than just breathing, more to life than just waiting to die, and, most of all, that there were better purposes in life than just revenge.

10

Alee returned to public school at the start of her junior year and she was bound and determined to change the impressions that people had formed about her over the years. Her family, Dani, even the doctors, thought she was "special." They saw her as a gift, a rose, an angel, an old soul. Her classmates thought she was odd, sickly, and different. All of which translated to: "Fragile. Handle With Care." And Alee was tired of it. Being home sick all of her sophomore year hadn't helped her any either. Everybody knew she was different, and they openly treated her differently. Alee's delicate health made people feel uncomfortable. As a result, people never seemed to like being around her, and it made it hard for Alee to ever really get close to anyone.

Alee had never really caught the boys' attention either; at least it never appeared that they were looking in her direction. It may just have been that they were afraid of the unknown.

Afraid because she was "sick," afraid that they might hurt her. She had always been small, just over five feet tall, and all the boys her age and most of the girls, including Dani, had always towered over her. Alee was slender and graceful, and very pretty in her own right; or at least she could have been if she'd had any guidance in that direction. Martha was a stay at home mom who prioritized taking care of Alee—sometimes up to twenty-four hours a day—over trends or shopping or hairstyles.

At times, Alee's condition made her skin look almost translucent and delicate to the touch. Her best quality had always been her eyes. She had piercing ocean blue eyes. Her smile was nice, but nothing dazzling or inspiring. Her wild curls were a dull red, and hung around her face untamed and unkempt. She usually pulled them back into a ponytail or a bun because it was easier than trying to coerce them into a style. Despite Alee's rather average appearance, if anyone looked closely, they would notice that there was a good deal of natural beauty hidden behind those wild bangs and out-of-date flower-print clothing her mother always bought for her. Although she excelled in every aspect of school, Alee didn't know a thing about fashion, and her mother was even worse. Even the way she always carried herself, protective and defensive, made her appear to be untouchable. Her typical expression was attentive and hopeful, yet at the same time— sad.

Alee's parents forbade all sports and physical activities that could lead to too much exertion of energy. The only exercise they would allow was walking—not running—on the track at school. Her mother insisted that it was for her protection and that they were only trying to keep her safe. But, in Alee's mind it was just one more way to emphasize that she was different, one more way her parents forced her to be an outsider.

During their freshman year, Alee and Dani had tried out for the cheerleading squad, without Alee's mother's prior knowledge or permission. Dani didn't make the team but, much to Alee's surprise, she did—at least until she told her mom. Alee had been so excited and hopeful—this was going to be her chance to make an impression in high school. Alee, more than anyone knew that a first impression really mattered, and she needed her first impression to be a good one. Unfortunately, her mother didn't agree.

"What the *hell* were you thinking Alee?" she screeched.

"I just wanted to—."

"To what Alee, get yourself killed?"

Alee always thought her mother had a tendency toward the dramatic. "I wasn't going to—."

"You don't know that!" When Martha had her mind set on something, there was little that could change it. "You're quitting the squad tomorrow, and if I hear you haven't quit, we'll be talking to your father about this."

"So, tell him! I get it Mom. I know you want to protect me, but I also know that you and Dad want me to be happy. I'm not sick right now, and this—this would make me happy. Besides, Dad has always told me I can do and be anything I want. He says that I shouldn't let my illness hold me back."

"Alee, we do want you to be happy, but I couldn't live with myself if anything ever happened to you, and your father would feel the same way. Cheerleading isn't what he meant when he said you shouldn't let it hold you back. I'm sorry sweetheart. I just—."

"It's fine. I get it. I'll let them know tomorrow. I knew it was a pipe dream anyway. I guess it just felt good to make the squad." A couple of tears escaped her eyes.

"I know sweetie."

Martha pulled her daughter in for a big hug just as David was coming through the door. "What's going on? Why the tears?"

"Nothing's wrong. We were just talking about school." Martha kissed Alee on the forehead softly. "Now, go on up and do your homework." Her mother, although usually very soft-spoken and nurturing, could also be very demanding and controlling regarding sports and physical activity. That was the last time they ever talked about the cheerleading squad.

Alee had turned sixteen during the summer, and she had decided that she was going to make changes in her life. She made herself a promise that she was no longer going to be the outcast, the loner, the girl everyone was afraid of. She had been saving her allowance, and begged and pleaded with her parents to help her buy her first car. Although they were reluctant at first, they eventually gave in. David was somewhat of a car buff, and he took her out and helped her find the perfect car, it was a chrome-colored 1985 Chevy Camaro. She spent the last half of the summer with her dad in the garage, fixing it up. "A car is a huge responsibility Alee."

"I know Dad."

"I expect you to take care of her, keep her clean, and never let her fall below half a tank of gas."

"You do realize it's just a car, not a person, right? Why do you keep calling it a 'her'," Alee asked.

"Cars are like boats, planes, even motorcycles—they're all referred to in the feminine form," Alee just looked at her father like he was crazy. "Don't question it Alee, it's just the way it is."

She laughed, "OK, Daddy." They laughed together, and continued cleaning up the car.

"And, I don't want to find out that you ran out of gas," he continued.

"Dad, don't worry. I'll take good care of her, just like you do me." David stood up, and pulled Alee in for a long hug.

"I love you baby girl."

"I love you too, Daddy."

By the time school started her car was perfect in every way. There wasn't a dent or a scratch anywhere on the body, and she took care of it, washing it inside and out, every weekend. The engine purred like a kitten while in park and roared like a lion when she put her foot on the gas. She felt like she could do anything when she drove that car. She felt healthier, sexier, stronger, and a little bit dangerous, but she would never tell that to her parents. And the power she felt behind the wheel was nothing compared to how she felt when she stepped out, and everyone's eyes were on her.

It wasn't just the car. That summer she had really come into her own, physically and emotionally. She had grown two inches—bringing her up to a full five-foot-four—and she was more confident than she had ever been. She had learned how to tame and even style her otherwise wild hair. She still let her curls be natural and free, but she had grown out her child-like bangs. She traded in her old wire-framed glasses for contacts, even though she couldn't convince Dani to do the same. She donated everything with a flower print or ruffles to the local Goodwill, and bought a brand-new, age-appropriate wardrobe. Although her mother was sad to see her little girl changing so much, she was also excited and proud to be a part of the transformation. Martha took Alee shopping, and with the help of Dani and every teen magazine they could get their hands on, they picked out a ton of new clothes. As for her makeup Alee had to rely on what she read in the magazines, because her mother hardly ever used it. In her stylish new outfits, and sporting more carefree hairstyles, eye makeup, and lip gloss, Alee impressed everyone with the woman she was becoming, the woman who seemed to have been hiding somehow, for a long time.

When she pulled up to school on that first day, it felt like the first day of a new life. It was like she was the new girl on campus, and everyone wanted her attention. Wearing black leather boots with three-inch heels, low rise faded jeans, a flattering shirt, her bag over her shoulder, and the shiny hematite pendent hanging loosely around her neck from its silver chain, she was a brand new girl. She was ready to re-invent herself this year, and it was going to be a full head to toe makeover. Dani walked with her, grinning from ear to ear and nudging her elbow into Alee's side as people stopped to stare. Dani had dated a little from time to time, mostly chess club and debate team members. She had never received this kind of attention, and she loved every second of it, even if the majority of it was directed at her best friend.

A couple of boys wearing letterman jackets exchanged looks as she walked by. Then, as they walked through the hall, classmates Alee hadn't seen in over a year as well as people she didn't recognize welcomed her back. She didn't really know how to handle all the attention. Although she had changed on the outside, she was the same vulnerable Alee on the inside. *Was changing my appearance really all it took to be accepted?* she thought, as she smiled and waved on her way to her first class. They had almost made it to her locker when she saw him. He was tall, with amazingly wild brown hair, and the second he turned in her direction Alee noticed his bright green eyes. She stopped in her tracks, grabbing Dani's arm and pulling her close. "Who *is* that?"

Dani glanced up just as Kyle noticed Alee. "Oh, that's Kyle Fields. I told you about—." She stopped talking when she realized that Alee wasn't really listening.

Both Kyle and Alee were frozen in place, just staring at each other. Alee attempted a reply. "He's—."

"Hey Kyle!" Dani broke the silence.

"What? Oh, hey, Dani." He turned back to his locker, grabbed out a few things and then slammed it shut. Before he turned to jump on his skateboard to leave, Alee noticed that he sneaked a quick glance back over his shoulder at her.

"Oh. My. God. He's so—."

"Yes he is, now let's get to class, please," Dani said slightly annoyed.

The rest of the morning was more of the same. Alee was happy to be back at school instead of cooped up in her house being homeschooled by her mother. She even enjoyed seeing some of her old classmates, with a strong emphasis on some, and maybe even a teacher or two. Each class felt like a new adventure with more people wanting to talk to her and get to know her. By the time lunch rolled around she was feeling tired. She walked into the cafeteria, got her food and looked for a seat at a table in the corner somewhere where no one would bother her. As she passed table after table, people were scooting over to make room for her to sit down. She politely declined their offers as she scanned the room for Dani.

She turned around and found herself standing face to face with a dark haired girl. She was wearing all black, with black eye liner and black nail polish. "Sorry—excuse me," Alee said as she squeezed around the girl.

"You new?" The girl stopped her.

"Um—I guess. I was home schooled last year," Alee said as she quickly scanned the room looking for an easy exit. She finally spotted Dani sitting at the back of the cafeteria with a few other kids Alee didn't recognize. She hurried over to Dani's table, smiling and nodding at everyone trying to get her attention. "Hey, did you see that girl?" Alee said quietly, pulling Dani close.

"Which one?" Dani asked.

Alee nodded in the direction she has just come from. "Her. The girl in all black with the dark hair, who is she?"

"Oh, that's Phoebe. Do you remember Petra Wenham? She's a year ahead of us—always used to come in our homeroom during freshman year to help the teacher."

"Yeah." Alee wasn't really sure.

"Phoebe's her little sister. Honestly she's a little weird, they both are."

When Alee finally turned to the table, she hesitated to sit, realizing that these students sitting with Dani must be the people she had been talking about all last school year, but Dani was quick to introduce her to everyone.

Victoria was a pretty girl with long brown hair and stunning chocolate brown eyes. She was deep in conversation with Tyler who was sitting next to her, but she also seemed to somehow be flirting with a boy two tables away. It was a talent, Alee would soon learn, that only Victoria had.

At first glance Tyler was a typical jock. You could tell he knew how good looking he was, from his perfect hair to his light brown eyes to the letterman's jacket he wore like it was his most prized possession. He seemed to be engrossed in everything Victoria said, but Alee noticed his occasional glances toward Dani's end of the table. Why he didn't sit four tables over with the other football players and their bubbly cheerleader followers eluded Alee.

Damian, Victoria's twin brother, was about six feet tall with a slender build. He was quiet, and didn't even say hello when Dani introduced him. However, he seemed to be observing everything that was going on around him. His friend sitting next to him was talking animatedly, so it wasn't so surprising that he didn't say anything. But, when his eyes met Alee's, a look of something like fear washed over his face for a second. It was uncomfortable, and Alee quickly looked away. From that point, on Damian seemed particularly interested in everything Alee did, watching her out of the corner of his eye while pretending to still pay attention to his friend. It made Alee a little nervous at first but within a few minutes she was able to refocus her attention. It wasn't hard with the particular view she was given.

Directly across from Alee and next to Damian sat the very talkative Kyle. He was even better looking than she had thought that morning, she realized, now that she was only three feet away from him. He was tall and handsome, with an athletic build and was maybe a little rough around the edges with his shaggy brown hair and the skateboard at his side that Alee was well aware was against school regulations. Alee slipped into her seat next to Dani and looked across to find Kyle's welcoming smile. She gave him her best smile in return, with a bright, "Hey! Don't let me interrupt." She could sense a change in Damian's demeanor that made it clear that he didn't like the way Kyle and Alee looked at each other, but she didn't know why, nor did she care. Alee saw Victoria flick her eyes in Damian's direction and he quickly relaxed and turned his full attention back to Kyle.

Alee had never been on a date, let alone had a boyfriend. She had never found anyone that she was particularly attracted to, not that it would have mattered since her parents would never have agreed to let her date. But, sitting across from Kyle she felt a strong physical attraction pulling her attention back to him time after time. And Kyle—Kyle carried on his conversation with Damian as if nothing had changed, though he also kept glancing back toward Alee. His shirt fit tightly around his biceps and hugged his chest. She finally realized that she was staring, and her throat was starting to burn. She tore her gaze away, and reached for her water bottle.

Kyle paused in his animated interaction with Damian. When Alee looked back toward him, one corner of his lips curved up in a teasing smirk. "I have such sights to show you," was all he said. Alee could hardly breathe, let alone eat her lunch.

"Kyle's a little off," Dani laughed.

"Alee, is that short for anything?" asked Tyler at the far end of the table. He brushed his perfect blonde hair out of his eyes and the light seemed to glint off his pearly white smile. Alee could feel Dani softly nudge her side with her elbow, and noticed a pink blush heat her cheeks. Then Alee remembered—Tyler was the guy Dani had talked about day after day last year. They had been lab partners in Earth Science, and Dani had completely fallen for him, only she was too shy to actually say anything. If he wasn't interested too, why is he still hanging out at her lunch table? But, just as she thought it she noticed Victoria's well-manicured nails taping on the table, pulling Tyler's attention back to her.

"No, just Alee." She looked down at herself with a second of uncertainty, and wondered if they could tell she was a fraud in her black heels and tight jeans. Did they see through the mask she was wearing? Could they see the sick side of her that she was so desperately trying to hide under a new wardrobe and makeup?

"It's a beautiful name."

"What? Oh, um, thanks." She looked up at Damian, not really sure how she knew he had said it, but he just looked back with a blank stare.

"Who are you talking to Alee?" Dani asked confused.

"I thought…" Everyone at the table went quiet and turned their attention to Alee who was looking straight at Damian. "…were you not talking to me? I thought you—."

From across the table Victoria spoke up. "Ah, sweetie he didn't say anything."

"But, I thought—." Alee was confused.

"Trust me, he didn't say anything."

Dani leaned in whispering in Alee's ear, "Alee, remember when I told you about my friend who never talks?" Alee just nodded. "Okay, don't get weird, but that's Damian."

Alee just stared across the table at him, not sure if she really believed it or not. *How could he just not talk?* She thought.

She could see Damian's expression soften slightly before he dropped his eyes back to his plate in silence and the moment was gone. Everyone went back to talking around her but the mood was somehow different, more somber. Dani just smiled at her and went on eating her lunch, unaware of the unspoken tension. When Alee looked up again, her eyes met Kyle's. He quickly looked away and began rambling on to Damian about a movie they had seen the weekend before. She could feel herself begin to blush, and turned back to Dani and their light banter about their morning classes. She spent the rest of the lunch hour waiting, hoping that he would say something else to her. Anything else. But the end of lunch was signaled by a loud bell ranging through the speaker system, quashing Alee's hopes for further conversation with him.

The rest of the day lasted forever as she moved from class to class, trying to find her way, remember everyone's names, and survive. She was pleasantly surprised when it turned out that Damian was in her fifth period Literature class, and even more so when got to the parking lot at the end of sixth period to find Kyle and Damian leaning against the hood of her car, waiting for her. She couldn't hear what Kyle was saying, but as she walked up he quickly stopped talking and turned toward her. Damian gently grabbed her bag and opened her car door for her. It felt more calculated than courteous, and something about the way he looked at her made her a bit nervous, but she wasn't about to let him know it. "Um, thank you."

Kyle watched her from the front of the car. She started to feel warm all over. Her skin started to tingle under his gaze. She felt her heart race and her hands become cold. When Dani came running up to the car a few seconds later Alee felt a wash of relief flow over her, "Hey Alee, I told the guys about your car, and they just had to see it. I said we'd give them a ride home. You don't mind do you?"

"Of course not," Alee answered. She looked at Kyle and Damian, who smiled back. She knew her parents wouldn't approve of her having boys in her car, but what they didn't know wouldn't hurt them.

Damian and Kyle tried for the passenger seat before Dani brushed them aside, claiming her spot. "Yeah, I don't think so. You want a ride, you climb in the back," she directed.

They sulked in the back seat, as if they had been put in time-out, until they were out of the school parking lot.

11

That year, Alee really felt like she blossomed in school. It was two months into the semester and still everything seemed to be going her way. She'd always had good grades, but now she was also popular—something she wasn't used to. She enjoyed hanging out with friends, going to parties, all the things her parents would never let her do—at least not if they actually knew about them. She had ways of getting out of the house. They trusted her, and she knew from years of living with them just what information to give them and what information could remain unspoken. Friday night parties became Friday night "study sessions," and Saturdays at the movie theater became sleepovers at Danielle's house, which wasn't that far off because she usually did end up at Dani's, one way or another.

She didn't want to deceive her parents, but it was easier to get permission for activities that her parents approved of, and there was no reason to go into intricate detail of an evening's events. She knew her parents didn't allow dating, and kissing was strictly forbidden. Her mother would reiterate how kissing spreads too many germs, "And you can't afford to get sick Alee Marie Moyer." (Her mother always called her by her full name when she was trying to make a point.) But Alee also knew that it was her life to live and she didn't want to do it trapped inside her parents' protective glass bubble. Furthermore, she wasn't out kissing every boy in school; in fact, she hadn't actually ever been kissed. She did have her eye on a particular someone though, and hoped that maybe, just maybe, he might one day notice her too.

The rest of the year was a whirlwind of excitement and fun as she and her friends became closer and closer. The six of them, Alee, Dani, Victoria, Damian, Tyler, and Kyle, were pretty much glued at the hips. Admittedly they were a pretty odd combination of students, but somehow all of their differences actually made them perfect together. They did everything together and spent all their time in school and out of school together. It seemed almost natural that couples would eventually form in their tight circle. Although it wasn't surprising, except to Victoria, Dani and Tyler were the first to officially start dating. If Victoria had it her way, Tyler would have been her back-up date all year long. However, after a few weeks of trying to impress Victoria he woke up to her games and decided not to play any longer. Moreover, even if dating a slightly overweight honor-roll student wasn't what was expected of the high school football star, it didn't really matter, because Dani was the one Tyler was attracted to and he didn't see any reason to hide it any longer.

After school one day, Alee had turned the corner toward her locker when she overheard Tyler being berated by some of his football buddies.

"Dude, what are you doing? I mean we get it, practices suck when you're benched for the whole season with a bum knee, but you could at least come to support the team. When you started skipping out on practices to hang out with Victoria, we all kind of understood. But, now you're dating the fat chick?"

"It's not like that," said Tyler. "She's really—. You know what, never mind, just mind your own business."

Alee didn't understand why Tyler didn't defend himself, but she remembered being on the receiving end of some petty, nasty comments, and knew that sometimes it was easier to just let it go.

"What is she, amazing in bed? Cause honestly? I can't think of another reason you would choose her over Victoria. Besides, you could have any girl you want, and you pick the one—."

"That's enough! I'm out of here, and consider me off the team. I don't need this!" Tyler stormed off while his teammates laughed. They dispersed, and Alee went on to her locker, grabbed everything she needed, and headed out to the parking lot.

Dani's relationship with Tyler really made Alee look at her own life differently. Her best friend was having great new experiences, while she sat on the sidelines too afraid to get out and play. But what should her next step be? What did she want, exactly? Damian's mysterious behavior captivated her, but Kyle made her body tingle in a way she never knew possible. She wasn't sure what to make of either of them.

Alee had always had a hard time expressing her emotions, and wasn't able to tell Kyle how she felt. She had a hard enough time trying to figure out the weird friendship she was forming with Damian. And a secret part of her felt that her health issues wouldn't make it fair for her to fall for anyone, or to let anyone fall for her. Why chance falling in love if it was only going to hurt them in the end? If she was being honest with herself, Kyle didn't really seem all that interested in her anyway, at least not enough to pursue her, and Alee had given him plenty of opportunities.

Fridays were always movie nights for the group. Whether they went out or stayed in at someone's house it never failed that some, or all of them, were there. Alee, made it known that when they were going out she was willing to drive, mainly because the boys liked her car, and she figured it would be a great way to get Kyle interested in her. "You want to ride with me to the theater tonight?" she asked Kyle as they were walked out to the parking lot after school one Friday afternoon.

"What?" Kyle hadn't really been paying attention. Jennifer, one of the varsity cheerleaders had run up to him and was tugging on his jacket sleeve.

"Are you coming to the game tonight Kyle?" The cheerleader tilted her head to the side, invitingly.

Kyle tossed his skateboard onto the sidewalk in front of him and hopped on. "Yeah, I don't know. Doubt it."

"That's too bad. It would have been fun." She ran off giggling with her girlfriends.

When he turned back to Alee she could see a hint of pink that lit up his checks. Is that really his type? She was disappointed, but not entirely shocked. "Maybe, we'll see. Call you later?"

"I'm sorry?" Alee had already lost her train of thought, and forgotten that she was still waiting for an answer.

"The ride, I'll call later if I need one." Then he was off. Kyle lived close to the school so most days, unless it was raining or he had too much to carry, he would just skateboard to school and back. He didn't call Alee that night. It was the first time, but wouldn't be the last time he would blow her off.

When Alee turned back toward her car she noticed Damian standing there with Dani and Tyler. "Hey Alee, can Damian, Tyler and I catch a ride?" Alee just smiled, it seemed that even if Kyle didn't want to come alone, her car was never empty.

A few weeks later Alee was standing in the cafeteria line carrying her tray when Kyle zoomed past her on his skateboard. Without even noticing her he bumped right into the guy behind her causing *him* to dump his tray all down Alee's back. "That's what you get when you mess with one of my friends!" He was yelling at the guy he had knocked down, but didn't even notice Alee standing there, her back covered with spaghetti.

"Mr. Fields, what have I told you about riding that thing in my school?" Principal Gregory Davis called out from across the cafeteria. He wasn't really yelling, but his voice seemed to carry farther than anyone Alee had ever met. He was tall and slender, and very distinguished with his salt and pepper hair, but was no less intimidating than a rabid dog when he got angry.

"I was just…" Kyle jumped off the board, and flung it up behind his back and into his backpack in one swift move. "…getting off, Sir."

"That's what I thought." Principal Davis turned and was down the hallway before anyone even noticed he was leaving.

When Kyle turned back to give one last warning to the boy on the ground he finally noticed Alee standing there wiping off the remaining spaghetti. "Woo, what happened to you?"

She stood there stunned. "What happened to me? What do you think happened to me? You happened!" She left her tray on the counter and stormed off out of the cafeteria without so much as a glance back. He hadn't apologized, and that made her madder than she had ever been. But, after she got more or less cleaned up in the girls' bathroom, Kyle was the first person she ran into.

"Hey, sorry about that," he actually sounded sincere.

"It's fine." Alee's shirt was stained and the last thing she wanted was to be standing there with him looking like the cafeteria had thrown up on her.

"Here," Kyle pulled his leather jacket off and wrapped it around her shoulders. "Maybe this will help."

When Alee looked up, Kyle was smiling down at her, and she could feel her checks flush and her heart pound in her chest. "Thanks."

"What are you two doing?" Victoria interrupted. "Wow, giving her your jacket huh Kyle."

"It's the least I can do, after spilling her lunch all over her shirt," Kyle said without looking away from Alee for even a second. "Well, I should go. Keep the jacket. I'll get it back later."

Victoria's love life was a different story. She tended to look outside of their circle when it came to dating, or at least when it came to serious dating. She had a way with guys and never seemed to be lacking in the dating department. Older guys were more her cup of tea. More to the point, she never really kept guys around long enough for them to become a part of the group, and she didn't intend to allow her friends to get attached to any of her conquests.

The more Alee learned about both Kyle and Damian the more she liked each of them. She found herself wanting to spend more time with them, and daydreaming about them when they weren't around. She became more and more fascinated by each of them as the days passed. She had an instant physical attraction to Kyle, and she didn't try to hide it. She always tried to sit next to him at lunch, and worked to find ways, during conversations, to casually touch his arm. Her hope was that one day he would notice her in the same way. She couldn't explain her feelings, even to herself, because she had never felt that way before. All she knew was that when he was around something inside her felt free. She felt adventurous. She felt a hunger. She realized she needed to pull back a bit when Dani pointed out that it had been a week since she had seen her eat anything during lunch. Instead she spent the whole time staring longingly in his direction, listening to the conversations he had with everyone but her, and waiting for him to smile at her or even laugh at something she said. When he finally did, she froze, trying to stop time with her mind so she could hang onto the moment forever. Luckily, he didn't seem to notice. Aside from a few small moments she thought they shared, Kyle continued to treat her the same way he treated any other member of their group; which was a blessing and a curse.

Alee could recite, in full detail, every one-on-one interaction she had had with Kyle since the beginning of school. There weren't many, but she played them in her head over and over during long class lectures and in chemistry lab. There were only five lockers between Alee's and Kyle's, and she often found herself waiting until just before the bell rang, hoping to see him before classes began.

One day, just as she was giving up hope and getting ready to leave, she closed her locker, turned toward the hall, and bumped right into his chest. She knew it was him before she even looked up. He had the sweetest scent of anyone she had ever met, notable because she had never really noticed how anyone smelled until she met him. Stumbling back she felt his hands around her arms, steadying her. When she looked up and their eyes met she could feel her heart pounding, and she prayed he couldn't hear it. They froze, his hands still around her arms, eye-to-eye, and she felt a warm fire burning in her arms, and flowing through her veins. She forgot about class entirely and could have stood there forever if it hadn't have been for the slamming of a locker just behind him. He let go and the warmth quickly faded but he never looked away.

"Hey," she croaked. She gave him a crooked little smile before biting her lip to stop herself from blushing. It didn't work.

"Where's the fire?" He raised an eyebrow at her in what she could only hope was an attempt to by playful.

"Oh, I um—contained it in my locker. I don't suggest going in there."

He chuckled and smiled back. "OK, well I guess I'll keep my distance."

"No, I didn't mean—."

"I'll just see you at lunch," he said. Without waiting for a response, he continued down the hall to class.

Alee remained momentarily paralyzed by her embarrassment and frustration. Contained it in my locker? What was I thinking?

On the way to class, all she could think about were his smile, his smell, and his amazing green eyes. She started to analyze their conversation, word for word, searching for any hidden meaning behind what he said, or how he said it. At first, she thought maybe he had laughed at her joke, but then she worried that maybe he had actually laughed *at* it—and her.

Her feelings for Damian were different. He was mysterious. Where Kyle made his presence known, Damian sat on the sidelines, just taking everything in. Kyle liked to make an entrance, hence, constantly getting in trouble for riding his skateboard around school, but Damian preferred not to be noticed. The two were actually the perfect pairing. Kyle would talk Damian's ear off and Damian seemed content just to listen.

It wasn't a physical attraction that drew her to him—. Not that he wasn't good looking, because he clearly was. He had perfected his silent brooding, yet she felt that something about him was crying out for her attention. Damian wore his emotions on his sleeves. She could tell when he was upset, because he focused less in class or he chose to sit closer to Victoria at the lunch table rather than next to Kyle. When he was in a good mood the energy of the group almost seemed to center around him, but Alee couldn't really pinpoint why. She found that more intriguing, more sexy, than anything. She was drawn to him. Her need to understand him fueled a couple of weeks of trying to get to know him and connect with him. But she started to think that his silence might be his way of shutting her out and telling her that he wasn't interested.

Alee had thought that he seemed interested, but maybe he was just being polite in those moments. He had selected the seat right behind hers in math class, and he had even claimed the front passenger seat of her car as his, moving Dani to the back on a regular base. "What do you think you're doing?" Dani blurted out when she saw Damian sitting in the front seat one afternoon after school. Contrary to how Alee thought Damian would respond, by climbing out and taking his usual place in the back seat, he just smiled and leaned forward so Tyler and Dani could squeeze behind him into the back. From that afternoon on no one questioned him.

That seemed promising, but Alee knew that she didn't have a whole lot of experience with boys, so after a while, with no other signs of interest from Damian, she told herself that most likely she had been reading him all wrong.

Alee was becoming more and more discouraged every day when finally, after spending an entire lunch period ranting about the math class they shared and Damian not speaking up to defend her or even just agree at all she decided to give up. That was when Victoria, who she got along with but wasn't really buddy-buddy with, decided to pull her aside for a little girl-to-girl chat. "Hey, Alee, are you OK?"

"What? Yeah, I'm fine. I just—."

"Is it Damian?" How Victoria could have known that Alee had been thinking about Damian at that moment eluded her. "Listen, Alee, don't let him get to you."

"It's kind of hard not to. I mean what do I have to do to get his attention?"

Victoria's eyebrows rose. "You like him, don't you?" Alee could feel her checks flush, even though she knew she had nothing to be embarrassed about. "Wow, I would have guessed you liked Kyle, not Damian." Victoria was probing her for information.

"I didn't say I—I mean I do like Kyle, and—I don't know how I feel, OK?!" Alee turned away and started down the hall toward her locker, but Victoria was right on her heels. "Alee, come on, don't leave. Seriously, if you like him that's

cool, from what I can tell Damian really seems into you too."
That stopped Alee in her tracks.

"Really?"

Even for Victoria, Damian was hard to explain. He was
her brother, and she would always defend him, no matter
what, but he wasn't your average teenager by any means.
"Yeah, I mean I haven't seen him connect with anyone as
quickly as he has with you."

"Victoria, come on! Connect? Are you kidding, I've seen
two dogs fighting over a hotdog connect better than the two
of us have. It's like he can tolerate me, but can't actually
stand me long enough to hold a conversation." Realizing that
Alee had raised her voice loud enough that people were
starting to stare, Victoria grabbed her by the arm and pulled
her into the girl's bathroom.

"For being as smart as everyone says you are, you can be
really dumb sometimes."

"What?!" Obviously and justifiably offended, Alee
pulled out of Victoria's grip.

"What is it? You think Damian's avoiding you? Ignoring
you?" Victoria's judgmental eyes watched as Alee almost
squirmed in her own skin. "Well, he isn't. Damian isn't just
quiet Alee. He doesn't talk—to anyone. Damian hasn't
spoken in years. Ever since our dad died, he's just—well,
he's different. That's the only way I can describe it. But,
when you're around, he seems a little more like the Damian I
used to know."

"Yeah, OK. Whatever—. Dani told me about it. She told
me he never talks, but I mean he talks. He's just quiet or

something. He and Kyle are always talking, like non-stop. I've seen them together, everyone has."

"Kyle is always talking—non-stop—not Damian!"

Then, thinking back, it all seemed so obvious. She couldn't actually remember a single time when Damian had even said hello to her, or just participated in a conversation at the lunch table. He had smiled, waved, and even appeared involved in the group, but for the life of her, she couldn't actually remember him ever speaking. The funny thing was, she could hear his voice in her head, even describe what it sounds like. But that didn't make much sense. How could that be if she hadn't actually heard it?

"How did he die? Your dad I mean."

"I don't know. I mean I don't really remember it. My mom says it was an accident, but won't tell me anything else. I wasn't there."

"Was Damian there?" Alee was leaning up against the sinks as Victoria avoided eye contact by pretending to fix her lipstick.

"Yeah, he was there. From what my mom says he watched my dad die." She tossed her lip gloss back into her purse and snapped it shut. "Anyway, it was a long time ago. It really affected Damian though, and he hasn't spoken a word since. Be it fear or shock, the doctors don't really know. They hoped that one day he would speak again, but no one really knows for sure."

"How does he—."

"He doesn't let it hold him back, at least not any more. Anyway, you didn't even notice how different he really is."

Victoria wiped a stray tear from her check as she made her way to the door. "Look, I have to get to class. Just think about what I said, and don't write him off so quickly. I miss the connection my brother and I used to have, but I just want to see him happy. If that means with you then I'm OK with that." She was gone, leaving Alee confused and alone.

Intrigued, Alee started asking around, trying to find out anything and everything she could about him. Everyone had a story to tell. Some said he and his father had been in a bad car accident, others said it was a break-in at their house. The stories varied, but everyone agreed that Damian had been with his dad the moment he died, and Alee knew that had to be hard on him at only five years old.

Through the years, Damian had found his own ways to communicate with people. He kept a laptop with him at all times to communicate what he wanted or needed to say. His teachers did what they could to make him comfortable in the classroom, trying hard not to bring any unneeded attention his way. His emotions, what most people show through the tone of their voice and the rhythm of their speech, were a little harder to express. Damian was an amazing artist, and when he wanted to he was able to express his feelings, his deepest thoughts and even his fears very clearly—sometimes disturbingly—through art. With only a pencil and a pad of paper he could reveal his soul.

To some people this might have seemed tragic, and maybe it was at first, but as the months past and their friendship grew stronger, Alee realized that it didn't matter that Damian couldn't speak. He didn't see his life as tragic or sad, so why should she? She saw it through his eyes. She saw it as pure. He didn't have to hide his feelings or lie to make others feel better. He just was who he was, and he didn't try to defend himself to anyone. Alee understood, better than most people. Everyone deals with grief, pain, loss, and tragedy in different ways. How she handled her illness wasn't the same as how Damian handled the loss of his father, nor would her methods have worked for him.

The whole group had gone out to the movies after school one Friday, and the plan was for everyone to crash at Dani's house for the night because her parents were out of town. It didn't end up working out quite as they had planned though. Kyle, to Alee's disappointment, ended up leaving after the movie because his family was having a reunion the next day, and his parents insisted he be home when his aunt and her family showed up. Tyler didn't even come to the movies because he and Dani were in the middle of a stupid fight. So, after the movie, Dani, Victoria, Alee and Damian went back to the house and ate a whole large pizza. Then Victoria and Dani went up to Dani's room to read magazines, paint their nails, and listen to music.

Alee and Damian stayed on the couch long after the pizza was gone. They watched TV for a while, but the later it got, the braver she became until she finally got up the nerve to say, "Damian, tell me about your father."

Damian wasn't the type to cry, at least not in public, but no one had ever really been interested before—other than his therapists, who were paid very well to be interested. He looked at Alee, and it was the sincere concern he saw in her eyes that brought the tears. He had to turn away. Showing weakness wasn't something Damian liked to do.

"Is this the first time someone has asked you about it?"

Damian shook his head slowly.

"Is this the first time a friend has asked?"

Damian nodded.

They spent all night together learning everything they could about each other, and he never spoke a word.

It started slowly at first, Damian typing on his laptop, jotting things down on a notepad, drawing pictures—everything they had done in the past. However, eventually, as the night went on, they started to get tired and, much like children, the sleepier they became the less control they had over their thoughts and the less their concern for censoring themselves. Without really noticing a change, their communication became as fluid and natural as an ordinary conversation. She was talking freely, and he was no longer using pen and paper to answer. His voice was somehow in her head, answering her questions, and asking his own.

"My mom sent me to the first psychologist shortly after my dad died. I don't know if I was afraid to tell the doctor what had happened, or if I just couldn't. I still don't really know what happened. Not fully," Damian explained.

"What do you mean" Alee asked out loud.

"My father was murdered right in front of me, and now every time I close my eyes, I can see the face of the man that killed him."

"Murdered?"

"Yeah." They sat in silence as Damian remembered, and Alee tried to understand what he must have gone through.

Damian shared his feelings and his fears. He even told her about the first time he saw her, about how her blue eyes seemed to pierce into his soul in the same way the man's eyes had done on that night so many years before. She understood then why she had felt like she was getting mixed signals from him during those first few weeks. It all made so much more sense. That look of fear when they first met, the way he kept his distance yet tried to be friends.

"When did you first know you were sick?"

"I don't know. I guess I've really never *not* known if that makes any sense. Mom says I lived at the hospital more than I did at home in the first few years of my life. But I don't remember all that. I do know that over the years I have met more than my fair share of doctors and nurses."

She told him about her illness, all the surgeries she had gone through, the fact that according to ninety-nine percent of her doctors, she shouldn't even *be* alive. They bonded over the tragedies of their lives that night. For the first time they both felt like someone really understood them, and what they were going through. That was something that neither one of them had ever really had before, at least not on that level.

That night Alee fell asleep in the warmth of Damian's arms. When they woke up together the next morning something had changed between them, more than just the psychic connection that she wasn't really sure was real or a dream, but the way he looked at her, as if she was the only thing that mattered in the world. *"Are you OK?"* There it was—his voice in her head as clear as day.

Yup, it's real! "Yeah, I'm fine." She wasn't really sure if she was lying or telling the truth. Although she loved the feeling of being so close to someone, it also made life a little more complicated. She had already been confused by her feelings toward Damian verses her feelings toward Kyle: now her confusion was overwhelming.

When Alee fell ill near the end of the semester, her doctors made her stay out of school for the final month of classes. Her teachers and her parents were really good about letting Damian bring all of her homework to her. When finals rolled around, they worked with her to do at-home proctored exams. Those four weeks seemed to last forever, and she found herself spending most of her free time with Damian at her bedside, and what time she didn't spend with him was spent studying, sleeping, and traveling to and from doctor appointments.

Damian and Alee never officially dated, but everyone assumed that they were together. Even if they themselves didn't think of it that way. They spent all their free time together, mainly because he was the only one who bothered to visit her on a regular base. Dani was too busy with Tyler in their on-again off-again relationship. Victoria was a friend, but they had never been close enough that she would feel comfortable being around Alee when she was sick, and Alee didn't really want her around either, when all she really felt like doing was vomiting and crying. They hung out only with the group, or just Dani, as the common ground. None of that mattered though. Alee and Damian truly enjoyed each other's company, but despite their strong feelings for each other, they never developed a physical relationship. It wasn't something they cared to explain, it was just an unspoken bond.

Whenever Alee got sick, Damian was by her side the whole time, without question. It might have been different if he had been dating someone else, or if Kyle had shown an interest in Alee, but that hadn't happened, at least not in the way she had hoped.

Alee's parents didn't approve at first. Like most people, they didn't understand Damian. The fact that he didn't talk just seemed strange and wrong to them. However, after Alee explained about his past, that his father had been killed right in front of him, how that experience had traumatized him— their feelings started to change. The Moyers were no stranger to death—to killing, and the thought of an innocent child having to watch his father be killed didn't sit well with them.

Eventually Damian grew on them. Besides, Damian wasn't doing anything that could harm her, and he had made it clear, coming back day after day, that he didn't intend to stop visiting her. After a couple of weeks, her parents actually started to see the positive effect he was having on Alee, and they welcomed him in day after day, instead of rushing him out. His presence alone seemed to make Alee feel better, which in turn made her parents feel better. He would bring her homework and they would study, listen to music and hang out. He made her feel normal, even when other people maybe didn't see her that way.

Every day, Martha would answer Damian's gentle knock and send him up to Alee's room. Damian announced himself by tapping on the door with his knuckles before walking into her bedroom. Alee was always ready and waiting for him.

"Hey, how're you feeling?"

"I'm good, really good," she said, actually meaning it, even if she didn't look all that good. Alee had started losing weight, and she really didn't have any extra weight to lose.

"Well you look good."

She could see it in his eyes. Damian was worried, and trying hard not to show it. That was just like him too, always trying to protect her even if it meant telling little white lies to make her feel better.

Whatever the bond was between them, she didn't want it to stop and neither did he. They were private about how connected they felt because even they didn't really understand it, and they chose not to tell anyone else about the way they had learned to communicate. Damian was afraid people would look at him as even more of a freak if word got out that he was able to communicate telepathically.

She taught him how to meditate, and they found that they could literally spend hours in complete silence and not be bored at all. They were completely in tune with each other. Meditating started as a way to help her relax, but she discovered that she was able to manage her pain, which seemed to be coming more and more frequently. However, through their connection, Alee's pain somehow transferred to Damian. There were times during meditation that as her physical pain decreased, he would become increasingly ill:

vomiting, fever, even severe migraines. When they were done, he would feel completely drained of all his energy. His symptoms would last for hours, days, sometimes weeks. During those times she could feel him pull away, ever so slightly, in order to protect himself. She could sense his inner strength fighting the pain she caused him, and she tried to stop, but not knowing how it was happening, made it hard to control. It felt animalistic the way his emotions took over, yet she never feared him, or worried about his intentions.

Eventually, they didn't need the meditation to feel and understand each other's emotions. It became part of who they were, much like the way they had learned to communicate simply through thought alone. They were connected in a way that she had never been with anyone else, a way that most people never feel in a lifetime. She loved him and he loved her, but she quickly realized that it was no more than just a friendship, at least not yet. Not to her. Their love, although strong, was not romantic or passionate. It was more of a need than a desire. They felt protective of each other, and at times even possessive. They knew that they were meant to guide and guard each other. They knew they would do anything it took to make sure the other was safe. Neither one of them could imagine that bond ever breaking.

Despite—and also because of—their bond, Alee understood that Damian's heart didn't belong to her, but to someone or rather something else. Damian's soul was on a quest, and Alee could feel that his heart would not settle in life, let alone love, until that journey had been completed. She suspected it had something to do with his father's death, but he had already told her so much, she didn't want to pressure him into sharing even more if he wasn't ready.

Things would have been so much easier if they longed for each other, if their bond were not only of the mind but also of the heart. But, life isn't always easy, a lesson that Alee had learned thousands of times before. Their connection had been sealed, and although they didn't fully understand why or how, they accepted it without question and knew that they would forever be a part of each other, forever a part of each other's lives.

12

Jacinda stood alone in the center of the small empty cellar. The walls were bare, no furniture in sight. It was more like a closet than a room. It was as cold as the winter air blowing outside, but to look at her steady hands and calm demeanor you would never know it. The small, narrow windows near the ceiling were covered in dust thick enough to block out the moonlight. Outside, the wind began to blow. The distant cry of an approaching storm could be heard. With soft white sand that she scooped out from a bag held with her other hand, she drew the outline of a circle around the floor.

"Spirits here, spirits near, come ye, come ye, come ye that may. Throughout and about, around and around, the circle be drawn, the circle be bound."

Before she completed the last bit of the circle, she stepped inside and then sealed herself in. Taking a smaller silk bag from over her shoulder she knelt on the floor in the center of the circle. With the edge of the circle only an arm's length away from her body in all directions the fit was tight, but she was careful not to cross the sand. She knew how important this was, and that she only had one chance. She withdrew five candles from the bag, and placed them evenly around the circle, indicating the five points of a star.

As her hand passed over a pure white candle she softly spoke, "By the powers of the goddesses I ask for your strength—your power—your mercy." A flame began to glow softly, casting a light across her face. Slowly and with great care she shifted her position to face the green candle. "By the power of the earth I ask you to help her find her way." The candle flickered in the dark room. The yellow candle lit as the hiss of the wind outside grew louder. "By the power of the wind I ask you to guide her to me." She turned to the blue candle as a crack of lightening lit the room, and outside, the rain began to pour. Slightly startled, she turned toward the door and her soft blue eyes glistened with the glow of the candles. Lighting the candle she called out to the water, "By the power of the water that flows through all living things help her to hear my calls. The red candle burned the brightest within the circle, and flickered as the wind pushed stronger and faster through the cracks in the foundation. Outside, the lightening lit the sky, and the thunder shook the walls as if trying to take them down around her. "By the power of fire show her the path and light her way home."

"By the powers of the goddesses and the four elements combined, give me the strength to call her forth. Bring her to me so that she will one day see. By the powers of the goddesses and the four elements combined, give me the strength to call her forth." Her voice grew louder and more demanding as she spoke, "Bring her to me so that she will one day see!" Her chant continued as the storm grew more and more powerful.

Suddenly, the door blew open and the wind blew her long dark hair away from her face as she looked up with eyes as black as coal. Her sister Loraline, a beautiful woman with long, flowing, auburn hair stood in the doorway watching and waiting. "Is it done?"

"It is, but are you sure this is what you want?"

"I have been away from her for almost seventeen years," Loraline crooned, almost in tears. "She is my only child, my daughter. No matter who raised her she is mine. I want her back!"

"What will Granny Edith say?"

"Granny Edith should have been dead a long time ago, and is dead to me now. I know that sounds harsh, but you would feel the same way if you were in my shoes. I couldn't stop her from sending my daughter away, but if I don't fight for her now, what kind of mother am I?" She stepped into the room as close to her sister as she could without crossing the circle. "You are either with me or against me. What will it be?"

"You know I'm with you. I want her back just as much as you do." After hearing those words Loraline nodded to her sister and turned and walked out, leaving Jacinda there in the circle as one by one the candles burned out. When only one candle was left burning she lifted it close to her face and, before blowing it out, and leaving herself in darkness, she made one last small plea. "For what is done, is done. Goddesses watch over us, this path we have paved."

Over winter break, Alee's parents had taken her out of town to visit family and to meet with a specialist her doctor had referred her to. It was the first time in over two months that she and Damian weren't going to be spending their weekends together. He had pretty much locked himself in his house while she was gone. He told his mom and his sister that he just needed time to think, rejuvenate, before school started back up, but Victoria knew what was really going on. As did his mother, whether she wanted to admit it or not.

It was the same every year, always around the holidays, Damian started thinking more and more about their father, and he would sink into a deep depression. The nightmares got worse, his headaches came more often, and the older he got the more it seemed like their mother just didn't understand. Victoria tried to be there for him, but even she knew that she could never really know what he was going through. So when he secluded himself in the dusty old attic of their small house, she tried to leave him alone and give him as much space as she could.

There was a dusting of snow on the lawn below, and the small window that Damian was looking out of was still frosted over, but he knew that everything would be melting as soon as the sun came up. The flickering overhead light was just enough for him to read the old newspaper article describing his father's death. As he scanned the faded paper, which he had read a thousand times before, there were the words that always stood out, time and time again, "—still searching for a suspect—this animalistic attack—James Ward, twenty-seven,—died within seconds—leaving behind a wife and two small children—."

When they moved into this house a few years ago his mom had stored all of their father's old stuff in boxes in the attic. She had said that she wasn't ready to let them go, but she didn't want them scattered throughout the house like they had been for so many years. No one had even thought twice about what was up there except for Damian. From time to time he would go into the attic and rummage through his father's old clothes, books, and random items. It made him feel closer to his father, and over the past year he found himself spending more time submerging himself in the old dusty boxes. This urge usually came over him late at night after everyone had gone to sleep and he lay, restless, in his bed. As his seventeenth birthday approached, he felt like he needed his father more than ever, and he didn't know any way to connect to him other than through the things he had left behind.

Like most days he spent in the attic, hours had passed without him even noticing. Lost in the pages of an old photo album, and surrounded by piles of books all around him, he leaned back against an old dusty wooden crate. He had never been able to look inside because he didn't have the key to the rusty metal lock that held it tightly shut. He had often imagined what his father might have kept inside, but over the past few months, there was a new desperation to his curiosity. He tried picking the lock several times and had even taken a hammer to it once. But today when he leaned against the box something felt different. He turned to look at the crate and saw that the lock was no longer hanging through the latch where it had always been.

Damian glanced around the room. He thought maybe his eyes were playing tricks on him, showing him what he wanted to see but not what was actually there. He could have sworn that the lock had been there when he sat down a few hours before, but he hadn't really paid it much attention. His excitement drove him to move quickly. It took just minutes to pull off the boxes and books from on top of the crate, and he pulled it into the center of the small floor space he had filled with pillows and blankets and had been using as his personal reading area for years. The crate was about the size of an old record player, but was much heavier than it looked. The wood grain of the hard oak was clearly visible when he wiped away the layers of dust that had settled over the years. Taking a deep breath, Damian slowly lifted the lid.

"Damian? Damian, are you up there?"

Startled by his mother's voice calling from the bottom of the attic stairs, Damian woke up with a jolt. He hadn't even realized he had been sleeping. His dreams had been getting clearer and clearer, and he was remembering more details every time.

"Damian, please come down here for a minute," Karen called.

Turning to look at the crate behind him, he saw the rusty lock still hanging tightly shut. He pulled and twisted the lock as hard as he could, but it would not open. He knew now, more than ever, that he needed to get the lock open. He was determined to do it today.

Downstairs his mother was waiting patiently. When he climbed down the ladder she handed him the kitchen timer. "When it goes off, take dinner out of the oven."

His mother saw the confusion in her son's eyes, and she was hardly surprised. Damian had been in the attic since before the sun came up that morning, and she could see that he had no idea what time it was now. She tried to give Damian his space when he got like this. This time of year was equally hard on her, and she didn't want to make it worse by doing or saying the wrong thing.

"Damian, please pay attention. I have to run out for an hour, Victoria went to the mall with Dani, but I should be back before she gets home."

He took the timer and turned toward his room. Before he could take a step away she grabbed his arm and pulled him gently toward her. "I wish you wouldn't spend so much time in the attic. You're not going to find the answers you're looking for up there." Their eyes locked and her level gaze urged him to give up his search. The problem was that he didn't really know what he was searching for, and the more she protested the more he wanted find out what was in that locked crate. He smiled innocently, and gave her a kiss on the cheek before turning away. With that she turned and walked back down the hall and disappeared around the corner.

When he heard the car back out of the driveway and knew that he was finally alone he moved quickly. He had already tried everything he could think of to open the crate, and had searched all the boxes for a key, with no success. There was still one place Damian had not yet checked. He hadn't had the opportunity until that day. His mother kept a small jewelry box on her dresser that he remembered going through as a small boy. He used to try on his father's wedding band and play with his pocket-watch. But as he got older his mother stopped letting him do that. She said she didn't want him to misplace the ring, or break the watch, which was a family heirloom. She told him that one day, when he got older, they would belong to him, but until that time he should just forget they were there. It never struck him as odd until a few days ago when his mom had come out of the attic, where she never went, with what looked like a leather necklace in her hand. She had quickly gone into her room, and he could hear her opening and closing her jewelry box as he quietly stood outside her bedroom door.

Damian's need to know what was in the crate had become an obsession. He knew he didn't have long, and if he was lucky enough to find the key he would need to make sure he returned it before his mom got back. He pulled the small jewelry box down from the dresser, sat on the end of her bed and raised the lid. He was disappointed to find only the pocket-watch and a few of his mother's necklaces that he hadn't seen her wear in years. Damian had been so sure the key would be there, he didn't know what to do next. More disturbing than not finding the key was the fact that his father's wedding ring wasn't there either. His mother never took it out, and was very protective of it. He remembered at his father's funeral seeing his mother crying over his body holding his ring in her hand. She just couldn't let it go.

As he lifted the box to slide it back into its place between her cell phone charger and the stack of books she had recently finished, a small panel on the bottom of the box slipped out of place. He quickly turned it over to find a small open slit. Using his thumb, he pushed hard, sliding the panel open and revealing a small compartment. Inside was the old leather necklace he'd seen in his mother's hand. When he pulled it out there was a small silver key hanging from the bottom like a charm. His heart began to race, his hands were shaking, and he almost dropped the box as he stumbled to put it back in its place and rush out of the bedroom and up into the attic.

The crate was right where he had left it. He knelt down and gently, so as not to break the key in the lock, slid the key in. It was so old and the hole was covered in rust, but after a little wiggling he made the key fit and as he turned it he heard the pop of the lock as it fell open into his hand. He wanted to savor the moment, but knew he needed to get the key back before his mom made it home. Reluctantly, he turned his back on the crate and rushed back downstairs and straight into his mom's room. He put the key back where he had found it. He felt as if a weight had been lifted off his shoulders. Although he didn't know what he expected to find in the crate, he felt like he was finally going to get some answers.

"What are you doing in Mom's room?" He turned to see his sister standing in the bedroom doorway just staring at him with her questioning eyes.

Damian didn't feel like dealing with Victoria right now. He pushed past her and made his way to the attic staircase. Folding up the ladder, he shut the attic entry. He didn't want to leave the crate unlocked for long, but knew he would probably have to wait until after dinner before he would be able to make it back up here.

Crap! Dinner!

He rushed back into his mom's room to find his sister holding the kitchen timer. It had gone off at some point while he was in the attic unlocking the box.

"Good job, Damian. What has gotten into you lately? You're even weirder than normal, and you haven't spent any time with Alee lately. You two have a fight?" Her sarcasm was thick, but he could tell that she did genuinely care.

He grabbed the timer and rushed downstairs to the kitchen. He pulled the roast out of the oven and smoke poured out when he lifted the lid. It wasn't burned too badly, and by the time their mother got home the table was set and he and his sister were sitting quietly across the table from one another waiting for her to arrive so they could all eat together.

Family dinners had been a once a week tradition for years in their family, and the one tradition their mother was determined to keep alive.

That evening, after everyone else was sound asleep, he sneaked out of his room and made his way back up to the attic. The crate was already unlocked and he didn't want to waste any time. As he had done in his dream, he quickly moved the boxes and books off of the crate, and pulled it to the middle of is reading space under the dim light bulb. Then he quietly lifted the lid. He found news articles, mostly describing animal attacks or animal hunts, from the town he grew up in. Damian didn't understand why his father would have kept them locked up.

Under the articles, as if hidden, he found his father's wedding band. He slid it easily onto the ring finger of his right hand, and it fit perfectly, almost as if it had been made specifically for him. It looked just like the silver band his mother still wore every day. It was exactly how he had remembered it. He was always intrigued by its unique design like a braided rope. Damian remembered being mesmerized as a child by his mother's ring and would twist it around and around on her finger, searching for where the rope began, but never finding that spot. Now as he twisted and pulled at the ring on his finger he realized that taking it off wasn't going to be as easy as putting it on. He gave up the fight, deciding that it just wasn't worth it. The ring was eventually going to be his anyway, why not now?

The ring had been sitting on top of a package wrapped in brown paper and tied shut with a thin white rope. The paper crinkled in his hands as he pulled it off of the box, but not loud enough to wake his sleeping family below. Once the box was fully unwrapped he pulled out an old notebook, with slightly smudged writing on the front cover.

"Fear not the change or the pain—for courage and life are yours to gain."

A few pages into the book he found a list of names and next to each name was the name of an animal. He flipped through the pages and read the scribbling inside. Words like "—in our blood—shape shifters—transformation—" stood out. He went back to the beginning of the book and quickly scanned the list of names. Near the end of the list were his parents' names. Written next to his father's name was the word "panther," but nothing was written next to his mother's name. Even more confusing was the fact that at the very bottom of the list were the names Victoria and Damian. No animal names were written next to their names either. As crazy as it all seemed, Damian understood what it implied. Whether or not he believed it yet he wasn't sure.

With the box back in place and the notebook safely hidden under his bed, Damian tried to get a little sleep. He wasn't sure how he was going to explain the ring on his hand, but seeing as he couldn't get it off he would just have to figure that out in the morning. Maybe his mother wouldn't even notice. She never did seem to pay much attention to those kinds of things anyway. Besides, tomorrow was another day, and for the first time in a while he was looking forward to the possibilities it held in store.

The next morning Damian woke up to the sound of his name being shouted from somewhere outside.

"Damian? Damian, are you up yet?" If he didn't know that Alee was out of town with her family he would have sworn it was her voice he was hearing. When he rolled out of bed and opened the window a small stone flew through the air and hit him right in the center of his forehead. It wasn't big enough to hurt him, but it startled him.

He was rubbing his forehead when he looked down and saw that it really was Alee, smiling up at him. He threw on a pair of tennis shoes and bounded down the stairs two at a time. Flying out the back door onto the deck he grabbed her in his arms swinging her around.

"What are you doing here?"

He was hugging her so tightly she could barely speak. "I missed you."

As his grip loosened and their eyes met she tried to catch her breath.

"I missed you too."

They felt as if time were standing still. Something in the air around them was thick, and the only sound Alee could hear was the muffled sound of her own heart. Hesitantly, with his arms still wrapped around her, Damian leaned forward and kissed her lips. His lips were soft and warm and tasted like Chap Stick.

Alee hadn't planned on kissing Damian, and was still motionless when Victoria came out of the house to find them lip locked in a tight embrace.

"Alee? Damian? What are you two—? Oh. Oh?" She looked around searching for a distraction, but found nothing. "Sorry. Wow. This is awkward."

"I, um…" Alee quickly pulled away, out of Damian's arms, and started backing up toward the side of the house. "…I was just leaving." She looked back over her shoulder as she quickly made her way around to the front of the house where her car was parked. "I'll see you later."

Damian would have stopped her if he could have, but he could feel Victoria's eyes burning into his back, and he was already a little embarrassed, and didn't really want to hear what she would have to say about their kissing. Instead he headed to the garage, pulled out his bike, and took off down the dirt trail out behind their house. He needed air more than anything right then.

14

After the holidays, with everyone back at school, things were a little awkward between Alee and Damian. The first day back Alee made her way to their usual lunch table only to find everyone staring at her. "What's going on?" she asked.

Dani literally jumped out of her seat and grabbed Alee. "I thought we were friends. Why didn't you tell me?"

"Tell you what?" Alee was searching her brain, trying to figure out what Dani could be asking about. Then she realized that Damian wasn't there, and when she looked over, Victoria was covering her mouth trying to hide a smirk. "Oh."

"Oh. My. God!" Dani glanced back at Victoria. "It *is* true."

"Dani, it's not a big deal. Please just let it go." Alee sat down, but could feel everyone still staring at her. She ate in silence, secretly wishing she had been smart like Damian and chosen to spend her lunch period somewhere else. After gulping down her food, Alee gathered up her tray, said hasty goodbyes, stopped at the trash bin, and headed to her locker to get her books for her next class. The bell hadn't even rung, but she would have been more comfortable anywhere else in the world at that moment.

"Hey." She didn't even have to look up to recognize Kyle's voice. "So, um, you and Damian, huh?"

OK, things *could* get worse. She wanted to just sink through the floor, but she had to say something. "No. I mean, yeah, but no, we aren't a thing or anything. If that's what you're asking."

"Then, what—?" He was just watching her closely.

Is this jealousy? Is he actually jealous? She thought to herself with a hint of glee, but couldn't imagine it actually being true. "I don't know. We're friends, I guess." Friends, wow what a lame answer. She knew they were more than friends, but what they were she couldn't explain, nor did she really want to explain it, at least not to Kyle.

The unexpected kiss seemed to have a deeper effect on Alee and Damian's relationship than either one of them had expected, but what was worse was that it had affected everyone in the group. As a distraction, Alee was spending more and more of her free time with Dani and Victoria. At first she had to dodge questions every five minutes, but eventually their interests shifted. They did the usual girl stuff like shopping and sleepovers, but one day while they were all hanging out in Alee's room Dani pulled out the box of crystals and stones that she and Alee used every so often whenever Dani got the urge to explore witchcraft. It had been a while, because nothing ever came of it, but the girls had fun trying. This time she just started fiddling with them, and as soon as Victoria saw the shiny stones she was captivated.

"Are they real?" she asked.

"What do you mean are they real?"

"You know, are they real? The green one is it really an emerald?" Victoria was timidly sifting through the stones, but as soon as she saw the smooth and glistening green stone she gently lifted it from the box and held it in her palm.

"They're real, but that's not an emerald. It's called peridot," Alee answered. "They're all either crystals or semi-precious gemstones. You're not going to find any emeralds, diamonds, rubies, or anything like that."

Alee liked Victoria, but there had always been something about her that made Alee uncomfortable. The worst part was she had no idea why she felt that way, and it made her feel guilty somehow. They had spent a lot of time together, with the rest of the group, but never one on one. It was awkward at first, but Victoria was Damian's sister and Alee really did want to get to know her better. Considering that Victoria hadn't made the effort previously, Alee figured she was going to have to take the first step.

"Well, they're really pretty whatever they are," Victoria said. She held the peridot up toward the light and watched how the light reflected through it. "Why do you have them all?"

Good question, Alee thought to herself.

Before Alee could say anything Dani interrupted, saying, "It's really cool actually. She gets them every year for her birthday. Something special her parents have done since she was little." Then she turned to Alee for confirmation. "Right, Alee?"

"Yeah, right." It was a little more information than Alee had been comfortable giving Victoria, or anyone for that matter, and now that Victoria knew the whole group was bound to find out. "But they're really no big deal. And they're kind of private, so—."

Victoria looked down at the stones she and Dani had scattered across the bedroom floor and the peridot in her hand. Still not wanting to let go, she said, "Oh, right, sorry. I'll put them away right now. It's just that they're so pretty. I thought they were interesting, that's all." Alee had never seen Victoria look so innocent, almost embarrassed, but she didn't know what to say.

Dani had practically grown up in Alee's house; it was like a second home to her. The thought that anything there was private, even from her, didn't seem natural to her. She was watching the exchange between Alee and Victoria, and figured the only reason Alee could possibly have been uncomfortable was because she was still a little upset about Victoria telling everyone about her and Damian kissing. Besides, Alee and Victoria had never really connected and, being a good friend to both, she wanted to change that.

"Yeah, but we're all friends here right?" Dani pulled on Alee's arm, urging her to sit down with them on the floor. "Tell her what the peridot is used for."

Over the years Alee had shared a little information here and there about her collection with Dani, but no one else had even seen it until that day. Although Victoria seemed sincere in her interest Alee still wasn't really comfortable being pushed to open up. "Dani." Alee was eyeing Dani trying to get her attention so she would realize she wasn't comfortable.

"What?"

Victoria was pretending not to pay them much attention, but she couldn't help but notice when Alee pulled Dani into the hallway. "Seriously, Dani? What are you doing? You know I've never shown those to anyone but you. Why would you even bring them out?"

"What's the big deal Alee?"

Alee just sighed. She knew she wasn't going to get through to her. When Dani was around Victoria she was different, always trying to impress her, to the point of losing sight of everything else around her. "Nothing, never mind, I guess I'm just over reacting." Alee pushed past her and back into her room. "Here, let me see." She held her hand open for the stone. At least this way she could play on her own terms, only sharing what was comfortable, nothing more nothing less.

"Peridot is considered a healing stone," she said hesitantly, hoping if she gave her just a little information she might loss interest. "If you believe that stuff, supposedly it can help with gallbladder or kidney problems, but who really knows right?!" She shrugged and tossed a crystal into the box, instantly regretting treating her stones so carelessly. She hoped that Victoria would quickly move on to something else like magazine quizzes and painting her nails.

"Seriously? Cool." Victoria's eyes were wide with excitement, as she grabbed another stone from the pile. "What about this one?"

Alee bit her lip, but answered the question. "That's called hematite. It's used to help circulation, and to help supply oxygen to the blood stream."

"It's like your necklace," Victoria said while pointing to Alee's hematite pendant.

"Yup." Alee lifted the quarter-size pendant off her skin, and could feel the warm air wash over the cool spot. "It's one of my favorite stones."

"What's this one?"

Alee was surprised at how excited Victoria was, "That one is a rose quartz. It's a love stone."

Dani and Victoria both perked up at that. "A love stone?" Victoria asked eagerly her voice practically singing with excitement.

"It's supposed to open your heart to love," Alee smiled self-consciously as she answered.

Before long, without even realizing it, Alee had completely opened up and was teaching them all about the different crystals and stones in her collection. She had been so worried that Victoria would think her crystal healing theories were a little crazy or off the wall; she hadn't considered the possibility that she might be just as open to it as she and Dani were. Alee was surprised and more than a little excited when both Dani and Victoria were so eager, and without judgment, just wanting to learn more and explore the possibilities of what they could do with all this new information.

It wasn't so surprising that Victoria was especially anxious to know more about the powers of passion and love that some stones possessed. She saw it as an opportunity to enhance her personal life, as if her personal life actually needed enhancing, but who was Alee to stop her from trying? Especially when Alee knew that she herself would love to have a little extra help in the love department.

Dani took their shared interest in crystals and stones to the next level by incorporating her own budding interest in witchcraft and the occult. Alee always knew that Dani had a natural talent for writing. So, writing incantations didn't seem much different than the poems she used to write as a child, or those she wrote in English class. However, turning them into spells and making them do anything other than rhyming didn't prove to be very easy. Working together, over the next few weeks the three girls really started to connect with each other. As the weeks passed, Alee had hoped it would bring them together even more, but she didn't expect much in the way of magic, which was odd, because even as a young child she had known that when it came to magic, she couldn't entirely dismiss it.

Alee could remember times when she would lie in bed unable to sleep and she would stare up blankly, imagining the night sky just beyond the painted ceiling, until she could see it just as real as if she were lying on the cool grass in their front yard. She remembered the very first time she tried to call the elements using one of Dani's poems—the way the thunder rocked the walls of her room, and the lightening lit up the night sky If Dani had actually been there that night, she just might have been scared off from magic altogether, or maybe it would have reaffirmed her beliefs. Alee always rationalized those instances, telling herself that it was all in her mind, coincidence, or even a fluke, but she didn't really believe this. If she had she wouldn't have continued practicing so many years later. Not that she would ever admit that to Dani. All Dani knew was what they did together. Alee vowed to herself that if she ever saw real progress, she would talk to Dani about it, but the most that ever happened was the minor and very temporary effects she had on the weather, and once or twice she experienced something she could only describe as telekinesis. Simple things like her crystals coming to her, just by thinking about them. Crazy, right? That's what Alee thought anyway.

Alee probably would have tried to laugh the whole idea of magic off, if it hadn't been for Dani's insistent interest, at least in front of Victoria. But, Dani had a way of getting Alee excited about things, almost like a cheerleader can get a crowd at a football game amped up. Alee often thought that the school cheer squad really missed out when they decided not to put Dani on the team, but then again, their friendship probably wouldn't have been the same if she had made it.

With the help of Dani and the persistence of Victoria, Alee learned a lot about herself, and gained more confidence than she had ever hoped to have.

Although Alee and Damian were still close, during these times he wasn't around nearly as often. They still spent most of their weekends together, but always as a group, never just the two of them. In the evenings after school he spent more and more time alone reading through the old notebook he had found among his dad's things. He had told her that he needed space and Alee wanted to respect that. Damian just didn't want, or wasn't ready, to share what he was going through with anyone just yet, and with the changes Alee was going through he wasn't sure if he ever would.

Damian would join the girls on occasion, but it was as if he was there just because Alee had invited him, like fulfilling a friendship obligation: it often seemed like there was somewhere else he would rather be. Alee could never really put her finger on what it was, but she knew that something wasn't the same. He never really seemed to be paying much attention anyway, so it was a surprise when he finally came to her one night and told her, *"I don't know Alee, I just don't get it."*

"What do you mean?" He had pulled her aside after Victoria and Dani had gone down to the kitchen to get some soda and snacks.

"I can tell you're happy, all of you, but I just—I guess I'm just not comfortable with the idea of spells, crystals, or even magic in general. It doesn't seem natural." He took her hand in his, and pleaded for understanding. *"Please don't take it the wrong way. I'm not judging you; you know I would never do that. I lo—. You're my best friend. I don't care that you're doing it. I just can't."*

Alee was lost in Damian's soft grey eyes, as his voice echoed in her mind, caressing her thoughts.

"Alee, say something. Please."

"I just—I mean, I don't really believe in all this stuff. It's all just pretend anyway, but—you're telepathic. It just seems like it shouldn't really be a big deal to you I guess. But, no, it's fine, really. Like I said, it's all just pretend anyway." She said it, but she knew she didn't really believe that any more. "I get it if you don't want to be around it." He didn't have to explain anything. He was right, he never judged her, and so she wasn't going to judge him either. Alee knew this wasn't going to change their friendship, at least she hoped it wouldn't. Like he said, she was his best friend, and she felt the same way about him. It just meant that she had something she could have to herself, and share with her girlfriends.

Alee and Damian heard someone coming up the stairs and they quickly turned away from each other. Damian threw himself back on the bed and went back to reading the "People" magazine he had been staring at for the last two hours, and Alee went back to sorting her crystals.

"Hey, who were you talking to?" Victoria asked as she came into the bedroom. She didn't know about the "connection" Alee and Damian had, so explaining what was going on wouldn't be easy.

"Me! I mean, just myself, like always. Damian's just gracious enough to listen," Alee answered, smiling back at Damian. He looked grateful for her quick thinking. He wasn't ready to be the weird guy again in his sister's eyes. From that point on Damian opted out of hanging out with the girls whenever they decided to whip out the candles and crystals.

15

Early on a Saturday morning, Alee woke up to the sound of Victoria's car honking loudly in her driveway and Dani ringing the doorbell. Victoria and Dani had woken up early and were at Alee's house unexpectedly, to pick her up.

Alee's mom knocked on her bedroom door saying, "Wake up, Alee. Please go downstairs and tell the girls that it is too early to be honking the car horn. They're going to wake the neighbors."

Alee jumped out of bed and raced downstairs. Pulling the front door open, and sticking her head out, she called, "What are you guys doing? You know my mom is going to kill you, right?!"

"Get dressed. We're going on a road trip," Dani said matter-of-factly, and pushed her back into the house. "We'll be waiting in the car. Quietly." She smiled and jumped off the porch then took off skipping down the driveway and got into the car.

"Dani—."

"Go!" she whisper-yelled back, already softly closing the car door.

Alee laughed but then she shut the door behind her and ran upstairs. Her excitement was building with every step. She was anxious to know what was going on, but she figured there was no point in asking. They weren't going to tell her anyway, at least not until she had gotten in the car and agreed to go along with them. Once Victoria got an idea in her head, there was little you could do to change her mind. Back upstairs and in her room she quickly got dressed and pulled her hair into a ponytail. Grabbing her purse she ran out the door and headed downstairs.

"Alee!" her mom stopped her with just one word as she passed the kitchen door. "Come in here please." Her mother's voice was always so calm and quiet, but her intentions came through loud and clear. Alee could tell there was something on her mother's mind, and she was afraid that if she stayed too long she wouldn't be going at all.

She closed her eyes and slowly backed into the kitchen. With an innocent smile, she looked at her mom and dad who were sitting at the table drinking their coffee and reading the morning paper. "Good morning!" she said brightly. "I'm just going out for a little while. But, don't worry, I'll be back soon."

"What are you guys going to do today?" Martha was looking for information, but seeing as Alee didn't have any it wasn't that hard to answer honestly.

"I don't know. We'll probably just hang out, maybe get something to eat." After a few seconds she turned to leave. "I should go. They're waiting. Love you Mom. Love you Dad."

"Have fun, but don't be too late," David said behind his paper.

"Thanks Dad," she called back.

Within seconds the door was closing behind her, "We love you too dear—." But it was too late, she was already gone. Martha sat at the table sipping her coffee, and a single tear rolled down her cheek.

"Don't cry." David reached across to wipe the tear from her face.

"She just doesn't need us anymore."

"She will always need us." He leaned over and kissed Martha on the forehead, then went back to his paper.

They usually took Alee's car out on their girls-only adventures, so it was a little odd for her to now be sitting in the backseat not knowing where they were going, or how long it would take to get there, but she didn't really care. They talked about anything and everything, hardly paying attention to where they were going.

"Didn't we already pass that gas station?" Dani asked, for the second time.

"I don't know. You have the map not me," Victoria said, never wanting to take the blame for anything, but quick as a whip to pass it off.

"From what I can tell…" Dani mused, "…we should have been there, oh, about an hour ago." She turned to Alee and said, with greater certainty, "I think we're lost."

Alee couldn't help but laugh, "We're lost? You think? You woke me up early to get me lost somewhere on the back roads of Atlanta. I've lived here all my life and I've never been lost."

"We're not lost. We're just—turned around." Victoria snapped, snatching the map out of Dani's hands as she pulled the car over to the side of the road. "Just give me a minute."

"Seriously guys, you can get anywhere in Atlanta in under an hour. I know you've only lived here for a couple of years, V, but it's been what, two hours now?" The smile on her face proved she wasn't really mad, not even annoyed, but what she was saying was true. You *could* actually get just about anywhere in Atlanta in about thirty minutes, but that wasn't the point.

"Don't call me V." Victoria's face was expressionless, and Alee couldn't tell if she was serious or not, but Victoria's face quickly softened and the edges of her lips curved up in a smile. Alee started laughing, maybe from the awkward release of tension, who knows, but it was contagious, and Victoria and Dani couldn't help but join in.

"So where are we going anyway? Maybe I can give you directions."

Still laughing but trying to focus on the map too, Victoria chimed in. "I found a store I wanted to go to." Victoria had the biggest smile on her face, and she looked like a little kid just waking up on Christmas morning.

"We're going shopping? I should have known." She shook her head in disbelief, "You woke me up at six thirty on Saturday morning to take me shopping, seriously? There isn't a store in Atlanta I haven't already been to, and none of them are worth getting up that early for. The nearest mall is in Gaylord, and you're really going the wrong way if that's where we're headed."

Dani turned around in her seat, and was visibly excited as she started to explain, "Come on—you're having fun, ri-ight?" She was taunting Alee with her voice. "Besides, it's not just shopping. Victoria found a little hole-in-the-wall magic shop called the Black Onyx." She lowered her voice and extended the vowel sounds as she said it, for the dramatic effect. "They sell everything from crystals, to spell books, to—well—anything and everything we need to start making potions."

Alee, laughed. "Potions? You mean like real witches?" She was a little surprised, and maybe even scared by the thought. "You guys are kidding me, right? The spells never work—why would potions work? Why waste the money?"

Victoria put the map down and turned around in her seat. The three of them looked at each other for a few seconds before Victoria said, "No one said anything about witches; we're just going to look. It's not a big deal, trust me. But come on, you are the one who started all this stuff."

"Me?" Alee was shocked.

"Uh, yeah. You are the one with the amazing crystal collection. Right? Oh, no, wait. I'm sorry, my mistake, that's our other friend Alee." Victoria's sarcasm had a dark, ominous tone, like puss draining from an infected wound. Alee just stared at her, unable to respond, but wishing for a witty response that never came.

"Besides, you're the one with all the power," Dani exclaimed.

Alee couldn't quite wrap her head around what they were saying, "What do you mean power? What are you even talking about?" OK, secretly she had to admit that she had from time to time thought that maybe there might be something there, but how would they have even known? None of the spells she had ever done with Victoria or Dani ever amounted to much of anything. It was only when she was alone and uninhibited that anything ever happened; it was probably because she wasn't worried about other people watching her—judging her.

Victoria tried to make Alee feel less uneasy, "Alee, remember a few weeks ago when we decided to see if we could make a love spell work?" Alee, just stared at her. "Dani wrote a poem—."

"Spell!" Dani interrupted.

"Yeah, right, a spell. Anyway, then you put together some crystals for each of us to put under our pillow that night and then you read the spell...." Victoria and Dani exchanged an awkward glance, "...and, well, we had been trying that spell for about a week, without you. We've actually both tried spells on our own, but nothing ever worked. Not until that night when we did it with you. Don't you get it? You're kind of—special."

"Oh my God. What are you talking about, that spell didn't even work. Why would you—."

"Yes it did. I had written down David Morgan's name on my paper—who by the way I had been trying to get to notice me for weeks, —*un*successfully. Then two days later he asked me out. Don't you remember? We went to the movies, where I quickly discovered he has no idea how to kiss?" Victoria made a gagging sound, and Dani started to laugh.

"I haven't done anything, and I'm not special. Besides, it was only a matter of time before David asked you out. Like you said you've been giving him the 'sexy eye' for weeks. We were just messing around. It's not like this stuff is real. Love spells are just gimmicks to make teenagers like us interested in the idea of witchcraft. It's a way to commercialize it, just like Valentine's Day is just a made up Hallmark holiday. It doesn't mean anything!" Suddenly she got a sick feeling in her stomach. "Oh my God." She opened the car door and ran out. About ten yards away from the car, Alee fell to the ground and threw up. When Victoria got to her side, Alee was in a cold sweat, shaking, and hyperventilating. When she looked up, Victoria noticed that Alee's eyes were not their normal ocean blue. Her pupils had shrunk to the size of a pinhead, and the blue had faded to a pale grey, leaving her with a vacant sightless gaze. "I can't breathe!" Alee managed to gasp. Then she blacked out.

"Dani! Dani come quick!" Victoria yelled from the ground in front of Alee. Dani ran to her side and helped carry Alee back to the car. Victoria pulled out onto the road spinning the car around and speeding down the road in the direction they had come from. She drove as fast as she could, but, not knowing where they were her only hope was to find her way back home. Their cell phones weren't getting a signal and they hadn't seen any stores or even houses for miles.

In the back seat Dani franticly searched through Alee's purse looking for Alee's medication, thinking that might help, not really knowing what she would need or even how much. Ever since Dani had met Alee, Alee had been on numerous medications. It wasn't like taking a vitamin every morning, either. For Alee, keeping up with her pills was a necessity. It wasn't something she would just forget to do, and so Dani didn't understand what could have made Alee pass out. There was nothing in Alee's purse, why would there be? She had probably taken them as she was getting dressed, and since they never normally went far from home there wouldn't have been any reason to carry them with her. Dani began to feel very guilty for not having told Alee where they were going before they left her house.

Dani sat in the back seat with her friend's head resting on her lap as Alee moaned; Dani only hoped it wasn't from pain. She gently stroked her hair and told her that everything was going to be OK. It was more for herself than Alee, but she needed to say it anyway.

Driving aimlessly hadn't seemed like a very good plan, but shortly after they were back on the road they passed the same run down boarded up gas station they had already passed at least three times. I guess it's actually the fourth time that is a charm, she thought, because it wasn't until this time that Victoria noticed the small brick house off to the right side of the road with a wooden sign by the front porch that read Black Onyx in carved out script letters. "There it is." It was less than a whisper but Dani looked up with eager eyes.

It was a quarter to ten as Victoria pulled the car into the driveway and parked in the lot. The color had drained from Alee's cheeks and her skin seemed even paler than normal. Her body was heavy in Dani's arms. Had it not been for her slow, quiet breathing it would have been hard to tell if she was even alive. Beads of perspiration were starting to form around her hairline, but she had stopped moaning, which Victoria took as a good sign. Dani didn't see it the same way.

Dani was crying silently as she held Alee tighter and tighter. She felt completely helpless, "What did we do? Didn't you ask if she had her medicine with her? We never should have brought her here."

"Dani, snap out of it! No I didn't ask her. I didn't think about it, but neither did you," Victoria barked from the front seat. "She's going to be fine." But by the way her voice trembled Dani knew that even Victoria, whose confidence never failed her, was having doubts.

The parking lot was empty, save for a black Mustang with dark tinted windows parked close to the door. When Victoria ran in, she stopped in amazement, forgetting everything, not believing what she was seeing. The small room was dimly lit with blue tinted lights along the shelves that lined the walls from floor to ceiling. Every shelf was stacked with books, baskets, bowls full of every kind of stone or crystal; hundreds of jars full of every herb, oil, lotion, powder; and aquariums filled with creatures dead and alive. The store was stocked with everything that could possibly be used in a potion. Victoria stood there speechless, until a woman with long dark hair wearing a flowing white skirt and a lace-up bodice blouse appeared from behind a beaded curtain carrying a small crystal ball about the size of a tennis ball. She was beautiful and angelic as she walked across the room. She couldn't have been but in her mid-thirties, but something about the way she carried herself made her seem wise beyond her years.

Victoria turned in her direction, noticing the crystal ball that she was rolling back and forth between her hands. It was just a glass crystal ball, like the once you always see fortunetellers using in the movies. But, the center was a foggy grey almost like a cloudy sky just before a storm. It reminded Victoria of the way Alee's eyes had looked just before she passed out. "Can you help me? My friend is sick, and I need to get her to a hospital."

Without hesitation, the woman followed her out to the car and looked down at Alee through the window of the backseat. She gasped and, taking in a deep breath, whispered to herself, "Dear goddesses, it worked." The sides of her lips curled up ever so slightly as she told them to bring her inside. However, neither of the girls moved. Maybe they didn't hear her, maybe they didn't understand, so she quickly opened the car door herself. Dani was confused, and started to argue as the woman climbed inside to get hold of Alee.

"You can't take her out. She needs to go to the hospital." The woman didn't listen. She just pulled Alee out of Dani's arms and into her own. "What are you doing? Who are you?" Dani looked over to Victoria, trying to figure out what was going on. "Where is she taking her?" Victoria and Dani realized that the woman was moving quickly back to the shop, so with no other choice at the moment, they hurried to follow her back inside and then through a beaded curtain at the back of the front room.

In the back room, the woman lay Alee down on a couch and quickly moved about the room gathering different items before coming back and kneeling on the floor beside her.

"We need to call for an ambulance," Dani said quickly as she grabbed a phone off the wall above a desk that was cluttered with papers, books, stones, and everything else you could or couldn't imagine.

"No!" The woman turned to her and snapped. Her voice was commanding, like a schoolteacher catching a student cheating on a test. Both Dani and Victoria froze, confused about what was happening, unsure of what to do or say next. How could this woman not see that Alee had to get to a hospital, *now*? "This child needs more help than they can provide. She will stay here."

Dani almost stumbled over her words as she hurried to get out the explanation, "She's sick. You don't understand. She needs—."

"Blood, yes I know, and she will get what she needs. Now, please stand back and give her some room to breathe." She didn't stop moving the whole time she spoke.

"Are you a doctor, or a nurse?" Dani asked hopefully.

"My name is Jacinda Wenham. This is my sister's home. My family owns the Black Onyx. Therefore, while you are here you will listen to me, and do as I say." She placed a cloth soaked in a mixture of different oils and herbs across Alee's forehead, and with another she wiped down her face, neck, arms and legs. "Now, please sit down. You are nervous, that is to be expected, but it isn't going to help your friend. I need you to either calm down, or step outside." She hadn't answered Dani's question, but at that point it didn't matter. Both Dani and Victoria were engrossed in watching what she was doing.

They didn't move, and a few minutes later when Jacinda turned to look at them her soft blue eyes had hardened and turned almost black. With a calm, but direct voice, she repeated herself, "I said, sit down, or step outside." As if under her control, the two girls sat down simultaneously on a couch directly behind them.

As soon as Jacinda was sure that Alee was fully asleep, and her friends were motionlessly mesmerized on the other side of the room, she started working. Jacinda knew she wouldn't have long, but she already knew what she needed to do so she got straight to work. In a small stone cauldron she mixed more of the thick red liquid along with other powders and herbs. Once the mixture was complete she carefully poured it into what looked like small pill capsules, and sealed them with just a touch of melted wax. She made enough to fill a large pill bottle. If she calculated it right, and she was sure she had, it should be more than enough to last her through Alee's seventeenth birthday that coming summer.

She quietly tucked it into Alee's pocket, wrapped in a piece of paper held on with a rubber band.

Then Jacinda disappeared through the beaded curtain, and her footsteps faded as she went down the hall. In moments she returned, carrying a tall glass filled with a thick red liquid. She propped the still sleeping Alee up, and held her head as she poured a bit of the liquid into her mouth. Alee's body reacted almost instantly, sucking down the drink as if it were liquid life. The liquid moved slowly down the sides of the glass like syrup. Even in her sleep, Alee drank every drop before collapsing back on the couch. Moments later her eyes slowly opened and she looked around the room, keenly aware of her surroundings and more alert than she had ever been, but still too weak to stand. Her body had not yet caught up to her senses.

"What's going on?" She looked to her friends for answers, but they didn't even look in her direction. She looked to Jacinda, who was sitting on the floor next to the couch. She felt like she should be afraid, waking up in this strange room, but she wasn't, and she didn't know why. "Who are you?"

"You're fine. Just try to relax." Again Jacinda didn't answer the question, but Alee didn't seem to notice.

Gesturing toward her friends, who were both sleeping on the couch at the far end of the room, with what little energy she had, "What's wrong with them?"

"They were worried about you, but they're resting now. They'll be awake soon. I promise." Jacinda's voice was sweet like honey, and Alee could feel her body relaxing into it.

"Hmmm." None of it made sense to her, but she didn't feel a burning need to understand. Her body was tired, but her mind was wide-awake—alert. She didn't know when she had ever waked up feeling so—complete—so certain that everything was going to be fine.

Then Alee noticed the necklace that hung loosely around Jacinda's neck. It was a circular pendent about the size of a quarter only thicker. It was polished black hematite and in the center was a star. It was identical to the pendent that Alee was wearing. She pulled her necklace out from under her shirt and reached up to grasp Jacinda's necklace. She couldn't believe what she was seeing. "Where did you get this?"

"I've had it a long time, since I was a young girl." She took Alee's hands in hers and directed a level, commanding gaze at her. "Now you need to relax. Just lie back." She tucked Alee's necklace back into her shirt, and slowly lay the already sleepy-eyed girl back onto the couch. Just before she closed her eyes Alee noticed a small tattoo on the inside of Jacinda's wrist. It was a star in the center of a circle that seemed like it was miles away in the distance. It looked spherical and almost tangible, as if she could reach out and hold it. "A trick of the light?" Maybe, but she was too tired to really think about it. She tried to focus, but she was quickly drifting off to sleep again.

When Alee next woke up she couldn't remember how she had gotten to this place, but once again she felt wonderful, as if she had slept for days. A sense of peace and comfort suffused her. Although she didn't know where she was or why she was there she wasn't in the least bit afraid. It was a strange sense of calm, like nothing she had ever experienced, and although she thought that maybe she should be afraid, she just couldn't bring herself to actually feel it.

The clock above her head on the wall said three o'clock, but it felt so much later. She could hear her friends down the hall laughing and talking as they shuffled things around, moving from table to table and shelf to shelf. There was the clanking of hard objects and swooshing sounds as books came off of shelves. Everything sounded crisp and clear, and yet somehow she knew they weren't as close as they sounded. In another part of the building she could hear shuffling feet and whispers of muffled voices.

She got up slowly, because even though she felt great she was still a little uneasy. Something still didn't seem right. She looked around the room as she crossed to the door where she paused briefly before stepping out. Somehow she knew she should turn left, toward the colorful beaded curtain, and her friends' voices sounded louder as she moved toward it. But there was something more powerful pulling her further down the hall, to the right. Something she couldn't explain was almost calling out, silently, to her.

She turned around, going deeper down the hall. It was a long hallway that seemed to get darker and colder the farther she walked. She ran her hand along the wall as she went. It took time, but her eyes eventually adjusted to the darkness. At the end of the hallway she came to a large wrought iron door handle on what seemed to be a very old hardwood door. It felt smooth, with no seams, one solid piece of wood. In the dimly lit hallway it was hard to see, but under her fingertips she could feel something carved into the front, though she couldn't make out what it was exactly.

"You don't want to go that way. Not yet." The voice was beautiful and calming, but when Alee turned around there was no one there.

Just my imagination, it's all in my imagination, she thought to herself. She looked again at the door, and a wave of cold rushed over her. She turned and hurried back the way she had come, without looking back. Her friends' voices became clearer with every step.

As Alee entered the shop all eyes were on her. Victoria and Dani ran to her side the second they saw her, bombarding her instantly. "You're awake!" "Oh my God, you passed out." "How do you feel now?" "You have to meet Jacinda." "She practically saved your life." They didn't even give her time to think, let alone answer.

"Wait, what?" It was all she could get out.

"Are you feeling better?" Dani said excitedly, and Alee just nodded. "Oh my God Alee, you're not going to believe this place."

"Give her room girls." Jacinda came to Alee's aid. "You look much better, how are you feeling?"

"I'm good, great actually." Alee couldn't take her eyes off of Jacinda's soft blue eyes. "I'm sorry, who are you?"

"This is Jacinda!" Dani said it as if her name should answer everything, and somehow it did.

Alee looked around, taking everything in. "What is that smell?" she asked Jacinda as she searched the herbs on the table in front of her.

"It could be almost anything." Jacinda answered, laughing to herself.

Victoria and Dani were pulling Alee in opposite directions trying to show her the things they had found. Feeding off of their excitement Alee looked around in amazement as she slowly moved from shelf to shelf touching everything she saw. She ran her hands through bowls of crystals, and took time to smell all the different herbs and roots. Something about this place just seemed familiar, but she couldn't place her finger on what it was. Was it the smell? What were the noises? She knew she had never been here—she would surely have remembered this. Maybe a past life or a dream, she didn't know.

After about thirty minutes of watching Alee walk around in that dazed, almost trance-like state, Jacinda finally spoke up, "May I help you find anything, Alee?"

Alee turned and stared into those ocean blue eyes again, "No. No thank you. I'm just looking." Then, as if she was trying to convince herself, "I don't really believe in all this stuff." She knew it wasn't true; she had been interested in crystals for years, although she had never labeled that as witchcraft. Now, being here in a shop that was clearly designed with Wiccans in mind, it began to seem a little too real, and yet even more exciting than ever before.

"That's not really true though, is it?" It was as if she had read Alee's mind, as if she had known Alee hadn't meant what she had said the second it had come out of her mouth.

"I'm not really—I guess not." Without even realizing she had moved, Alee found herself standing only a few short feet from Jacinda. Almost hypnotized by her blue eyes she felt as if there wasn't anything Jacinda could say that she wouldn't agree with, and she was having a hard time looking away.

It started slowly at first, with a gentle touch on her arm, but soon Jacinda was guiding her through the store, gathering item after item from all different areas of the shop. The last thing she gave her was an old black leather-bound book that she pulled from underneath the counter at the back of the shop. She slipped the book into the bag without giving Alee time to so much as touch it, much less flip through the pages. There didn't appear to be a title on the cover, but Alee didn't question. She simply paid the amount she was given, which seemed extremely low for as much stuff as she had gotten. Again she didn't question. As Jacinda slid the bag across the counter and into Alee's hands she whispered in a serious tone, "Keep it safe, and keep it secret. Only share it with those you know you can truly trust."

Alee looked around for the other girls, who were already waiting near the door. Dani was thumbing through the pages of her new book while Victoria sifted through a bin of mixed stones near the entrance.

A small shiny black stone caught her eye. It was the size of a silver dollar and as smooth as ice. She held it in her hand, twisting and turning it, examining how the light seemed to reflect off every curve and angle. Victoria didn't notice as the stone's cold surface began to warm up, matching, then exceeding the temperature of her own hand—which she did notice. Before she had a chance to react, the stone started to vibrate and a sharp sting penetrated the palm of her hand as she saw that the glossy black stone was glowing brilliant white. A strong burning sensation went through her hand and up her arm, as if she had just stuck her hand in the flame of a burning candle. Instinctively she threw the stone to the floor, "Oh my God. What the—?" She grabbed her hand and saw that the flesh of her palm was bright red and already starting to blister around the edges.

Alee and Dani could only stare at her in disbelief before running to her aid. "Victoria, are you OK? What happened?" Alee asked quickly as Victoria pulled her sleeve over her hand and clutched it trying to dull the pain.

Jacinda focused on Victoria's eyes as she slowly crossed the room toward her. She paused briefly to pick up the small stone without ever taking her eyes off of Victoria's.

"Are you all right dear?"

"I'm fine. It just—um, never mind." Catching Jacinda's expression, Victoria felt a prick of fear and panic. "I'm sorry; I didn't mean to throw that."

Jacinda's interest was ignited, and she couldn't help but wonder about this young girl. "What did you say your name was?"

"I didn't." Slowly moving toward the door, Victoria glanced around for her friends. "It's Victoria." Then she turned, fumbling for the door. "Come on you guys. It's getting late. I have to get home."

She walked outside without looking back, hoping her friends were following. They were. Alee and Dani had gathered their things and rushed to follow Victoria out.

"Come again, Alee. Any time," Jacinda called out the door as the girls got into the car. The way she said her name didn't feel right, but she couldn't put her finger on what it could be.

As the door shut behind them, Jacinda looked down at the small black stone now sitting softly in the palm of her hand.

"Black tourmaline? It can't be."

Shaking her head in disbelief she went to the back room, selecting a large black book from one of the bookshelves as she passed. Laying it open on the counter, she flipped through the pages until, in amazement, she read aloud, "Black tourmaline is a stone often used to increase luck and happiness. When rubbed in the palm of the hand it is charged with magnetic electricity to intensify its powers." She quickly scanned the page and continued reading. "Black tourmaline can also be used to ward off and push away all negative energy, and eliminate threats or dangers that may harm or have the power to harm its possessors. It is often used in conjunction with silver to keep lycanthropes and other preternatural powers at bay."

Once in the car, Victoria took a deep breath as if her life depended on it. "What the hell was that?"

"Let me see your hand." Dani said, pulling Victoria's arm toward her. "Oh my God Victoria, does it hurt?" Right in the center of her palm was a bright red burn.

"Yeah it hurts. What do you think?!" She snatched her hand back, and tossed her bag in Dani's lap. "Here, you take this stuff. I don't want it."

"What? Are you serious? Victoria, it was your idea to come in the first place," Dani turned to Alee for help, "Alee, tell her she's being crazy." But Alee didn't say anything. She was just staring out the window. "Fine, whatever, I'll keep the stuff till you change your mind."

"I'm not going to change my mind."

"Victoria, it was probably some hoax or trick to get people's attention." Victoria shot Dani a disbelieving look. "I'll admit it wasn't cool, and I'm sure it didn't go as planned, but I doubt they meant any harm. My God, she practically saved Alee's life for Pete's sake." Victoria didn't answer, and Dani slumped back into her seat in defeat.

After a bit of silence, Dani couldn't suppress her interest any longer. She gave in and tore through her bag, examining all the cool things she had found, and hoping her excitement would get Alee and Victoria excited too. She had bought a book of beginner spells and she quickly started reading through the index as Victoria drove. "Love spells, protection spells, success spells, fertility spells, marriage spells and even revenge spells. Wow, are you guys listening to this?" No one answered. Obviously her attempts were not working. She just shook her head, and continued to read to herself. With the book came a silk satchel of the basic crystals and stones that were needed for a majority of the spells throughout the book.

Alee was a little confused as to the array of items she had purchased. Why Jacinda had recommended these things she didn't know, but she was intrigued by most and a little frightened by some. When she pulled a small silver dagger out of the bag she quickly replaced it, along with everything else, closed up the bag, and sat quietly in the back seat watching the scenery pass by, trying not to think about the dagger, which could have easily been mistaken for a miniature sword.

Victoria and Alee didn't say a single word as Dani rambled on the whole way home.

It only took about forty-five minutes to get home, Alee supposed that not getting lost helped, but even at that it was five o'clock when they pulled into her driveway, and she had apparently fallen asleep at some point because Dani had to tap her on the shoulder to let her know they were home. "Hey Alee, wake up, we're here." Alee's neck was tight and cracked as she moved to stretch.

"We're home?"

"Yeah, it seems Victoria actually does know how to drive without getting lost."

"Shut up!"

"Oh my God, so you *are* still talking to me?" Dani asked with a smile.

"I was never not talking to you, dork! You just never stopped talking, so how was I supposed to get a word in edgewise?" Victoria laughed as she reached to smack at Dani's arm, but Dani jumped out of her car door before she could make contact.

"See you later Victoria." Alee grabbed her bag and climbed out of the back seat.

"You OK?" Dani asked as they walked up to Alee's front porch.

"I'm OK, just tired." Alee and Dani hugged goodbye, and Alee walked up the steps. "Hey Dani," she called back over her shoulder, "you really believe in all that stuff?"

"You know I do, and come on Alee, if you're honest with yourself, you know you believe in it too."

Alee didn't answer. Instead, she sat on the rocking chair on the front porch for a few minutes as she watched Dani skip across her yard and dart into her house through the front door. "Hey Mom, I'm home," Dani's voice sang out through the open windows of their living room.

16

Alee could hear her parents talking in the kitchen when she came in the house, and her dad didn't sound particularly happy. "Martha, we can't just let her run loose whenever she wants. It isn't safe."

"I know that. You don't have to lecture me, but you didn't stop her either. How was I supposed to know she'd be gone all day? Besides, her birthday is just around the corner. She'll be seventeen, practically an adult—then what?"

"Then she will be seventeen, and we will face whatever comes at that—." he heard her shut the front door, "Alee is that you?" The tone of his voice changed instantly, to the calm gentle Dad she always saw.

"It's me. I'll be right there. I just need to go to the bathroom." She hid the items under her jacket and made her way to the stairs and up to her room. She didn't really know how her parents would react to her going to the witchcraft shop on the outskirts of town, let alone the items she had brought home. She wasn't really sure what to make of those items either. But she knew she didn't feel like trying to make up an explanation for them right now.

Before going back downstairs she ran to the bathroom, flushed the toilet, and ran the water in the sink for a few seconds. They lived in a fairly old house, and the upstairs bathroom was directly above the kitchen, so her parents would have been able to hear the toilet flushing, or not flushing for that matter. She didn't want to take the chance that her parents would figure out she was hiding something.

After an awkward dinner, with her father staring at her silently in a way he had never done before, almost suspicious, and her mother scooping food onto her plate every few seconds Alee waited in her room listening for the house to go to sleep. Quiet. Still. It was her favorite time of night. When she was certain that her parents had fallen asleep, she sat up in bed and spread the contents of the bag out in front of her. She took her time touching the stones that she was so eager to add to her own collection, smelling the herbs, and even feeling the weight of the solid silver dagger resting in her hand. It was small, but much heavier than she would have thought, and when she touched the tip of her finger to the pointed edge she was startled at how sharp it felt, as if it could easily slice through her skin if she just pushed a little harder.

When she pulled the rubber band off of the pill bottle and rolled open the paper she was surprised to see that it was personal, a hand-written note:

Sweet Alee,

There are so many things you have yet to learn. Some you will not believe and others that will come naturally. Always follow your heart and trust your instincts and you will never be led astray.

She couldn't get past the familiarity in which the letter was written. "Sweet Alee." It didn't seem like something a stranger would or even should write. She read it at least ten times before she even looked at the pill bottle. The label on the bottle simply read TRUST! And in small letters on the bottom of the label the name of the shop Black Onyx. She didn't know what to think, but would never actually consider taking the pills, especially not knowing what they were. Alee had never been into drugs, she didn't drink and she had never even smoked a cigarette, but her curiosity got the best of her, and she opened the bottle just to take a look. At least that was her intention.

As soon as the lid was off her senses went crazy, and all she could think of was the sweet aroma, like nothing she had ever smelled. She poured the pills into her hands and rolled them around as the scent filled the air around her. It tempted her like the scent of chocolate, only sweeter. She struggled with the desire to taste just one. How much trouble could one little pill cause? OK, bad idea, she thought as she quickly poured them back into the bottle. Alee, like most kids her age had seen the bad made-for-television movies about kids on drugs and she knew better than to think that just one pill couldn't hurt. But, even against her better judgment, she held on to the last pill and popped it quickly into her mouth before shutting the bottle tightly. She should have run straight to the bathroom, shoved her figure down her throat and forced herself to vomit, but she didn't.

The waxy outer coating seemed to melt almost instantly on her tongue, releasing a sweetness that seemed to warm her whole body as she swallowed. It only took a few seconds before she started to notice the changes taking place. She felt more alive than she had her entire life. Her body tingled from head to toe with energy, and she felt as if she would be able to run faster and farther than she ever thought possible. She became increasingly aware of the room around her. Although her bedroom was dimly lit by the lamp next to her bed the light seemed suddenly brighter. She could see every detail, no matter how small, of the items that scattered her room. The colors were more vibrant, and everything seemed almost alive around her. She could hear her father snoring down the hall, and although the windows were closed, she could smell a fire burning in a fireplace someplace up the road. She knew it had to be all in her head but at that moment she didn't really care. It felt like living in the most vivid and exciting dream she had ever had, but she was sure she hadn't fallen asleep. She had so many questions, but no one to ask. With everything lying on the bed before her, she was intrigued and energized by the power she felt radiating around her. She picked up the black leather book from under her pillow where she had hidden it earlier in the evening. There was a pentagram burned into the leather cover, and she slowly began to trace it with her fingertip. Over and over her finger seemed to glide across the cover until a soft heat started to flow through her finger and into her hand. It was as if she could feel the heat from the tool that had originally burned, branded, or scared the leather.

"What does it mean?" She asked out loud to no one at all, but the answer came to her almost like a vision. She could see the sign in the yard outside of the black onyx with the carved pentagram in the middle. She hadn't even really paid it any attention when she saw it before. Now seeing the symbol again on a book Jacinda had given her; it couldn't have been just coincidence.

Under the pentagram were the words, "Book of Shadows" She didn't know what the words meant, but they sent a chill down her spine. Alee wasn't afraid of much. She had escaped death so many times at such a young age that she had learned not to dwell on thoughts of pain or death, and once that is out of the way there really isn't much more to fear, besides spiders and snakes and bees of course. But shadows were different. It wasn't the shadows so much, of course, as it was what could be lurking within the shadows. Throughout her life there had often been times when she had felt that someone or something was watching her from the shadows, or from the distant darkness. She hesitated, unable to open the cover, not really sure she wanted to know what shadowy secrets the book held.

But curiosity won out, and she worked up the courage to open the cover and read the inscription inside:

"For those who came before us and for those who are yet to come. Within your blood you have the power and through your line the answers you shall find."

It was hand written in the most beautiful script she had ever seen. As she flipped through the faded yellowing pages, she was confused by the fact that there wasn't a single word written beyond the inscription and yet many of the page corners had been folded down as if marking important pages. The natural wear and tear throughout the book implied years of use, but for what purpose she couldn't figure out.

She drifted off to sleep wondering what it all meant and she made a promise to herself that she would talk to her mother about the symbol on her necklace first thing in the morning. It had been long enough, and she needed to know what the connection was between her birthday gifts and the Black Onyx.

But when morning came and the sunlight pounded on her bedroom window Alee heard her mother and father in a muffled disagreement somewhere down the hall. "What do you mean she called to find out if Alee was feeling any better?"

"I don't know. She only said she wasn't feeling well yesterday, but Alee didn't mention anything to me about being sick." Martha sounded apologetic and defensive at the same time.

"Call the doctor, and see if you can get her in first thing this morning. I'll call you on my lunch break to see what he says." David didn't even wait for Martha to answer before Alee heard the front door closing behind him.

Her parents didn't normally argue, but over the past year she had noticed there seemed to be more tension between them. After she was showered and dressed, and had gone down to the kitchen for breakfast, the idea of asking her mother about her necklace just didn't seem as important any more.

17

Eric stood in the corner of Alee's room hidden by a thick layer of shadows. It was more than just the simple parlor trick that most vampires could do. Like most vampires, Eric had learned early on in his transformation from human to vampire how to manipulate the shadows. But there were few vampires who, like Eric, had truly mastered the art of forming shadows into true walls of protection around them.

That night, like so many nights over the past ten years, he stood in the shadows watching her as she slept. There had been many times over the years when Eric had wanted desperately to take his daughter in his arms, but he knew that he wasn't able to care for her, not the way she deserved to be cared for. He was on a mission to fill a void, to find his wife's killer. Until he did Eric, knew he would never be able to give Alee the life she needed. The life she deserved.

He was tall and strong in stature with dark brown hair and sapphire blue eyes filled with a sadness that could be felt. Though his appearance had not changed—he was still as young as he had been on the day Alee was born—and he looked no older than that twenty-eight year old youth—the years had taken their toll on him in other ways. He had seen little rest over the years, as he searched constantly, without direction, defending his lifestyle only to protect himself, and hunting for food. Hiding who and what he truly was had been a drain on his body and spirit.

Eric hadn't chosen to become a vampire. It wasn't something you wake up one morning and decide to do. It's not a calling, or a career path. Instead, it is something that often chooses you; at least that is what he had told himself time and time again to make it through the years. When Loraline came into his life, centuries beyond when he should have been alive, he knew instantly that she was the reason he had been turned. It was his destiny to meet her, to love her, to eventually call her his wife. She was his calling, his soul mate. The fact that they were able to produce a child was, in his eyes, proof of that destiny.

At that moment, looking down at his sleeping daughter, hidden by the shadows, Eric could see that Alee was a true gift, a miracle, a vision of beauty in every way. Her wild red hair reminded him of her mother's. His heart longed to hold her, to tell her he loved her, and to protect her in a way that he feared he might never be allowed. Like so many nights before, she mumbled softly to herself as she drifted in and out of sleep. Most times her words blended together and were unrecognizable, but that night what he heard made him rush to her side.

"Spirits here, spirits near, come ye that may."

He sank to his knees, voice trembling in anguish, "What did they do?"

Her voice trailed off but then she slowly opened her eyes and saw him. A moment of fear flooded into her eyes, but he quickly knelt before her, whispering, "Shhhh—. Everything's OK, go back to sleep. You're only dreaming." His voice was like soft velvet as she closed her eyes and drifted off back to sleep, lulled by the sound of his voice. Eric slipped out the second story window, landing silently, steady and balanced, with the grace and ease of a dancer, as he had done so many times before. His weight made the crisp frost-covered grass crackle beneath him, then he disappeared into the darkness faster than he'd ever run.

Moments later, and not even winded, Eric was outside the Black Onyx. He stood on the porch just outside the door trying to calm down and prepare for what he might find inside. He hadn't been there since the night he and Loraline had left to start their lives together, so many years before. The memories came flooding back now: the look of anger and disgust that her family had given him when Loraline had told them that she was choosing him, over her own family; the sad look in Loraline's eyes as they drove away, leaving her family behind.

Eric had loved Loraline more than anything or anyone. She was his world, his soul, his everything. He had opened himself up to her and to her family, but he always felt that they would never fully accept him. His suspicions were confirmed in the accusation he heard in Jacinda's voice as she asked, "What did you do?" the night Loraline had died. He wasn't willing to accept her senseless death, and it hurt him deeply to have her family, especially her sister, believe that he could have had anything to do with it. Eric hadn't intended to return to the Black Onyx, to her family, until he was able to prove to them that he was innocent, and to tell them that she hadn't died in vain—that he had avenged her death.

Now, as he stood outside the door of the Black Onyx, Eric could feel all of the pain and anger rushing back as if it was happening all over again. His hands started to shake as he reached for the doorknob and for a moment he thought he wasn't going to be able to do it.

The Black Onyx had been his second home for a while. He had never gotten rid of his key, and taking it out now he prayed they hadn't changed the locks. They hadn't. The shop was empty and the ringing of the bell hanging at the top of the door echoed in his ears. As he looked around the room it was as if he had been thrown back in time. Not a thing had changed. The shelves were still cluttered with books and artifacts, the crystals and emulates were gathered on tables throughout the center of the room, the old-fashioned cash register sat in the center of the counter. It took his breath away as he slowly moved through the room. This would have been his home to share with Loraline, had her family accepted him and if they had decided to stay in Atlanta. As it was, Loraline was dead and for all Eric had known the shop could have been shut down. But it wasn't, which meant it was being run by either her parents, her sister, or her grandmothers. The farther into the room he moved the more Eric recognized a faint smell—traces of the perfume Loraline used to wear, and he desperately scanned the shelves and tables looking for the source of the hauntingly familiar scent.

He could hear quiet whispers coming from the back room, and he checked the clock on the back wall. It was a little after midnight. No one should have been up for at least another five or six hours. "I know you don't agree, but this wasn't your choice to make, Mother. She's going to be seventeen soon, you've kept me from her long enough. I have every right to be a part of her life." Confusion hit him like a ton of bricks. He would know her voice anywhere, but it couldn't be. It wasn't possible. He stopped himself from calling out her name, knowing full well that there must be a logical explanation. It had to be her mother, or her sister, or a cousin—anyone else. As he turned toward the back hallway she stepped through the curtain.

She was just as beautiful, standing there, as she had been so many years before. Her long flowing auburn hair, radiant, sky blue eyes, flawless porcelain skin, and her voice just as angelic as he remembered. Eric was frozen in time not knowing or understanding what was happening around him. Loraline slowly crossed the room and wrapped her arms around him, tentatively at first, and then as if she couldn't get close enough. It was a desperate, passionate and urgent hug, as if she had been waiting for a very long time for him to finally arrive.

Eric didn't know what he was supposed to be feeling as he slowly pulled away from her and looked into her eyes. He felt denial, shock, anger, and pain. He needed to know that it was really her, and not just an illusion his mind had made to help him deal with coming back to this place after so long. Without his even realizing it his whole body had begun to shake.

Eric tried to speak, but his throat was completely closed. He couldn't wrap his brain around the thought that Loraline was actually alive, let alone standing right in front of him. He had so many things he needed to know, so many questions to ask, most importantly: Why? Why had her family kept her from him for so long? Why had Jacinda let him believe she was dead? And why couldn't he feel her presence anymore?

Their bond had been strong. Strong is too weak a word to describe it. They were connected in a way mere humans could never imagine. The act of blood-sharing between a human and a vampire is a very private and sexual thing, but when you are already meant to be together it becomes intimate on a whole new level, *connecting* the souls—if you believe vampires have souls. So, standing there with her in his arms he couldn't understand why he felt only his desires and need to be with her. He could feel nothing of her needs and desires for him.

They had been soul mates torn apart too early. It hadn't happened right away, after Loraline "died," but over the years he had felt their connection slowly fading. Year after year pieces of him died as he learned to live without her. At one time they didn't even have to speak to know what the other was thinking. They were that in tune to each other, and now, knowing she was still alive, that loss hurt him just as much, if not more, as knowing her death had all been a lie.

The beaded curtain rattled and Eric saw Loraline's father William walk into the room. With superhuman speed and grace Eric moved across the room and with one hand lifted him by the neck and thrust him against the wall. Fangs exposed, barely able to see through his tears, Eric fought hard to control his anger as he demanded answers. "What did you do? Why did you keep her from me?"

"Eric, don't. This is not his fault."

"Loraline, don't defend him! I knew they didn't want us to be together, but this—" He was struggling to breathe as he continued to glare at her father

"Eric, please," she pleaded with him. She had never seen him this angry, and although she understood, she didn't want him to do anything she knew he would regret.

"Turn away Loraline. You do not need to see this!" Then as he leaned in, fangs exposed, he felt the sharp tip of a wooden stake press into the center of his back. He was faster and stronger and could have easily taken the stake out of her hands before she could have done any damage. What little damage the stake could have done. Wood can kill a young vampire, but only if it completely penetrates the heart; otherwise it just burns a little until it is removed and the flesh is allowed to heal. However, for a vampire as old as Eric even a direct blow to the heart isn't always deadly. He would have survived, unless she had dipped the tip of the stake in silver, and she hadn't. He would have felt the burning of the silver even through his clothing. "You know that won't hurt me."

"Eric! It's my fault not his. If you are angry be angry at me, not him." Loraline's voice was direct and desperate, yet it mesmerized him, putting him in a trance. Eric had opened his grip leaving William to fall to the floor, unconscious. As he turned around, he and Loraline were standing face to face with the long wooden stake between them.

"What happened? I thought you were dead. Why did you leave me?" Eric was trying hard to process everything but he still couldn't understand what could have caused her to leave him. He felt like the world around him was moving in slow motion and for a vampire slow motion wasn't a natural feeling.

Loraline could see that her father was already starting to wake up. Shaking, she lowered the stake, took his hand, and tried unsuccessfully to lead him into the back room. "I will explain everything, but first please come sit down and try to relax."

He pulled away from her and lashed out. "Relax? You want me to relax? Do you know what I've done? Do you know what I did because I thought you were dead? Because I thought you had been killed? Do you even care what I went through?" He pulled a glass jar off the shelf and threw it as hard as he could across the room. "I died the day you died. Not only did I lose you but I lost our daughter. I lost my whole life." He collapsed on the floor in the corner with his head in his hands and was sobbed uncontrollably. The commotion had brought Loraline's sister into the room where she quickly went to their father's side.

"I know how you feel," Loraline said, cautiously sitting down next to Eric on the floor.

"You have no idea how I feel." Eric snapped back at her like a snake to its prey.

"You weren't the only one who lost their family that night. But, you weren't around and my family made the only choice they could. I wasn't able to care for Alee. Hell, after I woke up I didn't even know who I was let alone who Alee was." Loraline fidgeted with her hands in her lap. "It wasn't until a few months ago that I really started to remember things. I don't know why or how…" She was absently playing with a ring on her left hand. "…I was given another chance. I remembered our house, the one out in McBain. I took a drive out there, not really knowing where I was going or why. When I got there, it was like a flood of memories came back to me. I could see you standing on the porch as if you were really there, and I knew who you were. I could hear cries—a baby crying—from inside the house. I instantly saw Alee's rosy cheeks and orange-red hair. I remembered everything. Everything except what had happened to us." Tears were streaming down her face.

"What do you mean?"

"I was in a coma for a long time. Granny Edith and Granny Estelle took care of me, but there was nothing even they could do to bring me back. I'm not really sure why I did wake up, but I realize now that they had made the right choice, or at least the only choice they thought they could make. I might not have agreed with it, but I wasn't able to care for her. Alee was safer in a life that didn't include magic, vampires, and all the other evils of our world—at least until she became of age and could accept and learn to control her powers as a witch." Tears were streaming down her face, "They didn't know what else to do, and I—I—. When I did wake up, I had no idea. I don't know what I would have done, had I known, but that doesn't matter now."

"Then what did you do?"

"I went on with my life, not knowing that anything was wrong. Maybe it was wrong of them not to tell me, maybe it wasn't. Alee has been safe all these years because of it. But, it's different now. Now that I remember, I'm going to get her back. I'm going to bring Alee home."

"Stop calling her Alee. Her name is Aleerah. I don't care what those people call her. Her name is Aleerah!"

"I'm sorry." Loraline looked sad and ashamed. "I'm sorry, I didn't know. Aleerah? It's a beautiful name."

"You named her. You said it sounded like a name meant for a goddess and that your daughter wasn't going to have a generic overused baby-book name."

She laughed, "That sounds like me." She took his hands back in her own and caressed his palms with the tips of her thumbs. "Aleerah it is, but Eric, she doesn't know that. She will always be Aleerah to you—and me, and hopefully one day she will even recognize that, but right now she's Alee, in her heart, and if we aren't careful we might ruin any chance we have at a life with her."

Eric held Loraline's gaze, listening intently. All he wanted was to make things right and he knew he couldn't blame her for the pain and suffering he had been through. "Is it already happening?"

"What?"

"The sleep-chanting, is that because she is coming into her powers?"

"What is she saying?" Loraline asked.

"I don't know—" He bit his lower lip as if focusing to remember every word she had said. "—Spirits here, Spirits near, something like that. What does it mean?"

Loraline's eyes widened and she turned to her sister who was still sitting at their father's side. A single nod from her sister told Loraline that the chanting was the result of the spell Jacinda had performed. "I had Jacinda cast a spell." She looked away. "I wanted to awaken her powers, if any. I hoped it would bring her home—to me."

Eric's eyes narrowed. "Did it?"

Loraline looked down, "No—"

"Yes," Jacinda cut her off.

"What!" It wasn't a question, but a demand. Loraline stood up almost abruptly and Eric was on his feet at her side before she even saw him move.

"She showed up." Jacinda stood up and faced them. "You weren't here, and I didn't tell you because she wasn't alone." Eric's jaw stiffened and every muscle in his body tensed up. Jacinda continued, "It wasn't her powers that brought her here. If I had believed in any way that it was I would have told you, but if what Eric says is true—if she is really reciting spells in her sleep, then it won't be long before her powers become active."

Loraline stood there, hands clenched into fists at her sides. She had never been a violent woman, at least not unless it was truly warranted, and never against her own flesh and blood, but this was different. Jacinda had kept something too personal. She had crossed a line. "Why would you lie to me?" She was slowly crossing the room toward her sister as she spoke.

"I didn't—."

"Don't lie!" Loraline reached toward her sister, who already out of reach but now nearly trapped as she backed toward the wall. With a single furious and forceful slap, Loraline drove Jacinda sprawling into the wall.

"Loraline—don't." Eric grabbed her shoulders trying to pull her into his chest, but she wasn't listening. Still, he pleaded, "You don't want to do this."

Jacinda's eyes were also pleading and her voice was trembling, "Loraline please, I can bring her back. I'll bring her back." Maybe it was the sheer terror in Jacinda's voice or Eric's restraining hands, but Loraline lowered her arm, and fell to her knees.

"Oh my goddesses. I'm so sorry." Her eyes met Jacinda's and she didn't know how to explain. "I didn't mean it. I—I just—."

"I know. It's OK." Jacinda came to her side and wrapped her sister in her arms. If it hadn't been for the sudden interruption of the phone ringing in the back room they may have just stayed there on the floor for the rest of the night.

"Oh no, that's probably Mom looking for Dad." They turned to find their father slowly starting to move around and open his eyes.

"Are you going to get that?" He was groggy as he looked around the room. "Eric. Good to see you son." Always true to his nature. No matter how the rest of Loraline's family had treated Eric, William had always treated him with kindness and respect.

They let the phone ring. No one was in the mood to get up, at least not yet.

"So now what?" Eric asked.

Jacinda knew that her answer wasn't going to be what he and Loraline were hoping to hear, but sometimes the right thing to do isn't the easiest. Taking a deep breath, she said, "Now we wait. She has already begun her transformation. It won't be long before it's over and she finds us."

"Transformation?" Loraline repeated it like a question, but didn't wait for an answer. "You mean her powers?"

"No. There is more to Alee than just her powers." She met Eric's eyes, but only briefly. "There is a lot of you in her." She didn't elaborate. How could she tell her sister that Alee's body was beginning to change, that although she didn't even know it herself her body had started craving the only think that kept her father alive. Blood!

Loraline and Eric sat side by side, not touching, not talking, not even moving as Jacinda helped her father to his feet. "I'll take Dad home." She led him through the curtain and back down the hall as Loraline and Eric sat listening to their footsteps get farther and farther away and at last, a calmness filled the air around them.

18

When summer break finally came, Alee and the gang decided to go on a two-week camping trip. They had been talking about doing something exciting for weeks, but couldn't come up with anything they could all agree on until Alee mentioned camping, and although her parents didn't want her to go, they also knew they didn't have a good reason to stop her. She was turning seventeen in just a few weeks and was old enough to make her own decisions. They had to trust that they had raised her to make the right choices, and that she knew her own limits, both physically and medically. Since "the incident," as her friends liked to call it, she carried a copy of her medical background with her everywhere she went. And her friends took great care to remind her to make sure her medications were in her purse wherever they were going.

Only Alee knew the real reason for the rapid change in her health. She was a little worried about the fact that she was down to her last ten pills, but figured with the stress of school behind her, she would be able to limit herself to just taking a couple of pills a week and still have enough to get her through the trip. She would worry about what to do after that, when she got back home.

It was just a simple log cabin with two bedrooms, a living room with a small stone fireplace, a kitchen, and a bathroom the size of a small closet. It wasn't anything special or out of the ordinary, but to them it was a five star hotel. This was the best time of their lives, and they had every intention of making this the best trip of their lives. On their way through town, they stopped at the local store to get snacks, drinks, and all of the necessary essentials to last them the full two weeks. Aside from short hikes or swimming off the pier, they had no intention of leaving the cabin once they got there. There were four beds and six of them, but that didn't matter. Between the couches and the floor, they were sure to find places to sleep. No one seemed worried, least of all Alee, who was secretly hoping this trip might bring her and Kyle closer together.

As the sun began to set, they realized that they would need to use the fireplace for heat. Even though it was summer, the nights would still get pretty cold this deep in the woods, and that meant they were going to need a way to keep the cabin warm. Kyle volunteered to go out and find some wood before it got to dark, and Alee was quick to jump at the chance to go with him.

Walking along the dirt pathway leading to the back of the cabin and into the woods, they exchanged a few glances but neither of them spoke. It felt strange having known each other for almost a year now, and yet they had never really had a full conversation. Kyle was known for making conversation with just about anyone, which didn't say much for how he felt about Alee. But they'd never found themselves alone in the woods at night, or alone anywhere for that matter.

If Kyle had ever been interested in Alee, he never showed it. Alee assumed if he wanted to ask her out, he would have—unless he was concerned about doing damage to their friendship. Or maybe he just didn't think he needed to ask her. When it came to dating, Kyle never really had to do the asking. Girls at school always seemed to take care of that for him. All he had to do was say yes, and he was good at saying yes, *very* good from what Alee had been told.

"He has dated like half the girls in our class Alee," Dani whispered into Alee's ear one afternoon when she caught her staring at him across the lunch table. "Do you really want to be added to that list?"

He was kind of seen as the bad boy, or the muscle of their tight-knit group, probably because of the leather jacket he wore year-round, and a wardrobe that consisted of mainly black, which seemed to attract quite a few girls. "Hey Kyle, you want to sit with us?" girls would ask him every day as he made his way through the cafeteria.

Alee secretly wished she was the type of girl to be more forward, but it just wasn't in her. Although, over the past nine months she had a strong feeling that he just might be interested in her. But maybe it was just the strength of her feelings for him giving her hope that he felt the same way. When he reacted with enthusiasm to the idea of the camping trip, she decided that if they were ever going to have a chance at starting a relationship, or even just a summer fling, then this was the time. She wasn't going to let the opportunity slip by.

Kyle didn't get excited about much. He rarely cared one way or another about what their plans were as long as they were out and about doing something, but at the suggestion of a group camping trip over summer break he made it very clear that he thought it was a great idea. A summer 'must do' was his exact phrase.

The decision to go on the camping trip was completely spur of the moment. The six of them had been hanging out on a Saturday night, as usual. Except on the rare occasion when Alee was in the hospital, or quarantined to her bedroom by her mother because she sneezed, or the occasional date night interruption, they had spent every Saturday night together since the beginning of their junior year. Tonight they were trying to decide what to do to make the summer before their senior year "special."

"What if we take a road trip? We could go to Mackinaw City. We live so close and I've actually never been," Dani suggested.

"I've been there like, a thousand times. Besides, don't you guys want to do something, I don't know—exciting?" Victoria didn't have any suggestions, but she was always ready to shoot down everyone else's.

"What about camping?" Alee suggested, and everyone turned to look at her. "OK, never mind. I guess it was a bad—."

"No, it's great." Kyle chimed in.

They all knew that eventually they would go their separate ways, scattering the globe, in search of higher education. Or, to put it more literally, they would be moving off to college to enjoy the wonders of co-ed dorms, Greek life, college parties, oh yeah, and of course higher education.

The camping trip was Alee's idea, but everyone seemed to embrace it as soon as she mentioned it. When she was a little girl Alee's mother and her mother's friends took Alee on a week-long camping trip every summer. The cabin wasn't far from her house, only about a half hour drive, but she remembered feeling like it was a whole other world. She remembered bonfires, singing, and dancing. She distinctly remembered enjoying herself, and the campground that they always went to made her feel safe and protected. She thought it would be a great summer getaway for the group, and she couldn't think of a better way to kick off the summer.

Being there alone in the woods with Kyle was more than she had hoped for on the first night. A thousand scrambled thoughts rushed through her head as they walked along the path, side by side, close enough to touch but keeping their distance. As the sunlight slowly began to fade away behind the trees and below the horizon she could feel her heartbeat quicken in her chest. It rang in her ears like a drum, getting louder and louder.

Alee searched for something to say as they took turns bending down to collect pieces of firewood to fill the cloth carrier that Kyle carried, but her mind was in complete disarray. Instead, she found herself almost hypnotized by the woods that seemed to close in on them as the light faded. The trees grew taller in this part of the woods, the leaves a shade of green she had never seen before, and they seemed to be painted on the branches overhead. The crickets started their nighttime symphony, and in the distance lightening bugs flickered as they fluttered about.

She remembered sitting by the campfire wrapped in a warm blanket, and watching the other children running around catching the lightening bugs in glass jars. She wanted so badly to catch the mysterious glowing bugs for herself, but her mother wouldn't let her. She had to enjoy them from a distance, isolated from the other children. Watching them now she felt an urge to start running; her mother wasn't there to stop her. But as Kyle's arm softly brushed against hers she forgot all about the lightening bugs, and was content to stay there by his side.

Shadows seemed to move beneath the trees, almost dancing to the sound of the wind. Only shadows—nothing more—or maybe rabbits, squirrels—nothing more. She had almost convinced herself when she thought she saw a pair of glowing eyes just beyond a large bolder, and stopped in her tracks.

Two steps ahead of her Kyle turned to see why she had stopped. "Are you OK?"

Alee stared into the distance, but the eyes were gone as quickly as they had appeared. His voice pulled her out of the trance, and she shook her head, "I'm fine. Just—daydreaming I guess."

"Listen to them, the children of the night. What sweet music they make." He said in an ominous voice.

"What?!"

He couldn't help himself, he started to laugh. "'Dracula!' Have you never seen the movie?"

She smiled, and with a quick glance back into the woods she caught up again and fell back in step at his side. "Nope, was it good?"

"Oh my God, the coolest!"

The cool still night surrounded them, sending a chill down her spine, as the comforting smell from the fireplace of a cabin in the distance filled the air around them. As they walked deeper into the woods the tree line thickened and the path narrowed, pushing them closer together until their hands brushed lightly. It caught her off guard, which seemed to be happening a lot more than normal, causing her heart to skip a beat, "We should hurry back. The others might start to worry." Alee didn't really want to go back, but she was getting cold. They'd already found more than enough wood for the night, and they were walking deeper and deeper into the woods and away from the cabin.

"We can go back if you want to," he said, playfully challenging her, and setting the firewood carrier down at his feet. He turned to face her and his vibrant green eyes met her the tranquil blue of her own.

She stood there looking up into his eyes, unable to move. He was almost a full foot taller than Alee. A sudden gust of wind blew her long hair across her glasses, covering her eyes. Kyle softly brushed her hair away from her face, tucking it behind her ear. He moved her closer and put his arms gently around her waist. With the warmth of his arms around her, her shivering lessened and she sank into his chest. There wasn't anywhere else she would rather be at that moment.

She was closer to him than she had ever been, and she could hear his heart beating faster and faster. She felt his arms tighten around her as she pressed her cheek against his chest. Her body seemed to warm up at his touch and she stopped shivering. The moment seemed to last forever—until Victoria interrupted.

"Hey! You guys coming back anytime soon?" Victoria called. Her voice, carried by the wind, echoed oddly around them.

Kyle pulled away, picked up the wood carrier, and they started back toward the cabin. He didn't say a word, or even look at her as he walked up the path. Alee followed a few steps behind Kyle, as she caught her breath and tried to figure out if she and Kyle had shared a hug or an embrace—or whether she was hoping that there might be more. Lost in her daydream, her steps slowed down even more.

Suddenly, she heard Damian's voice in her head. *"You need to get back inside."*

Until this moment, Damian had only been able to communicate telepathically with her when they were face to face. Alee couldn't understand how he was able to do it, but she understood the urgency in his voice. The darkness surrounding her and the sounds in the woods only increased the urgency. She picked up a few stray pieces of wood that had escaped the carrier and walked quickly toward the cabin. She couldn't even see Kyle on the path ahead of her any more. Halfway back to the cabin, she heard a rustling noise in the bushes. It was closer than the sounds she had heard before. Alee slowed down to try to see what it was but it was too dark to make anything out in the shadows of the trees.

When she came to the boulder she had noticed earlier, she saw the same bright eyes staring back at her, focusing on her every move. Alee stopped and squinted, trying to see what form surrounded those burning eyes. Why did I stay behind? You never stay behind. It's always the one in the back that gets killed first. She had always been a fan of horror films, but standing there in the woods she didn't particularly like the idea of living in one.

In a blink, a wolf sprung from behind the bolder and darted to the middle of the trail. Startled, she fell back, but she managed quickly enough to scramble back onto her feet. The wolf stood firm, glaring straight into her eyes. It had dark brown, almost black, eyes. The moonlight bounced off them reflecting a hollow darkness inside. Its fur was brown and black with a black mask that surrounded its eyes, and stretched down its snout to the black lips that were pulled back to reveal its sharp teeth. The wolf was stunning, and Alee couldn't help feeling a touch of awe mixed with her feelings of fear and helplessness.

The wolf crouched down as if preparing to attack; she heard a low growl and saw what looked like a smirk cross the wolf's face. At the same moment, Damian's voice yelled in her head, pushing through the noises of the woods. *"NOW!!"* His anxious and angry tone pushed her up the path heading straight to the cabin without looking back.

Alee slammed the cabin door shut behind her and dropped the few pieces of wood that she had actually managed to hang onto. She scanned the room and found Damian. She could see the relief in his eyes, and that was enough to confirm for her that it *had* been him trying to warn her, and not just her subconscious, but how he could have known about the wolf—she didn't know.

When she finally caught her breath and looked down she realized that her outfit was covered in mud, and the wood was scattered on the floor around her feet. Everyone stared at her as if she was crazy. "You OK?" Dani asked from her seat on the couch.

"Yup, just thought I heard something out there." She knelt down to gather the wood she had dropped.

Kyle turned briefly to see that she was OK, but then turned his attention back to the fireplace where he had already started to stack the wood he had brought in. He didn't make eye contact, or offer any assistance. What had happened between them in the woods seemed like a distant memory.

Looking around, Alee realized that Victoria was the only one not there. "Where's Victoria?"

"I was in the bathroom," Victoria said, coming through the bathroom door just in time to answer her question. She stood there staring at Alee. "My God Alee, what happened to you? You look like the earth threw up on you."

Alee didn't respond, and Victoria's attention shifted to Kyle's fire-building, hovering over him and telling him how to stack the wood. He just squinted his eyes and cocked his head at her. "Did you change your clothes?" She didn't respond. Then reaching over he pulled a small leaf out of the back of Victoria's hair." Wow, first night here and you already hooked up in the woods? How do you find the time?"

"Ha ha, very funny. I was on the porch earlier and it was windy," she said, snatching the leaf from him. "Idiot," she added, attempting to cover her embarrassment.

Something about the exchange didn't feel right to Alee. Maybe it was nothing, she thought. She was just shaken up from coming face to face with a wolf. She would make sure to stay with someone else at all times while in the woods.

The next day she woke up with a slight headache, but after taking one of her pills it quickly faded away. She decided to take an early morning swim in the lake that was just up the road from the cabin. When she got out of the bathroom, Victoria and Tyler were sitting quietly at the kitchen table eating breakfast. She slipped out the front door and headed up the dirt road. It was peaceful, and the birds chirping in the trees around her seemed to give her energy that she didn't know she had. When she got to the small pier that jetted out into the lake she realized that everyone had had the same idea. Although she'd miss out on a quiet morning alone, at least Kyle would get to see just how cute she looked in her new bikini.

After dipping her toes in the water to see how cold it was, she was pleasantly surprised to find that the water felt great. Everyone else was sitting around in a morning haze, and she decided it was time for them all to wake up a bit. "Who wants to race me?"

"What?" Dani cautioned, "You know you're not supposed to—."

"I'm fine Dani. Besides I feel great. And I'm on vacation so I want to have a little fun."

"I'll race you," Kyle said, jumping up. It was clear that he considered her a weak opponent. And like most guys, he liked having the chance to show off in front of the girls.

Standing on the side of the pier, they determined that they would swim to the far shore, ring the bell on the dock across the lake, and then return back. They convinced Dani to be the referee, and then stood ready to dive off the edge of the pier.

"On your mark," Dani said. "Get set—Go!"

Kyle and Alee hit the water in one, smooth, fluid movement. Dani's excitement got the better of her and she cheered in spite of herself. Damian leaned back on the pier, looking off in the distance, looking not quite at Kyle and Alee, but past them.

Kyle emerged from under the water and began free-style swimming across the lake. He was fast and didn't seem to be tiring at all. Dani stopped cheering when she realized that Alee had not yet surfaced. "Where's Alee? Oh my God, where's Alee?"

Damian heard the terror in Dani's voice. He quickly stood up and scanned the water for any signs of Alee. *"Alee? Alee, can you hear me?"* He called out to her, but there was no answer. The water was calm except for the gentle wake from Kyle's strong, smooth strokes.

"Go get help," Dani snapped at Damian, but he was already half way down the road running toward the cabin.

Dani yelled with all the breath in her lungs, "Kyle!"

He kept swimming toward the far shore. Dani kept screaming until he finally looked up, confused by the sudden change in Dani's demeanor.

He stopped swimming, thinking that she might just be trying to trick him in an attempt to help Alee win the race. However, when he looked around he couldn't see Alee anywhere. Just before he started back, he heard the distant sound of the bell ringing across the lake. He only saw a glimpse of Alee as she dipped back under the water and out of sight. When he turned back he saw that Victoria and Tyler had already returned with Damian and joined Dani on the edge of the pier.

Dani was in hysterics and could barely be understood as she tried desperately to explain what was going on. Suddenly, as Kyle swam toward the pier, he was pulled under, vanishing before their eyes. Dani screamed, as Damian kicked off his shoes preparing to dive in after him. But before he had the chance, Alee broke through the surface of the water with a huge smile on her face.

Alee finished swimming the final stretch and pulled herself up and out of the water. She sat triumphantly on the edge of the pier, only slightly winded. Not only did she finish the race, she won it. Kyle resurfaced seconds later, confused, and struggling to catch his breath. "Couldn't finish?" She mocked as he stared at her in shock. "Had to come back early? Oh, so sad."

As she leaned back to grab her towel off the chair behind her, she noticed that it wasn't just Kyle: everyone was staring at her in disbelief. "What's wrong with you guys?" No one answered. "Why are you all looking at me like that?"

"What the hell was that?" All eyes went from Alee to Dani. "What? You were all thinking it."

"Yeah, we just didn't think you'd be the one to say it," said Kyle, lifting himself out of the water.

Alee still didn't understand, "What? I won the race. I thought you guys would be excited. I am."

"You didn't—. You never—." Dani didn't know how to articulate what was going through her head because it just didn't seem possible.

As the loser of the race, Kyle had a particular interest in finding out what happened. "You never broke water. How did you swim the whole way there without coming up for air? No one can do that!"

Alee shrugged, "Apparently, I can." Sarcasm didn't come natural for her on a normal day, but this didn't seem to be turning out like any other so-called normal day. "You're just mad because you didn't win. You want to go again? I'll give you a head start." Her tone was playful, but no one seemed to appreciate it.

"No, Alee I mean *no one* does that. You were under for like five minutes. No one can hold their breath that long," Kyle reasoned with her. Alee wrapped her towel around her shoulders, and wiped off the excess water dripping from her hair.

"Then maybe I should join the swim team next year."

"Alee—" Dani chided.

"Listen I'm fine, and I have no idea how I did it—I was just focusing on swimming, and not really thinking much about breathing I guess. Can we just drop it, please?"

"As exciting as this adventure of Alee the Teenage Fish is, my eggs are getting cold," Victoria said as she turned back toward the cabin with Tyler following close behind.

As they lounged by the serenity of the lake, Alee briefly wondered how she had been able to hold her breath for so long. She had never been what one would call an exceptional swimmer, but she knew there had to be an explanation.

Over the next week Alee and Kyle found themselves in a number of intimate yet awkward situations. Damian always found a way to interrupt them a moment before she thought something might actually happen between her and Kyle. After it happened time and time again, she started to believe that maybe it wasn't merely coincidental.

She woke up one morning with a burning sensation in her throat. Drinking water had no effect and it got worse as the morning went on. She realized that since she had left her house over a week ago, she had only taken one pill the morning before the swim race. Afraid she was getting sick again, she quickly pulled the plain medicine bottle from her purse, and poured two of the dark red pills into the palm of her hand. She had never felt this way, and she was worried that one pill wouldn't be enough.

"What's that?" asked Dani. She was standing in the door of the bathroom watching as Alee franticly tried to wash the pills down with water from the facet.

"What? Oh, nothing. It's just my medicine." She had never kept secrets from Dani, and slipping the pills back into her pocket didn't feel right. "I'm just feeling a little under the weather."

"Are you getting sick? Do you need anything? Do you want to—?"

"No—don't alert the media just yet," Alee smiled reassuringly. "The last thing I want is everyone fussing over me."

Dani looked at her skeptically.

"I'm fine. Trust me. I think I'm just tired. I'm going to go out to get some fresh air. I promise I'll be back to normal by the time I get back for breakfast."

"Who said you were ever normal?" Dani called as Alee slipped out the back door and started down the path behind the cabin.

Alee needed some space and time to think, but after a few minutes of walking her hands began to shake, and she started feeling dizzy and nauseous. She realized that being alone maybe wasn't the best decision she could have made. When she looked around she recognized where she was at once. Reluctantly and unsteadily, she made her way into the woods just off the path, and sat down leaning against the hard grey bolder she had seen the first night.

Taking long deep breaths didn't seem to control her racing heart, but the burning sensation in her throat had started to dissipate. It suddenly occurred to her that she really had no clue what she had been taking over the last several months. She started to worry that maybe they were illegal narcotics of some kind. The fact that she was becoming more and more dependent on them scared her. She wondered to herself if this is what being a drug addict felt like.

Suddenly, a sweet syrupy scent drifted through the air around her and made her mouth water. She heard what sounded like rushing water through a stream and she realized how thirsty she was. She couldn't remember a stream anywhere behind the cabin, but as her thirst began to burn, she decided to find from the source of the sweet smell and the trickling sound. She turned to get up and realized she wasn't alone.

Damian was standing fifteen, maybe twenty, feet behind her. His crystal grey eyes, almost silver, seemed soft and sad. As he moved slowly up the path she noticed that the scent that had been tempting her was radiating from his body, and the closer he got to her the stronger it was. When he made it to her side, he reached down to help her up. She took his hand, and in an instant realized that what she had heard wasn't rushing water, but she wasn't willing to believe her own ears. She had heard the rhythmic sound of his blood flowing through his veins. She jumped back, pulling her hand away as if she had been burned. She was confused and afraid.

What the hell is going on with me, she thought to herself as she backed away, covering her ears with the palms of her hands. I need to get out of here. But, the pounding in her head was too strong. She fell to her knees overwhelmed and confused by the strange sensations, and near tears.

Damian moved closer, kneeled down in front of her, and looked into her eyes. They were burning red and orange like a fire.

"Your eyes—. Are you OK?"

She knew that Damian wasn't angry, but scared; and not for himself but for her. Concerned that something might really be wrong, he made as if to get help.

She grabbed his arm to stop him. "I'm OK. Please just— just don't go." She knew it was a bad idea to ask him to stay, but she was too scared to be alone. They sat for several long moments. He breathed with her as she tried to calm herself down. They stared into each other's eyes and he watched as her eyes faded back to the blue he was used to seeing. More was said in their silent moments than could be shared through spoken words, and yet this time he still couldn't understand what was happening, and she was too scared to try to explain. Sitting together reminded them both of the endless hours they had spent in her room when she was sick, saying everything by saying nothing.

After nearly an hour of sitting in silence, she turned to look at him again. Hesitantly, she asked, "Why are you afraid for me to be with Kyle? He isn't going to hurt me you know." She couldn't believe she was thinking it, let alone saying it out loud.

The way Damian looked at her, as if she were a wounded puppy he needed to help, only made her feel guilty. She wanted desperately for Damian to approve, to understand, but when she tried to explain, "He's good to me—at least I think he could be," Damian only scoffed. *Is this jealousy?* Damian and Kyle had been friends for the past two years so why would Damian have anything against him now? Had their friendship been merely a charade, and if so, to what end?

"No! I'm not jealous. God Alee, you can be so self-absorbed." He quickly let go of her hand, and turned to walk away. But Alee grabbed his shoulder, and made him look at her, but she couldn't keep him there for long. Every time she touched him the pounding of his heartbeat began to ring in her ears again.

"Hey, I'm sorry OK?" He nodded. "And, I'm OK. Or at least I'm going to be OK, and so are you. But, you have to let me figure this whole Kyle thing out for myself. Even if you think it's a mistake."

Damian forced a smile and nodded his head, but she still saw sadness in his eyes. He leaned in and kissed her softly before he turned and walked away. It almost felt as if he were saying goodbye. She was left standing utterly alone in the woods.

This time it felt different somehow, maybe because it was daytime and the sun was shining brightly above her, or maybe because she felt mysteriously stronger. Whatever she had gone through, whatever the change was, it continued throughout the last few days of the trip. Each day seemed to go a little more smoothly than the one before, although she and Kyle still weren't as comfortable together as Alee had hoped they would be. But the trip wasn't over yet.

Two days before they were scheduled to leave, Alee decided that if Kyle wasn't going to make a move, then she would. She found herself sitting next to him on the couch during the group's nightly movie, and she moved over close to him and leaned her head on his shoulder. He didn't move at first, but in a few minutes she could feel him lift his arm and place it around her shoulder. That small gesture was the moment she had been waiting for. She sighed with relief and sank into his side. They stayed that way long after the movie had ended and everyone else had gone off to bed.

"Whatever you do, don't fall asleep," Kyle whispered in Alee's ear.

"Why do you do that?" Alee asked, turning her head up to see him.

"Do what?" He was smiling.

"Quote movies all the time." She laughed. "The first time I met you, you said, 'I have such sights to show you.' It's from 'Hellraiser,' right?" She raised her eyebrows and smirked.

"Yeah, it is." Kyle raised his eyebrows, amazed. "You remember that?"

"Obviously!"

"It's Halloween, everyone's entitled to one good scare."

"Hello, that's an easy one—'Halloween.'"

"They're heee-re." He stretched out the word just like the character in the movie.

"Hmmm, it's not 'Psycho.' He smiled. "'Poltergeist,' its 'Poltergeist,'" she announced proudly, like she had just won a spelling bee.

"OK, try this one. I'll go check it out!" He was smiling with pride.

"No fair, that's in almost every horror film. It's the last thing the first dead guy always says." They laughed together, and ended up spending the rest of the night talking about old movies, until they finally fell asleep with "The Shining" playing on the television. When the sun started to shine in through the window she woke up still wrapped in his arms. She couldn't remember falling asleep, but she loved waking up and seeing him smiling down at her. "Hi," she smiled as she looked up into his emerald eyes.

He just smiled back at her, "This is no dream! This is really happening!"

"'Rosemary's Baby.' Really?" shot back as Kyle tilted his head down, hugged her closer and kissed her softly on the lips. It was their first kiss, and she wished it would last forever. His lips were warm, soft, and slightly moist. As they kissed she could feel a connection forming between them and she prayed he could feel it too. It was as if they were wrapped in a warm light, their bodies merged as one. She couldn't tell where her body ended and his began. Everything just felt right, as if this was the way it was always meant to be. Time seemed to stand still as the world around them melted away. Their souls were connected and in that moment they could feel each other's hopes, dreams, and fears. It was like nothing she had ever experienced. The longer it lasted the more they could feel and sense from each other, and the harder it was to separate. Somewhere in the distance, beyond the wall they had built around themselves, a faint scream seemed to be echoing around them.

As Kyle pulled away, Alee took a deep breath as if to breathe him in. A familiar taste filled her mouth as she licked her lips, and realized his lip was bleeding. She quickly but softly wiped the blood off of his lip. "Oh my God, I'm so sorry. I didn't mean to," she apologized, avoiding his eyes.

He gently lifted her chin and looked deep into her eyes and kissed her again. The moment their lips touched, and the taste of his blood was on her tongue again, she wanted more. She craved his kiss like nothing she had ever experienced. A quiet moan of pleasure and pain escaped his lips and he told her to continue, and they were locked in a desperate and passionate kiss. She wasn't sure what had happened or why, but from that point forward they were connected, soul to soul and heart to heart. She had no idea what she was going to tell her parents, but for now she was going to enjoy every second she was able to spend with him. For now that was enough.

Suddenly, the screaming came again. She could hear the fear and pain as it got louder and louder. Shock and realization hit her like a truck moving a hundred miles an hour. "Oh my God, Damian." She said and quickly hurried to her feet.

Alee ran straight to his room, but Victoria had gotten there first and pushed her out of the way before shutting the door in her face. All Alee could see through the crack in the door before it shut was Damian curled in a ball on the floor crying, and grabbing at his bag as if he were in pain.

Alee wasn't used to Victoria being so rude, at least not to her, but somehow she had managed to get on her bad side on this trip. It had started that first night, when she and Kyle had gone out to get the firewood together. "Smooth, Alee," Dani had said later that night when she and Alee were alone.

"What do you mean?"

"I thought Victoria was going to rip you to pieces when you jumped up to go get the firewood with Kyle tonight." She was laughing, but Alee didn't see what was so funny.

"Why? Victoria doesn't like Kyle."

"Yeah, but who else is she going to hit on here? She's already dated Tyler, and besides he's with me." Dani gave a wicked little smile. "And, Damian is her brother, so yuck. That only leaves Kyle, and you basically laid claim with that little move."

"I didn't lay claim!" Alee said, all the while hoping that maybe he saw it that way too.

Even as Alee ran that scene through her mind, as she waited outside Damian's room all she wanted was to help her friend, and Victoria wasn't about to let her in. Banging on the door a few times, Alee called out to him, but the only responses she got back were undistinguishable grunts and screams.

After a few attempts at opening the door by force Alee resorted to just pacing back and forth in the hallway, listening to what sounded like a physical struggle between Victoria and Damian.

When the door finally opened, Damian and Victoria walked out with their bags packed and jackets on. Damian wouldn't even look Alee in the eyes. Victoria moved quickly and grabbed the car keys off the table.

"We're ready to go. We'll be in the car waiting while you guys get ready," she snapped, shutting the door behind her.

Everyone stared at each other in confused silence. Slowly they all went their separate ways to start packing and cleaning before leaving the cabin behind.

They rode home in silence, and when they finally made it home, the world seemed somehow different. Alee's parents seemed even more quiet and concerned than usual, and her bedroom seemed smaller and more confining. Alee felt that something had changed, not only in her friendships, but in herself. She felt like a piece of herself had been lost, yet her new connection to Kyle made her feel oddly whole. She had tasted freedom, out there away from everything, and she wanted more of it. She craved it. She needed it.

19

"Goodbye kids. I'll be home in a few hours," their mother called up from downstairs, as unaware as ever of the things going on around her.

"Bye Mom, we'll see you later," Victoria called down the stairs before turning back to her brother.

Damian and Victoria sat in the attic, quietly waiting to hear their mother pull out of the driveway and the garage door close behind her. Victoria had so many questions to ask, but didn't know where to start.

"You have to tell her," Victoria demanded. "There isn't even remotely another option, there's no good reason—or bad reason—why you shouldn't tell Mom."

"No I don't."

"Yes you do. Don't you get it? This is huge. I don't understand why you didn't tell her as soon as we got home."

"What's the big deal?" Damian tried to sound casual but he was desperate to avoid being hounded with questions.

"What's the big deal? Damian, the big deal is that you've been secluded in your own little world for years now, only speaking to your therapist, and then only under hypnosis," Victoria just shook her head at him, "You have no idea how hard this has been on her, do you? How hard it's been on both of us. Damian, you are *talking*."

Damian didn't say anything; he just looked down at the floor. His world was changing all around him. He had no control over it. He was scared. So many things were running through his mind and he didn't know what he should or shouldn't tell his mom even though he wanted to tell her everything. He was just too afraid she might think he was crazy, or worse.

"You don't have to freak out, and you don't have to be scared. Everything is fine. Everything is going to be fine now," Victoria sounded excited and scared all at the same time. He had never seen his sister this way, and honestly, he was a little amused.

"I know, V," Victoria hadn't heard Damian's "secret" twin name for her since they were children. It was almost as good as hearing him speak after so many years. "I get it, trust me. I haven't spoken in years, and yeah, I'm pretty excited to be—I don't know—back, or—normal again. But that isn't all that's going on here, and you know it," He stopped himself before he said too much.

"I—know."

"What? What do you think you know?"

"I—I don't know. I mean I know something is happening, but I don't—I can't explain it," She started to stumble over her words. Something Victoria never did.

"Explain."

"I can't—I don't know how. I just know something was—different. I wanted to talk to you—but then at the cabin when you—."

"Why didn't you? What happened to me at the cabin? What was that? I don't think I've ever been in so much pain before, at least not physically,"

"I really don't know—I swear," Now, for the first time ever, Victoria was having a hard time making eye contact.

As sensitive as Damian was, it took a lot to make him angry. But knowing that his sister had been keeping something from him hurt him deeply. It probably shouldn't have bothered him, considering he had also been keeping something pretty significant—reading his father's old journal—from her.

She sat down next to him trying to come up with the right words. Victoria had always been the kind of girl to just go with the flow, and not question why things happen. She didn't mind change; in fact, she rather liked it. Everything in life was a new adventure to her and she thrived on the excitement, but she knew her brother wasn't as open to change. "I don't really know much. I can't answer all your questions. You probably know more about what's happening than I do. But, whatever it is—I don't think—well, I don't think that it's—bad."

"How do you know? How can you even say that? Did you see how sick I got, or weren't you watching?" He was upset now, and practically dripping sarcasm. He wasn't even trying to hold back his emotions and it felt good to let out some pent-up aggression. Having held everything in for so many years, anger seemed to come so much more easily now. "I felt like my body was being torn apart. What was that?"

True to her nature, Victoria snapped back, "You tell me. You're the one who spends all your time up here in the attic reading these old books and searching through Dad's old stuff. What do you think is happening, haven't you learned anything? Because—if you ask me, this is big, much bigger than just you and me."

Just like when they were kids they sat there and bickered back and forth—for almost an hour. Falling back into old routines felt natural and comforting after so long. Before long they realized they had stopped fighting and started talking. It had happened almost seamlessly in the conversation. Victoria sat quietly listening as Damian relived the memory of the night their father died, and through tears he told her the story as he remembered it. There had been so many things left unsaid over the years; so many things for them to share and learn now.

Victoria seemed more excited than anything, and not in the least bit scared. Her strength seemed to give Damian courage, and even made him a little excited at the prospect of their future. Even as uncertain as it was, it still seemed better than no future at all.

"So, let me get this straight," said Victoria during a lull in their conversation. "You're telling me Dad was a cat?"

"Not a cat. He wasn't a cat. He was a panther. You make it sound like we could have held him in our lap and cuddled with him before bed…" Victoria giggled. "…God, if you're going to make jokes or mock me—."

"No, I'm sorry. Go on." She didn't mean to mock him, as the smile she was holding back would suggest, but she urged him on. "Please, Damian, continue."

Damian stared at her for a long time before continuing, "For years I thought I was crazy, but deep down I knew I wasn't. You've seen my drawings. I knew I didn't just make it up, or dream it." He started rummaging through the stack of books around them, but couldn't find what he was looking for.

"Wait here." In less than a minute he had gone up and down the old creaking attic staircase and come back with the old notebook held tightly in his hands. Flipping through it he found a quote that he had read at least a hundred times.

"Only through the blood can the lineage be passed, but only a pure soul can truly transform, and fulfill the destiny."

"What does that mean, pure soul? What destiny?"

"I don't know, but it goes on to talk about crazy stuff like witches, night walkers, and then more about shape shifters."

"Shape shifters? Is that what—?" Victoria's mind was already flooded with ideas, images, and a million different thoughts. Her train of thought de-railed, she wasn't sure what to say next.

"I think so. I mean—I don't know. There's a list of names—I only recognize a few. But, each of them has an animal listed next to it except you, me, and—."

"And who?" She demanded, as if she couldn't take even a moment of silence.

"Mom." Damian searched through the pages at the front of the notebook, trying to find the list.

"Oh my God, oh my God!" Victoria exclaimed, snatching the book out of his hands, seeing it there in print made it all seem so real to her now. It actually gave reason to rhyme—order to chaos—allowed her to understand things that had happened recently. "I thought I was imagining things. I thought that my mind was actually starting to fail me like yours after Dad—." She stopped herself, and their eyes met. "I'm—that's not what I meant. I'm sorry, I—." Victoria never said sorry, and when she said it to Damian just then, he knew she meant it.

Damian could hear the regret in her voice. "It's fine, honest. I haven't been myself for a long time. I get it." He gave her a small, tender smile, and she knew that she was getting her brother back.

"But there is something I want to tell you. I wanted to tell you right away, but I didn't know if I was dreaming, or maybe sleepwalking. Then when it happened again—."

"When—what, happened again? What are you talking about?"

"When I—changed, maybe," she said.

"When did you—? How many times have you—?" Damian asked, more than a little shocked. It had never happened to him, and although he was open to the idea, he didn't actually believe it was real. He never would he have thought it was happening to his sister, even if he did think the possibilities were there.

"Only twice—I think. The first time was a few months back after I had gotten into a big fight with Mom. She was mad at me for being out so late one night without calling. I tried to explain to her that Alee had gotten sick, but she wouldn't listen."

"I remember that fight."

"Yeah well, I was angry. I climbed out of my bedroom window and just started running. Before I knew it, I was waking up in the woods the next morning. I felt so sick, and I ached all over like I had worked out and pulled just about every muscle in my body. My clothes, what little I had left, were completely shredded and filthy. I couldn't remember anything about the night before except the fight. By the way I looked anyone would have thought I had been attacked, but I don't think that was it. I'm sure I would have remembered that. I mean—I don't know—. I didn't know what had happened, not really. But then, when it happened again, I didn't pass out, I was conscious the whole time. I could feel what was happening, almost as if I was watching it through my eyes, but someone else's body. I guess I kind of figured it out then, but I thought if I said anything you would just think I was crazy. I mean, it's not really possible right?" Victoria was looking straight at him, and Damian knew she wanted him to tell her it didn't happen, but he couldn't do that.

He pulled the book back out of her hands to get her attention. "When was the second time?" She wasn't listening. "Victoria, when was the second time?"

A little embarrassed she turned away, "At the cabin—the first night."

"That was you? Why were you following Alee?" She just looked at him, confused. "Why, Victoria?" He was angry now, realizing that the danger he had sensed when Alee was alone in the woods with Kyle was his sister, and not Kyle like he had thought.

She was shocked and a bit embarrassed, "I didn't mean to—. I was angry. She gets everything she wants; everyone treats her like she's so special, so delicate. I couldn't take it anymore. Besides, it's not like I did it on purpose. I went outside to try to calm down, and the next thing I knew I was following them along the trail, but it wasn't me—. It was—. I was—.

"Wait, how did you know I was following Alee? You were busy with the others in the living room picking out movies."

Damian didn't say anything for a long time. He didn't know how to explain, without sounding crazy, that for years he has felt that he might be—clairvoyant—perceptive—intuitive—telepathic—psychic—psycho?. Yup, they all sounded crazy. He hadn't always been that way, but after his father's death it had started slowly, only happening once in a while. However, over the last couple of years it had happened more and more. The only person he had ever shared it with was Alee. Alee was safe. Alee would keep his secret. But to tell his sister now, what would that mean? How would she react? He was afraid, to say the least.

She nudged him on his shoulder to knock him out of his trance, "Damian, you still with me?"

"What?" looking up, he realized his silence had lasted a lot longer than acceptable. "Yeah, I'm fine, why?"

"How did you know it was me?" Victoria sounded calmer now, willing to listen.

"Oh that. Well, its little things I guess. You remember that time Mom was driving us to school, but we ended up over an hour late because the traffic was so bad?"

She chuckled, not really understanding, but remembering the incident like it was yesterday, "That was what? Like, eight years ago, right?"

"Yeah, I know—just hear me out. We sat there in traffic not moving, and the whole time you and Mom were singing to the radio and playing I spy." Damian took a deep breath before he continued, "I sat there staring out the window at a woman covered in blood. She just stood there not moving, not saying a word. She just watched, staring into the distance at the traffic jam, as cars slowly passed her."

"What are you talking about? There was no bloody woman next to our car. I would have seen her."

"Nobody saw her there, but her picture was in the paper the next day. She had been hit by a car as she was crossing the street at the corner of Governors and Franklin. That accident was what was causing all the traffic." He sat back waiting for her to laugh, but she didn't.

"What else?"

"What do you mean what else?"

"Does it happen a lot?"

Damian didn't know how or even if he should answer that, but he had been the one to start this, so he figured he needed to be all in or not at all. "No, not a lot, or at least it didn't use to. Until about a year and a half ago it hardly ever happened, maybe two or three times a year, but—."

She was intrigued now, "But what changed to make it happen more often?"

He thought for a moment and suddenly, he knew. "We moved to Atlanta. Oh my God, that's it. For some reason it started getting worse when we moved here." He mumbled to himself, trying to sort through everything that had happened since they moved here. "Or maybe I just noticed it more. It started affecting me more, forcing me to react. Maybe if I hadn't interfered—."

She could remember being so mad at him, a thousand times, for ruining things for her, and now she wondered if he had known something she didn't, and had been trying to protect her. "The night of the Homecoming dance last year. I was supposed to go with Jake Shivley."

"He and Tom Andrews were planning to—." He couldn't say it, and he didn't have to.

"Thank you."

He nodded in response. They sat there in the still calm of the quiet attic as everything sank in. "He was a jerk Victoria. He didn't deserve you anyway. You're better than that."

She nodded, and wiped a tear from her eye.

He let his mind drift as his fingers instinctively flipped through the pages of the book. "You know what this means don't you." His expression changed from one of acceptance to one of knowledge, age, and wisdom.

"Yeah. You're psychic. That's so cool." She was smiling now. Not the reaction he had expected when he told her. It was a *thousand* times better, and he was inundated with relief. "Does that mean it will happen to me too?"

"I don't know. But, I didn't mean me. I meant you. You made a full transformation."

"What?" She was baffled at how he had gone from one topic to the other.

Still flipping through the pages of the book, but with more intention this time, he was actually getting excited. "The book only lists one animal next to each person's name, right? So, I assume that means each person can only shift into one animal. That would mean you've picked your animal, or your animal has picked you—I'm not really sure how that works."

"I didn't pick anything. I'm not even sure how it happened. It's not like I did it."

"I know, but, if you can learn to control it—oh my God, the possibilities." Stopping at a faded page in the book, "Listen to this: "Metamorphs, skin-walkers, therianthropes, lycanthropes and shape shifters all refer to those beings with the power to change in form or shape, most commonly humans who transform into animal form. Once they have made their first complete transformation rarely are they able to change their chosen form. However, there are a rare few shape shifters who can transform their appearance into multiple animal forms. Only twice thus far in the history of the Hedley line has this happened—."

"Did you say Hedley?"

"That's what it says, why?"

"Damian, don't you remember anything about Dad's family? His mother, Grandma Margie's maiden name was Hedley. When she married Grandpa Phil, she took his last name, Ward. That means this book came from grandma, or grandma's family anyway. Who wrote it?" She snatched the book back and flipped through the pages.

"I don't know. It was with all of Dad's stuff, but I don't think he wrote it, at least not all of it. The writing is different throughout the book. There's no author's name on the cover—it's like a journal, and not something sold at Barnes and Noble. Most of the time it's written in first person, but other times it reads like a textbook or instruction manual. I haven't gotten through the whole thing yet, just kind of skimmed through it."

"Then we need to find out," she said, calculating a plan in her head. "We need to talk to dear sweet grandma."

Damian laughed. "Talk to grandma? Are you crazy? You know Mom hasn't talked to Dad's family since none of them showed up to the funeral. They've completely avoided all of Mom's calls ever since—."

"That is if she even ever tried to contact them." Victoria said, pointedly.

"Seriously, Victoria? Come on!"

"I suppose we could just ask Mom about it—"

"No! I doubt she knows anything anyway. Even if she did, we can't talk to her about this. At least not until we really understand what's going on."

"Good, then it's settled, we'll go see Grandma Margi this weekend!" Victoria crowed.

Downstairs the garage door started to open, and they quickly pushed everything back into place, rushed down the stairs, and closed the attic door. For now, their secret was locked up safe and sound.

20

Eric sat across the table from Loraline as she ate her dinner in silence. He hadn't slept all day, not wanting to leave her side now that he had finally found her again, but being cooped up in the house was starting to wear him down. He could feel the moon rising higher in the sky and slowly he could feel his energy coming back to him like the tide rising after a strong rain.

Being in such a familiar situation, as if they hadn't missed the last seventeen years, felt stranger than anything he had ever known, which is saying a lot considering he was a vampire. It had been almost two months, and he still didn't know what to say or think. But the worst part was that he still couldn't feel what she was feeling anymore.

The connection they once shared was bound by blood. They had shared one soul and one heart. When he hurt, she hurt. When he felt joy, she felt joy. From the moment Eric saw her, so many years ago, when Loraline was only a child, Eric had known she was his soul mate. He had known her family, having been one of the city's founding members, and although the vampires and witches didn't trust each other a hundred percent of the time, they were willing to work together to make Atlanta a safe, open society. Knowing that she was too young for him to pursue at the time, and understanding the ramifications of a vampire trying to bond with a witch—death at the wiccans' hands—he kept his distance, watching as she grew up. When she finally turned sixteen, Eric approached her. His plan was just to get to know her, but much to his surprise she was instantly taken with him. It wasn't long before they were sneaking around, hiding their relationship from her family, or at least the full extent of their relationship. She didn't kiss and tell, nor would he.

Loraline had explained why she chose not to seek him out after finally waking from her comatose state, but it didn't make it easier, nor did he understand it. Eric was left raw with the knowledge that she had chosen to move on with her family, and she had never looked back. The worst part was not understanding how their bond had been severed. She called it a cleansing, implying a bath or a baptism, but the way she described it sounded more like an exorcism. She said it was a wiccan ritual designed to cleanse the body of any impurities. In her case, it was to cleanse her body and blood of any remnants of him, and their past. "Impurities" was the word she used, as if their love had been a disease of some kind. Her family had completed the ritual only weeks after they had brought her home. She was still in a coma, and unable to fight them. Their hope was that if they could break the bond between Loraline and Eric, he would stop looking for her and the baby. They had never accepted Eric, and even less so after what had happened to Loraline.

They had exchanged blood, sealing a bond that could never be broken. At least Eric thought it couldn't be broken. The more blood that's exchanged, the stronger the bond; however in their case it only took a small amount of blood to seal them together. From that time forward Eric was constantly hyper-aware of Loraline's energy, no matter how far away she was—until she disappeared from his life.

It was only a small amount of blood, shared with her to heal her after a bad fight she had been in. To say the least, Loraline wasn't one to sit on the sidelines. She always wanted to be in the middle of the action. From time to time that meant getting a little dirty defending herself and her family. It was a few weeks after she had turned seventeen and she was beginning to come fully into her powers—beyond the simple fire and wind spells that most witches raised in practicing families are able to do from childhood. She was attacked just outside the local pizza place while waiting for Eric to meet her. She heard the guy's jeering voice. "Hey freak!" It didn't happen often, but every now and then she would get teased by humans just because her family owned the Black Onyx.

"Say that again!" She snapped back. Even though she knew there were rules against using magic in public, she couldn't help herself. The kid was a sophomore, two years behind her in school, thinking he was tougher than he really was. He swung his bag at her, intending to knock her down, but instead she caught it, and yanked him down to the ground in the process. "With rushing winds to push you down let floods of water wash you away!" He stared up at her, shaken by the fact that she had just overtaken him. She turned her back to him, and started to walk but, before she could get away, he grabbed her by the ankle and pulled. She flew to the ground, banging her head on the concrete sidewalk and blood quickly began to spread out, covering the ground. The boy pulled himself up and ran, but before she blacked out Loraline heard the winds pick up and felt the rain as it started to pour down around her.

Eric, ever aware of her state of mind, arrived at her side just after she passed out. It wasn't late, but the sun had already started to set. He gathered her into his arms and could feel that her pulse was dangerously slow, and her breathing was weak. He didn't hesitate before biting at his own wrist, and placing the open wound to her mouth. Without even waking up she quickly began to suck in the warm liquid. Twenty minutes later, just as Eric was turning into Loraline's driveway, she started to wake up. "Hey, are you OK?" His voice was as smooth as silk and as alluring as chocolate.

"I'm fine." Loraline was staring at him with longing eyes. "Kiss me!"

"What?"

"Kiss me," she said again.

"Loraline, we're at your house." She pulled herself across the seat, not even bothering to look outside, so that she was only inches from him. "You're not acting like yourself. I think we just need to get you inside so you can sleep this off."

"No, I don't want to," she whined like a child, and scrunched her face up into a pout.

Eric knew what was happening; she wasn't the first female to have drunk his blood. The reaction, like a euphoric high, was perfectly normal and should only last a short while, subsiding slowly over the next few hours. However, even though her behavior went back to normal within a few hours, her feelings for him never did. From that moment on, they were bonded, and there was no hiding it from her family. Shortly after her high school graduation Eric and Loraline skipped town, leaving behind her family and their prejudices, to start a new life, together.

Now, so many years later, Loraline was "cured" by the cleansing ritual her grandmothers had performed, and Eric couldn't sense a thing from her. It was as if he were sitting next to a stranger. He assumed that the "cleansing" had done its job. He hoped that for her it was worth it because for him, it felt like the end of the world.

Loraline was so close, and yet so far. She was so much the same, and yet so different. But even as angry and as hurt as Eric was, he still loved her and that wasn't something that could just be taken away by a ritual, at least not for him, and he hoped not for her either. Their little family had been torn apart, but he just couldn't stay mad at her for very long. There was something about her that he craved and needed to have in his life more than anything else. He clung to the hope that he could rebuild what they had lost, and he was already planning how to do it.

"You know I still love you," he said. Their eyes met, and her heart melted. But before she had time to say anything, Eric softly touched her lips with his fingertip. "I know that things are different now, and I don't want to rush this. I just want you to know that I'm going to fight for us. I'm going to fight for our family. I can get over the past, now that I have you by my side again. You know that Aleerah belongs with us, and I'm going to do everything in my power to bring her home to us."

Loraline looked down at the table. The years had been kind to her, but there *was* an obvious difference in their apparent ages. Eric still looked so young—not a day older than when she first met him, though maybe a little more worn and tired. She wasn't quite so lucky, though she did look much younger than her years.

Taking her hand in his, Eric spun the ruby encrusted ring around her finger. "You're wearing your engagement ring. Don't think I hadn't noticed." She looked up and her eyes met his, "If you really wanted our relationship to be a thing of the past you would have taken it off long ago, but you didn't." He could clearly see the tan line that years of wearing the ring had made. He was sure she hadn't gone even a day without it on her hand. Maybe she didn't know why she wore it, but that didn't matter. Something inside her compelled her not to take it off, and maybe that was what had brought his memories back to her so many years later.

He wiped away her tears and as they sat, arms around one another, she remembered what they had had, and all that she had been missing. "I don't know what you remember, and what you don't," he began, "but before I lost you there were a series of attacks in the neighborhood, rouge lycanthropes. I remember you were afraid to go out in the woods behind the house at night. Then you told me that a few times when you were out during the early evening you felt like you were being followed. It's funny…." He was staring into her eyes. "…it only took days of living together and you had already reversed your nights and days. You took to the night like it was the most natural thing in the world." He just shook his head at the memory. "I didn't even take to it as easily when I was turned. It took getting burned by the sun my first week before I realized I had to make the change. But, you didn't care."

"I did it for you."

"You always did so much for me. And I should have listened to you more. You were right, ninety-nine percent of the time you were right. Do you remember the attacks?"

"No."

"You had a theory—who you thought was doing it. After you were gone, I—I became restless. I started looking into the attacks, thinking they had something to do with who you thought was following you and who had hurt you, and you were right all along. It took time, but I finally took care of him." A few days before Loraline had been attacked in their house, she had told him that she thought she knew who had been following her. She had thought it was one of the old lycanthrope families that had left Atlanta during a shift in leadership. The night she was attacked she learned the truth, but she never got the chance to tell Eric, and she didn't know how to now. It was far worse than he could have ever believed, and she wasn't ready to hurt him that way. "Your family is safe." Eric assured her, "I made took care of that, years ago."

The color drained from Loraline's face as she realized what he was saying. "What did you do?" Loraline searched her brain for a moment until finally she remembered. The memory was like a waterfall pouring into her brain and flooding her thoughts. "Oh goddesses above, did you kill him?"

"Of course."

"When? How long ago?"

"I don't know. It took time to find him—maybe five years after I lost you."

"Why would you *do* that? I asked you not to interfere," she cried, and, overcome with frustration and fears she dashed out of the room.

When he found her down the hall she was whispering on the phone, and he could only make out a few words: "He said he took care of him—I don't know—yes, maybe. I don't know, because he thought he was helping! What does it mean?" Her voice was becoming frantic, and she peered down the hallway. Her eyes fell on Eric who stood silently, just watching her from the dark hall. "He's dead—I know—. Do you think it will happen again? It could explain why everything is moving so quickly. The timing would make sense. He says it was five years after he lost me."

As Eric stood in the dimly lit hallway surrounded by all the witchcraft artifacts and tools of her family's past, he realized there was still so much that he had not yet learned about her. In all the time they had been together she had never really opened up to him about her family's history. His only knowledge came from what he had learned from her relatives during his early years in Atlanta—before she was born and during her childhood. He knew that many of her ancestors had been burned at the stake during the witch trials, and still more were persecuted in the years that followed. Yet, what he found most interesting was that Loraline and he had bonded so strongly, when she came from such a strong line of witches who for generations had fought against the vampires.

Watching her on the phone he noticed the gentle rise and fall of her chest as her breathing became labored under her increased stress. "Mom, I know how you feel, but please just give him a chance this time." He moved to help her, but she just shook her head and turned away. Loraline had always been strong-willed by nature, not wanting help from others.

"I'll see you in a few minutes," Loraline said as she hung up the phone. She turned quickly, and started down the hall. As she passed Eric she tugged at his sleeve. "Come on. We don't have much time. It may already be too late."

"Too late for what?" When she didn't answer he pulled her toward him, forcing her to look at him. "Loraline, please talk to me."

"We'll explain everything when they get here." He knew the whole family would be there soon. It was hard enough coming back after so many years to find her there, and having to face her sister and her father. Now to have to face her mother, who had been avoiding him like the plague ever since he returned, and the rest of her family, it was a lot to deal with. Eric took a deep breath trying to calm his suddenly shaky nerves.

She moved quickly, pulling him through the beaded curtain and into the shop. She began loading his arms with things she pulled from shelves and drawers all around the room. He followed like a puppy after its master— she always did have a way of making him, and everyone else around her, follow her lead. It was a gift, or a curse, depending on who you were and what she wanted you to do. He still wasn't sure what was happening, but he knew that when she got like this it meant to shut up and listen because something important was about to happen.

Her mother was the first to arrive, and it was obvious that she was uncomfortable, but with William at her side she managed to hold her head up as she made her way toward him. "Eric." She managed to keep her voice from trembling as reached out to hold his hand. "I'm sorry." That's when he looked her in the eyes. "I'm sorry that I let you down. I wasn't a good mother-in-law, but if you'll let me—I'd like a second chance."

"I—thank you." What else could he say?

It didn't take long before the small living room in the back of the shop beyond the colorful beaded curtain and down the hall was filled with Loraline's family, and other members of the Underground, the society that founded Atlanta so many years before. He knew many of them, from a life that ended years ago when everything crumbled around him. He sat, quietly observing everything around him as if he were just a fly on the wall. They remembered his reputation for being "human friendly." He was lucky none of them knew all the things he had done over the past sixteen years. They might be looking at him slightly differently.

Quickly, the men moved through the room, clearing out the furniture and other items cluttering the floor space. Eric didn't know why it was happening or what was coming next, but before long he found himself moving the couch into the hallway and the bookshelves and the coffee table into the back bedroom. Wow, if I ever need to move, these are the people to get to help, he thought. Once the room was completely clear, all of the men left to gather in another part of the shop. Before Eric could leave, though, Loraline grabbed his arm

"You'll need to stay." It wasn't a request and no hint of a smile crossed her face as she spoke to him.

He watched as the women spread throughout the room, making arrangements for the women of the Wenham family who were now gathering in a tight circle in the middle of the empty floor. Loraline pulled Eric aside, and quietly began to explain what was about to happen.

Loraline came from a long line of powerful witches. The Wenham family could trace their lineage back to the first crusade against witches in 1022 AD when the first witch was burned to death. Although they lost many ancestors during the Salem Witch Trials of 1692, the few who managed to survive were able to hold onto the family traditions and pass down the stories and the history of those who had passed. But with such a history also comes enemies. There would always be some who felt that the Wenham powers were unnatural or evil. The Wenham family had learned to be fighters, and they had learned to survive.

Through the years, they had found ways to make peace with the clans who lived in neighboring territories—even forming alliances for mutual protection. Their most powerful ally, if you could call it that, was the Cummings clan of shape shifters—an alliance dating back to the early 1700s. It was in the early 1800s that the Wenham family and the Cummings clan elders, as they were called at that time, had made a formal alliance. However, years later, when Loraline was a young girl, her great grandfather changed the conditions of the alliance. Using the Wenham's influence in Atlanta, he declared that as long as the Cummings wished to live within the city territory then their powers would be bound by a powerful spell. They would be allowed to live in peace—they could even remain members of the Underground, but they couldn't use their shape shifting powers.

The Cummings clan hadn't been seen or heard from in nearly five years. The Wenham family had assumed that they had moved out of the area, or maybe even died off. Eric's first experience with the Cummings had been in 1880. He could remember it clearly, because he had been scouting for a new territory. He and a few of the other original founders of Atlanta had chosen the land because of the dense woodland areas and the extremely low population. However, the Cummings, the Wenhams, and a few other families had already settled there. Eric's family hoped to form an alliance with the current residents, but not all of the families were willing. The Cummings were among those who accepted the new development, but then they continually fought the changes that were made over the years. It was clear to Eric that the Cummings were not the type to follow rules unless it benefited them in some way to do so. He had lost many friends and family members to their hands and he was convinced that it was the Cummings who were behind the rouge lycanthrope attacks throughout Atlanta, Blain, and other northern counties prior to the attack on Loraline and Eric. It only made sense that Eric and Loraline would come to the conclusion that it was a member of the Cummings clan who had attacked them—and whether Loraline's family choose to believe it or not, Eric was convinced it was a Cummings who had attacked them that night.

Five generations of Wenham women sat around the circle. Edith, the Covent's crown, her daughter Estelle, Estelle's daughter Elizabeth, and Elizabeth's daughters Jacinda and Loraline, and finally Jacinda's oldest daughter Petra. Everyone's attention was focused on the matriarch, Edith, Loraline's great-grandmother, who sat with her daughter, Estelle to her right. Edith was a small woman, ninety-five years old, and as thin as a toothpick, but she carried herself with such confidence and strength that no one would dare to get in her way.

"We knew it was a possibility that one day the threat of the Guardians would return. We have survived far worse fights in our family's past, and this too shall pass."

With an up thrust hand Edith cast a spray of sand across the floor in the center of the circle and began the ritual. She turned to her daughter Estelle and asked, "Do you have the book?"

Loraline's grandmother brought Edith a large black leather book similar to the one Jacinda had given Alee, and placed it unopened on the floor beside her.

"Within our blood we have the power..." Edith chanted, "...and through our line the answers we shall find!" She lifted a sharp silver dagger from her lap, made a small cut in the palm of her hand, and squeezed a few drops of blood onto the cover of the book. The book flew open and the pages began to flip back and forth on their own. There wasn't an open window in the whole building let alone in the room, and yet Eric could feel a strong current of air whip through the circle. He felt Edith's power wash over him.

His normally faint heartbeat now speeded up, and his lungs were closing in on themselves, and even though he didn't need air as much as mortals did, he gasped for breath. His body ached as if it couldn't get enough air, and he hungrily filled his lungs.

Loraline took his hand in hers and leaned in close to him and whispered, "Just remember not to let go."

Eric wasn't sure if she was actually talking to him, or if he was hearing her thoughts in his head. Don't let go. Don't let go, he repeated it to himself a half a dozen times— Loraline's grip tightened, and she shook her head in his direction. Although Eric had been around witches from time to time throughout his past, he had never participated, willingly, in one of their rituals. Vampires and witches didn't really intermingle in that way, and he wasn't at all sure what to expect. The closest he had ever come to a Covent's circle was only a few years after he had been changed. He had been captured by a family of witches and held captive for almost a month. They beat him and starved him, waiting for the upcoming solstice where they planned to stake him as a gift to the goddesses. It was only by sheer luck that he was able to escape. A young child, a girl only eight years old, who was mesmerized by his fangs, got a little too close, and he was able to feed. He didn't like remembering that night, but he fed for survival, and didn't care who he killed. He was a different vampire back then than he had become over the centuries. Ever wary of witches, he had allowed himself to align with only a few covens, the Wenham's being one of them.

As if they were thinking as one, the members of the circle held hands at the same time. Edith's voice filled the room as she chanted, "Air, fire, water, earth, elements of astral birth. In this circle, rightly cast, safe from curse or blast. Attend to us, I call you now! We ask you here to show us how!

"From cave and desert, sea and hill, by wand, blade, and pentacle, I call you now, come to me! This is my will, so let it be!"

As if the ceiling above had opened up, the air began to spin, slowly lifting the sand off the floor and forming a funnel cloud. From within, a soft voice no louder than a whisper could be heard, "The time has come for she of the blood to reunite. Together witches far and near shall stand together in this fight. Band together and hold your ground—for thine enemy shall come without a sound." The sand gathered in mid-air, showing them the shape of a dog, or a wolf, running wild through the trees of a dense forest. "Beware the one that exhibits the brand—for at your side he may well stand."

A crack of thunder, and the sand fell to the floor. The room went silent, and Edith's voice filled the room, "Air, fire, water, earth, in our blood is your re-birth. Guide our hearts in this great fight; let our blood be complete this night!" The circle raised their clasped hands, and Edith commanded, "Awaken now the one who sleeps. For she, alone, the secret—keeps."

The room filled with voices as the circle repeated, "Awaken now the one who sleeps. For she alone the secret, keeps. For she, alone, the secret keeps." Over and over, for what felt like hours, the chanting continued.

Eric saw that the beautiful blue, green, and brown eyes of the women in the circle now burned black as coal. Loraline's hand tightened as if she knew what was coming, and the sand exploded in a burst that broke the circle at every connection.

21

Miles away, sound asleep in her bed, Alee took a deep breath and sat straight up. "It's *my* blood."

With her heart pounding in her chest, Alee franticly jumped out of bed and started rummaging through her closet. It had been months since she had thought about the book she had gotten at the Black Onyx, but for some reason it was the only thing on her mind when she was jolted out of sleep. When she finally found the leather-bound book she grabbed it and, rushing out of her room and down the hall, she carefully closed the bathroom door behind her. Alee felt different somehow, more alive. She hesitated as she stood with her hand on the light switch. She wasn't sure what she thought she would see when the light came on but she knew something felt different. She flipped the switch, and blinked as her eyes adjusted to the bright light. Her eyes *burned*, in fact, and she squeezed them tightly closed, dropping the book and grasping the counter with both hands to prevent herself from fainting.

Alee consciously calmed herself and opened her eyes, and there, in the mirror—. Her eyes were as black as coal, and her once auburn hair was as black as the night sky. Her first thought was, NO! No, no, no, no, no. But images from the dream that had just awakened her came streaming back, and she knew exactly what she had to do. Alee sat down on the floor and, placing the "Book of Shadows" on her lap, she opened the cover to reveal the silver dagger that she had hidden inside. She read aloud the inscription she had read so many times before, "For those who came before us and for those who are yet to come. Within your blood you have the power and through your line the answers you shall find—."

"It's my blood," she intoned. Holding the dagger with a shaking hand Alee quickly, so as not to lose the nerve, slit the inside of her palm with the tip of the blade. She bit her lip to keep from crying from the sharp pain that rushing through her. She squeezed her hand to allow the blood to form a pool in her cupped palm. She turned her hand over and firmly placed her bloody palm over the inscription of the book.

Her blood spread out, filling the page until all she saw was red. She lifted her hand and watched as the blood soaked deeper and deeper—throughout the book, but then receded— gathering itself to form words—then paragraphs—paragraphs that read as instructions—and spells. Horrified but fascinated, and somehow feeling that she had seen this before, she leaned back against the wall—not wanting to disturb what was happening. Without looking away from the book, she wound a hand towel around her wounded palm.

When it seemed that the pages had settled and the blood had dried, she began to woozily flip through the pages—she must have lost more blood than she expected. As if seeing the book for the very first time she couldn't believe that her blood was all that had been needed for her to see the secrets that it held—her blood, which until now had only filled her life with pain and sickness.

Alee continued to read, well into the early morning hours, not realizing or caring that the world around her was starting to wake up. When she heard her mother opening her bedroom door down the hall, she quickly locked the bathroom door and turned on the shower. Glancing toward the mirror she noticed that her eyes and hair had returned to their natural crystal blue and auburn red. The black that covered her hair and burned in her eyes the night before was gone. The burning of the cut in her palm confirmed that it hadn't all just been a vivid nightmare.

"What are you doing up so early Alee?" her mother called from the hallway.

"Um..." she stammered as she quickly stuck her head out the door trying to seem tired, as if she had just woken up. "...I'm just not feeling very well. I thought a hot shower might help."

Alee's mom rushed over and put her hand on Alee's forehead before Alee had a chance to close the door. "Are you getting sick?"

It had been months since she had shown any signs of getting sick. Now every cough or sneeze scared her mother into phoning the doctor's office and leaving frantic messages until the advice nurse called her back to calm her down.

"No. I'm just tired—not enough sleep."

Pulling her hand back, her mother exclaimed, "My God Alee you're as cold as ice. I'm going to go call Doctor Mitchell. Take your shower, but make it quick and then get back in bed and rest." With that she turned and headed down the stairs for the first of a series of calls.

Moving quickly, Alee gathered all of her stuff off the bathroom floor and ran to her bedroom. She slid the book and silver dagger back under her mattress, and searched her purse for her pills. She was shocked to find only one pill left in the bottom of the bottle. "Where did—. When did I?" There was no time to question so she popped the pill in her mouth. She looked again at the small print on the bottom of the label— "Black Onyx"—and tossed the bottle back in her purse as she ran back to the bathroom, and jumped in the shower.

She knew she needed to get more pills, but she wasn't really sure how she was going to get back to the Black Onyx any time soon. Now that her mother thought she was sick there was no way she would let her go out for the day. She had to come up with a plan, fast. As she thought, her mind began to get lost in the sound of the water. She could hear thousands of individual drops landing on the warm tile floor. Each drop was distinctly different in tone and pitch, but similar enough that she had never really noticed the separation before. The longer she listened the more it sounded like music filling the room around her.

The sudden and loud pounding at the door pulled her out of her trance-like state and back into reality. "Alee, are you OK? Did you fall asleep in the shower Sweetie? You've been in that shower for over an hour now. Are you OK?" Martha asked, obviously worried.

Over an hour? That can't be right.

"Yeah, Mom, I'm fine. I'm getting out now. Just give me a few minutes," she called.

Back in her bedroom, she waited patiently for her mother to leave the room and give her a moment of peace.

"Are you sure you're OK honey?" she asked.

"I'm fine, Mom. I promise. I was just a little tired, and as you can see my temperature is normal." She pulled the thermometer out from underneath her arm, and quickly handed it to her mom.

"I know. You just felt so cold this morning. I can't understand why—."

"But I'm better now, and I'm just going to take it easy today. So don't worry about me."

Glancing down at her watch, "Well, if you're really sure. Dr. Mitchell's nurse said that as long as you don't have a fever, just make sure you rest and drink lots of water."

Noticing her mother checking the time again Alee said, "I will. Don't worry. And, I don't need a babysitter. If you have something to do, go ahead. I promise I'll let you know if I need anything."

"It's just that Suzi was going to come over this morning. We were going to—."

"Mom, its fine. Do what you need to do."

"I'll be right downstairs. If you need anything just yell." Then, leaning down to kiss Alee's forehead, she whispered, "I love you baby girl."

"I love you too Mommy." Alee didn't call her mother Mommy very often, but it seemed to calm Martha down at times when she was overly worried, and Alee knew it.

Before leaving, Martha said. "Your dad should be home from work around five o'clock tonight. I'd like to have a family dinner, if you're feeling up to it." Without waiting for an answer she turned and headed downstairs.

Alee pulled the book out from under her mattress and sat back, propping herself up against her pillows. It didn't take long before she was once again submerged in her own little world.

22

Damian and Victoria walked up the long dirt path to the house on the hill. He didn't remember there being so many trees, or the house being so far off the main road. "Are you sure this is the one?"

"I'm positive. See there?" Victoria pointed to an old tire swing hanging from the branch of an old oak tree. "That was ours. We used to come here all the time before Dad—." She didn't finish her thought—there was no need.

"I guess I just blocked it all out. I don't remember any of this." Damian shook his head and kept walking.

Victoria gave him a slight shove in the arm. "You're telling me you don't remember when we were four and you were trying to push me on the swing but I came back so fast the heel of my shoe hit you right in the forehead and knocked you down?" He just shook his head as if only half listening.

"You had to be taken to the hospital for stitches. How did you think you got that scare on your forehead?"

Damian rubbed the small raised scare just below his hairline. "I don't know. I never really thought about it. Does it really matter?"

"I guess not. I just thought—." She just stared at the ground in front of her as they walked on.

Damian knew his sister better than anyone, maybe even better than she knew herself, and he could tell he had really upset her, but this time he had no idea why. "What?"

"Nothing—. Never mind. Let's just hurry."

Damian grabbed his sister's arm and turned her toward him. "Seriously, what?"

Victoria glanced back at the house, still too far off for anyone to hear their conversation. "I just don't get it. I don't understand how you just forgot everything. I mean, yeah what happened to Dad sucked, for all of us, and you especially, but, what about me?" Victoria was shaking as she spoke. "Dad died, and you just left me. All those years, you left me on my own." She tried not to let it, but it hurt every time she felt like he was pushing his past—their past—away. Maybe that was why this trip was so important to her; maybe they would get some of their questions answered, and maybe she would start to get her brother back.

"I'm sorry. I didn't know." There was nothing else he could say. Damian had never seen his sister so weak, so scared. She had always been his rock and he hadn't even thought about how she had felt since their father died, or how his own condition had affected her. 'How could I be so selfish?' he thought to himself.

"What?" she asked

"What?" He replied, thinking, *"Did she hear me?"*

"Yes I can hear you." Victoria was backing away, but not scared—more, curious. "How did you do that?"

"Um, I don't know. It just happens."

"It just happens? Happens with whom? It's never happened with me before."

Damian wasn't sure how to answer, or if he should tell his sister, but he didn't really have a choice. "With, Alee." Victoria's jaw tightened and he could see her fists clench at her sides. "It's not a big deal, really. I'm sure it's just part of all the other crazy stuff going on right now."

Victoria just stood there focusing, staring at him. *Seriously, why Alee? What is it about that girl?* She focused hard on the thought. No reaction. "Humph—." Victoria just turned away and started walking faster toward the house. "We should hurry." She kept glancing back over her shoulder as Damian walked ten paces behind her.

When they finally made it up to the house they were greeted by a beautiful golden retriever. It didn't bark or growl, but simply sat at their feet bowing his head waiting for them to pet him. "I don't remember them having a dog."

Damian laughed. "I'm sure if they had a dog when we were four, it'd be dead by now."

"You're probably right."

As they played with the dog, the front door opened and a heavy-set older woman was stared at them, astounded.

As if she were five years old again, Victoria's eyes lit up and a warm pink glow lit up her cheeks, "Grandma Margie?"

"Victoria? Damian?" The woman hurried down the stairs and grabbed them, pulling them close and holding them so tightly they could barely breathe. "Oh my God! Look at you! I can't believe you're here. What are you doing here? Where is your mother?" She let them go and eagerly searched the tree line behind them.

Victoria took a deep breath and said, "She isn't here."

"What? You came by yourself? Why didn't she come?" Then, conspiratorially, she asked, "Does your mother know you're here?" The lack of a response was answer enough. "Come inside now," she said, keeping an arm around Victoria's shoulders and taking Damian's hand. Then, a little less certain, "We should give her a call. So she knows you're safe. What is her number?"

"No, we can't!" Victoria held her ground knowing that this was the last thing their mother needed to know.

"My God," Grandma Margie stopped suddenly. "How did you even get here? Where are you living now?"

"We're still in Atlanta," Victoria said, thankful that she had changed the subject.

"Atlanta?! When—why did you move so far away?" Grandma Margie was flabbergasted.

"A couple of years ago Mom just couldn't take being in our old house anymore, without Dad," Victoria looked over at Damian—she wasn't mentioning the problems he had had, and Damian nodded in appreciation.

"Well, I certainly can understand that," She averted her eyes, and pulled them in for another hug. "We should get inside. We can call your mom, later. All right?"

"We only came because we needed to talk to you, and she wouldn't understand."

Grandma Margie cocked her head and peered into Victoria's eyes, deeper and more intensely than Victoria was used to. Grandma Margie already knew what she would find, but had to be sure. "My dear, your mother knows more than you might think," She looked into Damian's eyes, but seemed a little disappointed or distracted when she broke contact. "Umm, you——.You must both be hungry. Come inside— please."

Grandma Margie sat them at the kitchen table and they soon had plates of sandwiches and potato chips in front of them—and glasses of ice water. As Grandma Margie sat down across from them, she gasped, looking at the ring on Damian's hand. "Who gave you—?" She sounded almost angry but then she took a deep breath and started over. "Where did you get your ring?"

Damian wasn't sure how much he should tell her so quickly, but figured the ring had belonged to his father, and it was probably just as good as any place else to start figuring out about their family's past. Besides, she must have seen it a thousand times in the past so she might actually know why their mom would have locked it up for so long, instead of burying it with him. "It was my dad's."

"Yes, I know. Did Karen give it to you?" She sounded more suspicious then curious.

"No, Mom didn't give it to me. I recently found it in a bunch of Dad's old stuff. I wear it because it reminds me of him. It makes me feel closer to him somehow."

"Yes, I suppose it would," Turning to Victoria she glanced down at her hands before asking, "And, do you have something to remember him by?"

"Just my memories, but that's enough for me," Victoria wasn't sure what to think of this conversation as it didn't seem to be getting them anywhere. Victoria never did have a long attention span, and she was quickly becoming annoyed by Grandma Margie's unimportant small talk. Victoria had always felt like she and her mother were a lot alike. That was the excuse she always gave for the two of them fighting all the time. Sitting there, listening to her grandmother try to make small talk after so many years, she started to wonder if her mother had felt the same way about their grandma so many years ago—annoyed.

Grandma Margie turned back toward Damian. She could tell she was going to have better luck getting through to him. "Has your mother told you the story behind that ring, and the one she wears? I assume she still wears it."

"I didn't realize there was a story," he said. It wasn't really what they were there to ask about, but Damian figured it was just another opportunity to learn something about his father that he didn't already know.

"The rings match, do they not?"

"Yeah, but that's not shocking. Most wedding bands match, right?" Victoria replied, not understanding why their grandmother was so interested in their father's ring.

"Don't be mistaken," she snapped, "They are not simply wedding bands. They're heirlooms forged by your grandfather's own hands, your mother's father," she almost hissed, carefully clarifying that it had not been her husband who had made the rings. "Karen has worn hers since she was a child. Your father's was a gift he had to accept if he wanted to marry your mother. How much do you know about your grandfather?"

"After Dad died we lost contact with everyone. As far as I know, Mom hasn't spoken to anyone in years. Mom told us stories about when she was little, and of course about Dad, but not much else,"

"Well, we all deserve to know about our pasts. I'm not one to speak negatively about anyone, but I will say this, your grandfather was a very controlling man, and even after his death your mother and grandmother refused to remove the rings he had insisted they wear," Sadness spread across their grandmother's face. "For most people, feeling bound or controlled isn't easy. For your father, who wasn't raised the same way as your mother, I'm sure it was even harder. But your mother had lived for so long under her father's control that she didn't know how to survive any other way,"

Confusion swept across Damian and Victoria's faces as they heard the words bound and controlled. Neither one of them understood what she meant, but they knew it didn't sound good.

"James, however..." She paused and Damian and Victoria drew in a deep breath. No one had spoken their father's name in so long it was heart-wrenching to hear her say it so casually. "…James didn't grow up in that environment, but he agreed to conform to her family's ways when they got married. He loved your mother very much. He was a free spirit and he knew that once your grandfather was dead he would finally be able live again. He tried to convince your mother that it was safe to take their rings off, but she wouldn't listen."

"What do our parents' wedding rings have to do with their safety? That doesn't make any sense," said Victoria.

"Because, my dear, this is not just a ring. It's a curse,"

Victoria lowered her voice, and quoted, "They are one; the ring and the Dark Lord. Frodo, he must never find it."

Their grandmother didn't seem amused. She looked to Damian for help. "What is she talking about?"

"It's from a movie," Damian explained, holding back a laugh. "It came out a while ago. I think I dragged her to see it like ten times, in the theatre, but until now I thought I was the only one obsessed with it."

"Yes of course it is. Your father was the same way with movies," She shook her head absently. "But, this is not a movie. It's a curse, and you would do best to remember that," Damian's face went pale and Victoria let out a small laugh but quickly stifled it, as the word curse registered in her mind.

Damian casually fidgeted with the ring. When it wouldn't come off, he started pulling at it vigorously. It wasn't proving to be an easy task. It almost felt as if it was getting tighter every time he turned it, but after several attempts it finally came off, scraping a thin layer of skin away from his finger as it slipped over the knuckle. His knuckle was starting to swell and bleed a little—a few drops of blood dripped onto the table in front of him. Margie jumped up and ran a washcloth under the faucet. Damian's eyes shifted between his grandmother and the ring on the table in front of him.

"You know nothing of your ancestors do you? Of your past or what your future may hold? She's left you completely in the dark, hasn't she?"

"We knew enough to bring us here! But, no—Mom hasn't told us anything," He pulled the old notebook out of his backpack and placed it on the table in front of her. "Will you explain what this is? If you tell us what it means then maybe we'll understand."

Damian and Victoria watched Grandma Margie's expression change. As she slowly slid the notebook across the table, her expression registered surprise, then fear, excitement, then sadness. She picked up the book and held it gently in front of her.

"Oh God—I never thought I would see this again," When she looked up, her expression had softened as her eyes met Damian's gaze. "Have you read it?" Damian just nodded, "Then, you already know. Why do you need me?"

Victoria stood; her anticipation could not be contained any longer. "So, it's true. It's really true?! How do we control it? Can we control it? Why does it happen? Why me and not Damian? Does our mother know? Is she—?"

"Calm down child," Grandma Margie said, taking Victoria by the hand and sitting her back down. "I know you have a lot of questions, and that is understandable, but give me time. I promise your questions will all be answered," She stood up, crossed to the front door and whistled into the yard. As she held the door open, the golden lab ran in and down the back hall. She walked over to the refrigerator. She poured four glasses of tea and brought them back to the table. As she sat back down an older man, even taller than Damian, appeared from the back hall, and came to stand beside her.

"This is your grandpa Phil. Do you member him?" Phillip leaned down and kissed Margie on the forehead as she watched Damian and Victoria carefully for a reaction. Victoria's eyes lit up like a child on Christmas morning. "Darling, this is Damian and Victoria," Her smile never left her face as she spoke their names.

"Yes Dear, I know who they are," He sat at the table next to his wife as she slid the book and the ring in front of him to see.

"They have questions," Margie said. Over the many years they had been married, less and less communication was needed for them to understand each other.

"Of course they do," Their Grandpa Phil's voice was deep, comforting and warm. Damian and Victoria felt instantly at ease, like everything in the world would be all right if only he would continue talking. His soft, grey-silver eyes were identical to Damian's, and the more he looked at him the more Damian saw himself.

Damian turned back toward his grandmother. "You said the ring was a curse. Why?" He had been wearing it for months, and couldn't imagine that it had been anything more than a ring until that point.

"Well, well, you *have* been talking, haven't you?" Phillip asked Margie, surprised.

Carefully picking it up and making sure not to put it on her finger Margie held the ring flat in the palm of her hand. "Did it fit you perfectly, like it was made just for you?"

"Yes."

"Did it slide on easily, but prove to be difficult to remove?" she asked, as if reading from a script.

"Yes. I couldn't remove it until just now and well—." Damian held his hand up showing his grandfather the bloodstained washcloth.

"If you've read the stories in this book then you know what you are. It should be no surprise to you that you come from a long line of lycanthropes and shape shifters. Although there hasn't been a true shape shifter in our family for centuries," Hearing Margie say it out loud made it seem so much more real than just reading it and talking with Victoria.

"What is the difference between a lycanthrope and a shape shifter? The book makes them sound like one in the same."

Their grandfather took over. "A lycanthrope takes on the form of one single animal. A shape shifter have the able to take the form of many animals, and sometimes, if they are powerful enough, they can even take on the form of other humans."

Damian and Victoria didn't know what to say.

"What does all of that have to do with the ring?"

"This ring, as well as your mother's and those of her family, are made of pure silver. Pure silver can hurt lycanthropes, even kill them if used the right way. However, when infused with the powerful spell that your great-grandfather placed on the family rings, they are capable of much, much more."

As he spoke, it became clear that Phillip was a born storyteller. The words flowed like water in a stream as he spoke. "Many years ago, your great-grandfather, Virgil Cummings, your mother's grandfather, made a truce with a coven that lived in the adjacent town. Both families agreed to live in peace, but in order to ensure that your mother's family obeyed, the coven bound our family with a powerful spell, and these rings.

"What do you mean, coven?" Damian asked.

"A coven is a family of witches. This one, the Wenham clan, was very old and very powerful."

"Wenham? As in the last name Wenham?" Victoria asked more as an aside, but loud enough that her grandfather heard her.

"That's right,"

"We have a girl at school—what's her name?" Victoria thought for a minute, and then it came to her. "Petra! Petra Wenham, she's so weird. Always dresses in black, and hangs out with some pretty odd kids. I think she has an older sister who graduated last year," Then suddenly her trip to the Black Onyx flashed through her head.

"My name is Jacinda Wenham. My family owns the Black Onyx," Her angelic voice echoed in Victoria's mind as clearly as the day she had met her. How did I not realize it before? She wondered. Her grandmother continued, interrupting her thoughts.

"The Wenham coven could trace its lineage much further back than the Cummings, and with age comes knowledge, and power. That was the reason why it was so easy for your great-grandfather to be manipulated or maybe just scared into complying,"

"What did the spell do?" Victoria asked eagerly.

Sadness once again filled their grandmother's eyes. "It bound their powers. It forced them to live the lives of mere humans."

"Why would they agree to that?" Victoria was appalled. She had only just learned what she was, and still had so much to learn, yet even she couldn't understand why her family would have given it up.

"I honestly don't know. Maybe they just wanted something normal, not to have to hide who they were," Grandma Margie said. "But that decision, made for whatever reason, affected so many people. When your father made the choice to marry your mother—." she couldn't control her tears now.

Taking his wife's hand in his, Phil said, "Your grandfather told him he had a choice to make. Either he could give up his powers and marry your mother, or he could keep his powers and walk away from her forever," Phillip exchanged looks with his wife. "We respected his choice, but hoped that one day he might convince her to change their fate. All they had to do was take the rings off—to make the conscious choice to break their connection with the clan—and they would be allowed to live the life they were born to, the life of a shifter. But, that wasn't something your mother was able or willing to do."

"When your father was killed," Grandma Margie said, sending chills down Damian's spine, "out of respect for your mother and her family's way of life, and for your safety, we choose not to pursue what we believed in our hearts—."

"Wait!" Damian interrupted, "Wait a minute! Are you saying you knew who killed him? That you knew, and you just chose not to seek vengeance against some witch who murdered our father—your son? Out of respect? What about respect for our dad?" he yelled. "How the hell did that help us anyway? We live a lie, not knowing our past. And our mother lives in denial, not willing to teach us."

"I did not say it was a witch who killed—."

"You didn't say it, but you implied it," Damian snapped.

"I implied no such thing," Margie took a deep breath, not sure what to say, but understanding that saying nothing would be worse now than a half truth. "Believe me, it wasn't an easy choice, and there isn't a day that goes by that we don't worry that we made the wrong choice."

"You did!" Damian spat.

"We did what we had to. I have to believe that what we did was for the best and that because of our actions you were both given the opportunity to grow up, an opportunity you might not have had if we had acted differently. Chances are, any retribution we pursued would have only led to more bloodshed, and I wouldn't have been able to live with myself if it had been either one of you that got hurt."

Damian didn't know what to say, or how to feel. "I'm—."

His grandpa shook his head, "I'm sorry. You have every right to be angry with us. I'm just thankful we now have this opportunity to make things right. You have the right to know the truth, and I am sure you have more questions. Please, continue."

"So, these witches—are they evil?" Damian asked, picturing Alee, Dani and Victoria sitting around reading spell books and trying to make potions. Not that he ever believed any of it really worked, but now the idea that magic was real and witches were real shed a whole new light on a lot of things. He couldn't even look at his sister.

"No, dear. Witches aren't necessarily evil. Many can be very powerful and that can make them a possible threat—or it can make them very good allies, depending on the situation. But, it was not a witch who killed your father."

"But you said that Mom's family had made a truce with witches right?"

"Yes that is correct."

Damian was trying to think logically. "OK, so—when you make truces with your enemies you decide to stop fighting. So—so maybe Dad didn't abide by the truce? Maybe he did something that they didn't like? Is that possible?"

"No. I understand why you would think that, but it's—complicated," Phillip sat back. "Let me see if I can make it simpler. "Witches are not our enemies. In fact, for the most part, witches, lycanthropes, and shape shifters live in complete harmony. I believe that the Wenhams meant well by their actions—I do. Besides, there are far worse creatures out there than witches. Those we truly do claim as enemies,"

Damian was almost afraid to ask, but needed to know. "The Cummings and the Hedleys are shape shifters; the Wenhams are witches. What other 'creature' could be out there to fear?"

Phillip had no intention of prolonging his grandchildren's discomfort. They had come this far and they deserved to hear the truth. "Night-walkers," he whispered.

"You mean—"

"Yes. They're called the walking dead, nightwalkers, blood demons; there are literally hundreds of names, but the most common is "vampire." They are not only dangerous, but they are the reason our race exists. In every culture—the Romans, the British, the Celts, and Native Americans—you will find some form of folklore about men who could control their form, turning themselves into animals, or animals that can transform into humans. However, what the stories don't tell you is *why* there are shifters—*why* lycanthropes exist. Such powers were not birthrights in the beginning. Men begged, pleaded, and prayed to their gods for the strength they needed to protect their people from those that walk in the night. God granted the power to only those he felt worthy, to a select few in each society. Now that right is carried down through our blood," Damian and Victoria sat open-mouthed, listening as if every word was a clue to a mystery they hadn't known existed.

"Throughout history, Lycanthropes and shape shifters have been the guardians of the human race. That responsibility carries with it great risk and great danger. We protect society from vampires, and the fact that people don't know that vampires exist only makes our job that much more important. But you have to understand that shape shifters would not be accepted in today's world. We would be seen as different, freaks—even crazy. We must keep our abilities hidden, for our own safety."

Victoria and Damian listened intently—motionless. Then there was silence, as they fit the pieces together in their heads. Victoria broke the silence with a whisper. "Did a vampire kill our father?"

"Yes..." Damian said, his voice trembling. The memory of that night came flooding back as it had so many times, but this time with so much more detail and clarity. "...I remember him. I *saw* its eyes burn red, and the blood drip down its chin," Damian was starting to feel the way he had felt that night, but he didn't know how to try to explain that. "Its skin was almost translucent—almost white against its black clothes," His vision started to blur, and his stomach churned. He leaned over and threw up on the kitchen floor.

"Damian?!" Victoria yelled reaching out for him.

Margie was at his side instantly. "He'll be OK. Just breathe, Damian. It's OK."

Victoria held her brother's hand tightly in her own. 'Please be OK, please be OK.'

'*V, I'm fine.*' Their eyes met, and a small smile lit up her face.

'You heard me?'

He nodded in response. He realized that, when he allowed it, the telepathy came much more easily than when he tried to force it.

"You're already linked?" Both Damian and Victoria snapped their attention back to their grandfather's compelling voice. "That's a good sign."

"What do you mean we're linked?" Damian asked, eyeing him up and down.

"It happens among our kind. Being linked is how we communicate in our animal state, and it often comes in handy in our human form as well," He looked at his wife and smiled. She nodded back.

"Did you say something? Why couldn't I hear it?"

"Some things are private, Damian," Margie said with a smile. "As you get older you'll learn to control it, too," She slid his tea across the table for him. "You should drink some more. Are you feeling any better?"

"Yes, thank you," He took a sip of the tea contemplating his next question. "Is it only shape shifters who can communicate like this?"

"No. There are other societies that communicate telepathically as well."

"Can we, I mean shape shifters, communicate with people who aren't shape shifters?" Damian stumbled over his words, but it didn't matter—his grandmother understood what he wanted to know.

"When you learn to control it you will be able to communicate with anyone with an open mind and spirit. It is easiest with other shape shifters, or with others who have already developed their physic abilities. Although rare, it can happen when you just have a very strong connection to another person. Like a soul-mate if you will."

"A soul-mate?"

Margie nodded leaning into her husband's arms and the four of them sat in silence.

Victoria let go of Damian's hand and turned back to her grandfather. "You're telling us we fight vampires?"

Margie answered before her husband had the chance. "Not all of us. But, yes, some do. Vampires are our only enemy, and it has been so for centuries. There have been communities, Atlanta being one of them, where Vampires and Shifters have tried to work together, but it never lasts long. And when it does end, it usually ends in bloodshed. Typically, if there is no danger near, then there is no need for the change to occur. However, when a vampire is close by, one who seeks to threaten, then the change becomes more urgent, forcing a shifter to fully evolve into their animal nature," She held up the ring for them to see. "That is what the ring is designed to prevent. However, once you've made your first full transformation, you'll always have the power to shift."

"So, you're saying that in order for a shape shifter to make their first transformation there has to be a danger present?"

"Yes. Or there has to be a *perceived* danger."

"And if vampires are our only enemies, then by 'danger' you mean vampire, right?" Damian wanted to make sure he was one hundred percent clear on what they were telling them.

"You catch on quickly," his grandfather smiled. "Yes, by 'danger', I mean vampire."

They sat in silence for quite some time, adjusting to this new information.

"I have a question," said Victoria, trying hard to control her emotions. Everything they had learned so far was so unreal; she needed to fully understand everything. "Damian was wearing the ring. I wasn't. Is that why he hasn't... transformed?"

"Most likely yes, but," she looked into Damian's eyes, "There is a chance that you might never change."

"What? Why not?"

"You see, Karen started wearing her ring as a very young girl, and as far as we've been told, she never made her first transformation. That means there's no guarantee that she would be able to pass on the gift to either of you," Grandma Margie took Victoria's hand in hers and said, "You have the gift. I can see it in your eyes. I knew it the minute I saw you. May I ask you something?" Victoria nodded. "What animal have you chosen?"

"I didn't choose it," Victoria said, sounding embarrassed, "Maybe I did something wrong, but it just kind of happened."

"It isn't something you choose, Phillip interjected, "At least not how you think a choice is made, through thought or rational reasoning. Your spirit makes the choice. When it happens, as it did for you, the choice is made because your spirit has made its connection,"

Victoria answered with a new sense of calm and awareness, "A wolf. I shifted into a wolf."

"Ah, I knew you were special," Her grandma smiled, bringing back so many memories of when they were children. Out of the corner of her eye, Victoria could see a glint of pain flash across Damian's face. "The wolf is one of the purest animals a shifter can take. It's the original— hence all the many fairytales and folklore stories about werewolves. The transformation to wolf was once very common, but over the years, shifters have been able to bond with such a pure animal soul less and less. You are lucky indeed."

"Why lucky?" Victoria felt bad for Damian, and she was still curious about what was happening to him. She felt certain that he would soon be joining her.

"A shifter lucky enough to take the form of the wolf becomes a member of the Elders." Margie explained. "Even many of the true shape shifters were unable to take the form of the wolf," Phil nodded, encouraging her to go on. "The Elders are a group of shifters that govern our people. They make sure that the rules are being followed and take care of things when they are not. Not only are they the guardians of humans, they are the protectors of our race. It is their job to make sure we are protected."

"Wow, so—.I'm an Elder now?" Her natural cocky attitude started to show again. The thought that someday she would be in charge of a race of people was a dream—one she didn't know she had—come true.

Margie laughed. "No, it doesn't quite work like that. You have to earn your place as an Elder. And when you do, *they* will find *you*. For now, my dear, just get comfortable in both of your bodies and read the rest of this journal. There is so much more for you to learn."

Damian half smiled at his sister. He wanted to be supportive, and he was happy for her, but the thought that this gift of power that ran in their family had just passed him by didn't seem fair. He didn't know why it meant so much to him, but it did. He knew, somehow, that he was meant to follow in his father's path, and to live the life his father had not been able to live: the life his father had given up for love.

"Is there a way to *make* it happen?" Damian asked.

"You can't make it happen, not if it isn't meant to be," Margie answered. "You can learn to control it, but that takes time. Learning to control the transmogrification takes a lot of focus—and clothes. For some it can be very painful. For others it happens as simply and easily as changing their outfit. If you really want to try," Margie said, cautiously, "Begin with meditation. Focus on the animal within you. If it's there, you'll feel it. Victoria, you would focus on the wolf. You've already made your transformation, so you're already starting to learn to control it. After you've done it a few times your body will start to remember the feeling, and it will become easier each time,"

For the rest of the afternoon, Margie and Phil told family stories, illustrated with pictures in old photo albums. When his grandmother set a piece of homemade apple pie down in front of him, Damian had a moment of déjà vu. It was the first childhood memory he had of his grandparents. He remembered sitting at that same table when he was three, maybe four years old, with his hands covered in apple pie, grinning from ear to ear. He could hear his mother's laughter from down the hall and could see his father walking in the front door. It felt so real that he jumped out of his seat, ready to run into his father's arms. But his father wasn't really there, of course. He turned back to his grandfather and asked, "Do you know the vampire that killed our dad?"

"That is in the past," Phillip said calmly, hoping that Damian, too would—could—leave those memories in the past. He knew, though, that if Damian was anything like his father, there was small chance of that happening.

"I don't feel that way. He was my father. I needed him—I still need him every day. I need to know. Please," Damian didn't beg and he knew better than to demand the information from them, but he clearly didn't have any intention of leaving without it.

Phillip paused for a long moment. Finally, he looked at Margie who nodded almost imperceptibly. "Promise me you won't do anything to get yourself hurt," Damian just nodded. "His name is Ermanes, son of Chalkeus. At least that was his name years ago. I'm not sure what name he goes by now. He is very powerful, and very old—though his appearance and his actual body is that of an eighteen year-old. A few years before you were born, I've been told, he left his family—of the time—to marry the great great granddaughter of the late John David Turner. David Turner was married to Edith Wenham—of the Wenham family we were speaking of earlier. You'll recall that the Wenhams were the clan with whom your great-grandfather had made the truce. Edith was the witch who put the spell on their rings. As far as I know, she still leads their clan, and still stands behind her husband's alliances."

Damian's confusion started to boil over into anger. "Married—a witch and a vampire?"

"That is what I was told, but that was many years ago, and your grandmother and I choose to live a life of peace. We stay out of other people's business and expect the same in return. We have made few enemies in our lives. We hope the same for you, but know that the life of a shifter isn't always easy. If you're carrying with you the weight of your father's death, then you will have a very long road to travel."

After saying their goodbye, and promising to come back to visit, Damian and Victoria walked down the hill, back to their car. Somehow everything seemed just a little more familiar, a little more like home.

By the time they got in the car to head home, they were feeling a little more prepared for what might come next. They didn't understand all that they now knew, but at least they knew they had each other to lean on. They also knew they had grandparents who truly cared about them. But most importantly, Damian finally had some direction. Ermanes, son of Chalkeus. It was only a name, but at least he didn't know where to start, with the Wenham family, and he was determined to find him.

The ride back home was mostly silent, as Victoria and Damian tried to process everything they had just learned. They also tried to figure out what they were going to tell their mother once they got home. Somehow, that seemed like the hardest thing they would have to face all day.

Getting out of the house proved difficult at best, Alee had hoped that her mother and Suzi would go out at least for a little while, but instead they sat in the living room drinking tea and talking. Suzi didn't leave until a little after five-thirty and Martha poked her head in Alee's bedroom door just about every half hour to check on her. "Are you feeling all right dear?"

"Yes Mom, I'm fine. I promise,"

She sat on her bed half reading, half staring at the clock as it ticked on second by second. Her father was supposed to be home by five o'clock, but it was already eight o'clock and getting later. She could hear her mother opening and closing the front door, pacing the kitchen, and making sure the dinner in the oven stayed warm. David wasn't the type to be late, and if he had to be, he usually called. But the phone hadn't rung all day. Alee made her way downstairs and could feel her mother growing more and more worried by the minute. The tension was thick in the room.

"Hey, Mom. Are you OK?"

"I'm fine honey," But, Alee could tell she wasn't. "I just don't want dinner to burn, that's all."

"Why don't we just eat now? I can make Dad a plate and heat it when he gets home." Martha just stood there for a minute.

"OK, yeah that's a good idea dear. Why don't you go on up and wash your hands while I get the plates ready,"

"OK," Alee tried to sound positive, even smiling back at her mom as she headed back upstairs. Just as she was opening the bathroom door she heard the phone ring. Her mother answered before she even had a chance to get to her room.

"Alee, it's for you. It's Kyle,"

No matter how worried she was about her dad's absence she couldn't stop herself from smiling at the thought of Kyle on the other end of the phone. She hadn't seen him in a couple of days because he had been visiting some of his cousins out of town. Alee was trying to give him space, and not calling him every twenty minutes. She didn't want to seem like the needy, or even worse, jealous, girlfriend while he was away, but she was excited to hear from him, and didn't even try to hide it. "Hey, I was just thinking about you."

"You were?" His voice enveloped her. Even through the phone it had an alluring, silky quality. She felt her cheeks blush and she could feel the blood hot just beneath her skin.

"I was,"

"Good! I missed you," They hadn't been together long, but it already warmed her heart to hear him say he missed her, after only a few days. "I have a surprise for you,"

There was no possible way to hide how giddy with excitement that made her, so she didn't even try, "What is it? Tell me—tell me—tell me," She was almost bouncing up and down as she insisted in his ear.

As she waited for Kyle to answer, she heard a car door slam. "Finally!"

"What?"

"Oh nothing, I think my dad just got home. He's late and Mom has been worried. But, that means I have to go down for din—." She stopped short as the doorbell rang, and there was a loud knock at the front door. "That's not my—. Oh my God, are you here?"

"What?" Kyle asked, confused and surprised. "No, I'm not there; I thought you said your dad—."

"It's not my dad, he wouldn't ring the bell or knock." The doorbell rang again. "You're really not here?" she was starting to worry.

"No. Why? Alee, what's going on there?"

"I wonder who's at the door," Alee started toward her bedroom window and could hear her mother open the front door downstairs. It had an old rusty hinge that her dad had talked about replacing for years, but he hadn't gotten around to doing it.

"Can I help you?"

"Are you Mrs. Moyer?"

"Yes, what is this about?"

"I'm Officer Manfra. This is Officer Tandy. We need to talk to you about your husband. Do you have a minute?"

Seconds later, Alee heard her mother scream in pain.

Alee dropped the phone and rushed out of the bedroom door, and flew down the stairs. She could hear snapshots of a conversation "—car accident—the car was totaled—died instantly—in custody—so sorry—" She felt like she was moving through molasses as she reached the front door. Everything seemed to be moving in slow motion, and she was having a hard time registering what was happening.

The two officers stood at the front door. Her mother was on the floor, weeping, with the officer's card clutched tightly in her hand. Alee looked to the officers for an explanation, but she already knew what they were going to say.

"We are so sorry, Mrs. Moyer. We will be in touch with the details. Someone will contact you when his body is ready for pick-up by the funeral home," Alee slid to the floor, wrapping her arms tightly around her mother as the words "his body" repeated themselves in her mind a thousand times.

When Alee looked up, Officer Manfra jerked back almost tripping on his own feet. When he found his voice, he squeaked, "If—. Um, if there is anything we can do, please let us know,"

He walked quickly back to the patrol car, pulling his speechless partner with him. And just like that Alee's world changed forever. As they closed the car door, she heard one officer say, "Did you see that girl's eyes? It's like they were on fire."

"Damn it Tandy, I knew we shouldn't have moved back here." He revved the car engine and started down the road.

Somehow, Alee found the strength to help her mother off the floor and help her to lie down on the living room couch. She paced the room, desperately wiping the tears from her face. She felt empty and scared, yet more focused than she had ever felt in her life. She didn't know what to do with all of her newfound energy and determination. Then, it was as if a light switch had been flipped. She knew exactly what to do. She went straight to her mother's side.

Looking deep into her mother's eyes, she said slowly, softly, "It's time to sleep now. Close your eyes, and drift away. I'll wake you when the sun brings a new day," Within seconds, Martha had stopped crying and she was as sound asleep and as peaceful as a baby.

The unbelievable fact of her father's death weighed heavily on Alee's heart, but the anger was even worse—anger that was building from deep within her. She couldn't seem to pull herself off the couch where she sat clutching her mother's hand in hers. The longer she sat there the angrier she became. The angrier she got, the more she noticed her throat starting to burn.

She rushed to the kitchen and drank down an entire glass of water, but it did nothing to ease the thirst she was feeling, which only increased her anger. She felt the need to lash out at someone—anyone. She didn't want to be home when Kyle arrived. She didn't think she would hurt him but she didn't trust herself either. She headed for the front door, ready to leave.

Too late.

Kyle's truck was pulling into the driveway. The light from his headlights flooded the porch and he jumped out of the car and ran straight to her, wrapping his arms around her. Alee just stood there—silent—her mind racing as she tried to decide what to do next, and fighting off every urge she was having. She hadn't yet hugged him back, and as he realized it Kyle slowly pulled away. The first thing he noticed was the long black curls that hung around her face.

"Wow—. Your hair—. You look—." As he softly brushed her hair out of her eyes and tucked it behind her ears, their eyes met for the first time. Her eyes burned a fiery red and before he could react, she pinned him to the wall.

Alee could smell the sweet blood flowing through his veins, and her throat burned with uncontrollable hunger. She wasn't thinking about her mother's grief or her father's death. She couldn't focus on anything but the sweet smell that surrounded her, filling the air, making the burning in her throat cry out for just one taste.

Without even thinking, she licked his neck, and felt his pulse beneath her lips. A quiet "mmmmm" sound of approval escaped his lips and she bit down hard enough to break skin. He didn't struggle or fight. He didn't even try to scream. His blood hitting her tongue was like a deep breath of the freshest air possible. She felt alive. She felt free. But that feeling only lasted a moment. She realized what she had done, and the fear and pain she was sure she had caused him forced her to pull away. She clasped her hands over her mouth, horror-struck, as she wiped away the blood that covered her lips. She could see in his eyes that he was confused, and she longed to explain, but didn't know how.

To her surprise, Kyle didn't pull away but instead leaned forward and kissed her. "You are so beautiful. I love you," His voice was unwavering. It was the first time he had actually said those words.

Why now? Why then? Why wasn't he running in fear— in anger—in disgust, if nothing else? Alee could barely look at him, she was so ashamed of what she had done. His eyes were so gentle and she sank into them as she tried desperately to find the right words to say.

"That didn't happen. Tell me that didn't happen. I'm—so sorry," It was all she could manage before she turned to run out the door.

Before she had taken even one step, though, he grasped her arm, pulling her back to him. "It didn't happen."

"What?" Now *she* was the one who was confused.

"It didn't happen. If that's what you need to hear, then it didn't happen," He pulled her closer still, and wrapped his arm around her waist, but she tried to pull away. "Don't go. Please,"

She was shocked—embarrassed—afraid. How could he want her to stay after what she had done? Why wasn't he freaked out? She was freaked. He should have been freaked! "I have to."

"Then I'm coming with you," it wasn't a question and he wasn't asking permission.

She could already feel the burning sensation in her throat starting to fade away slightly, but wasn't sure how long it would last.

She headed out the front door, not looking back to see if Kyle was following. She knew he was. She climbed into the driver's seat of Kyle's still-running truck. She watched him turn the lock and close the door. Kyle had never allowed anyone else to drive his truck, but he didn't' seem to care. He made his way to the passenger door and climbed in and buckled up. They were on the road in less than a minute.

Alee and Kyle drove in silence. The burning in her throat faded in and out of intensity, but was never really gone completely. Every second that she sat next to Kyle was like waving a cigarette in front of an addict who was trying to quit. She had to force herself to pay attention to the road and focus on objects outside of the truck. Eventually, she turned the radio on to drown out the sound of his rapidly beating heart that continued to taunt her. She didn't understand what was happening, and she was actually quite disgusted by what she had done. But then she'd get a whiff of his sweet scent and her horror was replaced by a violent thirst.

Although Kyle didn't understand what was happening or what she was going through, he could sense the pain she was in and he sat quietly trying to breathe as little as possible so as not to disturb her concentration. He didn't ask where they were going, or pressure her to talk. He knew that when she was ready to talk Alee would let him know. Besides, he was just content to sit and be there with her. They could have been doing nothing, and he would have been just as content.

Her jaw was stiff and sore. Her gums hurt worse than after a visit to the dentist. She kept running her fingers across the front of her teeth. Her eyeteeth seemed sharper than she remembered and she pulled the visor mirror down to get a better look. It was a subtle change, if it was even possible. She shook it off, trying not to think about it. If she thought about it, she would be forced to face the fact that she had bitten her boyfriend, and she wasn't ready to think about that. Not yet.

The road stretched out in front of them as far as the eye could see, and she felt like she had been driving for hours. She would drive for days to escape if she could.

She could feel her body getting weaker as every minute passed, and she was finding it hard to keep her eyes open.

"Where are we going?" Kyle asked as the trees grew denser along the sides of the road.

"The Black Onyx," she said without further explanation. She could feel a pull in her chest drawing her closer— farther—faster—as she pressed harder on the gas. The truck sped up. She was following only her heart and her instincts. Then suddenly the truck stopped. Alee wasn't really sure if she had done it, or if it had stopped itself, but when she looked up she recognized the small wooden sign in the yard of the old house.

Her heart pounded in her chest, and the burning in her throat was back worse than ever. Kyle just looked at her, perplexed and uncertain. She slowly pulled the truck forward into the empty parking lot in front of the shop. They sat in the car staring at the doorway, and then the door opened. It wasn't the beautiful woman she vaguely remembered from the last time she was here, but another woman. She was even more beautiful, with long curling red hair identical to Alee's own. She was wearing a long flowing black skirt and a tight black bodice that laced up the front. Alee recognized something familiar in the woman's eyes that sent a chill down her spine.

"Oh my God," Kyle's voice was pinched. "She looks like—."

"Me."

"Alee, what is this place?" It was just past nine o'clock and the parking lot was deserted. "I'm not sure this is a—."

Her eyes snapped in Kyle's direction and he could see that arguing wasn't a good idea right then. "I'm going. You can come or stay here, but don't try to stop me!"

Before he could answer, Alee was already out of the car with the door slamming behind her. In the short time it took him to get out and shut his door she had moved faster than he thought was possible and was already at the door.

As she stood there, standing face to face with the exotic woman, closer than she would normally feel comfortable, she felt as if she were looking into a mirror. It was obvious that this woman was older than she was, but if she didn't know better she would have bet money that she was seeing her reflection twenty years into the future. At that moment Alee didn't care who she was or why she was there. All she cared about was making the burning stop, and fast.

Alee closed the space between them even more as she leaned in listening to the steady rapid thumping of her heart.

The woman smelled like flowers, but underneath the masking of perfume Alee could smell the sugary sweet smell of her blood. It smelled like honey, and chocolate, and everything— and nothing at all. "You smell—mmm," She was almost moaning with pleasure and she could feel everything inside of her wanting to reach and take this woman in.

"ALEE!" Kyle yelled, trying to get her attention, as he ran to catch up. "Wait up!" She didn't respond.

"Alee?!" The woman's voice was angelic in Alee's ears. "Oh sweet goddesses, is it really you? I'm Loraline, I'm your—."

With one swift move Alee pulled Loraline close, attempting to bite at her throat, but Kyle, acting on instinct, pulled her away, causing them to stumble, inadvertently, into the shop.

As soon as they crossed the threshold, Alee fell to the floor, screaming in pain and grasping her ears to dull the sound of the high-pitched ringing that felt like it would burst her eardrums. As she looked up at Loraline, she silently pleaded for mercy.

Loraline reached for her, but Kyle quickly moved his body so that he was between them. "No one touches her," he growled. He was down on the floor, kneeling at her side, pulling her close and holding her to his chest. "What did you do to her?" Although he didn't understand what was happening, Kyle knew that he would do anything for Alee, and he was prepared to fight if it came to that. "Alee? Alee, sweetie what's wrong?"

A crescent of tooth imprints where Alee had bitten Kyle's neck had started bleeding again, but Alee was so distracted by the pain in her ears that she didn't notice the blood as it dripped down onto her cheek. When Kyle noticed the blood on Alee's face he quickly wiped it away searching for the source. He had no idea he had been bitten. When he touched a hand to his throat and discovered that his neck was throbbing with pain, he became nauseated and light-headed. "Am I bleeding?" He was staring down at his fingertips covered in his own bright red blood, unable to focus on anything else.

Alee, virtually paralyzed by the deafening pain, was able to grasp Kyle's pant leg, and tug on it to distract him for just long enough. When he saw her lying there, clearly in pain and unable to help herself, Kyle forgot all about the blood on his hands.

Alee curled up in his lap, trying unsuccessfully to dull the pain and block out the ringing. He had only a few options before him. He looked at the woman. "Either you make it stop, or I will," It wasn't a plea for help or even a request. It was clear by the tone of his voice that it was a threat, and he was praying inside, with everything he had, that he was sounding convincing. He wasn't really sure what he would be able to do, other than to try and get Alee out of the shop. She hadn't had any problems until she had crossed the entryway and maybe leaving would help, but he couldn't guarantee it, nor was he certain that the woman would let them leave.

He didn't understand the woman's response, because Loraline demanded, "Remove the crystals,"

Kyle glanced around, and noticed for the first time that they weren't alone. No one moved. They all just stood there frozen, staring at Alee as she cried out in pain. Loraline snapped at the other woman in the room, "Jacinda! Break the link. NOW!"

"Loraline—I can't."

"Do it!" Eric said as he came in through the kitchen. Kyle could feel the man watching him before he even looked up. He was watching Kyle's every move. The man wasn't threatening, but Kyle still didn't like the possibility of having to fight him. Something about the way he moved, silently, and with great ease, made him an ominous potential opponent. He came over and started to kneel down at Alee's side, but Kyle quickly scooped her up and away. Eric raised his hands, "I'm not going to hurt her," But Kyle wouldn't loosen his grip.

Jacinda snapped at him, "Listen to yourself, you know we can't do—."

Loraline cut her off, shouting, "Be gone!" With focus and determination, she raised her right arm and opened her right palm toward the corner of the room. A shock wave burst from the palm of her hand and hit the counter, causing a crystal that was concealed on an inner shelf to explode into a thousand pieces.

As soon as the crystal shattered, the ringing in Alee's ears began to fade, and she used what little strength she had left to sit up, still curled in Kyle's embrace.

"NOW!" A new voice issued the command, and two young girls quickly began to move about the room, gathering more hidden crystals. As each crystal was removed from the link, Alee's hearing returned a little more, and more pain subsided. Loraline stood between her family and Alee's fragile body as if to warn the others not to touch her—. She was protected. "We called her here; you can't just let her suffer like this. Why did you even put out the crystals? What did you think would happen?"

"I'm sorry, but we didn't know how she would act when she showed up. We didn't know what state she would be in." Jacinda explained, "You have to believe I never wanted to hurt her, but—but I had to think of our family too."

Alee slowly stood up, with Kyle's help, feeling scared yet humbled by the power she could feel around her. The ringing was gone, but the headache it caused remained. She noticed that the pain and fear had drawn her attention completely away from the burning in her throat—the burning drive that became the only thing that mattered. She no longer felt that thirst that had been so strong, and so urgent. Even standing right next to Kyle, so close that she could smell the sweet scent that surrounded him, she didn't feel the urge to— for a lack of a better word—attack. She looked around the room, studying the faces of those around her.

Alee kept one hand on Kyle, both for balance and for comfort. She took in the handsome, fair-skinned man standing near the beaded curtain, the two young girls hovering behind the dark-haired woman near the counter, and the elegant red-haired woman who had met them at the door. Alee was most interested in the red-haired woman. Their eyes met, and Alee noticed that the rich blue of her eyes seemed to move like ocean waves. Mesmerized, she couldn't look away. She wanted only to dive into those eyes and get lost forever.

"Are you all right?" Loraline reached out to her. Her voice was beautiful. Like a song, it rang in Alee's ears and she latched on to every syllable. "I'm so sorry, I didn't know——."

"I'm fine," Alee answered.

Jacinda was hesitant and kept her distance as she spoke to Alee. "I'm sorry. The headache should pass soon,"

Reluctantly pulling her gaze away from Loraline's blue eyes, Alee looked around the room again. "Is this your shop?"

"It belongs to my family, my sister," Loraline gestured toward the dark haired woman, and quickly placed herself between Alee and Jacinda.

"It's all right sister. You know I won't hurt her," Jacinda murmured.

Kyle also positioned himself between Jacinda and Alee. Alee took a step backwards toward the door, gripping Kyle's hand tightly in her own.

Maybe this was a mistake, she thought. She quickly stopped herself when she noticed that the slender gentleman had somehow made his way to the entryway without her even noticing, and was now blocking any chance of an exit that they might have had. Gazing at the man, Alee noticed that his skin was perfect, as if made of porcelain. People had always told Alee that she had porcelain skin.

Though he was slender in build you could see every muscle clenched under his tight black t-shirt. His eyes, sapphire blue, were more beautiful than a man should be allowed. How did he move so quickly? She had all but forgotten about Kyle until she felt his hand squeeze even tighter around hers and she realized that the man and Kyle were engaged in a stare down. The man wasn't just staring, though. He was *glaring* at Kyle, and it made Alee uneasy. It was as if he was ready to pounce if Kyle made just one wrong move. Alee caught Kyle's eye and saw his confusion and fear. He squeezed her hand and she could feel the fresh sweat on his palms.

Jacinda directed her full attention back to Alee, "Is there something you needed?"

"Yes. I was in here a few months back," As she spoke Alee glanced around the room and it seemed as if all eyes were staring back at her.

"Yes, I remember," Jacinda took Alee's hand in hers and opened it, palm up. She softly ran her fingertips along the lines of her palm. "But, he is new," she said as her eyes swept across Kyle's face and back to Alee.

Kyle stepped closer to Alee—not in fear, but to show her and everyone else in the room that if they had any intentions of harming her they would first have to go through him. He had every intention, no matter what, of protecting her.

Jacinda scanned Alee's palm again, and her grip on Alee's wrist became slightly tighter as she spoke more directly than Alee had expected but still in a hushed whisper, "There is something you desire!?"

Alee was confused by the woman's choice of words. Was she still speaking of Kyle? Was it a statement or a question? Desire? Although it seemed odd it was also somehow fitting. Alee didn't know where to start, and with so many people around she began to feel slightly claustrophobic. She even thought, she just might be going crazy. Then she remembered the empty pill bottle in her purse and, pulling it out, she asked the only question that didn't seem completely insane to her at the moment, "What are —were these?"

Jacinda reached out and took the bottle from Alee's open hand. "You took them."

It wasn't a question, but Alee answered her anyway, "Yes," Kyle was startled, his expression clearly showing surprise—and disapproval.

"All of them?" Even Jacinda seemed a little concerned. "Yes."

Kyle whispered in Alee's ear, "You took some random pills and you didn't even know what they were?" he was confused, and angry. How could she risk her life like that? Anything could have happened. Alee's only reply was to gently squeeze his hand, and hope that was enough to reassure him until she was able to explain more, or at least enough to make him stop looking at her like she was a child who had made a stupid mistake.

"They are—or rather, they were, what you needed," Shaking the bottle it was empty. "Though, you shouldn't have needed them all. Not in such a short amount of time."

"Were they—?"

"Blood, yes!" Jacinda was very matter-of-fact.

"Jacinda!" Loraline interrupted. "When did you—. Why?"

"She was sick and she would have only gotten worse, maybe even died, without them,"

"I just wanted to thank you for—for helping me that day," Alee said.

"Of course," Jacinda said, looking at Loraline with a smirk and an 'I told you so' look on her face, and then back to Alee, "I'm glad they helped."

"Yes, they did—." Alee shuffled her weight from leg to leg, and hemmed and hawed a few times, "Um, I was actually hoping I might…" Alee didn't know why she felt the way she did, but something about what she was asking for seemed almost wrong. Maybe it was the way Kyle had tightened his grip on her arm, or maybe it was the twinkle of delight in Jacinda's eyes. "…I thought that maybe I could get some more."

"Of course you can," Jacinda answered.

"No! Alee, you can't do that," Kyle wasn't about to just stand around watching God only knows what, "What are you thinking, she just said they had blood in them. Why would you ask for more?" He needed to get her out of here and fast.

Jacinda stepped in to stop Kyle from changing Alee's mind, "They won't hurt her, I promise," It did little to calm his nerves, but Jacinda didn't seem to notice, or care. She turned to Alee, "They won't hurt you, and I will make you more, if that is what you want. But, these aren't what you need any more. Your condition is progressing, and the desire will only get stronger. The pills will take the edge off, but what you need is—."

"What have you done?" The voice of an older woman coming through the curtain startled Alee, and interrupted Jacinda.

"Granny Edith, this is——." Jacinda started to say.

"I know who she is!" Followed by her daughter Estelle, Edith walked straight to Alee and lifted her chin, looking her over as if inspecting a horse "Well, let me look at you. Turn around!"

In an instant Alee and Kyle had been separated and she was being spun around and poked and prodded by this seemingly frail, elderly, gray-haired woman, "She's small. I would have expected her to be taller," She shot a sideways look toward Eric, who glared back at her not saying a word.

Kyle was held, if you could call it that, against the wall, unable to move or speak. Alee could see him struggle to get free, and there was no one physically holding him there, and yet his struggles were unsuccessful.

"You have beautiful hair, but do you not eat child?" Her hand was around Alee's wrist showing just how thin and fragile she was.

"Granny Edith, please. Hasn't she been through enough? She doesn't need this right now," Loraline sounded more pleading than angry.

Edith didn't hesitate to put her foot down, "If she is going to be a part of this *family*..." she emphasized the word, "...then she will be treated as such,"

A hush went through the room, but it didn't seem to faze Granny Edith.

"Mother!?" Estelle spoke directly, "Nothing has been decided yet. She doesn't even know."

Edith simply continued her inspection, ignoring the disapproving sighs and whisperings around the room. Alee was dumbstruck, unable to process what was going on. When she looked up, the old woman had ceased her examination, and even though Alee wasn't being restrained, she found that she couldn't find the courage to move.

Edith had moved away from Alee, and stood, now, face to face with Kyle, "Your name is?" She waited, but he didn't say a word. Not for lack of trying—he simply couldn't seem to make his vocal cords work. It was like when you try to scream in the middle of a nightmare, but nothing comes out. Realizing his struggles, Edith waved her right hand through the air in front of his face and as simply as that his voice found its way back to him.

"Alee are you OK? Leave her alone. Who are you people?" He would have continued but found that his voice left him as quickly as it had been returned.

"I asked your name young man," Edith wasn't being rude, but she wasn't about to be disrespected by some teenage boy, who didn't know his place. Clearly, she was accustomed to being listened to—and obeyed.

Alee suddenly felt a surge of energy flood through her, and she was by his side faster than she ever thought she could move, "His name is Kyle, and he is with me," She put herself between the two of them, trying to show that she wasn't someone to be messed with.

"Ah, *now* I see the family resemblance," She shot a quick smirk toward Loraline and Eric, and for once her cold hard face seemed to soften just a bit. "She has your spunk, Loraline."

Edith shot Kyle a meaningful look. "Don't worry young man, the girl is safe. She's among family," Then turning her attention back to Alee she reached out and took her hand. "Come child, I believe it's time for us to talk," She tried to lead her away, but Kyle wouldn't let her go.

Edith just looked at Alee. "Alee?"

"I'll be OK," Alee nodded to Kyle and, to her surprise Kyle slowly let go of her hand, and watched as Edith led her back through the beaded curtain.

But before they reached the beaded curtain, Edith turned back and called to Kyle and the others over her shoulder. "You may follow."

Edith led Alee down the long dark hallway that Alee vaguely remembered from her previous visit. Alee ran her free hand along the wall to the right. She could feel doorway after doorway as they passed. She could feel the air around her getting colder the farther they walked, almost as if they were walking into a freezer. Something deep inside her was telling her to turn and run, but it was too late for that, even if she didn't know it yet.

When they finally stopped in front of a large wooden door, Alee noticed the others following not far behind. The hallway had no lights, and no windows to let the moonlight in, but Alee was able to see everything around her in vivid detail. She could see Kyle squinting and being led by the slender man.

Instead of opening the large wooden door, Edith turned to the left and opened a smaller door leading into a dimly lit room. As the door eased open, Alee saw her mother sitting silently on the couch at the far end of the room. Alee ran to her, grabbing her and clinging to her as if Alee were in the middle of the ocean and Martha were a life raft. Martha's eyes were bloodshot from what Alee could only imagine must have been hours of crying, but then again, she had just left her mother only a little over an hour ago. It had only been a little over an hour, right? The thought came and went as quickly as lightening in a storm.

"Mom, are you OK?" When Martha didn't answer Alee turned toward Edith with fire burning in her eyes. For the first time since she had arrived, she was ready to fight. "Why is she here? What did you do?"

"Those questions don't matter now. You are home and that is what matters."

"What are you talking about?" Alee screamed, fighting the urge to run. "I'm NOT home. This is not—."

"Alee, please stop," her mother pleaded with a trembling voice. "Please," she said, turning to Edith, "She's all I have. I love her so much. She's my little girl—my baby."

"That is where you are wrong." Edith slowly and purposefully crossed the room, demanding the attention of everyone around her. "This child does not belong to you. She is no more your child than she was the day she was born. She belongs here, with us. I told you, years ago, that the arrangement was only temporary," Edith placed a hand on Martha's shoulder, trying, unsuccessfully, to comfort her. "You have served your purpose and we are grateful."

"But, my husband—"

"Yes, that was unfortunate, and I am sorry for your loss," The casual tone of Edith's voice betrayed her indifference. "There was nothing more we could have done."

"So it was you?"

"I think you already know the answer to that. Do you really need to ask? You both knew that our agreement was only for the duration of your custodianship of Aleerah," Aleerah? Who's Aleerah? Martha wondered. Edith sounded as if she were confirming the details of a business transaction, as if the death of Alee's father was of no consequence. Edith continued, "He was meant to die years ago, and if it were not for our arrangement," she said bitterly, "you would not have had the last sixteen years together. You should be thankful."

"But—."

"No. It is time to let go. I understand that you have a strong connection to my grandchild, but those feelings will fade with time. Just as I imagine it would with any parent who has lost their child. You will always have your memories, but it would be wise of you to bid her farewell and kindly accept the ride home that is waiting for you. When you wake in the morning you will feel sorrow, but everything else will be as natural to you as life itself."

Alee was shocked when Martha lashed back at the old woman. "You have never lost a child. You have no idea what this feels like. Don't tell me it will fade! Don't tell me this is natural! Nothing about this is natural! You couldn't possibly understand, you freak of nature—you sadist!" Alee was taken aback, she had never seen her mother so angry. It almost made her sorry for the old woman.

Martha began crying again, uncontrollably, and Alee held on even tighter. "It's OK, Mom. Don't worry. Nothing is going to happen. I won't let it."

"I may not have lost a child, but I know loss. Your husband saw to that," Edith's eyes shifted to black. "Don't think for one second that we have forgotten what your husband did. He has served his time. And we have no more use for you," She was standing directly in front of Martha, and was no longer even attempting to sound civil. She reached out and, with uncanny agility and strength, pulled Martha off the couch and out of Alee's grip in one smooth, angry gesture. "For his crimes, and for the way you protected him, maybe you should meet his same fate and—."

"NO!" Alee screamed. "Please, don't hurt her,"

"Granny, please," Loraline whispered. Alee would have known that voice anywhere. Even though she could hear the urgency and the pain in her voice, the words still sounded peaceful and angelic.

"Loraline, have you forgotten? Will you turn your back on your family, again?"

Humbled, Loraline lowered her head looking across the floor, "No, of course not, Granny,"

Edith gestured to the people amassed in the small room. "Do not forget how they hunted us down for centuries. He has paid his debt and kept the child safe, but that alone does not excuse him for his crimes, and for those of his blood line,"

She was a natural leader, born with the skills of communication and persuasion. Alee was convinced that if this little old woman stood up and told everyone in that room to take a step off a bridge or walk into a burning building each and every one of them would have done it willingly, and some eagerly, just to please her.

Edith motioned to one of the young girls, who quickly stepped over to a wet bar on the other side of the room and poured two tall slender glasses of ice water, which she brought to Alee and Martha. Something about the girl, and the way she moved, looked so familiar to Alee. With a bittersweet smile, the girl handed them each a glass. "Can I get you something to eat as well?" she asked before Edith quickly waved her away.

At the thought of eating, the burning in Alee's throat began slowly coming back.

"Relax," murmured Edith. "Have a drink, say your goodbyes," she turned to Martha and said, "And then you will be on your way."

Martha took her glass in both hands and quickly guzzled down the cold wet liquid. But then her hands started to shake and the glass fell crashing onto the cold hard floor, where it shattered. She clutched her chest with one hand, and rubbed her eyes with the other. "What did you give me?"

Alee examined the liquid remaining in her own glass, and she started to feel dizzy and light-headed. She took her mother's hands in hers in an effort to calm her down and to regain some sense of balance herself. But the second she touched her mother she could feel the blood rushing through her mother's veins, and her throat burned like it was on fire. Alee quickly let go and jumped off the couch. The urge to feed was overwhelming. She had to get away from her mother as fast as she could.

Pressing against the wall and squeezing her eyes shut, Alee tried desperately to focus on anything except the sound of the heartbeats echoing throughout the room. She could hear each beat, each rhythm unique to the individual person. With every beat her throat burned hotter and with more intensity. Then she heard Martha collapse. Alee opened her eyes and saw someone pick Martha up and carry her toward the door. As Alee started to go to her—desperate to stop them from taking her mother away—she licked her lips and felt the soreness in her gums getting worse. She pressed herself even further against the wall and watched her mother disappear from her life.

24

Alee and Kyle sat on a sofa at one end of the room, and Edith sat on a sofa on the far side of the room with her daughter Estelle. Elizabeth stood behind them with her arm around her daughter Loraline who was holding Eric's hand. Everyone else had exited the room shortly after Martha's body was carried out.

The small room was lined with tall built-in bookshelves made of a solid dark wood. The shelves were crammed tight with ancient leather-bound books, journals, boxes, and jars filled with what looked like spices, oils crystals and a number of things Alee couldn't identify. On the wall to the left was a large, open stone fireplace with a hand-carved wooden mantelpiece covered in candles of every color. The room should have felt claustrophobic, but instead it felt homey and almost comforting. If it wasn't for the fact that Alee was feeling like she was forgetting something important, something urgent, maybe even dangerous, she might have been able to enjoy herself. As it was, she was fighting her instinct to flee.

"Now, as I said before, it's time that we talked," said Edith, her voice was more gentle and grandmotherly. Previously, Alee had gotten the distinct impression that Edith was driven by her own personal agenda. But now Edith seemed to be offering guidance and protection. "There are so many things you need to know, and I am sure you have questions of your own," Alee nodded, but waited patiently for Edith to continue.

"I am your great-great-grandmother Edith Wenham. But you can call me Granny. This is my daughter Estelle. Elizabeth is Estelle's daughter; Loraline is Elizabeth's daughter. Next to Loraline is Eric. He is…" Edith scowled. "…Loraline's—."

"He is my husband," Loraline interrupted. "Or, fiancée I suppose,"

Alee sat quietly, taking it all in while her mind raced. Who does this woman think she is, calling herself my Granny? She doesn't even know me. Her grip on Kyle's hand got tighter and tighter.

"Loraline is your mother," Edith continued. "That would make Eric your father," Her eyes squinted into narrow slits as she peered back at Eric and Loraline over her shoulder. Alee noticed as Loraline let out a deep breath as if she had been holding it—scared to breathe somehow. Alee was so focused that every little sound echoed in her ears. She could hear the soft thumping of her heartbeat begin to quicken in her chest.

"Loraline is my mother?! she thought. It was almost as if Alee had known it all along. She had no doubt that it was true—that this familiar stranger standing before her was in fact her mother.

While everyone's eyes were on Alee, Kyle asked, "Then who are Mr. and Mrs. Moyer?"

"Moyer," Alee whispered, as if saying it for the first time. How could I have forgotten who I am? Her entire past—her father's death, her mother in tears—had all but vanished from her memory as she sat there so intently focused on Edith's words. She instantly felt guilty and ashamed.

Estelle answered, "They were working to pay off a debt to our family. They were assigned to care for and raise Aleerah until she became of age."

"My name is Alee, not Aleerah. Why do you keep calling me that?"

"Your name is Aleerah. Alee is a nickname, a shortened version of your birth name. It's cute, but it isn't who you are. Aleerah is a family name, from generations past. The fact that your mother chose this name for you shows great commitment to our family line," She was speaking to Alee, but all the while watching Loraline out of the corner of her eye.

So many questions were swimming through Alee's head. "What kind of debt could my parents possibly have to work off? They had plenty of money and could have paid whatever they owed you."

"The life of my husband is what they owed me," said Edith.

"And mine," answered Estelle.

Silence filled the room. Then Edith continued. She spoke of Mr. and Mrs. Moyer with disgust. "Your '*parents*,'" she spit out the word as if it tasted awful in her mouth, "as you call them, would have had nothing but the clothing on their backs were it not for the money we provided them to care for you, the job we helped David get, and the house we gave them to live in." She moved across the room and pulled a scrapbook off of one of the bookshelves behind them. She opened it, tossing it lightly on the table in front of them. Inside the book where pages and pages of newspaper articles reporting unsolved murder investigations. "They used to be very dangerous. Maybe they still would be had we not found them when we did. Twenty years ago, they were very successful hunters. But they didn't realize how strong our family is. After they killed our husbands, they thought they could just disappear, cross the border into the next town, the next state. But, they didn't get far before we found them. From then on, they had nothing except what we allowed them."

Alee was confused—there was no way they could have been talking about the same people who had raised her, "What do you mean '*hunters*'? My dad never hunted. He didn't even own a gun. He was the gentlest man I've ever met. And my mom couldn't hurt a fly. She wouldn't even step on spiders. She made my dad take them outside,"

Suddenly, the pages of the scrapbook started to flip on their own. Article after article featured pictures of her parents as suspects, or persons of interest. As she scanned the newspaper articles, she began to realize they didn't hunt deer, boar, or even bear. They hunted people. Sickened, she slammed the book shut and pushed it away in disbelief.

"I know you think you knew them," said Edith, the growl returning to her voice. "But you have no idea who they were. Deep inside. They knew they were being watched at all times. They knew better than to slip into their old lives. If they so much as spoke of hunting again, we would have known and the consequences would have been severe."

Loraline stepped in to help explain. "You see Alee, the punishment for killing a member of the Underground is death."

"What is the Underground?" Alee asked timidly, not knowing how much more she wanted to hear, but happy to hear that voice again.

"The Underground is an ancient society created thousands of years ago. They have established communities around the world and although Atlanta was already inhabited when they decided to make a home here, our Founders have made Atlanta what it is today. In every town, in which they have a presence, there is a founding council, or the original settlers. The council governs, so to speak, what happens within the city limits, as well as what is allowed.

"Then why haven't I ever heard of them before?"

"Only members born into the society, or those invited to join, ever learn about the Underground or of the council

directly. When the Moyers crossed into our territory and
began hunting, they violated our laws. Their punishment
should have been death, but Granny Edith and Granny Estelle
made a plea to the council and they were given the authority
to show mercy and spare their lives in return for services. A
few weeks after you were born, I was attacked," She held
tightly to Eric's hand, but never looked at him as she spoke.
"I was in a coma, for a while, and when I woke up I didn't
remember who I was let alone who you were. Your father
thought we were dead, and your grandmothers made the only
choice they could. You were given to the Moyers. They were
assigned to raise you and protect you. The only way to keep
you safe, and provide you with a normal life away from all of
this, was with people who truly understood the dangers of
your world and our world—people strong enough to protect
you and yet weak enough to know their limits."

"Why did I need protecting? Why couldn't I have just
been raised here?"

No one answered for a long time. The silence lingered
for a while, until Granny Edith spoke. "You are not just a girl
Aleerah. Until you understand wha—who—you are we cannot
answer that for you."

"Fine, but you mentioned my father," Alee almost started
to laugh as she shook her head at the image of her parents,
Martha and David Moyer being who Edith said they were.
Then the thought occurred to her that although they had
raised her for seventeen years, they weren't actually her
parents. Maybe it was just a job or a chore to them. She
remembered her mother sitting at her bedside, night after

night, when she was sick. She remembered the long drives, just she and her dad, when she had to go down South to see specialist after specialist. She remembered how loving and caring they had always been. No matter whether she was sick or well, they were always there for her. Then she looked up at Loraline and Eric, people she was only just now meeting, and thought to herself, "If you're my parents then where the hell have you been all my life?!" She was angry and hurt. She couldn't wrap her mind around the idea that her father wasn't her father. That this stranger, who didn't know how she liked peanut butter on her pancakes, or how she liked Oreo cookies and milk before bed when she wasn't feeling well, or anything else about her could possibly be her dad. Then she looked at Eric. "You? You're my father?"

"Yes," Eric answered.

Alee furrowed her brow and shook her head. "You can't be my father. You're, what, in your mid-twenties, early-thirties? There's no way,"

As Alee considered this, the tension and stress of the last few hours reached a breaking point. She thought of Eric as an adolescent father and she giggled. She thought of her parents hunting witches and she chuckled. Then she thought of these strangers around her actually being her family, what it would be like to live as a witch, and she laughed. Her laughter turned into guffaws until she was gasping for breath. Suddenly, the air was as thick as smoke, and almost as suffocating. Her hands were shaking, and her voice trembled ever so slightly, "I'm thirsty," It was a whisper for his ears only, almost a plea or a cry for help. Her eyes met Kyle's.

"Your eyes," he said, "They're red, blood red,"

In seconds, Eric was by her side with a mug of thick red syrup. "Drink this. It'll help,"

She took it, but didn't drink it right away. She brought it to her lips and smelled the contents. Sweet. Metallic. Tempting. The burning got worse.

As she took her first hesitant sip, Kyle leaned slowly away from her. She brought the mug back up to her lips and drained every last drop. She looked up again and noticed that Kyle had moved to the other side of the couch. It wasn't fear in his eyes or even anger, but disgust. Alee's heart sank in embarrassment, and she fought the urge to just break down and cry.

Loraline noticed Kyle's reaction and spoke to him. "It's natural,—" she began, but was cut off by Kyle.

"It's not natural! She just drank blood, right? That's what it was right? People don't drink blood! What is natural about that?" Abandoned by her protector, Alee began to cry softly.

"It's natural for her kind," Loraline finished her thought.

After Alee had stopped crying, Estelle moved to the couch to sit by her side. "Your history goes back much farther than you could possibly imagine," she began. "It is much older, and completely different than the family tree you did in grade school. Although I wish the Moyers could have told you about your real heritage, it was for your safety, and ours, that we couldn't allow it. You see when it comes to members of the Underground, all births must be registered. Yours was not," She glanced back disapprovingly at Loraline. "It will take some doing, but I am sure there is a way to correct that error without drawing too much attention," Then quietly to herself, "I hope."

Alee and Kyle sat silently listening intently to every word, but at the mention of her parents tears started to fill her eyes once again.

"Alee, you're a witch," Estelle said matter-of-factly. "No matter the circumstances of your childhood, you have come into your powers, and it is your birthright to join our society," Although she had been resisting understanding—pushing the thoughts away—Alee already knew that what Estelle was saying was true. Still, hearing it now came as a shock.

Estelle comforted Alee, cooing, "Don't let the word 'witch' scare you. The stories that you heard as a child about witches riding on brooms, using children or animals as sacrifices to evil spirits to gain power aren't real. At least not to the extent that books and movies make them seem. Of course, there have been dark witches throughout history that have done some versions of those terrible things. The stories do come from somewhere I suppose. But not all witches are evil. In fact, most people practicing witchcraft today are what we call white witches," Turning to her daughter Elizabeth, she said, "Bring me the "Grimoire" please."

From the top shelf of one of the bookcases Elizabeth pulled out a large, leather-bound book. It looked as if it had been through a war or two in its time. Loose pages were hanging out, the binding was creased and barely holding together, the cover was cracked and faded; but even with all those signs of age it was beautiful.

As Estelle opened the cover, a reverent hush fell over the already silent room. Alee saw that the inscription on the first page was the same as the one in the "Book of Shadows" she had hidden under her bed at home:

"For those who came before us and for those who are yet to come. Within your blood you have the power and through your line the answers you shall find,"

"This book and a few others like it hold the history of our family. They tell the stories of our ancestors, and they share the secrets from our past. It is a living, growing, record of our family's traditions and experiences. Each generation contributes, adding spells and potions they have created and used successfully: rituals, traditions, and even stories of the enemies or allies they have made and the battles they have fought—both victories and defeats," Estelle looked to Edith in a moment of sad recognition and remembrance.

"The 'Grimoire,' or 'Book of Shadows,' as it's also called, is specific to each coven and is marked with their family's symbol on the cover. Each witch will also create their own, with their personal experiences that are often passed down from generation to generation. I believe you have your mother's," Alee looked at Loraline who nodded in agreement. "Once you have returned it, she will help you begin your own book and much like this one…" patting the book in front of her. "…it will be bound and protected by a spell tied to our bloodline, to your blood,"

Alee remembered sitting on the floor of the bathroom holding the book on her lap and the weight of the silver dagger in her hand—the way the empty pages seemed to soak up her blood—How the words seemed to appear as if from out of nowhere, imprinting the pages with her blood.

"OK, so witches are real. What else?" Her eyes met Eric's. "Vampires?"

"Yes," Alee knew what he would say before Eric even answered.

"Vampires are—." she started but couldn't finish.

"Dead," It was Kyle. He wasn't questioning the fact that vampires existed, but merely pointing out the fact that from everything he knew vampires were in fact dead. "So, if you're saying you're a vampire then you can't be Alee's dad? You're dead," He leaned forward, intrigued.

"That is a common misconception, a myth," Eric said. "Vampires are not dead. We are no deader than you are. Only more evolved."

"But—." Kyle was shaking his head.

"Think of it as a virus. The virus attacks through the blood stream, slowing the heart rate, so slow that we have the ability to appear dead, even when inspected closely. Yet, our hearts beat just enough to allow our bodies to survive. We have an increased immune system that allows our bodies to heal at an inhuman rate. Our basal metabolism is also increased, which is why our natural body temperature is lower than yours, causing our skin to feel cold to the touch," Kyle and Alee were listening intensely, on the edge of their seats. "Just like yours, our body temperature increases with physical exercise, allowing us to burn calories and digest food. Therefore, we are able to eat regular food, although we don't require the nutrients."

"Then why eat?"

"Because we still enjoy the taste of food," Eric said. "We get all the nutrients we need through the consumption of blood. But, because our own blood is infected, so to speak, we need an intake of non-infected blood on a regular base."

"How often?" Alee asked, trying not to sound as disgusted as she felt.

"That depends on the age of the vampire, and how far along they are in their change. The amount decreases the older the vampire gets, but it will never become unnecessary," Alee looked away, and Eric quickly changed the subject. "There are of course other changes: increased strength and speed, improved night vision—" then with a smirk, "—other abilities. And, of course we have our weaknesses: sunlight, silver—." His voice trailed off and silence filled the room around them.

Kyle and Alee had grown up watching all the old horror films, and his favorites were those that were based around vampires, werewolves, and zombies. Quietly whispering into Alee's ear, "OK, he's not as creepy as that guy in 'Nosferatu,' but much cooler than Brad Pitt in 'Interview with a Vampire.'" He had managed to make her laugh and the tension between them eased a little.

"I'll take that as a compliment," Eric smirked with pleasure.

"OK, wow—really good hearing," Kyle said.

"Just another one of the many improvements," Eric said with a smile.

"I'll keep that in mind," Kyle looked at Alee with wide eyes, and just kind of shrugged. Kyle wasn't scared—. He just wasn't sure he really believed it yet, but he also didn't not believe it.

"I never was a fan of Brad Pitt's impression of a vampire. Louis de Pointe du Lac was actually a much—" he contemplated the words, "—meaner man. Some would have called him insane."

"You act like he was real, like you knew the guy or something" Kyle laughed, but Eric just stared at him with a blank face, showing nothing yet saying everything.

"OK then."

Jacinda asked, bemused and slightly intrigued, "You're not afraid?"

"No—maybe—I don't know—. You haven't killed us yet and he hasn't eaten us yet, so—does it really matter?" As Kyle spoke Alee turned to face him.

"Yes it matters. It matters to me," Alee looked around the room and everyone's eyes were on her. The fire crackled in the fireplace and the lights flickered overhead, but no one seemed to notice. She was the center of attention, and everyone wanted to know what she was going to say next. "I don't know if what they're saying is true, and I sure as hell don't understand what it all means. But, if it is true then what you think of it does matter, at least to me."

"Then no—. I'm not scared. Maybe a little confused, like you, but not scared. Not of them—" Kyle nonchalantly gestured waving his hand in their direction, not taking his eyes off hers, "—and certainly not of you," It was the perfect answer, and it seemed to give her strength. Knowing that he was still there at her side, she felt almost invincible.

Looking directly at Eric this time, "If you're a vampire how can you be my father? How is that even possible?"

Eric was holding Loraline's hand in his, and a soft smile lit up his face. "It is possible. It's rare, but it is possible. You are proof of that,"

"I won't go into the details of how babies are made—that's your mother's job. But, with vampires and humans it's roughly the same concept. In theory, if the vampire's body temperature is increased for an extended period of time then the body has the ability to—reproduce," Elizabeth was obviously uncomfortable as she spoke of her daughter's sex life in such educational ways.

"The child of a male vampire and a mortal woman is known as a dhampir," said Loraline. "They say dhampirs are rare, but really, on Earth today they were nonexistent until you came along," she smiled. "In fact, the Grimoire doesn't tell of another one who has survived past the age of six weeks. They normally starve within the first few weeks of life. That is, if they even make it through the birth. Even such a pregnancy is rare. Special,"

Alee took a deep breath to clear her thoughts. She had been sick all her life, and fought death a thousand times over. The doctors never had any chance of helping her fight a disease—because she didn't have one. All of her health issues were a result of her biological parents. "Did they know? Did my parents, the Moyers know what I am?"

"No," Edith finally said. "They were aware that you came from a line of witches, but they didn't know about your father. Nor did I when I gave you to them. We had been told that your mother and Eric had cut ties." That last statement had a bit of a bite to it. She shared a look with Loraline, and whispered, "I'm sorry,"

Alee supposed maybe she was actually lucky that day so many years ago when they gave her up. Who knows what her life might have been like as a half-vampire/half-witch outcast crossbreed? At least she was raised in a somewhat normal family with as close to a real childhood as someone in her condition could have.

Suddenly, as if a floodgate had been opened, all of the myths about vampires sprang to mind. "If I'm a vampire, then why can I be out in the sun?"

"You're only half-vampire. As a dhampir, you are very strong, even if you don't know it yet. In time you will come into your full range of powers, and prove to be far stronger than even I am. You will develop all of the strengths of a vampire, but you will not share our weaknesses."

"Except for the—" she couldn't finish it.

Eric could tell what she was thinking by the sound of disgust in her voice. Eric had been a vampire for hundreds of years, and had accepted his fate, but he could see in her eyes she felt it was more of a curse than anything else. "Yes, except for the thirst. But, even that you will learn to control, in time,"

Kyle turned to Alee, his voice as gentle as he was able to make it, "You believe them don't you? What they're saying, you believe it's true?"

A tear fell from her eye, and rolled down her cheek. He caught it with a gentle rub of his thumb along her jaw line. "I do. I feel it. I've seen the changes with my own eyes. I couldn't explain them before, but they make sense now, at least as much sense as they can make I suppose."

He just pulled her close and held her as silent tears ran down his face. The room went quiet as if they were the only two people left in the world.

"I love you Alee. I always will."

"But?" she offered.

"Always," Kyle assured her.

She couldn't bear the thought of losing him. After losing her father, and then her mother—. A sudden pain stabbed her in the chest as if someone had ripped out her heart. It was the feeling of loss. Alee turned to Loraline and wiped the tears from her eyes.

"My father, the man who raised me, is dead. What's going to happen to my mom?"

"Nothing, she has paid her debt. No harm will come to her, at least not from us," She directed it to everyone in the room as if giving an order. "She will live a long life, I'm sure."

It was meant to comfort Alee, but there was no comfort in knowing that her mother would spend the rest of her life alone. There were tears in Alee's eyes, and her voice trembled as she spoke. "Will I ever see her again?"

"You can, but you must understand that she will no longer know you as her daughter. She won't be able to connect you to the past you shared with her, or with the memories she has of her daughter," Estelle was so matter of fact, so sure of what she was saying. That confidence almost made everything worse for Alee.

"You mean she'll forget me? Forget having raised me? What about everyone else who knew me as her daughter, my friends at school and the members of our church?" Panic was growing inside of Alee at the thought of her entire life being wiped away, as if it had never even happened.

"It isn't as simple as that," Estelle thought for a while trying to figure out exactly how to explain. "They will not forget you. She will not forget having raised you. But, she won't recognize you as her daughter any more. That will be your only protection. Your mother will believe, and through her, others will believe, that you have died."

"Died? Died how?"

"All of your life, everyone, including you, has believed that you were sick. It would not come as a shock to anyone if it were announced that you had fallen fatally ill after forgetting to take your medications during a two-week camping trip," Estelle continued.

Alee and Kyle just shook their heads in disbelief. They had said they had been watching her, and if she didn't believe it before she knew now that it was true.

"I know it isn't an easy solution to accept, but it is a necessary one," Edith said. "Aleerah, it's the only way for

Mrs. Moyer to move on. We are trying to make it as easy as we can for everyone involved."

"Your mother will wake up in her home tomorrow morning, alone, with the knowledge of her daughter's death and her husband's car accident. She will find that she had already made the funeral arrangements during a period of mourning which she doesn't remember. Your friends will come, and everyone will say their goodbyes. They will have a chance to grieve. It is the easiest transition for all of them, as well as for you."

Shock struck Alee at the thought of her own funeral. "But—you said I could see her again. How? How, if she won't recognize me? Our house—her house—is covered with pictures of me—of us—of my family," There were tears pouring from her eyes, and her voice was trembling uncontrollably.

Loraline stepped forward, picked up an antique silver hand mirror from the mantel, and brought it to Alee. "Before you look, understand that you are still the same person you have always been. That will never change," She looked at Kyle. "Make sure she knows what you see when you look in her eyes. She'll need you now more than ever."

Alee didn't understand, what could she possibly be talking about, but then she lifted the mirror, and instead of seeing herself reflected in the glass, there was a girl she had never seen before. Her eyes were the same ocean blue, but that was the only resemblance to who she was. Her hair was golden blonde and as smooth as corn silk. Her skin was still as delicate as porcelain, but sun-kissed with a golden glow. Even her lips seemed fuller somehow.

"You see, Alee is gone," Loraline smiled reassuringly, but Alee wasn't assured of anything.

"But—how?" asked Kyle. "I see her. I mean, I see Alee. My Alee." Alee hadn't changed in his eyes. The woman in the mirror wasn't sitting next to him—she was a reflection of someone he couldn't see.

Loraline took the mirror back, lowering it so that Alee couldn't see her reflection any more. "It's an appearance-altering spell. You still see her for who she is because you have experienced this night together. But give it time. The more time you spend apart, the more her appearance will alter, until you will see her as the rest of the world does. It may take weeks or only days. It may be as soon as tomorrow that you wake up and can no longer see her as you do now. Although, even though you will see her differently, you will still know who she really is. Everyone else will believe that Alee is dead, and they will accept her now as someone new."

"As who? Who am I now?" Alee cried.

"That's up to you."

"But, I'm dead. I have nothing. I have no one," Alee sounded as if she were about to break down again.

"You have me," said Kyle.

She turned to look at him, and she knew he was thinking the same thing she had been thinking.

Her hands started to shake, as she asked, "And Kyle? Will I lose him too?" She couldn't bear to look away from him, not for a second, not without knowing.

"That is up to you both. But, understand that if he decides to stay in your life he too will have to make sacrifices. Your identity and your powers must be protected. You have to understand that, as we said before, there has never been another dhampir to survive. We aren't sure how our society will react when they find out what you are. Therefore Kyle would be putting himself at risk to protect what he knows. He would be putting everyone around him— his family, his friends, your friends—in danger if what he knows about you gets out," Turning to Kyle, she added, "Kyle, I know you say you love her, but there is no turning back once you've made that decision. We can just as easily take this memory away from you if that is what you decide."

Alee could hear his heartbeat quicken and his hands shook, but his voice was steady and calm. "I love her and I'm not leaving her…" Looking her in the eyes, he whispered, "…ever."

Elizabeth moved forward and took Kyle's hand in hers. "Then you must be protected. If you are going to join our world you will both have to learn the rules and follow them," Turning to her daughter, "Loraline, get your sister, and ask her to bring Phoebe. She'll want to bring in the kit, Alee will receive the mark today. There is no reason to delay it any longer."

"Yes, Mother," She turned to leave.

"Elizabeth, I'm not so sure—." Edith didn't even have time to finish before Elizabeth cut her off.

"I realize, granny, that you don't think this is a good idea. You didn't want Loraline and Jacinda to summon her in the first place. But they did. Aleerah is of age and she is family, and, as you said before, she should be treated as such."

"Do not speak to your grandmother in that tone Elizabeth," Estelle spoke up from her quiet seat across the room. "You may not agree with the way she leads this family, but that does not give you the right to openly disobey or be disrespectful to her. She is still our crone. It would do you well to remember that."

"I'm sorry Mother. I meant no disrespect. I only meant to help."

"Carry on," Estelle instructed.

Elizabeth turned back to Alee, ignoring her mother's watchful eyes as Edith quietly left the room, "Your transformation has already begun, and is moving at a much faster pace than we ever imagined it would. Your mother and father will explain what you need to know now," she said, nodding to Eric. "The rest you will learn in time. However, the most important thing right now is to make sure you are both protected."

Eric brought over another cup of red syrup—red syrup—red syrup—it's just red syrup. Alee was thirsty, and it did help ease the burning in her throat that had, over the past twenty-four hours, become a constant irritation. She worried that she would never be able to get rid of it completely. When she drank, Kyle didn't even flinch.

Elizabeth continued, "The necklace you wear, the hematite charm with the infinity symbol carved in the center, is the symbol of the underground. It is worn by all members, be they witches, night walkers, or any other member, as a way to identify each other. It is also a form of protection."

"Not all members" Eric corrected her.

"No, you are correct. Not all members bear the mark. There are some societies in which our founders have yet to allow the honor of the mark."

"Why?" No one turned to Alee as she asked. Their eyes were all trained on Eric and Estelle who seemed to be in the middle of a staring contest. "Why are all members not allowed to wear the mark?"

It was Eric who finally answered. "Politics."

"That is what you're going to tell her? Politics. That's all?"

"In every culture there are political reasons for some societies or races not being treated as equals. It may not be right, but it is the way of the world. The Underground is no different. I did not make the rules, nor do I agree with them all, but I am not at liberty to change them. So yes, my answer is politics. If you wish to elaborate more, then be my guest. I don't feel that the answer needs any further explanation at this time. Her understanding of the Underground will come much more easily as she is immersed in the society and as she learns her histories and her future."

"Alee—" Elizabeth continued cautiously, "—the Underground is not so different from the world you have always known," She glared into Eric's eyes.

"Your necklace, like mine..." She pulled her necklace out for Alee to see. "...bears the infinity symbol which is the mark of the Underground. It represents eternal life. It was chosen by the founders of the very first Underground society, in London, thousands of years ago, all of whom were vampires," She looked up at Eric who stood listening quietly to her explanation. No more interruptions—good. "Some members wear it on a necklace, as we do," As if on cue everyone around her began to pull their necklaces out for Alee to see. When Alee took her own necklace out from beneath her shirt it was easy to see that they were all identical, although some were smaller and others were larger. They were all made of black hematite and they all had the exact same infinity symbol carved into the middle.

"What does this necklace protect me from?"

"It insures that no harm shall come to you, at least not by the hand of a member of the Underground, so long as they know you bear that symbol. We have laws and we follow them," She glanced around the room and everyone was staring back at her. "However, it isn't the only protection you will need. No one knows you—you're an outsider. We need to make sure that you are recognized as one of us without question. Therefore you also need the mark of our coven."

"Which is?"

"The pentagram."

Alee's mouth dropped open and her eyes were wide. She gripped Kyle's hand tightly in her own. "Pentagram? You mean—" Alee's only knowledge of pentagrams came from horror films where pentagrams had been used in devil worship or black magic.

"Yes, the pentagram, but don't worry, pentagrams are not used in the ways Western society would have you believe.

The five points of the star represent the five elements; earth, air, fire, water, and the spirit. The pentagram is the chosen symbol used to identity members of our coven. The Wenham clan, if you will, has great power throughout the Underground. We are the largest coven within our society and bear the greatest power. This symbol identifies you as a protected member of our family. All who are born of the Wenham blood line, once they come of age as you have, not only burn or carve their symbol onto their "Book of Shadows" like other wiccans and wear the symbol of the Underground, they also accept the brand of our coven as a permanent part of their being. It's not only a birthright but an honor as well."

"What does that mean, 'a permanent part of their being?'" Nothing about that sentence put Alee's mind at ease.

Elizabeth turned to her mother for guidance. Estelle slowly rolled up the sleeve of her blouse and turned her wrist inside up so Alee could see the pentagram that had been burned into her flesh. What remained was a raised, white scar easily visible and easily identified. Alee, gasped in horror and fear. She tried to speak but nothing came out. She pulled her wrists close to her body not willing to let them burn her even if they did believe it was for her protection. Kyle pulled her closer to him on the couch.

Estelle's voice softened. "Don't worry, child. The days of branding are long past. The tattooed symbol on the inside of the wrist is easier and just as effective."

The memory of her first visit to the shop came flooding back. Just as Alee was about to ask about Jacinda's tattoo both Loraline and Jacinda came back in followed by a girl Alee vaguely recognized from school.

Kyle recognized her too. "I know you," he said, as Phoebe turned to look him in the eye, but she didn't say a word. "You go to Atlanta High don't you? You hang out with those—those, creep—" Phoebe gave him a look that said quit now or suffer the consequences, but he couldn't stop. The word-vomit had already begun and there was no keeping it in now, "—py kids. I mean different—different kids," Everyone was looking at him. OK, so different wasn't all that much better than creepy.

With raised eyebrows, Phoebe didn't even hesitate, "And you hang out with that bitch Victoria and her freakishly mute brother,"

"He's not a freak!" Alee snapped, standing up for the first time in hours. Her legs were wobbly beneath her, and she quickly sat back down, moving closer to Kyle for support.

"Right, he's completely sane," Phoebe said sarcastically before really looking at Alee for the first time. "You, what are you—?"

"Phoebe!" Jacinda snapped at her daughter. "Aleerah, this is your cousin Phoebe."

"Cousin?" Phoebe, Alee, and Kyle all said at the same time.

"I'm sorry about her poor manners" Jacinda apologized, as Phoebe rolled her eyes.

"It's fine, really," But Alee couldn't take her eyes off of Phoebe.

"As I was saying," Estelle continued. "A tattoo of the symbol is just as effective as the traditional branding. Jacinda, Loraline, please show Aleerah your marks," Both women rolled up the right sleeve of their blouses.

She got a closer look at Jacinda's tattoo. The pentagram sat in the center of a beautiful circle, which became much clearer the longer she stared at it. She saw now that it wasn't just a circle but a sphere, a full moon even. And the more she stared at it the more real it became, as if actually was shining and omitting light. What she wouldn't give to go back in time before that day—before her life began to change—before she lost her father—her mother—her *self*.

Loraline's tattoo was different—the symbol was centered in the middle of her delicate wrist with a rose wrapped around it. The petals were white with thin red veins going through them. A blood rose—that rare and beautiful flower. It was the same rose that she had seen year after year on her birthday cards. "A blood rose," she whispered. Loraline just smiled.

"All of the Wenham family, blood or chosen, bear the mark of our line," Loraline's voice was angelic.

Alee turned to Eric "Do you have one?"

He nodded rolling his sleeve up. A pentagram was burned into his wrist, branded just as Estelle's had been. "I am not of Wenham blood, but your mother chose me—" His eyes met Elizabeth's with a threat in them so strong it almost stopped Alee's breath, "—I wear the mark just as your grandfather William does. An *outsider* brought in," There was an emphasis on the work outsider, but nothing more was said.

Kyle was shaking his head. "Yours is branded—why not a tattoo? How did they—? I mean, you're a vampire right? You heal and everything. So, how did you get the scar when you were branded? Shouldn't it have just have, I don't know, vanished?"

"Because I am not of the blood, the mark had to be done in the traditional way. It was branded with burning silver. A vampire is unable to fully heal a wound created with silver as long as some of the silver remains," He ran his wrist over the mark then quickly rolled his sleeve back down.

Phoebe pulled up a chair and made herself comfortable in front of Alee. She went straight to work, focused on the task at hand. She opened the wooden box revealing small glass vials of ink, sterilized needles wrapped in sealed bags, and what looked like an electric pen. A portable tattoo machine Alee guessed. Alee's eyes, full of fear, met Kyle's as Phoebe lifted her hand to begin.

"No, wait!" Phoebe just looked at him. "Alee is afraid of needles. She's not ready," He was being a gentleman—her savior, and it was more romantic than anything anyone had ever done for her, and yet Phoebe seemed slightly disgusted, or maybe it was jealousy. "Isn't there something you can give her for the pain?"

"If she drinks, it will help to calm her nerves," Eric said as he brought her another drink. Alee willingly took the drink and downed it nervously.

The pain wasn't nearly as bad as she had expected. Just as she was starting to realize the pain, Phoebe was finishing up and putting her supplies away. When Alee looked down at her wrist there was a simple pentagram. It was about an inch in diameter, small and delicate. "It's so simple."

"It's beautiful," Loraline said, smiling at her niece. "You did good Phoebe."

Phoebe took Alee's wrist again and began wrapping it. "You need to give the skin time to heal. You can un-wrap it tomorrow evening, but make sure you keep it clean and use this throughout the next week or so," Phoebe handed Alee a small bottle of clear ointment then stood to leave.

As Phoebe pulled away Alee grabbed her wrist. "You don't have one,"

It wasn't a question, but Phoebe answered anyway. "No. I'm not old enough yet," Then she turned to walk away.

"Phoebe," Alee said, stopping her again. "I'm sorry I snapped at you earlier."

"It's OK. I'm sorry I said what I said. I didn't mean it." Then with a smile she turned to leave, carrying the box out with her.

25

Damian and Victoria made it home just in time to have dinner with their mom before they headed up to the attic for the rest of the night.

Sunday morning had come faster than they expected, and considering that it was the middle of summer, Damian and Victoria had decided to take an overnight excursion to meditate, read their father's journal and try to control, if possible, what was either their destiny or their curse. They left their mom a note on the kitchen counter that morning just after she left for work:

> Dear Mom,
> We're going camping in the state park for the night. We'll be back by Monday night. Don't worry.
> Love, D & V

They parked the car at the main entrance around eight o'clock in the morning, and began their long hike through the trails. Damian's plan was to follow the trail guide until they were just shy of the river, and then to veer off and build their campsite just off the riverbank. Although Victoria wasn't really the outdoors type, Damian had often spent his weekends doing day-long hikes through the local state park when he was younger. He had taught himself how to read a map, and work a compass, and was confident he would be able to maneuver his way through the trails here, too.

By the time they had found the perfect spot it was already noon. They had been walking for nearly four hours, not counting the frequent breaks Victoria repeatedly demanded. Had Damian been doing the hike alone, he figured he could have made it in less than two hours.

It took forty-five minutes for Damian to put up the tent, unpack their rucksacks, make a fire pit, and gather wood for the evening. Victoria sat on the riverbank with her bare feet dangling in the cool water. "I can't believe you made me walk all that way," she whined.

Damian rolled his eyes. "And, I can't believe you're wearing a brand new pair of hiking boots. I told you they'd give you blisters."

Damian sat outside the tent with a fire burning as he cooked hotdogs and toasted buns. Victoria was reading the journal aloud, while walking in circles around the fire pit.

"Victoria, be careful."

Victoria, ever confident, "I've got it—"

As she stepped forward, her shoelace caught on a piece of firewood and she stumbled forward, dropping the journal into the fire. Instinctively, Damian reached into the fire to grab the journal. He flung the book to the ground and Victoria stamped it out but an ember on Damian's shirt sleeve caught fire. The flames spread quickly, burning his entire forearm. Victoria poured the contents of her water bottle onto Damian's arm, drowning the fire. Searing pain tore through his body as he tried to pull the burned sleeve off of the melted flesh of his arm. He screamed as if his whole body were on fire. Victoria watched in horror as he began to convulse violently, scratching at his shoulders and trying desperately to tear the shirt away from his skin.

She tried to calm him down by wrapping her arms around his shoulders, but he shoved her away screeching through the pain, "Dooon'ttttttttoooouccccchhhhh." His voice was distorted, but she moved away and didn't try to touch him again. Suddenly, Damian propelled himself forward with his feet and dove through the air landing on what should have been his hands, but instead were the fur-covered paws of a beautiful snowy white wolf.

"Damian?" Victoria asked, uncertain and cautious. She slowly approached, not knowing if he could understand her, and worried that if he couldn't he might attack. She crouched down until she was eye to eye with the wolf, advancing in the same way you would an unknown animal. "Damian, are you OK?"

The light grey eyes of the wolf followed her as she moved, and he cocked his head to the side almost as if concentrating or thinking about something.

"I'm—OK."

Damian's voice was in her head. Damian sat across from her and they stayed like that for almost ten minutes just watching each other.

"What's it like?" she asked him.

He didn't answer, but instead lowered his head, as if bowing to her. Then standing up, he turned and ran into the woods. By the time the sun had gone down, Victoria was sitting by the fire with a blanket wrapped around her shoulders reading the journal and waiting for Damian to come back. Hoping he would. She desperately wanted to know everything.

The sound of twigs breaking in the woods just off to her right caught her attention, and she stood up quickly looking for anything she could use as a weapon. But when Damian walked through the thick trees wearing only the torn up shreds of the clothes he had worn earlier. Victoria hurried to his side and wrapped her blanket around him. He was tired and held his right arm close to his body. But aside from the reddened skin covering his arm from the top of his hand to his elbow, and a couple of minor blisters, he seemed to be all right. "Oh my God Damian, are you OK? It's already seven o'clock. Where have you been?" Victoria asked eagerly.

"I'm fine." He sat down next to the fire, just staring into the dancing flames.

"Look at your arm—shouldn't we go to a hospital or something?"

"V, I'm fine, really," he said as he pulled the blanket tighter around him. "It actually doesn't even hurt anymore."

Victoria finally sat down next to him, and pulled the journal back into her lap. "So—. Tell me about it."

They sat by the fire long into the night talking about his experience, and reading the more difficult entries of the journal over and over trying to interpret the meaning. It was almost five thirty the next morning, long after Victoria had fallen asleep, when Damian discovered a passage they had probably passed over at least a dozen times.

"For inexperienced shape shifters it is easy to get lost in the in-between. Most shape shifters, even those with years of experience, may require a personal artifact in order to aid them in their transformation back to human form. The use of a talisman, in the form of a charm, is the easiest and most commonly used. Such a talisman needs to be a representation of something that is personal to the shape shifter. It should be handcrafted by the shape shifter himself, stained with his blood, and worn at all times, be it in human form, or animal form."

Damian drifted off to sleep by the glow of the burning embers, as he read the passage over and over.

They spent the next morning walking the riverbank gathering as much driftwood, and other pieces of wood that they could find. They built a fire and, for breakfast, Victoria made toast and peeled oranges from their bags, while Damian sifted through their haul. He pulled his camping knife set out of the bag that he always carried when hiking, and started whittling away at a smooth piece of wood about the size of his fist. He wasn't sure what he was making, but followed his instincts, excited to see where they would take him.

Damian and Victoria worked on their talismans for a couple of hours. Victoria had created what looked like an abstract, hollowed-out heart with an infinity symbol wrapped around it. It was beautiful, and perfectly reflected Victoria's passion for life and love.

Damian's talisman, on the other hand, was raw and pure by comparison. He used the natural shape of the wood following the grain allowing it to almost form itself. When he finished, he held in his hand a delicate yet perfectly shaped sphere, covered in tiny wave like carvings.

"What is it?" Victoria asked as she examined his carving from over his shoulder.

"I don't know."

"It's pretty though." They sat there for a while in silence. "Blood huh?"

"Yup." Taking a deep breath Damian used the tip of his knife to prick the tip of his finger then passed the knife to his sister as he squeezed out a little blood, and smeared it into the wood. The result was a rust colored stain that seeped into the wood.

They strung fishing wire through the talismans to use them as necklaces, and spent the rest of the afternoon practicing controlling their transformations. It wasn't easy, and was even painful at first, but with each transformation it got easier. "We need to pack up," Damian said, as the sun began to set.

"Come on, just one more time," Victoria pleaded.

"It's getting late. We have a four-hour hike back to the car. If we don't leave now we won't make it back until morning."

"We could pack up, strap the bags to our back, and then shift. We'll be back at the car in less than an hour!" She was so proud of herself.

"V?!"

"Come on, live a little!" Victoria implored.

"Fine, but if we lose any of the gear in the shift you're coming back for it not me."

"Deal!"

The sun was starting to set as they packed up the contents of the tent. They stopped short when they heard a low growl outside. Victoria looked to her brother, ""Damian, did you hear that?" Looking through the window of the tent, they saw a wild mountain lion sniffing around their camp clearing.

Damian grabbed his knife and slowly unzipped the tent, waving his sister back. As he slipped out, the mountain lion mirrored his movements, taking a few steps back to give him room. They stood there for several long moments, and Damian realized that the mountain lion wasn't going to hurt them. He stuck his hand into the tent and waved his sister out, being careful not to make any sudden moves or startling noises.

"What's it doing?" She asked, slowly exiting the tent to stand behind her brother.

Damian just shook his head, unsure.

The mountain lion slowly nuzzled its nose under the blanket lying on the ground near the fire pit until it was fully covered. Damian and Victoria watched, waiting to understand what was happening. Slowly, the blanket began to writhe and expand. Then, standing before them wrapped in the blanket was their mother, Karen.

Victoria stumbled over her own feet and fell backward through the tent flap. Damian just stared. Karen didn't look happy.

"Don't you ever—and I mean ever— leave like that again!" Karen had never been the type of parent to yell. She had always coddled her children, almost too much. But there in the woods, she didn't hold back. "Do you know how stupid it was of you to come out here alone? Did you really think I didn't know what you were up to?"

They couldn't move or speak. They'd been told that their mother had never made her first transformation. It wasn't supposed to even be *possible* for her to be there right then, or to have found them the way she had.

"You're a—. How did—. What—?" Damian couldn't even form a complete sentence, but those few words were enough to turn his mother's look of anger into one of pure joy and amazement. It was the first time she had heard her son speak in over twelve years, and she ran to him, pulling him to her chest, and hugged him with all her might.

26

It was only three in the morning and still dark outside when Alee's father came to wake her up. It was a little startling, and a whole lot cool, how quiet and stealthy Eric could be. The fire in the fireplace had burned out, and it had to be about ten degrees cooler than she had remembered. Kyle was asleep on the floor next to the couch she was lying on. She didn't even remember falling asleep, but was thankful for the rest she had been able to get. She slipped on her shoes and stepped around Kyle, unsuccessfully trying to be as stealthy and quiet as Eric had been. She softly laid her blanket on top of Kyle's to make sure he stayed warm.

She followed Eric out the door and down the hall. "What time is it?" He didn't answer, as he kept walking, leading her through the beaded curtain and into the shop. "What's going on?" Alee wasn't yet fully awake, and couldn't quite wrap her head around what was happening. If she had been more aware, she might have been more frightened, and less cooperative and curious.

There were a few candles still burning in sconces along the walls of the shop, and the smell of cinnamon and apples wafted through the air. The only sound she could hear was her own footsteps on the hardwood floor underfoot. The world seemed to be asleep, until she heard the creaking of a door opening behind them. Instinct kicked in, and she turned with a speed that surprised her. She saw Loraline step through a door that led to what appeared to be a kitchen off the back of the shop. She was carrying a black fleece jacket in one hand and a thermos in the other.

With sleepy eyes, Alee looked back and forth between Eric and Loraline. Loraline handed him the thermos, and kissed him softly on the cheek. "Please, take care of her." She turned to Alee and handed her the jacket. "It's a little cool outside. This should keep you warm."

As Alee pulled it on, a dull pain shot through her arm. She moaned in discomfort and pulled her arm tight against her side.

"Are you OK? What's wrong?" Loraline sounded like a regret-ridden mother who wanted desperately to earn her child's acceptance.

"It's nothing. Just the tattoo, I guess. It burns a little." Rubbing her arm, "When can I take this bandage off?"

Loraline started buttoning up the jacket. "It'll feel better soon. You can take the bandage off this evening."

"We should go," Eric said. She followed him to the door, but before they stepped outside she felt Loraline's hand on

her shoulder. "Aleerah." When she turned to look at her—
mother, Loraline gave her a long hug and said, "Stay close to
your father."

Father. It still felt weird to think of this man as her
father. Her dad had died, and she hadn't even had time to
grieve. Eric was a stranger to her. How was it so easy for
them to find a place for her in their lives, as if they had been
there every day for the past seventeen years?

"She'll be fine. I promise." Alee could see that Eric had a
way of putting Loraline at ease. But the knowledge that he
was a vampire still seemed so unreal to Alee.

Before she knew it they were walking down a path
behind the shop, leading toward the woods. The full moon
overhead gave a delicate silver glow to the sky, lighting their
way. In the peace and quiet she realized how beautiful the
trees were under the haze of the moon.

Alee followed Eric closely, staying about three steps
behind him the whole way. When he stopped she stopped.
When he turned she turned. She wasn't sure where they were
going, but it seemed natural, somehow, to be there with him.
She could smell the pine trees all around her, and it reminded
her of Christmastime. It was a warm, welcoming scent and
made her smile as they walked.

They walked for twenty or thirty minutes, and came to a
large clearing at the edge of the tree line. Eric crouched down
low to the ground, and motioned for Alee to do the same. She
didn't see any movement in the clearing, and nothing, not
even crickets were making a sound. She had a restless feeling
that she already knew what they were there to do, but she

didn't want to believe it. Alee had never been very good at hiding her emotions, and she suddenly began to feel nauseous. She started to back away from him but he stopped her with a single touch of his hand on her arm.

"You're a hunter, Aleerah," Eric whispered softly, but his tone was as direct and commanding as she had ever heard. "It's in your blood, and you have to learn how to control it. If you don't, you could get hurt."

"But—"

"Trust your instincts. I'll be here to guide you." He twisted the lid off of the thermos, and as soon as the seal was cracked she could smell the sweet warm blood inside, and her throat became an inferno. She reached for the thermos, but instead of handing it over he held it just out of her reach and poured the contents out onto the ground. Something inside of her snapped, and her gums began to hurt—worse than ever before. Her fingers rubbed along the edge of her front teeth and found the sharp points of her eyeteeth slightly longer than she was used to. They weren't fangs, not in the Hollywood sense of the word, but in reality the idea was the same. Her eyes were as red as rubies and a low snarl rumbled in her throat.

"You're hungry. That's good, use it."

She peered at him through narrowed eyes, not focusing on what he was saying, but on the landscape that surrounded him.

"There's a deer twenty yards into the clearing." Her head snapped in that direction, and suddenly she could hear the blood rushing through the animal's veins. Her mouth began to water with anticipation, and he could see that she wanted to pounce. "You're not ready yet." She growled, watching him out of the corner of her eye, while still keeping the deep in sight. "Watch me, and I'll show you what to do." He took off swiftly, but as silently as a ghost.

She watched carefully. Suddenly the deer was down, and Eric was straddled on top of it, holding it down as it thrashed about, fighting to break free. He looked up at Alee and their eyes met. A simple nod, and she was at his side, but when she saw the deer up close, and looked into its soft black eyes, reality slapped her in the face.

Alee was so thirsty. Her throat burned horribly, and yet she couldn't bring herself to feed. "I can't. Oh God, I can't." She looked to Eric and pleaded, "I'm not ready." He let go and stepped aside. The deer hurried to a stand, and ran off into the distant woods without turning back. Alee just sat there with her head in her hands and sobbed, "I'm so sorry."

"Don't. Don't apologize. I know you didn't ask for this, and it isn't easy, but—." He took her hand in his, and held it tight. "I promise, it gets easier."

"But, why do I have to—."

"You can't survive without blood. It's who you are. It's who we are." His look reached deep into her soul, "It will come naturally after your first time, I promise." She shook her head. "Aleerah, you will die without blood. We can eat regular food, but it isn't enough to sustain us. It's a miracle you have lived this long, only receiving blood through transfusions once in a while. It isn't enough."

"I can't—I—"

"I can make it easier for you—if you want me to."

Alee didn't know what to say. Not knowing or understanding what Eric was able to do made her cautious. The idea of feeding made her nauseated, but the idea of dying if she didn't feed was terrifying. She closed her eyes, took a deep breath, braced herself and nodded. "Please."

Eric's hands were unnaturally cold as he placed them on her cheeks and it sent a chill down to her bones. "Open your eyes." She did, and as her gaze met his, she realized that although he looked so young and handsome, he possessed the knowledge of a thousand lifetimes.

His pupils spread across the iris of his eyes and beyond until from corner to corner all she saw was black. "Follow the smell and let your instincts guide you. Don't think about the kill—think about the taste. Think about the burning in your throat. Think about the thirst."

As if in a trance, she was on her feet, running in the direction the deer had gone. Eric followed behind as she slowly built up speed. She was weaving in and out of the trees, ducking under low branches, and leaping over fallen trees as if they weren't even there. The deer was about a hundred yards away now, but she could smell it. She charged ahead at full speed and tackled it to the ground. Stunned, the deer didn't try to fight back. Alee's "fangs" were exposed. She bit deep into the flesh under the soft white fur of its neck.

When Alee had her fill and the deer was drained of all life she could feel a rush of energy and warmth flowing throughout her body. She looked up to see Eric standing at her side. A smirk played on her lips as she wiped the blood away with the back of her hand, "Again?"

Eric nodded and she was off running. She wasn't hungry any more, but the hunt was invigorating. The cool fresh air in her lungs, the wind in her hair, and the feeling of true liberation, was like nothing she had ever experienced. Two more deer later, they were resting below a tall oak tree watching the first hints of a sunrise come up on the distant horizon. "We should get back," Eric sighed.

"Do we have to?" Alee sounded like a kid in a candy store not wanting to leave.

He laughed. "You need your rest. Besides, it's almost daylight."

"But the sun doesn't—"

Eric shook his head, and stood up. "It doesn't affect you yet, but the more you change the more it will. And although I can tolerate it I prefer to be inside during the early morning hours." He extended his hand out to her and pulled her to her feet.

"How will it affect me?" she asked timidly.

"It will make you tired, drained of energy. It will decrease your body's ability to heal itself." She swallowed, almost chocking on her own breath. "You won't burst into flames if that's what you're worried about, but things like hunting become virtually impossible. Eventually, with time, your days and nights will shift. Your body will require rest during the daylight hours—less than you need now—but at least a few hours until you're older, and you will be naturally wide awake through the evening hours."

"Hmm." She thought about it for a moment then stretched, jumped up and down a couple of times then smiled. "Race you back." And she was gone, with Eric in close pursuit.

By the time she made it back to the Black Onyx her eyelids were getting heavy, and all she could think about was sleep. She slipped off her shoes, and quietly curled up on the couch as if she had never left, already asleep by the time her head hit the pillow.

Less than an hour later, Kyle sat up to see—not Alee, but Aleerah— just a few feet away from him. Her golden hair spread out across the pillow, and her delicate yet sun-kissed skin had a slight glow in the dim light. "Wow." She was beautiful, and yet, for a moment, he longed for just one more glimpse of the Alee he had fallen in love with. They had told him that with time he would see her this way, but he didn't expect it to happen so quickly.

He pulled his cell phone off the coffee table, only to find the battery dead. There was a land-line phone on the end table, and he quietly lifted the handset. The dial tone blared in his ear, and he dialed the number for his voice mail service. He had missed over two dozen messages, and they were virtually all the same: Dani crying, his mother telling him about Alee's death, Dani scolding him for being gone with everything going on, and more of the same. He stretched and, as silently as he could, he folded the blankets he had been using, gathered his things and left the room—closing the door behind him.

Kyle found a bathroom down the hallway and managed to tame his bed-head with some water. He rinsed out his mouth, trying to get rid of the morning breath as best he could, and made his way back down the hall to the main shop. When he walked through the curtain, he found Loraline and Eric already there.

Loraline was like sunshine in the morning. He could see where Alee got her looks. If he hadn't known the truth he might have thought they were sisters. "Good morning Kyle. Can I get you anything to eat?"

"I'm not really hungry, but if you have coffee—"

She led him through the door, behind the counter, and into the kitchen. "Do you take cream and sugar?" Loraline asked.

"No sugar, just cream please." He sat at the table while Loraline fixed his coffee.

"Be careful, it's hot," she said as she handed him the cup.

Kyle took the cup and sipped the hot coffee. The rich scent woke him up right away. "Wow. That's really good."

"What's your plan for the day, Kyle?" asked Eric, and Kyle started to wonder if vampires even needed to sleep. Eric looked like he had been up for a while.

"I got a voice mail, well about two dozen actually, friends letting me know about Alee and her dad—I mean—Mr. Moyer—. Anyway, I have to head home for their—you know." His throat started to tighten and his palms were sweating.

"Funeral?" Loraline asked. "But, it's so soon."

"Dani said that Mrs. Moyer didn't want to wait. She's having a short service at the cemetery, and a small gathering of family and friends at her house afterwards." The tension was thick, and Kyle was finding it was awkward trying to have a normal Sunday morning conversation with a witch and a vampire.

"It's probably best that you slip out before Aleerah wakes up," said Loraline, wiping down the counter as if it was just another morning.

"Right—Aleerah—it is going to take some time getting used to that."

"Should we expect you back this evening?" Loraline asked.

Kyle was flattered that Loraline had taken such an interest in him. But something about the way Eric distanced himself made him uncertain of Loraline's motives.

"I'll be back. Just tell Alee—Aleerah—that I'll come back as soon as it's over and I can leave without anyone getting suspicious." He downed the rest of his coffee while walking to the sink, rinsed his cup and put it down as if he'd done it a thousand times.

Eric held the donut he had been about to take a bite of and nodded his head, "We'll tell her. And Kyle, she'll be fine. She's going to need her rest today, and she has some work to do before she'll be ready to go back to school in a of couple weeks, but I promise you, she'll be fine."

Kyle choked on his coffee. "Back to school? You mean, Atlanta High—for our senior year? Seriously?"

"It's important for her to get an education and to graduate. The fact that she now knows who she really is does not change that. If anything it makes it more important. Her days are going to get harder for her, and it's important that she finish school before the transition becomes too overwhelming and draining on her," Eric said somberly.

"That's great—actually. Thank you." Kyle didn't know what else to say.

"You should probably get home. I'm sure your parents are worried about you." Loraline had already made him another cup of coffee, and handed it to him in a travel mug she had pulled out of the cupboard.

"Thanks again," he said as he accepted the mug.

Loraline surprised him by pulling him in close and wrapping her arms around him for a hug. "Go now, but come back when you can. She's going to need your support."

27

Alee's funeral wasn't something Kyle was looking forward to, but knowing he and Alee would be spending senior year together made the day at least a little better. The Black Onyx was only about a twenty-five minute drive from town, if you knew where you were going and, considering that he had been beginning to think that Alee would be shipped off to some weird Transylvanian version of Hogwarts or the Xavier school for Higher Learning, this seemed like a much better option. He didn't know much about her new world, and he didn't know where—or even if—he fit, but they were still going to get their senior year together. And if all went well, the way he hoped, they would be together long after that.

Kyle had to go home to shower and change before the funeral. He wore a black pinstriped suit, his only suit actually. He had gotten it for his cousin's wedding a few years back, and he remembered how much Alee had liked it when his mother had shown her the photos.

Arriving at the cemetery just after nine it was still fairly cold for a summer morning. There was a cool breeze and cloudy grey skies that threatened to rain, but it hadn't started yet. Cars were lined up on both sides of the cemetery path for at least a quarter of a mile in both directions. It seemed like everyone in town had turned out for the funeral of David and Alee Moyer.

As Kyle walked along the cemetery road toward the black canopy and rows of small black chairs in the distance, he could feel the heavy weight of loss surrounding everyone. As he got closer he could hear muffled cries, and quiet whispers. "She was so young—do you really think it was an accident—her whole life ahead of her—he loved her so much—I can't imagine how Martha must be feeling—." He tried not to think about Alee's father, or even Alee. The thought of her funeral, even knowing she wasn't really dead, was just about more than he could handle.

Alee's mother wore a long black dress, black heels, and a black wrap around her shoulders, and a black veiled hat. The veil covered her eyes but couldn't hide the tears that soaked the handkerchief that she held tightly against her cheeks. She was trying to stay strong, but with her husband and her daughter gone, there was little hope for that. Seeing her so weak, Kyle couldn't imagine that there was ever a time when she had hunted and killed witches and vampires. This woman who had always been so kind and gentle, who had taken such good care of Alee—how could she be the same woman Edith had told them about? It just didn't seem possible. Then again, a lot of seemingly impossible things had been happening these days.

Kyle took his place standing next to Mrs. Moyer, focusing on his shoes as people from all over town came to pay their respects. Tyler stood to Kyle's left. On the other side of Alee's mom, Danielle sobbed. She had just lost her oldest and best friend in the whole word. Life was crumbling all around them.

"Where are Damian and Victoria," Kyle asked Tyler quietly as the pastor stood up to address those in attendance.

"Don't know. I texted Damian, and left five messages for Victoria but never heard back.

"We are gathered here to celebrate the lives of David and Alee Moyer, father and daughter, taken from our world to serve God in his ultimate plan." Sorrow fueled Father Johnson's service as he celebrated David's and Alee's lives with their family, friends, neighbors, co-workers, and Alee's classmates. As the service ended Kyle saw Victoria, Damian, and their mother pulling up.

"It has always been a tradition of our church to assist our loved ones in their burial," the pastor continued. "Their family members as well as friends are invited at this time to lay a shovel of dirt into each of the graves. If you should choose to do this, remember that we do it so that we are not leaving the burial of our loved ones to the kindness of strangers. This is the last good deed you are able to do for them, an act of kindness that can never be repaid." Father

Johnson bent down, pulling the shovel from the mound of dirt between the two graves, and nodded toward Alee's mother.

One by one, starting with Martha and Alee's friends, everyone in the congregation made their way to the graves and slowly poured a single shovel full of dirt into each grave. When it was Kyle's turn he almost couldn't do it. Martha put a hand on his shoulder. "It's OK," she said. Martha, a grieving mother and wife, had found the strength to comfort him. "Alee is in a better place now." Through her sorrow she smiled at him, and after he finished at the grave she pulled him into her arms and hugged him close. "She loved you very much. I could see it in her eyes and hear it when she spoke your name."

"Thank you." Kyle didn't pull away right away. Not until he noticed the first drop of rain that landed on his face. When he looked up to the clouds overhead, a bright streak of lightening split the sky and a loud crash of thunder made his heart race, and everyone around him look up. People started to disperse—back to their cars and out of the cemetery.

Damian was the last person to take up the shovel. He looked down into the open graves and clung to his sister's hand as they silently prayed at Alee's gravesite while people walked past, saying their goodbyes and dropping red and white roses on the mounded earth. Martha stood between the graves, watching as each rose fell. She fell to her knees, and finally gave herself over to the pain and grief. No one touched her or spoke to her. It was clear that she needed to be alone, and for the next half hour she didn't move, as her close friends, and Alee's, remained at her side, silently waiting and watching as the rain poured down around them.

The majority of the funeral guests gathered at the Moyer home after the service. Some brought food: casseroles, salads, fruit baskets. Others brought flowers and plants, accepted symbols of new life.

Damian, Victoria, Tyler, Kyle, and Dani didn't stay at the Moyer home for long. They made their appearance, gave their condolences to Martha, and then went next door to Dani's house. By five o'clock they were sitting in a circle on the floor of the living room nibbling on a plate of brownies and a bowl of chips. It was so familiar, just like they had done so many times before. The only thing missing was Alee.

Dani was telling everyone the story of when she and Alee had first met. "I was only six when my parents moved us here. Alee had been born here, lived here all her life. I remember at six she was so tiny. I used to pick her up and carry her around the yard on my back. I had to be at least three or four inches taller than her, even then."

"The day we moved in, she came knocking on the door, and my mom answered. Alee was so excited when I invited her in. She just squeezed herself in between my mom and the door, and before our moms knew what had happened we were up in my room playing with my dolls." Dani tinkered with a half-heart charm that dangled from her bracelet. "We've been best friends ever since."

Kyle put his arms around her, and she buried her face in his chest. Ever since the camping trip, Dani had felt a little jealous of the time he got to spend with Alee. But sitting there

in his arms at that moment, she understood why Alee had
become so attached to him. He had a calmness that seemed to
radiate all around him, and it flowed over her now. She saw
for the first time how sweet and caring he really was. It was a
side of him that not many people got to see, and even fewer
got to experience. "Thank you," Dani said, smiling up at him
as she shifted away, and back to Tyler.

Damian had been eyeing Kyle all day. His sister and
mother were still the only ones who knew that he was able to
speak again. Maybe this wasn't really the right time, being
that one of his best friends had just passed away, but to him it
seemed like the perfect time—the only time. Damian was
finally able to tell Alee how he felt about her, to really talk to
her, and she would never be here to hear it. "I loved her."

Everyone turned to him and stared. He could speak?
What had he said? He loved Alee? Even Victoria was
surprised by what he had announced. Kyle just looked at him.
He knew that Damian and Alee were close, but he never
thought—love—? Kyle loved her too, and she loved him
back. He realized how Damian must have felt, seeing them
together, and what he must be feeling with her gone now, but
there was nothing he could do to help him.

"I loved her, but you got her," Damian whispered,
looking at Kyle as if they were the only two people in the
room. "Where were you? Why didn't you take care of her?
Why didn't you protect her?"

"Where was I? Where were you? And, what would it
have mattered anyway? She was sick, Damian. There wasn't
anything any of us could have done. Even the doctors

couldn't help her." Kyle couldn't believe Damian's audacity. "You loved her? How do you think I felt about her? Do you think I was just playing around with her? I loved her. I still love her."

"Stop it!" Dani hissed. "This isn't the time to be fighting."

Even though Kyle knew the truth—knew that he was going to leave here and go straight back to her arms that evening, he still couldn't control his anger, or his pain at the thought of her death. He *knew* that she was still alive, but she would never be Alee again. Kyle saw now what that meant, and how it affected everyone who loved her. He would still be with her, but what about everyone else who loved her? What about all of her friends? What about her mom? It just didn't seem fair. It was too much to give up. It was too much of a sacrifice.

Kyle couldn't take it anymore. He was surrounded by friends, and yet he felt completely alone. "I'm sorry. I can't—. I can't do this." He gave Dani a hug that lasted a little longer than maybe it should have, but somehow it felt more final than just a simple goodbye, and then he walked out the door without looking back.

He had already packed a bag when he stopped by his house earlier that morning so he drove straight back to the Black Onyx. He had to see her and make sure she was OK. He hadn't liked the idea of leaving her there alone all day, but he couldn't bring her to her own funeral, even if no one would have recognized her. How would he have explained bringing a date to his girlfriend's funeral? We met on the way? No, there had been no way to make that work.

It was dark by the time Kyle arrived at the shop, and there were no cars in the parking lot, but he could see that the house lights were on. He grasped the large metal handle of the front door, opened the door, and walked in slowly, looking around before stepping in too far. "Hello?" No one was there. He walked a little farther in. "Alee?" Suddenly his back was against the wall, with Eric's hand clasped tightly over his mouth.

Eric slowly lifted his hand away from Kyle's mouth, and asked, "Are you alone?" Kyle struggled to break free and Eric pushed him harder against the wall. "I asked if you're alone."

"Yes! I'm alone. What the hell?"

Eric let him go, but didn't step away. "I had to make sure you weren't bringing anyone else with you."

"Why would I? I get that you don't trust me, but I'm not going to do anything to hurt her. Can you say the same?" Eric didn't answer. "Where is she?"

"She's out back, but she knows you're here. Give her a few minutes to get cleaned up and she'll be out."

"Out back doing what? Its pitch black outside and there's nothing around for miles." Realizing now that he was alone in a secluded room in the middle of nowhere yelling at a vampire made Kyle pause. Eric watched Kyle scanning the shelves and tabletops, understanding that he was looking for something he could use as a weapon if it came to that.

Eric pulled a sharp wooden stake from his jacket pocket and held it out to Kyle. "Here," he commanded, but Kyle didn't move.

"Take it. It will make you feel better." Kyle reached out tentatively and took the stake, holding it tightly against his chest. "Just don't EVER use it on my daughter. Do you understand me?" As Kyle watched, the pupils of Eric's eyes expanded until his entire eye was black—not a spot of color or white to be seen.

"I understand."

Then, just as quickly as it had happened, his eyes were back to normal. Kyle looked down at the wooden stake. It was about seven inches long, sanded smooth all around, and had a sharp point. It wasn't heavy but it wasn't light either. There was nothing particularly special about it—just plain hard wood —but it felt good in his hands, like it fit. "Why would you give this to me? I mean—you're—." He stopped when Eric took a step forward.

"You don't trust me. I get that. I don't completely trust you yet either. This is a gesture of peace." Eric put his hands up to show he wasn't armed, and Kyle lowered the stake to his side.

"You're very important to my daughter, so you are important to me. I won't hurt you, but if this makes you feel safer, you should keep it with you. But you and Aleerah both still have a lot to learn about our society." Just then a door slammed somewhere down the hall. "She's coming. You might want to put that away."

Kyle slipped off his jacket, and the stake fit easily in the pocket. When Alee came through the beaded curtain, it was like seeing her for the first time. She radiated with life. Her skin, her hair, her eyes, her smile, she simply glowed. It was cliché—cheesy—corny, and yet tender and loving all at the same time—he was enchanted at the sight of her. Before he realized what was happening she was in his arms hugging him.

"Oh my God, you're never going to believe the day I've had." Aleerah seemed to be bubbling with energy as she danced around the room, pulling him with her. "Did you know I can run? I mean really run." Her smile was radiant. "Mom and Dad never let me run, but I can run. Like fast! It's so exhilarating." Kyle was having a hard time focusing on what she was saying. His mind was still on the stake in his pocket and the conversation he had just had with Eric. But he followed as she led him through the shop and down the hall. Looking back he saw that Eric was following after them.

Alee stopped in the middle of the hallway and asked, "Want to see something?" She didn't wait for him to respond, just opened a door and pulled him into a room in the back of the shop. It was a bedroom. "In here." As Eric approached more quickly, Alee called out, "We're fine. We'll be out soon." Then she shut the door and locked it before turning back to Kyle.

They were finally alone, and time seemed to stand still. Kyle stood near the door with his back to the wall as Alee sat on the edge of a bed, kicking her shoes off. It was a large, elegantly appointed bedroom, with a wall of bookshelves, a seating area with a tea table, and large windows overlooking the lawns and the forest beyond. But the walls of the room seemed to close in as Alee realized that this was the first time that she and Kyle had ever been alone in a bedroom together. In fact, it was the first time since her change that they'd been alone together at all. Alee wasn't experienced, in any sense of the word, and she hadn't even thought about what impression she might have been giving him now. She started to fidget with the blanket as she tried to think of something to say.

The bed was a dark wooden sleigh bed, with an antique quilt coverlet. But the bed was nothing to the amazing woman sitting on top of it. Kyle was finding it hard to breathe. As he stepped toward her she smiled, and the rest of the world melted away.

"Is this your room?"

"Yup. Pretty nice huh? It's a step up from the couch in the other room, for sure."

He looked around the room taking it all in. "So, you'll be staying here then?"

Aleerah nodded. "Where else am I supposed to go?"

"Yeah, I guess there really isn't anywhere else." Kyle strolled around the room, checking everything out as he went. "It's nice, really nice. I think it's about double the size of my room." A laugh got caught in his throat. He proceeded to ramble on about the books on the shelves, the furniture, anything he could think of to talk about.

As he passed her, she grabbed his hand and pulled him in front of her. Kyle stood there silently.

"It's OK, don't be nervous," Alee said.

Then he saw it —for only a split second—Aleerah's pupils expanded and contracted as she spoke. *Has she always been able to do that?* He wondered. Before he could open his mouth to ask, he forgot what he was going to say. When he looked down, Aleerah was un-wrapping the bandage covering her right arm. She smiled that breathtakingly innocent smile. "I've been waiting all day to take this bandage off, but I didn't' want to do it without you."

Aleerah's skin was completely smooth, healed around the tattoo as if she'd had it for years. With just the tips of his fingers Kyle traced her tattoo—the circle and the short sharp lines of the pentagram. Despite, or even because of its incredible simplicity, there was something a little ominous about it.

"Wow—. It's beautiful," he said. "Does it hurt?" Alee shook her head. He raised her wrist to his lips and kissed it softly. His lips were warm on her skin, and sent a shiver up her arm. When he looked up, her face was inches from his, and he leaned in closer until their lips were barely touching. Her body tingled with excitement and she wanted to pull him closer and devour him with kisses. Her body was warming up from the inside as she breathed him in. She could feel her throat begin to burn at the awareness of the blood rushing through his veins, just under her fingertips. With each thump of his heart hers began to pound harder in her chest.

Alee pulled him closer, until they were lying on the bed in a tangled embrace. He rolled her on top of him as he effortlessly pulled her t-shirt over her head and tossed it to the floor. The buttons of his dress shirt seemed to come undone all on their own, and his warm chest against her skin made her tremble with pleasure. A quiet moan escaped his lips as she ran her tongue along his neck.

Eric banged loudly on the door and commanded, "You're wanted. Now!" Alee bit her lip as she pulled away, realizing how far things had almost gotten. She pulled her t-shirt back on and took a couple of deep breaths to calm herself. She noticed that Kyle was doing the same as he buttoned his shirt and tucked it into his pants.

As Alee and Kyle stepped into the kitchen, they were greeted with awkward stares. Aleerah quickly glanced down at her shirt to make sure it wasn't inside out or backwards.

Elizabeth took Aleerah's hand in hers and whispered to the others. "Have you ever seen anything like this?"

Estelle stared, and shook her head. Elizabeth lifted Aleerah's arm, and the others were silent. Alee looked up at the tattoo on her wrist. It was as if the tattoo had come alive. The once-black ink was now luminous silver, glowing just beneath her skin. Surrounding the pentagram were vines, twisting and turning around her wrist. They hadn't been there moments before, and Alee was breathless at the sight.

Kyle looked down at his own wrist, rubbing it as if it were burning. When he lifted his sleeve there was a small pentagram on the inside of his wrist—a mirror image of Alee's tattoo, only there were no vines surrounding his. The skin burned, but the pain was already starting to fade.

Nobody said a word for a long time.

Elizabeth finally broke the silence. "That's not possible. He isn't even a—."

"They have been touched by the goddesses," Estelle explained, as if that should suffice. Aleerah and Kyle just looked at one another in hushed silence.

The End for Now

Keep reading for an exciting preview of

The next installment of

the Blood Angel Series
by Nina Soden

http://www.ninasoden.wordpress.com
http://www.facebook.com/BloodAngelSeries
http://www.twitter.com/Nina_Soden

1

The blaring alarm could have raised the dead, but Alee didn't even flinch. It was the pounding on her bedroom door that finally jolted her back to life. "Aleerah, wake up. You have to leave in twenty minutes." It was her mother. Not the mother she had known and loved all her life—no, this was the mother she never even knew existed until a few weeks ago—until the man she had always called daddy—the man she had known as her father—died—suddenly—and way too early in life.

She rolled over, turned off the alarm, and struggled out of bed. *What to wear?* It was the first day of school, and Alee was once again the new girl. The new girl in her senior year at the school she had attended the previous year. Something about that just didn't seem right. She had already reinvented herself once. Why should she have to do it again? Oh yeah, because her life had been turned upside down. She was now the actual birth daughter of a vampire and a witch, who were happy to have her back in the family. Besides that, everyone she had ever known in her life thought she was dead—had, in fact, attended her funeral. Yeah, that's as good a reason as any.

Kyle and Alee had gone over the plan a thousand times with her new—real—parents, Eric and Loraline, in these past two weeks, but Alee still wasn't sure if she was going to be able to pull it off. Pretending not to know anyone was going to be hard, but keeping herself from running up to her best friend Dani, and telling her everything, and apologizing for lying to her—*that* was going to be the real test. Alee would see Kyle every day, and it was going to suck not being a couple at school, but at least she knew that would change in a few weeks. They just had to play the game, making everyone believe their relationship was just beginning. It might even be fun to play the role of a brand new couple in a fun new relationship: flirting, passing notes and having their first date all over again—especially since they never really had a "first date."

The bathroom was thick with steam, and yet the air was cold on her exposed skin, as she stepped out of the shower wrapped in a plush warm towel. Her bathroom was huge, with marble countertops, a glass sink, and a natural stone floor and shower. Her closet door was just to the left of her shower, and inside was a wardrobe that made the local department store she was used to shopping in look like a thrift shop. After the dad who had raised her died, there was a large bank account left to her in the will. Since she was also supposedly dead, the money went to the beneficiary, Edith Wenham. Apparently, the Wenhams had been paying her parents to take care of her since she was just a baby. Being the stubborn people her parents had been, they had refused to keep the money. Instead, they had put it into an account for Alee. Even in the event that Alee didn't live long enough to use the money herself, they didn't want to have anything to do with it. They didn't want to take charity from "witches." Now it was Alee's, and she was having fun.

Her new life was going to take some getting used to, not that she minded this part of it. Not entirely anyway.

Her new parents hadn't had time to put together all of the paperwork for her new life. Everything had just happened too quickly. They had promised to have a driver's license for her within the month. Without a license, though, or even a car to call her own anymore, Alee would have to ride to school with her cousin Phoebe. Phoebe had just gotten her driver's license a few months before, but drove as if she had been driving for years. Phoebe sped around corners without even pretending to brake, while Alee gripped the edges of her seat and just concentrated on breathing without throwing up, rather than looking out the windows at the view.

"Take it easy, I know what I'm doing." Phoebe's lips curled up in a wicked smirk and the fact that she was looking at Alee, instead of at the car they were quickly gaining on, didn't really put Alee's mind at ease.

Alee just nodded, gripping the edge of the seat even tighter, "Yeah—I can tell. Just get me there without killing me—please."

Phoebe just laughed, but after one more quick right turn she slowed to a crawl. Atlanta High School was just ahead on the right, and she pulled into the parking lot and eased up to the walking path that led to the main entrance to let Alee out.

"You're not parking?"

"Nah, you have new student orientation—I have another hour before I have to be in class. But don't worry, I'll be back. You made me miss coffee this morning having to be here so early." She started to drive off as Alee was shutting the door, but then only five feet up slammed on the breaks causing the tires to squeal as they came to a stop. Phoebe lowered the window and yelled after Alee, who had already started up the path. "Hey, Aleerah, you want any?"

This was the first really nice thing Phoebe had done since Alee had arrived at The Black Onyx a few weeks ago. "Really?"

"Sure," Phoebe nodded, "I mean, we're cousins right? I guess that means we're on the same side—kind of like—friends."

"Yeah—thanks—just a—." No point finishing, since Phoebe was already driving away.

Phoebe called back, "I know how you like it. No worries—go have fun with the new kids. Don't forget to play nice." She was out of the parking lot and around the corner so fast it was almost as if she had never been there.

Alee stood there on the curb looking out at the sad, barren parking lot, took a deep breath, and then turned toward the admissions building.

Looking around the main office Alee realized just how strange this year was starting out to be. She had been in the school office lots of times over the past two years, and even a few times during her sophomore year when her parents had home schooled her. Now she was one of five new students sitting quietly, waiting for Principal Davis to get in. Gregory Davis, or Principal Greg as he liked students to call him, wasn't your typical principal. That is to say, he didn't walk around the school scolding students and rushing them off to class. He actually seemed to care about the students, their interests, and their futures. He was a good looking man for his age, which Alee figured must be around forty-seven or forty-eight, because he had the same distinguished salt and pepper hair that her father David—the man who raised her—had had.

The school secretary, Ms. Thatcher, an older woman in her early fifties, was sitting at the front desk sifting through stacks of papers and distributing them into the teachers' mailboxes along the back wall behind her station when the phone rang. "Hello. Yes, Mr. Davis, they're all here." She looked out and smiled at the five students sitting in the wobbly hard plastic chairs on the other side of her office countertop. Ms. Thatcher had always been nice to Alee, and having her there on her first morning was somehow making her feel a little better about everything. "Yes sir. OK sir. I'll take care of it." She went into the principal's office. "All right, I'll see you later this morning."

Later this morning? OK, so Principal Greg wasn't going to show up for new student orientation. That wasn't the worst news Alee could have gotten. She preferred Ms. Thatcher anyway.

There was a section of the front office countertop that could be lifted to allow people to walk in and out of the back office area—the kind you might find in a cheap backwoods bar—but this one wasn't covered with beer bottle rings, cigarette burns, or chunks of chewing gum. This one was spotless and fully functional. Atlanta High was pretty old, and a lot of it was falling apart, but every year money was put into renovating and re-furnishing one area or another. The renovations had started just four years ago, the summer before Alee's freshman year, and the first area to benefit was the main office. The school administration said that a prospective parent's first impression of the school was the front office. Half a million dollars had gone into beautifying and revitalizing the lobby, the front desk, the school counselor's office, and of course the principal's office. Where the money had come from no one really knew, and the school board wasn't saying.

The second section of the school to be renovated was the gym. It used to be just one big room, not much different than one of the classrooms, except for the two basketball hoops at either end. No bleachers—no locker rooms—nothing—and I mean nothing fancy. The new gymnasium, or "stadium," as a lot of the kids like to call it, was a completely different building. It was back behind the main school facility, and it not only had separate locker rooms for boys and girls, but separate locker rooms for the different team sports: basketball, football, even baseball. Not to mention the state of the art weight room and exercise facility. Everyone in town was still wondering why a small town like Atlanta would need such a high-tech school.

Ms. Thatcher came out of the principal's office with a stack of bright blue and orange school-emblem files, and raised the lift-up portion of the countertop. A smile brightened her face as she spoke. "These are your class schedules, locker assignments, school map, and some other information about our campus." Yes, she called it a campus. It made sense, seeing how different it was now from the old facility, which had been a single small building. The new campus consisted of: the main building, which housed all the academic classes, the cafeteria, and the school offices; the new state of the art stadium that was used for sports activities and gym classes; and the new Creative Arts Building that was for drama, music, and art classes. "But, we'll get to the paperwork later." Ms. Thatcher smiled. "First, shall we take a walk?" She acted almost giddy, which seemed out of place for someone her age.

Alee just nodded, keeping in line with the behavior of the other students sitting with her. Not a single one had said a word since she came in, and she wasn't sure she should be the first one to start the cycle of conversation. As a small child she had been overly outgoing, but she found that as she got older she was more of a silent observer. She was curious to know what grades they were in, but figured she would find out soon enough. Although she wasn't really a "new" kid on the block, no one else knew that, and it might be nice to have some friends right off the starting block.

"All right then, shall we begin the tour?" Ms. Thatcher was nodding and walking out the office door as she spoke. Alee imagined, from the woman's bubbly behavior that Ms. Thatcher had probably been a cheerleader back in her high school days—that is if they even had cheerleaders back then.

Great, a tour, Alee thought as they all got up to follow Ms. Thatcher out of the office. She rolled her eyes toward the other students, and a couple of them chuckled, but one, a dark haired slender young boy just stared at her. He didn't smile— he didn't even blink. She had noticed him looking at her a couple of times before while they were sitting in the lobby listening to Ms. Thatcher's phone conversation. Now it was more obvious, seeing as he didn't look away when their eyes met this time, as he had before, but somehow Alee wasn't uncomfortable, like she normally would have been. Instead, she felt almost intrigued by the intensity of his gaze. She wanted to know what he was thinking, but would have to settle for just knowing he was most likely thinking about her.

"This hallway houses all of the seniors' lockers. Let me see, how many seniors do we have here?" Alee raised her hand, looking around at the other students, noticing that the dark haired boy raised his hand too. "Wonderful, and what is your name young lady?" Ms. Thatcher asked her.

"It's Aleerah."

"Aleerah, such a pretty name. All right then, the senior lockers will be down this hall." The dark haired boy just nodded in acknowledgement. He had moved behind Alee and was standing just inches away from her.

"My name's Jathan by the way." He whispered it into Alee's ear.

Hmmm, interesting name—Jathan. She turned to meet his eyes, but he had already backed away.

Ms. Thatcher scanned her notes, "Let's see, the rest of you are sophomores—your lockers will be this way." She moved quickly for someone of her age. Looking back over her shoulder, she called, "Come along. Follow me."

Jathan hung back watching as the rest of the group moved down the hall. Alee looked back a couple of times but he just stood there. When they turned the corner toward the library, he was finally out of view. She wondered what he was doing—why he had decided to ditch the tour—and just how much trouble he might get in. *Oh well, not my problem,* she decided.

The library was the next big renovation that they had done after the stadium. It had been completed the summer before her junior year, and it was amazing. For a lot of high school students a school library isn't really a place they care to go, but Alee had never been like a lot of other high school students. She loved to learn. From the time she started school she was always a straight "A" student. When she first learned about the plans to renovate the old library she had sent a letter to the school board with a few suggestions, and when she started her junior year she was pleased to see that they had actually incorporated all of them into the design. Even though she couldn't prove that it was her influence that got the changes made, she was still secretly proud of herself.

The first of her recommendations had been wireless internet and multiple computer stations throughout the library. Next she had asked for quiet study rooms. They incorporated five soundproof glass rooms along the back wall, each with privacy blinds, comfortable seating, a conference room style table and chairs for group project work, and a computer station. Alee's last major recommendation had been to replace the ancient card catalog file with a computerized system. Now there were two dedicated computers near the front entrance for that purpose alone. They had also added a small coffee café, to which Alee was quickly addicted.

"This is the library; I'm sure you'll all want to spend a good amount of your time here." The brunette girl standing on Ms. Thatcher's right was snickering, but as Ms. Thatcher pushed open the door to the library her mouth closed, and the snickering ceased.

"Wow," she gaped, as she walked in circles around and around looking at the computers, hardwood floors, beautifully crafted study desks, green glass lamps, leather covered seats, and rows upon rows of shelves filled with books. Then she noticed the coffee café. "It's beautiful! What time does it open?"

Ms. Thatcher just smiled, "Not until after first period. Now, as I said—" Ms. Thatcher scanned through her papers. "—Miss Wilkins, I'm sure you'll all want to spend a good amount of your time here. We have found that a lot of the students find it very relaxing between classes, or even during their lunch hour. Here at Atlanta High we participate in altered scheduling, allowing for longer rest periods between classes. You'll find we aren't the typical high school." She led them back out the door and into the hallway, stopping briefly once they were all out. "Now—do we have everyone?" She seemed to be looking back into the library.

"I'm sorry." Alee interrupted, "I just need to run back to the bathroom for a minute. I think we passed it back down the hall, right?" Why Alee felt she needed to distract Ms. Thatcher from the fact that Jathan was gone, or to stall until he got back, she didn't know.

"That is correct."

"I'll only be a minute." Where he had gone off to wasn't really any of her business anyway, and just as the words started to tumble out of her mouth she was wondering why she even cared. She didn't know him. What did it matter to her if he skipped out on the tour, or if he got in trouble because of it for that matter.

The older woman smiled at her, "Thank you Aleerah—" glancing down at her list. "—Aleerah—Wenham." Her eyes narrowed as she looked back up at Alee. She held her gaze a few seconds longer than what was comfortable before she turned to look down the hall. "Since you seem so eager to run off, I'm sure you wouldn't mind just meeting back up with us down the next corridor and out back. We're heading to the arts facility, and I know you wouldn't want the others to have to miss part of the tour." She turned and, before Alee had a chance to say anything, was headed down the hall with the other three students following fast behind.

The arts facility had been the most recent renovation. It had been started during the end of her junior year, and completed this past summer. Alee was actually excited about seeing it. She and Dani had often talked about wanting to try out for a school play together, but her parents never would have let her. Now, with a brand new Broadway style facility, she finally would be free to try, but without her best friend to share it with, there didn't really seem to be much of a point.

"Great, just great." It was to herself, since no one else was around to hear her, but as Alee turned the corner she slammed right into Jathan's chest.

"Whoa, where's the fire?" Jathan's voice was deeper than she had expected, kind of rough, but still pleasant to the ear. *Where's the fire.* She had a flashback to the previous year when she had been waiting at her locker for Kyle. When she was finally giving up and heading off to class she ran right into him. He had said the same thing. *It's just a figure of speech*, she reminded herself.

"Where did you run off to?" Not wanting to sound startled, Alee tried for casual but didn't really succeed.

Jathan just went around her and off down the hall, not even looking back. "I had things to do. Where were you going?"

"I was—the bathroom."

"No you weren't. You were coming to find me." Alee stood there staring until he finally stopped walking and turned to face her. "So, are you coming? Then he gave her just about the most charming smile she had ever seen. His bright white, perfectly straight teeth were a dramatic contrast to his dark black hair, and his deep chocolate brown eyes.

Alee froze. When she finally found her voice, it was small and frail, no more than a whisper, "Yeah." But she still didn't move, and his eyes hadn't left hers.

Eyebrows lifted, Jathan held a hand out to her, "Then come on." *That smile again—wow.* Alee took his hand without thinking, and five steps down the hall she realized that his hand was still wrapped around hers. It felt warm and comforting. Something inside of her didn't want to let go of him, but she forced herself to pull away. She felt him turn toward her, but she didn't look at him, and he didn't say a word. She somehow sensed that one corner of his mouth turned up faintly in the slightest of smirks.

At the end of the back hallway Alee pushed open the door that led outside to the brand new arts facility. "They went this way."

"So, how do you know where everything is already?"

"I used to—I read the map on the office wall." She corrected herself before blurting out that she wasn't really a new student. Lying about reading the map just made her look like a complete dork. She could feel the judgment in the way he studied her.

But he just said, "OK—"

Judgment, judgment, judgment! "Let's just go." She stood there holding the door open waiting for him to exit, but finally just walked out and let him catch the door before it shut in front of him. The outside of the Arts Building looked just like the main school building except that it was one story instead of two. They had used the same colonial revival style of architecture on the Arts Building that had been used so many years ago when the high school was first built. The cast stone detailing of the entryway and the tall stone pillars framing the entrance at the top of the stairs matched those of the older building perfectly. If Alee hadn't known that the building was new, she would have thought that they had been built at the same time. That is, until they walked in and saw that everything in the new building smelled clean—rich—and well, *new*.

"—for you creative students." Ms. Thatcher was just finishing her tour of the building when she looked up to see them coming in. "Well, I'm so glad you could join us again." There was a hint of sarcasm in her voice that Alee had never heard before. Usually Ms. Thatcher was so sweet, but now she seemed watchful—even critical. She led the students back out the main entrance, gesturing toward the gymnasium. "Your gym classes will be over there." Then, as she scanned the group, she added, "Though I doubt that any of you will be participating in sports. So we'll just make our way back to the office." They all just looked at each other in amazement at the blatantly obvious way she had just judged them.

"Actually I'm a swimmer." *Where did that come from?* She had no intention of joining the swim team or any other team for that matter, but the way Ms. Thatcher had just assumed, even judged them all by their looks, Alee knew she couldn't just not say anything.

Ms. Thatcher stopped and turned quickly to face Alee eye to eye. "Are you now? Well then Miss. Wenham, I'm sure you will be happy to know that the pool is just as impressive as the amphitheater." Then, as she turned back around and continued walking she added, "Oh wait—you missed that part of the tour." Everyone looked at Alee, who just smiled and shrugged her shoulders, all the while wondering what she had done to piss off such a sweet old woman.

Jathan continued to eye her, as if looking to see something he might have missed the first time. "A swimmer—really?"

"Don't sound so surprised," Alee hissed under her breath, then rolled her eyes, and headed off to catch up with the rest of the students. "I run too!" she called back over her shoulder.

"Yes, yes fine," Ms. Thatcher responded, as if she really didn't care.

"No, I wasn't talking to—never mind." She turned back to glare at Jathan, but he just smiled.

When they had finally made it back to the office, Ms. Thatcher thanked them all again for making it in so early, handed out their student folders, and set them loose to find their lockers and locate their morning classes. Glancing at the clock on the office wall, Alee realized that she still had about ten minutes before the majority of the students would begin to arrive. She wasn't worried about finding her classes—she already knew the school like the back of her hand. What she really wanted to know was where her locker was and how close it was to Kyle's and Dani's.

After finding her locker, practicing the combination a few times, and committing it to memory, she tossed the new-student folder on the shelf, folded her class schedule, and shoved it into her back pocket. Before she could even close the locker door, Phoebe was standing right behind her, coffee in hand. "Your drink." She handed her a brand new travel mug with lid.

"Wow, thanks. I could get used to this, but you know you could have just gotten the regular paper cup." Then she took a sip of the coffee, only to find that it wasn't coffee at all. Not quite ready for what she tasted, Alee gagged on the thick red liquid that began to drip down her chin as she desperately tried to wipe it off with the back of her hand. She coughed, trying to catch her breath, as Phoebe handed her a napkin, which she used to clean off her lips and hand while scanning the hallway to see if anyone was close enough to notice. Luckily no one was around.

Her eyes flashed with anger as she turned to Phoebe, "What were you thinking?"

Phoebe raised her hands up as if surrendering, and whispered back, "I just thought you might need it. I was only trying to help." She smiled an innocent little smile, "I figured your first day of school—might be stressful, and—"

Alee cut her off. "It's fine. Thank you. I'm sure you meant well. I was just expecting coffee. I wasn't expecting—well, this." Holding up the cup she smiled, and they actually shared a laugh.

Phoebe held up her own cup, actual coffee, and knocked it up against Alee's. "Cheers."

Alee tipped back her mug and drank the *red syrup* as she liked to think of it, as quickly as it would come out. Then she turned, opened her locker, and placed the mug in the back of the locker on the top shelf. It wasn't as if she could really throw a cup of blood into the school garbage can. "Thanks."

Phoebe was smiling even more now. "Anytime."

want to read more?

~ book 2 ~
the Blood Angel Series
by Nina Soden

Want your copy autographed? Order directly from the Author at <u>http://ninasoden.wordpress.com</u>

Coming Soon

~ book 3 ~
**the Blood Angel Series
by Nina Soden**

533380R10238

Made in the USA
Lexington, KY
04 March 2015